Praise for Colleen Gleason and the Regency Draculia series

"Lush details, lavish love scenes and characters both noble and violent make this a thrilling ride not for the faint of heart."
—*BookPage* on *The Vampire Narcise* (Romance of the month)

"This is the most powerful and emotionally intense of Gleason's trilogy. She has mastered the world of the vampire, making her own mark on the genre."
—*RT Book Reviews* on *The Vampire Narcise*

"*The Vampire Voss* has all the right ingredients for a sit-down-can't-get-up-until-I'm-done kind of novel. The writing is delightful, and the story brings us into new realms of the traditional. I loved this book!"
—*New York Times* bestselling author Heather Graham

"Fresh, unique, sassy and fun, Gleason's Regency Draculia trilogy is one of a kind, and destined to become a classic. A must-have addition to the bookshelves of vamp enthusiasts everywhere."
—Maggie Shayne, *New York Times* bestselling author of *Twilight Prophecy*

"Count on Colleen Gleason for a scorching page-turner."
—Jeaniene Frost, *New York Times* bestselling author of the Night Huntress series

"Dark and decadent, sultry and seductive, Colleen Gleason's sexy Draculia series will hold you in its thrall. This is Regency romance the way I like it—with a bite!"
—Lara Adrian, *New York Times* bestselling author of the Midnight Breed series

COLLEEN GLEASON

The Vampire Narcise

MIRA®

Recycling programs
for this product may
not exist in your area.

ISBN-13: 978-0-7783-1378-6

THE VAMPIRE NARCISE

Copyright © 2011 by Colleen Gleason

For questions and comments about the quality of this book, please contact us at Customer_eCare@Harlequin.ca.

www.Harlequin.com

Printed in U.S.A.

This book is dedicated to my sister Kate.

PROLOGUE

Romania 1673
The Estate of the Voivodina of Moldavia

He couldn't take his eyes off her.

She was so beautiful, with her sparkling amethyst-sapphire eyes and swirl of dark hair. Her skin, so pure and perfect, alabaster and rose. Her neck, graceful and slender; her curves, so lush and feminine.

And her gowns...he envied her the gowns, too. The slide of silk that would be so blissfully erotic over one's skin. The brush of fox and mink trimmings, sensual against the belly or cheek, the gentle tug of a train catching along the cobbled stones beneath her slippered feet.

The laces and brocades, the gemstones sewn into the fabric of layer upon layer of skirts, the embroidery and ribbons. The weight of the clothing—it would make one feel like a doll, like a jewel to be coveted. A gift to be unwrapped—like the little nesting blocks he used to play with—from the heavy, beaded and bejeweled overskirts, to the frothy and light chemise and layers of underskirts, to the whale-boned lacings that turned her torso into such a curved, lovely package. What would it feel like to be trussed up so enticingly?

The elegant gloves, a tradition from Paris brought here to the deep, cold and dark mountains of Romania, made her hands appear slender and delicate. A bracelet glittered gold and silver on her gloved wrist; rings sparkled. Her fingers fluttered becomingly near her face as she bent to smile and chatter with the crowd of men around her.

He swelled with love and affection for his sister—for how could anyone resist such perfection? She was exquisite. Lively. A goddess of light and laughter and beauty.

And of course, she knew it.

She drew the men in, she coaxed with her eyes and teased with her jests. Her body moved with unconscious eroticism, her eyes lit with just the right bit of naiveté, her shoulders, bare, ivory, shadowed by the delicate curves of collarbone and throat. Her movements, graceful and smooth.

The men fawned and praised, their eyes hot and wanting. Strong, broad shoulders strained the broadcloth of their coats, bronzed, elegant throats above white or black shirts. Firm, muscular hands and powerful thighs encased in breeches that outlined every masculine attribute, and heavy, solid boots that slid and held firmly when mounted on a horse. These were men.

And here was Cezar. Pale. Slender. His hands too big, his brows too heavy, his shoulders too narrow. His thighs seemed like sticks when he sat on a horse, and his face... spotted and a bit pasty, even for his Romanian heritage.

His jaw still ached on occasion where it had been broken two years ago by a group of other young men when he was twenty, and it had healed improperly so that he had the added indignity of a faint lisp. From the same event, he'd acquired a slight limp.

He was Cezar: the second son of the most trusted confidant of the *voivode*, overlooked or scorned by men and women alike—even on the occasion of his brother's wedding to the eldest daughter of the most powerful ruler in Romania.

But even she, the wealthy, beautiful offspring of the ruler of Moldavia, couldn't hold a candle to Narcise. Even on the occasion of her wedding, the bride couldn't maintain the attention that inevitably slipped to her new sister-by-law.

Narcise was incomparable.

And Cezar, as he had since he first set eyes on his younger sister, both loved and loathed her with deep, abiding passion.

He wanted to kill her…and yet, he wanted to *be* her.

And that was why, as his fangs—still so new and uncomfortable in his mouth—slid free, filling the inside of his lips like a mouthful of potatoes, he settled into the shadows. Unnoticed. Watching. Waiting.

Planning.

Soon, all of this would be his. All of them who laughed at him, who beat him, who scorned him…they would all worship him and cower before him.

They would look at him with hot, lustful eyes.

And his beautiful sister would become his pet.

~ I ~
Revolution

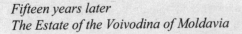

Fifteen years later
The Estate of the Voivodina of Moldavia

Narcise curled her fingers around the slender grip of her saber and steadied her breathing. Her fangs had sprung free, filling her mouth.

Her opponent leered at her, his own fangs thrusting long and bold as he lifted his own blade. Its silver gleamed red-orange in the low candlelight that danced around the edges of the chamber. The man was taller than Narcise, and much stronger, and thus he was certain he'd take her down.

That bravado, that certainty, was apparent in the haughty glint of his burning red eyes, the swagger in his step, and the ready bulge behind the flap of his trousers.

He wasn't fighting for his sanity.

But Narcise was fighting for hers.

She wore her hair scraped back in a tight knot to keep it from flying into her face. Her clothing was nothing more than a short, tight tunic that bound her breasts close, along with slim-fitting trousers. They allowed her not only freedom of movement, but also provided nothing loose or flowing for her partner to grab on to. Her feet were bare.

She started it, knowing her best chance was to take him off guard and to keep him that way. She rushed toward him, then feinted nimbly to the right as he lunged awkwardly and swiped his sword through empty air.

She heard the little gasp of anticipation for a good fight. It came from the spectators sitting just above them in the balcony, but Narcise spared no attention for her brother Cezar and his companions. She fought for the right to leave this chamber alone tonight, to be sent to her private room unaccompanied and untouched…instead of with the man who now spun on his feet and leaped back toward her.

Her lips closed around her fangs, she pivoted and ducked beneath the swing of sword blade. She felt the heat of her own eyes, burning with fury and intent, and knew they glowed just as red-gold as the candles studding the walls and the blaze of fire in the corner. Blood rushed and pounded in her veins, her body's reaction to the desperation and fear she tried to quell.

Her opponent grinned as he vaulted over the table after her, his feet landing heavily on the stone floor on the other side. There were two chairs in the space as well, and a tray of food and wine that wouldn't get eaten—for Cezar liked to set the scene. It wasn't merely a battle, like that of the Roman gladiators, where the fighters were released into the arena. No, he had to make a story around it, create a setting.

It enhanced the pleasure of watching his sister fight for the right to sleep alone that night.

Narcise felt the stone wall behind her, and a flicker of fear as her attacker stepped closer, blocking her view of the space behind him with his bulk. He grinned down at her, his fangs glinting and his lips wet and full. Her mouth dried and she fiercely drove the apprehension back.

I will not yield.

She glanced to the left, drawing his attention that way, and then streaked like a cat beneath his arm to the right, somersaulting herself over the table and landing with a little bounce on two steady feet. A soft murmur of approval from the balcony reached her ears, but Narcise didn't give in to the distraction of those who watched her as if she were some trained fighting bear.

No sooner had she landed on the far side of the table than she vaulted back, once again taking her larger, slower adversary by surprise when she used her hands to spring from the tabletop and slam her feet into his hard belly.

He gasped, stumbled backward, and she followed him, her saber ready as she landed on the ground, standing over him. Before he could blink, she had the blade settled at the side of his neck, and, firmly in her hand, the wooden stake she kept jammed into the knot of her hair.

"Yield," she said, pressing the metal edge into the side of his neck.

If he did not, she had no compunction about using either the sword or the stake to send him to hell right then and there.

"I yield," he growled, his eyes flashing with red fire.

Narcise kept the stake in her hand and the blade poised just-so. "Drop your weapon," she ordered. She'd been caught unawares before by a challenger who'd yielded, only to attack her moments after she released him.

That had only happened once. And that was why she had yet another stake shoved in her tight sleeve.

With a furious grimace, he tossed the sword to the floor and, still with the blade in place, Narcise kicked the other one far away, under the table. She noted with grim satisfaction that the bulge of his cock had softened into nothing more than a little bag of flesh, hardly even filling out his breeches. She liked it when the bastards wet their trousers, but apparently this one hadn't been sufficiently frightened for his life.

"Too easy!" shouted Cezar from the balcony, his lisping voice rising with mirth. "She bested you too easily, Godya! You lasted a mere fifteen minutes. What a sot!"

Narcise ignored her brother and, keeping the blade in place, stepped back and motioned for the man apparently named Godya to rise. "Slowly," she warned, her eyes never wavering until he'd risen and she'd backed him out of the chamber, courtesy of the edge of her blade.

She'd made the mistake of underestimating her rival only once before. No one could ever say she didn't learn from her errors.

Not until the door closed behind Godya did she lower her blade and turn to look up at Cezar.

"So sorry to have ruined your evening's entertainment," she said, taking no care to hide her loathing for the man.

"No sorrier than I, dear sister," he hissed morosely. "I can't remember the last time you were bested and gave us a real show."

Narcise did. It had happened eleven months ago, when she'd tripped over the blade of her saber as it caught on the rug. She'd lost her balance and rhythm, and that was the end of the battle. Cezar's colleague, whose name she'd never cared to learn, had wasted no time in slamming her onto the table, holding her hands pinned above her head as he used his own blade to cut down through her tunic and tear it away.

In an effort to add to the entertainment for the audience above, he'd fondled her breasts with rough fingers, then, breathing hot and hard, shoved his fangs into her shoulder. He sampled her for a moment, drinking deeply as she fought against the reflexive rush of arousal that always came when her blood was released thus.

Then, with her torso bare and her wrists pulled behind her back, he'd dragged her off to what she thought of as The Chamber for the rest of the night.

She hadn't lost a battle since and, in fact, had sent three Dracule permanently to hell during three previous engagements.

Now she sneered at Cezar. "What a pity I didn't provide enough entertainment. I'm certain it would be worth watching if you had a big enough bag between your legs to take me on yourself."

And then I could skewer you with a stake and I would be free.

But of course, he would never risk it. Nor would he dirty his pasty-white hands.

Her brother was older than she in both mortal years as well as *vampir* years. He'd been twenty-two when Lucifer visited him and offered him a life of power, wealth and immortality. That was more than fifteen years ago, and he looked exactly the same as he had at that time. Even the crooked tooth and the awkward set of a broken jaw that had never healed properly remained unchanged. It was that malformed jaw that gave his voice the faint lisp.

Cezar had waited three years, until Narcise turned twenty, before he arranged for her to be offered to Lucifer. During that time, their elder brother, who'd become the *voivode*, or ruler, over Moldavia through his marriage, had conveniently died…and Cezar had married his sister-by-law, thus becoming the new *voivode*. Their father and the original *voivode* had died just after their brother's wedding, and Narcise had come under Cezar's control shortly thereafter.

She always counted herself fortunate that she'd managed to lose her virginity to a man she fancied she loved before being turned into an immortal Dracule. And that female Dracule couldn't get with child—for they didn't have their monthly flow.

Since then she'd had little power over her own body.

The door behind her opened and Narcise didn't have to turn to know what was there. The rush of weakness flooded her and she gritted her teeth against the wave of paralysis.

It was, she thought dully as two of Cezar's thugs approached, a good thing that her brother liked to watch her win more often than lose. For, despite his earlier comments, Cezar would have the loss of a titillating form of entertainment, as well as a bargaining tool, if he didn't have his sister to beat up his friends and enemies alike.

Narcise remained still as her brother's men flanked her on each side. One of them fastened a cuff around her wrist. Woven of three brown feathers that were soft and delicate against her skin, and yet burned as if they were a branding iron, the bracelet leached her strength by its very proximity.

Her knees trembled but Narcise kept herself as tall and straight as she could. It never ceased to amuse her that, despite them being armed with the one thing in the world that could weaken her, there needed to be two strong, burly Dracule who escorted her back to her chamber.

That knowledge was the only thing that kept her hopeful as, day after day, she lived an eternity under her brother's control.

The knowledge that they were all terrified of her.

God and Lucifer help them if she ever got free.

Paris
September 1793

The first time Narcise set eyes on Giordan Cale, she was fighting for her safety.

It was yet another of countless evenings of entertainment for Cezar, and this time, he was seated off to the side on a raised dais with a single companion: a broadshouldered man with tight, curly hair and handsome, elegant features.

Normally Cezar liked to display his sister's capabilities to a small crowd of spectators. It was his way of advertising her abilities. But tonight, there were only the two of them watching from the unobtrusive corner as she fenced and fought with some man who'd angered her brother.

Her orders, tonight, had been to fight to the death, and Cezar had warned that she wouldn't be released from the small arenalike chamber until she either killed her rival, or he bested her—which didn't mean death for her, but something worse.

The poor fool was no match for Narcise, who'd been taught in swordplay and other acrobatic fighting skills by the best trainers Cezar could find. He wasn't about to have his favorite amusement killed by an overzealous suitor or an angry enemy.

Tonight, her opponent was a "made" *vampir*, one who'd been turned Dracule by another *vampir* instead of being invited into the Draculia by Lucifer himself.

Narcise wasn't aware of what he'd done to insult her brother, for, in truth, Cezar could interpret the twitch of an eyelid or a simple cough as an insult. She didn't particularly care.

Nor did she spare much pity for the man. She couldn't afford to if she wanted to remain unscathed.

But as she whirled around to face her adversary, readying the saber for its cleaving blow, she glanced over and happened to catch the eye of her brother's companion. He was watching her intently, and she had the brief impression of a tanned wrist and hand settled with its index finger thoughtfully against his mouth.

She also noticed, in that blink of an eye, that, rather than focusing on her, Cezar sat back in his seat, covertly studying his companion. Without pause, Narcise finished her flowing movement, slicing the head from her opponent with a clean stroke.

Ending with her back toward the dais, and her audience, Narcise remained thus as she wiped her blade with a pristine white tablecloth. Then, with no acknowledgment to her audience, nor to the dead *vampir* whose damaged soul was filtering permanently down to hell, she stood, waiting for the door to be opened and her guards to appear. Grateful that tonight's competition had been relatively easy, she slipped the clean saber into its sheath.

She could hear the murmurs from behind her, the slightly sibilant hiss of her brother's voice, and the answering rumble of his companion, neither of which induced her to acknowledge them. Any intimate of her brother's was automatically an enemy of hers.

It wasn't until weeks later that she even learned his name.

Giordan Cale was all about money.

His ability to earn it, find it, inherit it, save it—and

then, to multiply it several times over—was what got him into the predicament he was in: an immortal lifetime in which to spend more money than Croesus ever dreamed of. In fact, it seemed that Giordan couldn't lose money if he tossed buckets of it into the Seine, or had the servants burn it in his fireplace, for the funds simply reappeared in some other form—of a long-shot investment coming due, or even an inexplicable inheritance.

And it was precisely his flair with funds that drew him to the attention of Cezar Moldavi.

But of course Giordan had heard of the man…and his sister…even before Moldavi arrived in Paris, for the world of the Dracule was exceedingly small and tightly interwoven. Despite the vast geography of the earth, the members of Lucifer's secret society traveled and resided in only the largest, most cosmopolitan of cities: London, Vienna, Prague, Rome, Morocco and of course, Giordan's beloved Paris. And they tended to congregate at the same private clubs, interacting in the same high levels of society, a happenstance which Giordan used to his financial benefit. He was the owner or a majority shareholder in the most luxurious and private of these havens in every major city except London. And, he determined, it was only a matter of time until he was established there as well.

He had an eternity to make it happen, no?

Cezar Moldavi had come to the City of Light after spending several decades in Vienna, where, apparently, there had been an unfortunate incident with another of the Dracule—along with some increasing, unpleasant attention being given to Moldavi's propensity for bleeding children. There were those who risked their lives in order to hunt those of the Draculean world, sometimes even successfully. Giordan understood that Moldavi had decided it was best to evacuate from Vienna before one of those so-called vampire hunters was lucky enough to stake him to death.

Aside of that, one couldn't stay in one place for more than two or three decades without one's non-aging appearance being remarked upon, which required these powerful men to uproot and move their households every few decades or so. And now, after living in Vienna, Prague and even Amsterdam, Moldavi seemed intent on not only making his home in France, but also establishing himself as the leader of the Draculean underground therein.

Paris herself had changed during the last five years, during which Giordan had been in Morocco. Now, his City of Light roiled with tension and fear. Nerves crackled on the very *rues*, unease simmered in the Seine—for The Terror lived and seeped into every corner of the city. It had begun with the execution of the king by guillotine—and then shortly after, his wife Marie Antoinette, sniffing vials of her personal perfume tucked inside her bodice, met the same fate. And now every day, as Robespierre and his cronies struggled to maintain the burgeoning revolution, more and more people were dragged under the shining silver blade and relieved of their heads.

One who was required to live on the lifeblood of man—or whatever other living being one chose— might find it convenient that the mortals in Paris were being slaughtered in great numbers (for it wasn't only the Widow—the guillotine—that caused their demise; there were shootings and beatings and other random murders fueled by desperation and suspicion), for it certainly provided a vast opportunity for sustenance. But while Giordan Cale had no qualms about killing in general, he found such rampant, widespread actions distasteful and unnecessarily violent.

This was, apparently, only one of the many ways in which he and Cezar Moldavi differed.

In fact, there were painfully few ways in which he and Cezar Moldavi were in agreement. After spending only a brief time with a bottle of excellent wine (which Giordan had sent over) and discussing a possible investment with Moldavi, Giordan came to the conclusion that his friend Dimitri, known as the Earl of Corvindale across the Channel in England, was being kind when he described Moldavi as being the lowest form of a bollocks-licking, bitch-in-heat, Lucifer's-cock-biting bastard.

Giordan had just decided that, since he had no interest in continuing any form of discussion with Cezar Moldavi, he was going to excuse himself with great expedience and decline to watch the swordplay entertainment he'd been promised. But before he opened his mouth to do so, the man's sister entered the opposite part of the chamber, below the dais.

Everything in his mind whirred into silence and he found that his body, too, had stilled.

She was carrying a long, sheathed sword, with a slightly curved blade. A saber, then: a type of single-edged weapon just coming into fashion. In fencing, one most often used a straight, slender blade such as an épée, or even a blunted foil. The lethality of this blade was Giordan's first indication that the woman wasn't merely engaging in sport.

"My sister, Narcise," Moldavi murmured. He gestured to their empty cups on the table, and his steward moved quickly to fill them.

Giordan realized his breathing had ground to a halt and he reminded himself that, even though a vampire couldn't die from suffocation, one did have to breathe or become weakened.

She was lovely. Incredibly lovely.

He'd heard about her, of course. Who hadn't? Rumor had it that Cezar Moldavi's sister was bait, a tool, and even a bargaining chip for her brother. But Giordan, who'd met—and had—many lovely and exotic women during his travels hadn't expected to be so thoroughly entranced, and from a distance.

From his seat on the dais, Giordan studied her, attempting to be objective. And yet, one could be objective and still describe her as the most beautiful woman one had ever seen.

She was tall for a woman, and her rich, black hair was pulled into a large, tight knot at her nape. Her skin glowed like a pearl; it was fair and yet rosy luminous. He caught a brief glimpse of startling blue eyes that tended toward the violet end of the spectrum. They were outlined by dark lashes that made it appear as if she wore liner, as the Egyptians had to emphasize their eyes. But for her, it was a natural occurrence, and such artifice would be unnecessary.

And her face… Her features were incredibly perfect, magnificent really, with a lush, dark pink mouth and a straight, delicately formed nose.

If her face was exquisite, one could hardly expect that her figure would match it with such perfection…but it did. And the clothing she wore, unusual garb that clung to every curve, including her bound breasts, displayed the fact that Narcise Moldavi was this millennia's Helen of Troy: the face and figure that could launch a thousand ships.

The only element marring the perfection of countenance and form was the dull fog that veiled her expression, clouded her eyes. She was an empty doll, an emotionless puppet.

So distracted by his examination of her figure was he that Giordan didn't listen to the short commands given by his host, nor did he notice at first when another man joined them in the room.

But then he saw. Her opponent appeared larger and stronger than she, and like Narcise, he carried a deadly sword. But his was a broadsword, dual-edged, and heavier than her more elegant weapon. For the first time, Giordan understood that this was no simple fencing bout with foiled blades.

He turned to his host, intending to ask—and demand, if necessary—not to observe such an unmatched battle, but Cezar made an abrupt gesture. "Watch," he said. And then to the rivals, who stood mere feet away from the raised table, he said, "To the death."

Giordan stifled a reflexive response, and felt his muscles ready themselves to interfere if it became necessary. And surely it would.

Even the fierce expression that transformed Narcise's face didn't ease his concern, yet the change in her countenance Giordan found fascinating and quite striking. Her eyes flashed with loathing and determination, but she appeared so slight and much too elegant next to her burly rival.

And when she whirled into action, all taut grace and feline movement, Giordan's breath caught yet again. He was alternately entranced and tense, watching and waiting like a parent seeing their child make a jump on horseback for the first time.

Her dark hair gleamed in the light flickering from the sconces studding the walls, her slender arms were quick, and her teeth, fangs extended, were bared with ferocity. But her eyes did not burn red, and she seemed calm. Very much in control.

Giordan watched closely, his concern easing, as he saw her weight shift on her feet, and how she changed her center of balance to launch herself smoothly over one of the chairs, then used her momentum to fling that very chair back toward her rival. Admiration grew as he noted her employment of excellent fencing technique while moving her body in a more forceful, combative fashion than such an activity normally required.

He almost missed the nearly imperceptible circle made by her wrist in a counterparry, which might have caught him off guard if he'd been her opponent. Pursing his lips, Giordan's eyes narrowed and he leaned forward to watch more closely, trying to understand her strategy. This was most certainly not a fencing match, with parries and ripostes and the formal dance of back and forth and lunge…and yet she went through those motions like an expert.

And then…she ducked nimbly beneath her lumbering opponent's arm, spun around behind him, sliced her saber down the back of his shirt and then met his blade as he twisted and swooped toward her with a great, ringing clash of metal.

The clang reverberated in the close room, followed by the slide of metal against metal. Then once again, she stepped out of the routine and somersaulted away as the man, now obviously frustrated by his lack of progress, lunged for her.

After that, the neat fencing bout deteriorated into a battlefield matchup of two lethal weapons. Giordan felt his arms tense once again, readying to interfere, and he spared a glance toward Moldavi. But his host was watching him, as if to gauge his guest's reaction to the battle, his gaze contemplative and yet hooded.

As their eyes met, Moldavi raised his glass and sipped, then slid his attention to the battle beyond.

Giordan's attention returned as well, just in time to see Narcise rise up to make a perfect arc on her feet, her blade free and ready, and in one burst of speed, she clove the head from her opponent in a powerful stroke.

She completed her turn, then stood, her slender back toward Giordan and her brother as she wiped her sword. The back of her shirt clung damply to her lower back, but not one strand of inky hair had escaped from its fat knot. Nor did her shoulders or arms seem to be moving with labored breaths.

She never looked back at them as she replaced her saber in its scabbard and stood, waiting.

Giordan was about to speak when a door opened and two large men—vampires—walked in. As he watched in astonishment and growing revulsion, they flanked and escorted Narcise from the chamber.

She never once acknowledged Giordan or her brother, a fact which both fascinated and irked him.

At that moment, Giordan decided that he might indeed continue discussing his next Far Eastern spice ship with Cezar Moldavi.

Giordan's private club and residence in Paris was what he thought of as his flagship establishment. Everything from the women and other entertainment, to the wine and liquor, and the other vintages, exuded luxury, pleasure and perfect taste. But of course, it was also ridiculously expensive. And every night, and through much of the day, Draculean patrons—along with a limited cadre of mortals—filled the seats and clustered around illegal gaming tables. For despite what the city's residents had begun to call the Reign of Terror, life—and business—did go on.

There were dinner parties, theater and balls, the women shopped for fashionable gowns, and men visited their clubs—though now, they did it with worried glances over the shoulder and a definite strain in one's smile. The whispers and low-voiced conversations in corners were no longer confined to gossip about who was doing what to whom, but were filled with warnings and worries. Who would be next?

Little of this, however, affected those of the Dracule. In fact, not only did government and authority mean nothing to the vampires, but such upheaval only made their lives easier. The more chaotic, the better.

Which was why Giordan suspected that Moldavi was more than a little involved in the ongoing rivalry between Robespierre and his so-called "terror as a virtue" campaign, and that of Hébert and the proposition of his atheist cult—both factions which promoted reason over religion, government over church. While the two factions argued, fought and executed, the turbulent fallout was beneficial to Moldavi who sought to exercise as much control as possible over his mortal counterparts.

Giordan had extended a particular invitation to the cloistered Moldavi to join him at the club this evening. He wasn't at all certain that the man would accept, for he rarely left his subterranean residence, but he was hopeful that the possibility of continuing discussion on their potential business arrangement would draw him out. Aside of that, people rarely declined an invitation from him, simply because Giordan's parties and fetes were known for being lavish and exciting and, quite often, with unique entertainment. He didn't specifically ask that Moldavi bring his sister, but he knew it was likely that Narcise would accompany him.

Through the time Giordan had been absent from Paris,

Moldavi had become entrenched in the underworld of the French Dracule. And on the rare occasion that he participated in social activities, he was usually accompanied by his sister. The better, Giordan had come to learn, to tempt friend and enemy alike into engaging with Narcise in battle.

There would be few men—mortal or otherwise—who could resist an opportunity to win a night with a woman such as she. The most troubling aspect of that particular arrangement was, in Giordan's mind, whether Narcise's brother forced her to engage in those gambles, or whether she did it of her own free will. If it were the former—and he was fairly certain it was, a suspicion supported by the empty expression on her face—there was yet another reason for him to disdain Moldavi, for exercising such influence over a woman was just as abhorrent as bleeding children to death.

And so when Giordan, who'd been sipping a very fine French brandy with two companions in his favorite private parlor, was advised that both Cezar and Narcise Moldavi had arrived, he merely nodded to himself. The bait had been taken, and he hoped to have his curiosity assuaged.

He was more than a bit curious to see what Narcise would be like in a less combative, restrictive environment, whether that dull glaze would be gone from her eyes, and whether a woman who looked like her, and fought with the ferocity of a man, had any social skills at all. Or whether she was merely a well-trained puppet.

Giordan was master enough of himself to admit that his interest and attraction had been piqued, and sharply. And honest enough to note that he would suffer even the presence of the repugnant Moldavi to pursue it.

It didn't take long before the invited guests found their

way to Giordan's presence, and his host duly welcomed the siblings, introducing them to Eddersley, Voss, and indicating the latter's latest mistress, Yvonna. She was a mortal, and her eyes had sunk half-closed due to the earlier employment of an opium pipe. Now, she sagged quietly in a corner chaise while the men conversed.

Clearly Cezar Moldavi had been in his early twenties when he'd been turned Dracule. His facial features and the swarthiness of his skin betrayed a strong Romanian heritage despite an underlying pastiness; in fact, Giordan knew that Moldavi had only permanently left Romania within the last decade, although he'd made extensive trips throughout Europe prior to settling in Paris. His *voivodina* in Moldavia had been very remote, yet the army within was the most fearsome and powerful in its nation.

He was many pounds lighter than Giordan, and slighter as well, but he had a square jaw that made his face seem oddly proportioned, verging upon awkward. His dark brows hung thick and straight over small blue-gray eyes, and his hair grew unfashionably like a thin walnut cap over his forehead and ears. He had surprisingly elegant hands that were covered in rings, and he was fashionably attired in a long-tailed, cut-away coat of dark red brocade and dun-colored knee breeches. His waistcoat did not stint on color, of course, for dull hues were only for the lower class. Moldavi moved with a barely perceptible limp that had to be from an injury prior to becoming immortal.

"We've met, albeit briefly," Voss, the Viscount Dewhurst said, nodding to the new arrival. His attention strayed, as of course it would, to Narcise.

"Ah, yes," Moldavi replied, his face flattening in annoyance. His French wasn't perfect, but certainly serviceable. "In Vienna. On that most unfortunate evening some years ago. If I recall, you left before the fire that destroyed the house, did you not?"

But of course Giordan knew about the incident that had burned Dimitri's house in Vienna. "Some years ago" had actually been more than a century, but such was the life of an immortal when decades became mere flashes in time.

Voss and Moldavi had both been there in Vienna that night, and had both contributed to the tragedy in their own ways—although literally passing by each other as Voss departed and Moldavi arrived.

"Perhaps you might recall I was there as well," Eddersley said in his deep, cultured voice. He had large, knobby hands and wrists, and lots of dark, curling hair. His attention, as it was wont to do, barely touched on Narcise and instead glanced more contemplatively over her brother. But the short, slender Moldavi was no more Lord Eddersley's preference than Narcise was. He veered toward elegant, fair-haired men with broad shoulders and significant height when it came to feeding, and other pleasures. "But we haven't formally met."

"It was a rather…eventful night." Moldavi sketched the briefest of bows to the lanky, strong-featured man without comment, and Giordan fancied he saw him even sniff in disdain, for Eddersley made no effort to hide his preference for men. The latter gave no response aside of a similarly brief nod and then glanced at Voss, a little annoyed smirk twitching at the corners of his mouth as he greeted Narcise politely.

Next to her dark, awkward brother, Narcise appeared a swan. Giordan had to work to keep his attention from fastening on her and remaining there. But in the short moment his eyes swept her figure, he noted the detailed arrangement of her dark hair, tonight soft and loose around her porcelain face, and the sharp, sharp notice of her eyes.

The dullard look had gone.

Diamonds and ice-blue topazes glittered in her hair and at her throat. She wore a silk gown in the *robe à la Anglaise* style, which meant there was a significant expanse of bosom exposed and, if one were to get technical, ripples known as gathers all along the back of the bodice and bustle. The blue-and-cream-striped overdress and lacy underskirts lay flat in the front, but were gathered up in the back to create a silhouette that Giordan found most appealing: the elegant rise of a lady's rump, then the skirts falling in a short, smooth train to the floor. Fine lace decorated the edges of her sleeves and bodice, and even peeped from the layers of crinoline beneath the skirts.

He knew from experience that the weight of corset, chemise, as many as four crinolines, along with underskirt and overdress was significant, and he wondered how she felt to go from the light, clinging attire that she wore while fighting to such restrictive, heavy ones. He also contemplated the pleasure of peeling away her clothing, one layer at a time, like those curious paper boxes from China that nested one inside the other. Each one revealed a new delight and design just as did the layers of a woman's clothing.

"Please, sit," Giordan said, realizing he'd allowed his thoughts to go wayward. He gestured with his glass of brandy to encompass the chamber's hospitality, and one of the footmen poured a glass for Moldavi.

It was decorated in a relatively restrained style in comparison to that of other wealthy French residences—including Versailles. Giordan preferred the spare, simple elegance of the early Greeks and Romans over pastel colors and gilt. Thus, the furnishings were solid, yet inviting and comfortable, with cushions and pillows arranged freely. Large paintings hung on the otherwise bare white walls, except for one corner where a small collection of framed etchings of Parisian streets clustered. He kept them there to remind himself from whence he'd come.

"I am gratified that you saw fit to accept my invitation," Giordan added, sipping from the glass.

"I accept very few," Moldavi said as if bestowing some great favor. "But I am most interested in continuing our discussion begun last fortnight. And I have come to understand that one does not wish to miss a party given by Monsieur Cale." His lips moved in a brief smile. As if to punctuate his reference to joviality, a burst of laughter erupted from the public parlor below.

"Indeed," Giordan replied as Moldavi sat in the chair next to him, gesturing to his sister to alight nearby. "But before we turn our thoughts to business, perhaps a bit of pleasure first? I've just added some new vintages on which I would appreciate your opinion. We were just about to sample them."

"I would be delighted," Moldavi replied in his low, sibilant voice.

For the first time, Giordan scented Narcise—or, more accurately, he was able to identify and extract her specific essence from that around him, and it was just as decadent and alluring as the woman herself. Musky, spicy, dark, and yet elegant. Notes of smoky vetiver…clary sage… and sweet ylang-ylang. Lush, sensual, tempting.

Giordan swallowed, feeling his gums begin to swell as they prepared to thrust his fangs forth, and the further deep stirring of desire inside him. Narcise Moldavi was potent on so many levels.

She'd chosen to sit, not where her brother had indicated, but in what Giordan sensed might be more than a bit of defiance, on a chaise just to the right of her host. He didn't fool himself into believing she'd chosen proximity to him because she wanted to be near him, for it was the farthest available seat from her brother.

Turning his thoughts and attention from her, Giordan rang a little bell next to him on the table. "Then let us commence."

The door to the chamber opened and his private steward and valet, Mingo, stepped in. He was one of the few made vampires that Giordan employed, simply for the fact that he rarely chose to sire a new immortal. They were most often more trouble than they were worth, and there were plenty of other makes available for hire—most of them foolish mortals who'd been lured into a false sense of security by choosing to live forever. But Giordan found it necessary to have a Dracule, and one that he trusted, in the position for obvious reasons—otherwise, it would be like having a wine steward who had no taste for the beverage.

"Send in the newest acquisitions," he commanded. "And prepare a new plate, if you will."

Moldavi leaned closer to Giordan and murmured, "My sister has recently fed and will decline any offerings tonight."

Giordan was aware of the waft of patchouli and cedar that accompanied Moldavi's movements, along with a note of something mildly unpleasant. "I have already fed as well," he replied with a bland smile. "However, the purpose is not for sustenance, but merely to enjoy a sampling of an excellent varietal."

Moldavi smiled, displaying his fangs. In the right one, a bit of gold glinted. "I merely wished to explain in order to forestall any offense. Please understand that none would be intended, but she will not partake."

Indeed. Giordan kept his features smooth with effort, and his attention from sliding to the woman in question. *We shall see about that.* However, he merely said, "I do hope she will change her mind."

"She is quite stubborn," Moldavi said with a low chuckle, absently tapping his fingernail on the glass.

Before Giordan could find some unassuming response, the door opened and in filed two men and four women. There was no way to immediately identify them as mortal versus Dracule, but they were, indeed, mortals who were here to provide whatever Giordan's guests required.

"And here we are," he said, looking around at his companions, including Narcise. She fixed him back with a calm stare, and he felt certain she would have heard the exchange between him and her brother. Draculean hearing, along with sight and smell, was superhumanly acute.

"As you may be aware, I am particular about the sort of libation offered to my guests, both here and in my other establishments," Giordan explained. "Please note that all of them are willing participants…provided they are tipped well…and that they are kept in the most comfortable and regimented accommodations."

"There are no restrictions, of course," Eddersley said. His fangs had slipped free a bit, and his eyes glowed softly.

"Indeed, none," Giordan replied, knowing precisely why his friend had asked. One of the six was a strapping blond man from Russia. "As long as you cause them no lasting or mortal injury, and as long as you can afford the fee," he added with a brief smile, "there are no restrictions. Now, if you will allow me to introduce our selections. They are all new here at Château Riche, and tonight is their debut. I've found Damaris, the dark-skinned girl there in the blue gown, to be extremely rich and full of body. She is my favorite of them." He smiled at her, his fangs extended just a bit at the memory.

Moldavi looked at him sidewise and then back at the young woman, whose hair was scraped back into a high, exotic tail. Her skin was the color of dark tea and she was tall and slender, from Egypt or somewhere in the vicinity of the Holy Land.

"We keep each of them on a specific diet, strictly to maintain the integrity of their blood," Giordan continued. "Have you noticed how the taste can differ, depending upon the type of food intake, as well as origin? Rather like the types of soil that grow grapes or hops. The diets are as individual as they are. Some of them, like the lovely Drishni there, in the red gown, eat only vegetation. Others eat highly spiced foods, or drink an inordinate amount of champagne. And so on."

Once again, he gestured to his guests to partake, and then crooked a finger for Damaris to join him. She wafted over, her blue gown flowing loosely over long limbs. Unlike the ladies who wore high fashion, she didn't have the layers of crinoline and corset to peel away. One could see everything she had to offer as the silk clung to her from breast to hips to pubis.

As Damaris settled on the arm of Giordan's chair, just between him and Moldavi, Mingo entered the room again. He was carrying a plate with the pressed and rolled hashish. Without waiting for his master's direction, he arranged it on the low, central table and lit the small pyramid-shaped block.

"Please," Giordan said, looking at Moldavi with a nod of hospitality. Damaris, also well-trained, offered one wrist to each of them as she sat on the chair arm.

Giordan felt Moldavi's eyes on him as he extended his fangs and slid just the tips into the curve of her elbow. The release of blood into his mouth, warm and rich—and in this case, heavy with a note of spice—filled his senses. The taste, the smell, the way his body leaped and responded, skin prickling and warming, had his own blood surging.

For him, as well as for all Dracule, it was difficult to separate the primitive need for sustenance from the accompanying titillation and arousal that came with penetrating flesh and ingesting hot, thick blood, of the intimate slide of mouth against skin—and most of the time, it was neither necessary nor desirable to do so.

But tonight, now, Giordan was merely sampling. He had no need for sustenance, nor was he interested in engaging in any other erotic pleasures in his current company—although that wasn't due to any modesty on his part.

The simple fact was, despite the taste and smell of the exotic Damaris—who was beginning to breathe heavily as her own pleasure increased with both men feeding from her arms—it was the awareness of Narcise, and her smell, her essence and presence, that attracted Giordan. But he sensed that it would be best not to reveal his deep interest to her brother so overtly. So he kept his gaze strictly away from her.

As the sweet, peppery smell of burning hashish filtered through the chamber, and the arousing flow of blood settled over his tongue and rushed through his body, Giordan felt his world turning warm and red, hazy and lulling. He withdrew from Damaris and he'd barely turned away when another of his "vintages"—the Viennese girl Liesl—appeared in front of him. She was petite and blonde, and her lifeblood was just as light and pure as her appearance. She offered a slender shoulder, bared by a low-rising bodice, and as he tugged her onto his lap to take a taste, he allowed his attention to slide toward the chaise where Narcise was sitting.

Had been sitting.

She was gone now.

Combing through the miasma of pleasure and sensuality, Giordan paused before sliding his fangs into the delicate woman in front of him. The smoke from the hashish had cast a filter over the room, and Mingo had turned the oil lamps down to a soft glow. It took Giordan a moment to look around and see a lone figure standing near the corner, looking at a painting on the wall.

Instead of slipping his fangs in, he softly murmured instruction to Liesl to join Damaris with Moldavi, and to block the guest's view of the chamber.

He was under no misapprehension about Moldavi's need to control his sister. He'd also sensed that any attempt to speak privately with Narcise would be thwarted by her brother.

Aside of that, she would need to be approached with care. Despite the spark of life he'd noticed in her eyes, surely she must be skittish and leery of any male.

"Keep him occupied and distracted, and you will be well-compensated," Giordan murmured into Liesl's ear, then nicked her with his fang. Just to taste, for it was his duty as host to ensure that everything on the menu was exquisite. And it was. He slicked his tongue briefly around the edge of her ear and she shivered, her hands settling onto his shoulders as she sagged into him, clearly wanting more.

"More of my lord would be compensation enough." Her fingers slipped into his hair and she pressed her breasts into his collarbone.

But Giordan flashed his eyes in warning, for there was a fine line between making one's services available to a guest and overstepping one's bounds. His vintages must learn to finesse the difference. He eased her firmly from his lap. "Go on," he said quietly.

He took great care in extricating himself from the chair, attempting to be unnoticed by Moldavi, who seemed very content with Damaris. He watched as Liesl positioned herself, along with Damaris, nearly in the man's lap. And then, as much as every muscle in his body desired him to do so, Giordan did not walk directly over to Narcise.

Instead he wandered toward Voss, who seemed to be more than a little delighted by Drishni, the third of the female vintages, who was kissing one of the two male specimens. But of course Giordan must pause and ask whether Voss was enjoying himself, and if there was aught he needed, and they had a brief conversation about the variety of vintages, including those of the male gender.

"It is true, occasionally I prefer the taste of male lifeblood," Voss said, his softly glowing eyes never leaving the intertwined couple.

Both of the mortals had been bitten and fed upon, and the unique scents of their blood, and the combination of their essences mingling along with the aroma of desire was heady to Giordan as well. "I find it bold and strong, and a welcome change from the thinner feminine sort," Voss continued. "But Drishni… She is lovely as well. Pure and sweet."

She was Giordan's most recent addition, lately come from India. In fact, she had presented herself on his doorstep one day after hearing that he hired exotic girls. Giordan nodded complacently to Voss. "But that is precisely why we offer such a variety. To meet the varying needs of anyone."

Feeding on a male Dracule was not at all the same as fucking him, although Eddersley would of course prefer the latter. Gender mattered little when it came to feeding, but because of the intimacy that action promoted, most often a Dracule fed on a mortal of the opposite gender.

Yet, it was a rare *vampir* who hadn't had at least some intimate interaction with a member of the same gender, even if it was in a sensual, pleasure-induced ménage or orgy. Arrangements like that of this very evening were common and often led to such experiences. That sort of unfettered eroticism was part and parcel with the infinity of immortality, the need to puncture and draw blood from a living body…the knowledge that one could do whatever one wished as a member of the Dracule, and have little to answer for.

Even Giordan, who still fought horrible memories from his childhood, had been caught up in red-hot moments of pleasure when he wasn't entirely certain whose hands were stroking him, whose skin was sliding against his or whose body part he was driving his fangs into.

But there was no question that the woman across the chamber, who seemed to have moved on to examine another painting, was the only thing on his mind tonight.

Giordan made his excuses from Voss, smiling wryly at Yvonna, who'd slumped into a stupor as her lover indulged as only he knew how, and confirmed that Eddersley had slipped into a private alcove and was clearly occupied. Then he was finally able to skirt the edge of the room toward Narcise.

Whether by accident or design, she'd positioned herself in the only corner of the chamber out of eyesight of her brother. It was also the most well-lit area of the room.

She seemed to be entranced by Jacques-Louis David's second rendition of *Paris and Helen*. It was a painting that Giordan had had specially commissioned for this particular parlor, and for which he'd paid an exorbitant price because of some of the changes he'd requested.

And how apropos that Narcise should be drawn to an image of the same legendary woman with whom Giordan had compared her.

The spicy hashish scent clinging to him, slipping into his nostrils and curling around inside his head, he allowed his mouth to settle into a faint smile as he drew near…and considered how to approach her.

Although she must sense his presence as he came to stand next to her, Narcise gave no indication.

This, in turn, gave Giordan a moment for admiration—the ivory curve of her neck and bare shoulders, the thick blue-black mass of hair sparkling with pale blue topazes, the perfect slope and tip of her nose, and the full, dark pink mouth.

He needed a moment, too, to steady his breath, control the swelling beginning in his gums…and elsewhere. For, truly, the very proximity of the woman sent his thoughts to the wind and his stomach to quivering.

As he stood there, next to and slightly behind her, forcing himself to stare at the painting in tandem with her, Giordan felt a wave of annoyance and frustration at his powerful reaction. He didn't understand it, and he didn't care for the way it made him feel.

But, yet, he remained. Curious and infatuated.

"Is it the talent of the painter that has you so entranced?" he said at last, stepping into her line of vision. "Or merely the need to separate yourself from the others in the room?"

She turned to look at him then, covering him with

deep blue eyes that made his belly twist awkwardly. By the Fates, he felt like a bloody schoolboy. Not that he'd ever been one. A boy, yes. In school, no.

"Well, Monsieur Cale, I must credit you for a most creative approach." Her French wasn't even as practiced as her brother's, barely passable, and despite the brilliant hue of her eyes, the expression therein was nevertheless cool and remote. And, perhaps, fearful.

"Indeed? I thought it a rather mundane one, myself," he replied, switching experimentally to English.

Narcise returned to looking at the painting. "Monsieur David is making quite a name for himself," she replied, following his language shift to the Anglican. Here, she clearly had more confidence. "And with good reason. He is very talented. Such attention to texture and detail."

Giordan found himself absurdly pleased that she seemed willing to converse, and could string thoughts together with ease—for not every woman could. Those who could not made for very dull bed partners and companions.

And the dull glaze in her eyes was gone. Wariness lurked there, but that he could manage.

He smiled. "And yet, is it not ironic that a painting commissioned for the king's brother is in reality a harsh statement about the superficiality of the royal family? Choosing fleeting physical pleasures over responsibility to one's country?"

"Monsieur David is clever like that," Narcise replied. "But this is not the same painting commissioned by d'Artois."

"But of course you are correct," Giordan replied, wondering on what occasion she'd seen the original. "The first *Paris and Helen* was a bit too floral in hue for my taste—that flowing rose-colored gown too soft and feminine for this chamber. And it was missing some important details, no?" He smiled down at her, allowing a bit of mischief into his eyes.

"Hmm…yes, I don't recall Paris showing his fangs in the previous edition." The expression in her face eased a bit and the resulting softness made her even more lovely.

His heart stuttered, but he added smoothly, "Nor the marks on Helen's arm from said fangs."

"No, of course not. I don't believe the comte would have appreciated his mistress being portrayed as the victim of a Draculean lover," she replied, once again focusing her attention on the work of art. "You do know that if my brother sees us conversing privately, he will put a stop to it."

Just as she had followed his change of language, Giordan easily followed her non sequitur. "He is well-occupied for the time."

"Don't underestimate Cezar," Narcise told him. "Too many have, and most of them are no longer here to warn you themselves."

"And so you take it upon yourself to point out the obvious? I am just as able to take care of myself as you appear to be, mademoiselle. Wherever did you learn to fence with such skill?"

She stiffened next to him, but did not turn, leaving him to scrutinize her profile. "And how would you know of my skill with the saber, Monsieur Cale?"

2

Narcise stared up at the painting and tried to concentrate.

He was standing too close to her, this man named Giordan Cale. This man who'd hardly glanced her way all evening as he played host…but who, when he did, made a rush of heat flood her body.

She had lied, of course. By implication. By implying that she hadn't noticed him watching her that night when she'd killed a man to keep herself free. Or, at least, implying that she didn't remember him.

But she did remember him. Very well. In fact, she'd made a sketch of Cale later that night, in the privacy she'd won by sending her opponent to hell. Despite the fact that he was a friend of her brother's, Cale had provided an interesting subject for her creative mind.

She'd drawn the thick curling hair that capped his skull with glossy brown texture, shadowed in the square chin and fine lips in a strong, handsome face. Now, after seeing him tonight, she realized she hadn't quite got the shape of his eyes, nor the correct angle of his jaw and the proper shading of his cheekbones in that first sketch—

but she'd been working from a brief glance. That glance from a distance hadn't given her the details, either: the blue flecks in his brown eyes, the small scar near his right eye, the element of controlled determination rumbling beneath his easy smile.

And now he stood near enough that his particular scent rose above that thick, hazy smoke and the strong aromas of mingled lifeblood and arousal. The hair on the back of her neck prickled, as if he were so close that his breath brushed over the sensitive skin there.

She prayed that he was right, that Cezar was too occupied to notice.

Cale hadn't yet responded to her gentle taunt asking how he'd known of her skills, and at last she could no longer keep from looking at him. But when she turned, she had to resist the desire to step back. Instead she drew in a shallow breath and steadied herself.

Too close. Much too close.

Not because he threatened her—at least, not in the way other men did, with their leering faces and hot eyes and determination. But because he affected her with a strong tug, deep inside.

His appealing face was right there, a breath away, and he was looking down at her. She was tall for a woman, and her chin was almost level with his. The corners of his brown eyes crinkled a bit, and she saw not the lust she expected, that she was accustomed to in a man's gaze, but a sort of taunting challenge laced with levity.

As if to say, *Oh, this shall be the game, no?*

"Your skill with the sword," he said at last, neither acceding to nor challenging her lie, "is legendary. At least among the Dracule."

An unexpected bitterness swept her. Unexpected because she was adept at keeping that emotion well in check. Her swordplay and her beauty, known throughout the Draculean underworld, contributed not only to Cezar's power and fame, but also to her captivity. If she had neither, would her brother even care?

Of course, if she had no beauty, she would never have become part of this world. He would have let her die—perhaps even helped her—just as he had their brother and father, and even his wife. Instead Cezar had found a way to preserve her, along with himself.

Uncertain how to respond to Cale's statement, Narcise gave a brief nod of acknowledgment. "My brother has employed a variety of excellent trainers to tutor me." The chamber had become close and warm, and the lure of pleasure and satiation tugged at her. Her gums filled and a little flutter grew stronger in her belly.

"He must take care of his investment, no?" Cale replied. His voice was light, but she saw a flash of anger in his eyes and tightness at the corner of his mouth.

Her throat had gone dry and she found it difficult to swallow. Was it possible he understood? "My brother certainly doesn't wish any serious injury on me," she said, keeping her voice steady. It was a true statement, though barely so.

Cale hadn't released her gaze, and she found herself trapped in it, looking at the blue and black flecks in his rich brown eyes. "I was prepared to intervene that night," he said, his voice a low rumble.

Narcise felt the bottom of her belly drop. She couldn't speak, couldn't think at first; her lips had formed a silent O. She clamped them closed as she tore her eyes from him.

"Monsieur Cale," was all that she managed to say, even as her heart pounded and an odd fluttering rushed through her. "That would have been foolish."

All pretense that she hadn't remembered him was now gone in the face of astonishment and gratitude. He would have intervened? He would have helped her?

What would Cezar have done?

Suddenly she felt warm and shaky, breathless—and foolish, for the light-headedness was sudden and unexpected. The air had turned so thick, lush with the sweet-peppery smoke, and the deep, dark allure of fresh blood. Her fangs were trying to thrust free, her hands trembling. Before she quite realized what was happening, she felt his fingers close around her wrist, and another strong arm sliding around her waist.

"Some air, mademoiselle," he said, leading her away. "It has become too close in here. And you have not fed."

"No," she protested, determination penetrating the haze. Cezar wouldn't permit such a thing. She dug her heels in, despite the pressure on her arm, despite her need to escape the dangers of this place.

"When is the last time you fed?" Cale demanded, his mouth too close to her ear. Warmth flushed through her; his scent enveloped her along with the heat of his body.

The world swirled a bit, glazed with red heat, then as she blinked and steadied herself, she focused. "I will feed in the morning," she told him. "When we return." *If Cezar permits.*

That was his way of enforcing her good behavior on social events such as this. He didn't starve her; that would be foolish. But he withheld just enough, just long enough, that she was in need. And pliable. And she knew better than to partake without his permission.

The air had cleared a bit and Narcise realized that, despite her efforts to the contrary, Cale had managed to guide her out of the close, warm chamber. Nervousness seized her, and she yanked out of his grip. "Please," she said, forcing her voice to be sharp and strong instead of desperate. "I must return. Cezar will be searching for me."

Cale was looking at her searchingly, his eyes still too close, his mouth near enough that if she turned her head, the pouf of her hair would brush against it. He'd caught up her hand in his, drawing her toward him. "Very well," he replied. "But you must feed. I can see the need in your eyes."

Somehow, the rumble of his voice, the low dip of the syllables, was so intimate that a little pang twisted inside her. There was compassion there, compassion and admiration…and anger.

He made no move to stop her when she tugged free of his grip, noticing for the first time that they were in a dim corridor. A door behind her was ajar, and beyond she could see into the chamber they'd just vacated.

Heart in her throat, she peered into the hazy, golden room, her fingers on the edge of the door. Even through the filtering smoke, she could see the chair in which Cezar sat, its back facing her, his head barely rising above it. He couldn't see her from that position, thank Fates, and Narcise noticed the other two figures settled in front of him.

He did indeed seem to be well-occupied.

Her pounding heart slowed a bit, but before she stepped back into the chamber, those strong fingers were back, gently curling around her wrist.

"Do you see?" Cale said, drawing her back toward him, away from the door. "He has no notice of you."

"But—" she began, and then she stopped, her breath catching.

He'd moved sharply, jerking his arm, and all at once

the scent of fresh blood permeated the air. "*Merde*," he muttered. "What have I done?"

What have you done indeed. Narcise felt almost dizzy from the rich aroma as it seemed to embrace her, sliding into her consciousness. "Monsieur," she managed, her fangs suddenly filling her mouth, thrusting sharp and hard as her veins pulsed with the rush of need. She was under no illusion that his sudden wound had been an accident.

"You would do me a great service," murmured Cale, eyeing her steadily. "If you would attend to this." He lifted his arm.

He'd hardly needed to move, for despite her resistance, Narcise's attention had already slipped down to his bare wrist. His cutaway coat was gone, his shirtsleeve pulled away to expose a golden forearm, muscular and smooth but for the ooze of dark red blood.

"Please, mademoiselle," he said, and she felt the wall crushing the full bustle at the back of her gown. "You need to feed, and here I am in need of assistance."

Narcise should have been angry at him for such a trick, but she didn't even bear that strength of mind at the moment. The blood…his blood, his scent…that of the man whose presence had set her off-kilter, who hadn't made a single reference to her beauty or to wanting her…who'd been willing to intervene in a sword fight.…*his* blood tempted her, and in her weakened state, she had no real chance to deny it.

As if knowing she were light of head and uneasy, Cale slid an arm around her waist, positioning it between the hollow of her back and the wall behind. She had the sensations of heat and solidness enveloping her, the alluring scent of his presence, the warm cotton of his shirt.

She licked first…just a delicate slide of her tongue

over the pool of blood collecting in the hollows of his wrist. He gave a little start, the tiniest of jolts, and she felt his arm tense beneath her mouth. Heavy and rich, his lifeblood settled over her tongue and lips and a great surge of desire rushed through her.

But somehow she held her instinct in check and swirled her tongue over and around the small wound, inhaling his scent, tasting his life. Pure, hot, lush…strong. He was powerful. She could no longer wait, and sunk her fangs into the surging veins on the inside of his wrist.

Now he flowed into her mouth with the delicate rhythm of his heartbeat, the veins filling and surging against her mouth. She drank, breathed, her knees buckling so that she sagged against the wall and into his arms. Lust and need swelled her body, in her veins and beneath her skin, pulsing and dampening her far beneath layers of clothing.

The wall was solid behind her, and Cale to the side, his arm still curved around her waist. She was faintly aware of his body trembling against hers, of the rough movement of his chest. As she held him with both hands, bending his hand back to open palm and wrist, their fingers curled together. She was aware of the heavy ring on his finger, biting into her smaller digits as he gripped tightly.

Narcise drank, sucking gently, her swallows quiet and rhythmic as the ambrosia filled her mouth, funneling through her body. She found herself caressing his warm, smooth skin with her lips as she pinned him with her fangs, using tongue and lips to sip up every bit.

There was a moment when she'd regained some of her strength and she glanced up to see Cale's eyes fastened on her. Blazing red, they glowed like a banked fire beneath heavy lids. His lips had parted, his fangs thrust long and tempting. His expression shot a sharp pang into her belly, and down. Hard and strong, exploding into heat and dampness.

Narcise looked back down, away from that gaze burning into hers, steeling herself for him to pull away and tear his fangs into her throat. But instead of revulsion, she felt another rush of desire at the thought. Her belly trembled, her breasts and tight nipples thrusting against their silk chemise, her lungs constricted.

She pulled her fangs free, reality and fear sweeping into her glazed mind. *Cezar.* She swallowed, tasting the last bit of his essence, and felt him release her. Narcise bumped lightly against the wall, suddenly standing on her own balance, and looked up at him. His eyes still glowed in an orange-red ring around the hazel iris, his lips still parted, showing the tips of fangs. Cale's chest moved as if he'd been running, and for a moment, that fear…that thrill…that he might reach for her and crush her against the wall rose to clog her thoughts.

But he didn't. "*Merci,*" he said in that delicious, low voice that said much more than the simple syllables. "But perhaps you might finish?" He'd slipped back into French again.

Narcise knew what he meant, and for a moment she was terrified to risk tasting him again. But at the very least, it was courtesy. And at the most, it was one more moment of pleasure before she must return to a world of fear and desperation.

With delicate fingers this time, she lifted his arm and, casting him one quick glance, she kissed the wound. She used her tongue to slip away the last vestiges of blood, knowing that her saliva would cause the blood to stop flowing and the wound to heal quickly. And then Narcise released him and stepped back, waiting for him to lunge at her. And wondered how soon it would be before Cezar came out to find them.

"Perhaps," Cale said, still in French, still in that low voice, "if David had been witness to such a display, his painting might have had more authenticity. A bit more... heat."

Narcise could do nothing but nod dumbly. Her head was clearer than it had been for a while, but her body still hummed with desire.

And when Cale turned to pull on the coat he'd slung over a nearby table, she managed to say, "Cezar will know." A knot formed quickly in her belly as the reality set in. He would know and he would exact a punishment from her.

Cale looked at her, his eyes no longer burning, but now inscrutable. "But of course he will know. In fact, perhaps he likely even planned this. But I will ensure you'll have no repercussions, mademoiselle. You may trust me."

Trust me.

The last time she'd believed those words from a man, they'd come from Cezar. More than a hundred years ago, on the night she was visited by Lucifer. Narcise choked back a bitter laugh. And look what trusting a man had given her: an infinite life of captivity.

Cale offered her his unwounded arm, and she slipped her fingers around it. Lifting her chin high, she allowed him to return her to the chamber, ready to face what would come.

She would either live through Cezar's anger, as she had so many times before...or he would kill her in his fury. And that, she thought, could very well be the lesser of the two evils.

Cezar Moldavi was fully aware of his sister's disappearance, and with whom.

Certainly he was, for he rarely allowed anything out of his control to happen. Those days of being pummeled and pushed and bullied were long behind him. Now, everything he did was carefully planned, every possible outcome examined, accepted or rejected, and Cezar Moldavi had long since destroyed anyone who could remember him as the sniveling, snot-nosed coward he'd once been.

Except for his sister, whom he loved.

And hated.

Despite the stimulation of two lovely mortal women who fondled and stroked and tempted him to feed on them, his mind was elsewhere. He knew precisely when Narcise and Cale left the chamber, how long they were gone and who had fed upon whom by the time they returned.

And although he was disappointed with the turn of events, he'd expected it. It had been one of the possible—and, in fact, most probable—outcomes. He would have liked to have been surprised, but the fact that he wasn't surprised wasn't such a great tragedy, for, again, he'd been prepared.

Cale was a striking, powerful man, absurdly wealthy and well-thought-of in both the Dracule and the mortal worlds. He was used to getting all that he desired.

And so was Cezar.

But then again…nothing had truly happened between Cale and his sister. Cezar could smell it: a brief feeding, nothing more. Narcise would pay for her disobedience… but not in the way she might anticipate.

And that was why Cezar allowed himself to be convinced by Cale's smooth explanations for what had obviously happened. The scent of satiation was everywhere in the chamber, clinging to Narcise; there was no way to hide what had occurred. And so, admirably, Cale didn't attempt to do so.

"And see how I injured myself," he said, gesturing to his wounded arm. "I imposed upon your sister, and was able to convince her to assist me. I'm deeply gratified that she agreed, for I fear my shirtsleeve would have been stained otherwise." His smile was charming, even reaching his eyes. Yet, behind the smile, there was a hint of warning. "And Mingo—you understand how valets can be—would be beside himself."

"Certainly," Cezar replied, approving of the very well-cut lines of the other man's clothing. Not as ostentatious as some of the other high fashion here in Paris, with the brocade cutaway coats of pastel, but nevertheless extremely well-made and perfectly fitted. He must get the name of his tailor. "I'm certain Narcise had no real qualms about assisting our host." His expression and voice were bland, and as he glanced over, he saw the flare of nervousness in her eyes.

Good. *But do not expect the sword to drop so soon, my dear sister. I have need of you first.*

If nothing else, Cezar Moldavi had learned to plot and plan and manipulate instead of rushing in. And until he got what he wanted from Giordan Cale—which was more than a mere share in his next spice ship to China—he would look aside and allow Narcise to help him.

At the very least, it would provide some very stimulating activity.

Giordan looked out over the glittering lights. There were gently rocking carriage lanterns, and higher, stable streetlights. The glow of oil lamps, from bright yellow to dull amber, shone from unshuttered windows. The City of Light, named for being the center of education and enlightenment since the medieval monks built their narrow streets, was a more apt nickname than most realized.

He was high enough, here on the silent rooftop, that the shouts and cries from below were indiscernible, mingling with the low hoot of owls and the distant rattle of bridles and carriages. Bonfires blazed in red-orange pockets as spectators waited, reserving their places for the morning's executions. Giordan fancied he could even see the wicked gleam of the guillotine blade in its large black frame.

He wondered how long this madness would last, how long the likes of Robespierre and Hébert would escape a similar fate. Giordan had lived more than a hundred years, and one thing he'd come to realize was that fanaticism and violence had a way of turning on to those who wielded them.

A cool breeze ruffled his curls as he lifted a glass to sip his favorite Armagnac. Warm and pungent, the brandy's potency was a different experience than that of the lifeblood he'd enjoyed earlier this evening, courtesy of Damaris. Not for sustenance did he enjoy the liquor, but for pleasure and weight and taste, and the different sort of looseness it gave him.

So it was for the Dracule: when they ate cheese or fruit or pastries, or any sort of food, or partook of wine or ale, it was purely for pleasure. Texture, taste, scent. A reminder of their enjoyment from mortal days, a social activity. But not at all necessary.

He allowed the brandy to settle on his tongue, swirling it thoughtfully in tandem with a myriad of thoughts, a spectrum of emotions. A burst of laughter erupted below, coming from one of his balconies on a lower floor. Ah, good. His guests were enjoying themselves.

What more could a man ask?

Friends, companionship, social engagements… He was rarely alone. He need never be lonely.

Yet…he'd escaped from his own lavish party to find solitude on the private rooftop. Potted lemon and orange trees, surrounded by luminaries, released their scent into the breeze. A long ledge, planted with rosemary and thyme, contained the low bushes as they sprouted fragrantly. There was a bench if he chose to sit, and even a small pit should he wish to burn the neatly tied fagot resting in it. A fat beetle scuttled across the edge of the bench and Giordan smashed it with his boot.

Pity that he could only utilize the space once the sun went down, for he wondered how different Paris would appear in the daylight. What the creamy rows of houses and their peaked roofs would look like, neat and perpendicular and shoved together like rows of pointed teeth, knit together like the patterned stitches of a shawl.

Perhaps if he had such an unobstructed view, he might see La Chapelle-Saint-Denis from here: the place of his origin, of his birth.

Not his literal birth. He wasn't certain where that had been; in the countryside, he suspected. But the place where he'd lived—no, no, where he'd existed. Merely existed.

Those memories still pierced him, still caused his throat to close up. Still, more often than he cared to admit, had him waking, desperate, in the middle of the day, wondering if there would be enough bread for dinner or a place to sleep. Remembering the scrap of wool he tried to huddle beneath during the snows. Fighting off the memory of rough hands and the stink of unwashed men unlacing their breeches, shoving him into dark alleys.

Here he was, rooftops and decades away from those days, from his own Terror.

And, here in Le Marais, only a few streets from a new obsession: Narcise Moldavi.

A shadow moved on an adjacent rooftop across the way, but he'd already sensed the cat. Elegant and slinky, padding four-footed across the ridge, it turned and looked at him with knowing blue-gray eyes. The moon stroked its pale fur with a hint of blue and silver, leaving the creature to look almost luminous.

Giordan paused with the glass halfway to his mouth and lowered it, watching. Waiting.

The cat's long tail twitched and it gave a low meow, as if to taunt him.

But there was a street—albeit a narrow one—five stories below, between his balcony and the cat's roof peak. That was far enough that Giordan wasn't overly affected by the feline's presence. This was just about as close as he could get to a cat now without becoming weak or even paralyzed, a fact that he despised.

His only friend from those years living hand to mouth, dirty and cold, had been a large, fat orange tabby with yellow eyes. When things had started to change, when he'd had two sous to rub together, and then four clinking in his pocket, and then eight and then they began to multiply faster than Giordan could believe, Chaton (a decidedly uncreative name to be sure) had been with him.

The night Lucifer visited, deep in Giordan's dreams—or perhaps they had been nightmares—Chaton had been curled next to him on the bed, purring. This was long after Giordan had bought his own well-appointed home, with the largest, softest goosedown mattresses he could find, after his incredible financial luck had taken hold. And so it was that, when Giordan awakened the next morning after a hazy, dark dream in which the Devil had promised him immortality and power and even more riches, the first thing he saw was Chaton.

And that, horribly enough, was also the last time he would pet or hold or come near the companionable feline.

For, along with life everlasting and the requirement of fresh blood to live, along with the Mark of the Devil like evil black roots on his back, Giordan had also acquired his own personal Asthenia. His Achilles' heel.

Each of the Dracule had a specific weakness, the proximity of which tightened the lungs and weighted the limbs, making one feel as if they were trying to slosh through water. The nearer it got, the more helpless one became until, at the mere touch of the item, one felt as if one were being branded.

Thus, Giordan, who'd given up death and age, had also given up his pet to become his Asthenia as soon as he laid eyes on Chaton that morning.

It was a sacrifice he bitterly regretted, a hundred fourteen years later.

He turned his attention from the blue-eyed cat, who'd positioned itself to watch him with an unblinking stare, and toward the east. Toward the roof of Moldavi's home, which would soon be lit by the pink icing of dawn.

Cezar owned a narrow house near the edge of Le Marais, but most of his living quarters were located safely under the ground. Giordan had walked through skull-lined catacombs well beneath the *rue* to find his host. The subterranean lair was radically different from where most Dracule resided, and he couldn't help but wonder about the reasons for it.

Security, most likely. To keep both him and his valuable sister safe.

Giordan took another sip and at last allowed his thoughts to go where they wished.

It had been two weeks since the evening she was here, the night things had changed. Since he'd fallen in love with her...just like that.

Ever since the moment she'd fed on him, her full lips pressed to his skin, her teeth sinking into his flesh, he'd known. He'd never felt such strong emotion. Such...completion. Such—

A raucous burst of laughter exploded in the silence, and Giordan turned as someone called his name.

"There you are," cried Suzette, a made vampire who'd shared his bed—and blood—on many occasions.

She and a small group of his acquaintances were just emerging from the door that led to the rooftop. They chatted gaily, bottles of wine and ale dangling from their fingers. And, of course, in their wake trailed two of Giordan's well-trained servants, available to set right anything that might go amiss.

"Whatever are you doing up here alone, darling Giordan?" asked Felicia, another sired vampire with whom he'd traded bodily fluids. She slinked her way over toward him, and Suzette merely rolled her glowing eyes and turned to the man on her arm. Jealousy was not one of her vices.

He smiled at them, his host smile, his not-quite-mirthful-but-very-friendly-one, and gestured out to the City of Light. "But I was merely waiting for you to join me. The view is lovely, no?"

"Not nearly as lovely as this," crowed a drunken Brickbank, one of Voss's friends. He was leering down Suzette's exceedingly low-cut bodice, which, due to the size of her breasts and the way they were plumped up, had a deep, dark vee between them into which a man might slide his entire hand, sideways. Giordan knew this from personal experience, and although the thought might have tempted him in the past...tonight it did not.

"What sort of treat do you have planned for us this evening?" asked the Comte Robuchard, walking idly about the small space. "Some music perhaps? A blazing fire on which we can roast chestnuts?" He was one of the few mortals who knew about the Draculia, and who was invited to some of their activities. Paris was rife with secret societies, but the Dracule was one of the few that was truly underground and unknown, even by some of the upper class.

Ever the good host, Giordan pushed away his lingering thoughts of Narcise and immediately responded, "I thought perhaps I might jump from the roof tonight."

This suggestion—which he'd only just thought of— was met with squeals of delight and masculine roars of approval.

"That will be even more exciting than the night you danced among the flames in front of a crowd of varlets," cried Felicia. Her fangs had slipped free, and now they dipped into her lower lip as she smiled. "They thought they were witnessing the Devil himself!"

"It would be most exciting," Suzette agreed, her arm now slipped through that of a different one of their male companions. "Shall you do a flip, or merely swan dive from the edge?"

"Hmm," he said with a grin. "I must do something fantastic, no?" Giordan had begun to peel off his favorite coat of bronze brocade, and he tossed it to one of the ladies with whom he hadn't shared a bed. Loosening the ties at the knees of his breeches to give himself more freedom of movement, he looked down to the street below.

A fall or dive wouldn't injure a Dracule, unless, by some unhappy event, he or she impaled oneself on a piece of wood, through the heart. Or if some guillotine-like metal happened to be there on the way down to slice one's head from one's shoulders. Neither of which were the case.

Such a feat would, to be sure, frighten or startle any mortal who might witness it, but that was part of the thrill. This was no worse than a mortal riding a horse at full speed and leaping over a high fence: dangerous but hardly lethal unless something went wrong.

And nothing would go wrong for Giordan. He was an entertainer, not a fool.

"Bernard," he said, gesturing to one of the hovering servants, "go below and ensure that I have a clear area to land."

Once having ascertained that there was nothing that might hinder his fall from this angle, he undid the cuffs of his shirt, rolled up his sleeves and poised at the edge of the roof.

Amid the shouts of his friends, his companions, those who filled his nights with activity, he flashed a bold smile and jumped.

He'd purposely launched himself at an angle away from the roof, and caught the railing of a lower balcony on the same opposite building where the cat had been. He swung briefly, then released and somersaulted away from the landing, flipping so that he ended feetfirst onto the narrow cobblestone street.

The force of landing on half-bent legs caused him to stagger into another two steps, making it less than perfect—but at least he didn't land on his arse or head. Then, breathing heavily, Giordan looked up at the shadows lining the edge of his rooftop and executed a neat bow.

Cheers and applause filtered down, and a pair of hack drivers gaped from where they'd been chatting next to his faithful servant Bernard, but despite the commendation lauded upon him, Giordan didn't feel like smiling.

He'd entertained. He'd gifted his acquaintances with food and drink and entrée to his home and club. He had conversationalists all around him, at all times.

But inside, Giordan felt as if he was missing something.

And he knew exactly what it was.

3

Narcise swung around, saber high above her head, and slammed the flat of its blade against her much taller opponent's skull.

He staggered, his red eyes springing wide-open, and his arms flailed awkwardly.

Her teeth gritted in a feral smile, she followed through on the stroke, spinning on the balls of her bare feet, and then nearly gasped, and definitely slowed, when she saw Giordan Cale sitting next to her brother.

He hadn't been there a moment ago.

The angry roar of tonight's opponent dragged her attention back to the battle, and Narcise tightened her suddenly sweaty fingers over the sword's grip just as he lunged at her. She couldn't lose focus; she couldn't let her guard down.

She'd been ready to finish this off, and would have ended with the blade against his throat if the sight of Cale hadn't distracted her.

He was sitting slightly behind her brother, as if a chair had been pulled up for the late arrival at the table, which boasted several other spectators. Though they were in shadow, she could tell that his eyes were fastened on her, and even from here, she felt the heat in them.

I would have intervened.

Damn him to hell, he might have to intervene tonight if she couldn't get her concentration back. Not that Cezar would let him.

Narcise's thoughts had thus been divided as she vaulted over a low table, giving herself space to think and distance from her adversary. Now, she had her back to the dais where the onlookers sat, and though she could feel Cale's gaze boring into her shoulders, she was in no danger of locking eyes with him.

A burst of anger flooded her, fueled by uncertainty, and that gave her the rush of speed and strength to duck beneath the other sword's blade, spin around and take a slice out of her assailant's arm.

He cried out again in fury, but she was faster than his tall, lanky body allowed him to be—and than his lust-fogged mind could follow—and she snagged a chair, whipping it back at him. The crash of wood into flesh and bone, then its clatter onto the floor, told her she'd hit her mark even blindly. She followed through by pivoting on her toes, spinning back to face him. And then she was there, lunging, and used her blade to pin the man through his shirt and arm to the table before he could recover.

The stake was in her hand a breath later, and she positioned it over his heaving chest. "Surrender," she demanded.

He surrendered and she stepped back, removing her weapons carefully as she always did, and watched as he mopped his face with a sleeve. "Big-pussied bitch," he said, his expression ugly. All lust had faded from his eyes.

"Cock-sucker," she replied with calm and disdain to a common reaction. "No entertainment for you tonight."

She watched as he limped toward the door, which had been opened by Cezar's guards, and slammed the saber into her sheath. Then she drew in a deep breath and turned to wait for her own guards to take her to the solitude of her own chamber.

Hot, heavy eyes bored into her back, and she knew without any doubt that it was Giordan Cale who stared at her. She swallowed and realized her fingers were trembling, and that her body had begun to waver between hot and cold.

Three weeks ago, it had been. Three weeks, and not only had Cezar not punished her for feeding on Cale, but he hadn't remarked on it at all. Very odd, and certainly disconcerting.

And though Cezar hadn't seen fit to mention the incident that night, Narcise couldn't banish it from her thoughts and dreams. Even now, she felt her veins pulsing and surging with desire and unfinished need.

She became dimly aware of voices behind her, voices from the dais, and the low rumble that she recognized as Cale's…followed by a short laugh and then affirmation from Cezar.

"Narcise," her brother said peremptorily.

She had no choice but to turn and face the audience. A quick scan identified three pairs of male eyes, filled with lust and determination—likely future opponents—and her brother's bemused expression. Cale… He had stood and was moving *toward* her.

"What do you wish to say?" she replied just as shortly. *Don't look at him.*

"Monsieur Cale has expressed disappointment that he missed most of this evening's entertainment. And he has made a special request."

All at once, her body went cold, her stomach plummeting. Cale had a sword in his hand and he was examining the blade.

"He wishes to participate in a bout of entertainment himself."

A flash of light clouded her vision, then receded. Two battles in one evening? Despite the fact that she'd been overmatched for her previous opponent didn't mean that she could win against a second one in the same night.

Particularly against the broad-shouldered man stripping off his coat in front of her.

Cale didn't spare her a glance as he tossed it to the table, and commenced with unbuttoning his waistcoat. He flung that aside as well, then unfastened his cuffs and rolled his sleeves up to the elbows.

As she watched with rising trepidation, he glanced toward her bare feet and then pulled off his own buckled, heeled shoes…and then the stockings that went up to his knee breeches. Narcise glanced at his bare, muscular calves, then tore her eyes away.

She was to fight him?

And if he won, he would drag her off to The Chamber.

A knot in the pit of her stomach grew tighter and heavier. *I cannot let him win.*

"I wish to change weapons," she announced. A double-sided broadsword would be heavier, but it would give her that much more of an advantage.

"I was just about to suggest the same," Cale said, speaking to her for the first time.

She couldn't help but look at him, and to her dismay, the heat was gone from his eyes to be replaced by cool determination. Her belly pitched sharply, for she would have preferred to see an emotion she could use against him. Like lust or desire.

"I propose a stake only for each of us, mademoiselle.

You might remove the one from your hair, and also from the sleeve of your tunic, and choose only one of them."

Narcise hid her consternation at the prospect of fighting in such close quarters, hand to hand. She was lighter, she told herself. Lithe and quick.

But then again…this was a man who'd somersaulted from a rooftop four stories down, merely for the entertainment of his friends. Or so she'd heard.

"If you suggest stakes, that implies a conflict to the death," she said, keeping her eyes cool. "You are a brave man, Monsieur Cale, for you are no stranger to my abilities."

The room was so quiet the only sound was the heartbeat in her ears and the crackle and snap in the fireplace on the dais.

"If that is what you wish, mademoiselle, by all means I am agreeable." There was a flicker in his eyes, something almost soft, and then it was gone. "You," he said, commanding one of Cezar's servants as if he were his own. "A handkerchief or scarf."

"What, will you fight blindfolded?" crowed one of the audience. "What a sight that will be."

"No, I do not think that is what Cale has in his mind," lisped Cezar, delight in his voice. "He means for their hands to be bound together. Narcise."

This last was his order, and at first she simply couldn't make herself move. They meant to tie their wrists together so that neither could retreat. Or leap or lunge.

She had no breath. Her mind turned blank and fear took over. Already, she could feel his body on top of hers, his hands tearing at her clothes, his mouth and fangs on her.

How badly she'd misjudged him.

That interlude at his place, when he'd been more than

a gentleman, more kind and unassuming than she'd ever experienced…had been a lie.

He really was like the others: blinded by lust, fueled by bravado.

Narcise moved numbly toward Cale, raising her right arm—for she was left-handed in battle. They faced each other, and his strong, bare fingers curled around her hand as if they meant to arm wrestle. The feel of his hand cupping hers reminded Narcise of the intimate moment when their fingers had intertwined so that she could feed on his open wrist. The servant wrapped the scarf around their hands, binding them firmly, and she noted with apprehension that his arm was nearly twice as wide as hers.

Warmth flowed from his skin into hers, and she felt the slamming of a pulse where the delicate skin of their wrists met. Whether the beating was hers or his, she wasn't certain. But she was fully aware of his smoky, rich scent, and the size of his long, bare feet only inches from her own.

She couldn't look at him, instead focusing her eyes over his shoulder as they prepared to face each other.

"Begin," cried Cezar, and so it was.

At first, they minced in a maudlin circle, as far apart as their bonds would allow, delicate and arrhythmic as one attempted to read the other's strengths, strategy and steps. After one quick glance, she avoided his eyes, instead watching the rest of his body. Then Cale lunged, and she danced out of the way with ease.

But Narcise wasn't fooled; she knew he hadn't moved as quickly or sharply as he was capable. He was testing her, to see how tired she was from her first contest.

She concentrated on watching the signals: his eyes, the change of breath, the balance and shift of his feet and center, and she was ready when he lunged again. Their free hands clashed as she raised hers to block his blow, and a slam of pain reverberated down her arm.

Narcise swallowed a cry and attacked him before he could fully recover his stance, glancing a blow off his arm this time. Then without hesitation, she ducked beneath their twined arms and curled around behind him, but Cale was too fast, and he spun under and around at the same time, keeping her from getting to his back. She was tired, not moving as quickly as she normally would.

But she must.

Fury burned in her. She would kill him if she had the chance. There was no reason to hesitate, for if she didn't, he would have her.

And she couldn't bear that. Not after these last weeks of dreaming, fantasizing, hoping.

Bitterness galvanized her, and she whipped the stake, slamming it into the top of his shoulder with all of her force. He gave a surprised grunt, and she swore she saw a flash of humor in his eyes—but then she was dancing backward.

He tripped her with his next movement, and her balance stuttered. She caught herself with her right foot, but not before he twisted suddenly. The next thing she knew, their bound arms wrapped her back up against his torso like the movement in a dance, and he had his stake, poised over her chest. Her own tied hand was pressed against her belly with his, and her body acted as a shield from any blow she might attempt.

"Checkmate," he murmured into her ear, and damn him if the low timbre sent tingles shooting through her.

She tried to stomp on his foot to give her a target for her own stake, but he was ready for it and easily shifted, causing her to tip off balance again.

"Are you certain you still wish to fight to the death?"

Cale added, again close to her ear. "I had a different ending in mind."

Revulsion and hatred shot through her, and Narcise jerked hard at their tied hands, yanking his down with a savage twist.

He gave a huff of pain and for a moment she thought she'd taken him by surprise…but his bicep tightened immediately and he whipped her back against his torso hard enough to knock the breath out of her.

His stake came closer to her throat and poised there as one of his powerful legs shifted, curving in front of hers so that he tipped her forward but kept her feet immobile. Now she was slightly tilted toward the floor, her stake hanging from her left hand with no viable target.

"So now you must slay me," she said, grinding her teeth. "For it was agreed."

Cezar had been watching avidly, and now he began to clap his hands loudly and sharply. "Well done, Cale," he said, standing. "You are the first to best Narcise in years."

She threw her brother a dark look and said, "And that's only because he waited until I was weary. He could not have won if I were fresh."

Cale's arms tightened around her a fraction, and she felt the vibration in his chest as he spoke, "But the woman is correct…she was already spent. Therefore, I will deny my right to take her life—as she offered—and instead accept the customary spoils. If you agree, Cezar." He spoke lightly, but there was an edge to his voice that indicated he would accept no argument.

"Oh, indeed," Moldavi replied immediately. Narcise, who could interpret her brother's slightest inflection, heard the hint of displeasure there, but she wasn't certain whether it was because he'd wanted her dead, or because she'd lost.

Despite the fact that he forced her into such combative situations, Moldavi had a warped sense of pride about her; thus a flaw or loss in her performance was a reflection on him.

"Very well then," Cale said, and he released Narcise so that she was able to stand on her own. "Drop your weapon, *cher*. I have the only stake we'll need." He flashed a quick smile toward the dais, and the other spectators rumbled with soft chuckles.

The servant moved as if to untie them, but Cale stopped him with a raised hand. "No need for that. I will attend to it shortly." He looked at Narcise again. "Drop the stake," he repeated, a bit of steel in his voice. "I don't wish to have to fend you off."

Narcise realized that her knees were shaking so badly she could hardly stand. Her stomach felt as if it were going to erupt at any moment, and she was certain her pulse was pounding so hard he could hear it. She could scarcely force herself to uncurl her fingers to allow the stake to drop, but at last it fell to the stone floor with a clatter.

Cale glanced at her, a little frown between his brows, but she would not meet his eyes. Narcise drew in her breath and straightened her shoulders to stand proudly as he drew her toward the chamber door.

Why was she so terrified? She had outgrown the terror and paralyzing fear long ago. She'd learned to submit, to exist…to get through the demands of her own body's bloodlust, the reflexive response to fresh blood and penetration. There was nothing she hadn't lived through before. There was nothing he could do to her that hadn't already been done.

But she knew what the problem was. Not only had Cale betrayed her fantasy of him, but there was still that lingering *need*. The desire for his blood and the memory of his taste and touch still hummed deep inside her.

Narcise was aware of herself being directed out of the room and down the brief corridor to The Chamber, but she felt as if she were outside of her own body, watching this event.

Cale said nothing to her, nor to Cezar's servant, who led the way to the room of hell. It wasn't until they reached the heavy wooden door that her captor turned and offered their tied wrists to the servant. He obliged, using a dagger to cut through the handkerchief, and Narcise was free just as the door opened before them.

With a rebelling stomach and weak knees, she forced herself to walk into The Chamber.

She heard the sound of the door closing behind her, and of the metal bolt being shoved into place with its familiar, ominous *snick*.

Gathering all of her courage, Narcise turned to face Cale and said, "How do you want me? Shall I fight you and make it rough, or shall I lie there and let it be easy?"

4

Giordan stilled at her words, at the revolting offer.

Narcise stood no more than ten paces away from him, straight as a rail, her ivory face paler than usual and without its normal luminescence. The dark, scraped-back hair gave her an even starker appearance, verging on gaunt. Her fencing attire, those close-fitting tunic and breeches, had damp spots from perspiration and one red blossom on the shoulder from where someone had nicked her.

Her blue-violet gaze was cold and dark, without a hint of Draculean glow.

"Is that how you normally do it? Give an option?" he asked, legitimately curious and at the same time, repulsed by the very thought.

"Not at first," she said conversationally, though there was the faintest tremor in her voice. "I fought them all at first. It took me some time to realize that it was less painful, and often over sooner, if I lay there like a dead fish."

His gut tightened as his attention was drawn automatically to the large bed off to one side. The images flashing into his mind were unpleasant and dark; yet he couldn't deny that the vision of her lying on the bed, naked and spread out, was compelling. More than compelling. Desire flooded him, compounded by the fact that the very room smelled of her—of that heavy, rich ylang-ylang and vetiver—and of coitus and blood.

His veins began to swell as his fangs threatened to show themselves. He forced himself to look away from the bed…which wasn't an altogether prudent thing, for his gaze then lit upon a variety of other accessories in The Chamber.

Chains with manacles hanging from a plastered and painted, rather than stone, wall—which gave it an absurd appearance of civility. A rack of whips. A small metal box. Carved ivory phalluses, of varied sizes. Even small knives: too dainty to slice one's head from one's shoulders, but certainly dangerous enough to cut decorative nicks into one's flesh.

Giordan's belly churned, knowing that each of those items had been used many times over. And those were only the items he saw at a glance. *Narcise, Narcise…how can you be less than mad after this?*

"So which shall it be?" she pressed, her voice a little more tense now. She was as rigidly controlled as he struggled to be. "Surely it cannot be that difficult a decision."

"Where is the peephole?" he asked. For now, he must ignore her question. The very thought was enough to weaken his already stretched control.

She looked at him blankly for a moment, then her eyes skittered to the wall across from the manacles and chains. Cezar hadn't attempted to even hide the small holes through which he must observe. They were hardly larger than the arrow slits in a medieval castle, but there were several of them, at varying heights, in the plastered wall. Not obvious enough to distract one from one's pleasure, but certainly there.

Without preamble, Giordan walked across a thick rug to the wall and spoke into the dark slots. "I don't wish to be spied on, Moldavi." He could scent the stew of male need and lust through the holes, and knew that at least several of them from the previous room were there, prepared for even more entertainment. And, indeed, as he looked into the dark spots, Giordan saw the faint glow of several pairs of orange and red eyes, burning, blinking and then turning away.

He suspected that his host might be annoyed, perhaps even furious, at his statement, but Giordan was confident that the man wanted badly enough to buy into the spice ship he was sending to China, and that he would acquiesce gracefully.

His need for fresh opium was a strong incentive.

But of course, too, Cezar Moldavi needed always to be in control, and a conflict that he couldn't win—such as this with Giordan—would make him appear to be out of control.

So, once the male scents had faded and he knew they were all gone, he turned back to Narcise. She was watching him warily, and as far as he could tell, she hadn't moved.

"What is it to be, Cale?" she asked a third time. "You only have until dawn." The edges of her full lips were white with tension.

"Neither. I'm not going to touch you," he said.

A strained silence settled over the room.

"Are you mad?" she whispered. Her hand had moved, and he could see its faint tremble as she rested it against her throat. A bit of color rushed into her face.

"Just a bit." Giordan pulled his attention away and said, "Is there anything to drink in this torture chamber?" Blood whiskey would take the edge off his senses.

Narcise didn't reply; perhaps she didn't trust herself to speak, either. But she walked over to a cabinet he'd hardly noticed and pulled out a bottle of, praise the Fates, brandy or whiskey. As soon as she removed the cork, its warm, pungent scent filtered through the air, telling Giordan that while Cezar didn't provide his best brandy, it was still a far sight better than what most of the taverns in England served. The rush of the amber liquid sloshing into a small glass was the only sound for a moment. She poured a second one, surprising him faintly, and then turned to look at him. She left one of the whiskeys on the small table and stepped away, sipping from her own glass.

"Your name…it isn't French," she said suddenly. Although they had conversed briefly before, Giordan hadn't truly appreciated the low duskiness of her voice. But now, it curled around him like a smoky serpent and his belly twitched in response.

"No, it isn't, unless it is some shortened version of a name or place. Or perhaps my father was English. I don't know. I don't know much about my origins. I'm fairly certain my parents were from the countryside," he said, willing to follow the brief diversion, for of course he'd been telling the truth when he told her he didn't mean to touch her. Aside of that, conversation might perhaps relieve the pulsing gums pushing at his fangs and the bulge in his breeches.

He walked over to pick up his own drink, wondering if leaving it there was a play for control on her part, or if she didn't trust him to get close enough to hand it over. "They came into the city and then I don't know what happened. We were poor. I have vague memories of my mother, but nothing very solid."

"But you are no longer poor. Was that…" She hesitated, looking at him with desperate eyes this time. "Did He promise you riches?"

Giordan knew precisely what she meant. "Lucifer visited me after I was well on my way to becoming as wealthy as the king." The old niggle of unpleasantness wormed into his belly. "He merely promised that things would never change, and that I would enjoy great wealth for eternity. And I... But I'd lived on the streets, slept in the alleys and beneath the sewer bridges. Once you've been hungry every day for five years, and haven't had shoes or a clean shirt for a twelvemonth, you are desperate to keep that from happening again. At least...I was."

He took a large gulp and pursed his lips, ignoring the doubts and darkness that weighted him at the memories of his past. Why had he agreed to follow this conversational path?

"Did Cezar make you?" he asked.

"No," she replied. "But in a matter of speaking, yes. It was he who arranged for Lucifer to visit me. If he hadn't..." She shrugged. "If he hadn't, he would only have had a plaything for perhaps two decades instead of eleven."

Her tones were nonchalant; something that Giordan could hardly accept. How long had she been her brother's prisoner? And what could he do to take her away? "Luce came to you in your dreams, then?" he ventured, keeping his thoughts away from what he could not change. Yet.

"Is that not always how celestial beings deliver their messages?" she said wryly. "Or invitations?"

"I do not think of Lucifer as a celestial being," Giordan replied with his own dry smile, and felt a sharp twinge on the back of his right shoulder, where the Devil's Mark marred his skin. Luce's annoyance or anger with him often manifested itself through the rootlike weals that covered the back of his shoulder.

"No, of course he is no longer. But he once was friends with Uriel and Michael and Gabriel."

He noticed that her face seemed less taut, and as she chose a chair on which to sit—still a distance from him, but at least she was lighting somewhere—he sensed her beginning to relax. Because of course, their conversation had turned from dangerous things to angels, fallen and otherwise, and the world they had in common.

"And then Luce fell," she added, her face serious. Worn. "Just as we have."

"One does not have to live an evil, completely selfish life despite being Dracule," Giordan said, then gritted his teeth against the sharp searing pain.

Narcise fixed him contemplatively with her gaze. If she was experiencing similar discomfort, she hid it well. But then, she had a lot of practice. "I've yet to meet a *vampir*," she said, using the old Romanian term for the Dracule, "who does not live only for himself, at the cost of life, dignity or pain of others. Including myself. Is it not the way we've been made? What we agreed to?"

Giordan could scarcely account for the fact that they were having such a conversation. Surely Lucifer would burn them alive through their Marks, for he was finding it difficult to even breathe in the presence of scalding pain. At least it had distracted him from the lust and desire she caused in him.

Perhaps this blunt conversation was due to the whiskey. Perhaps it was because she felt the same connection—albeit unconsciously—that he did. Perhaps she'd never had anyone to talk with about such things. He could hardly fathom her and Cezar having a discussion of this sort.

"It is possible to live an honorable life as a Dracule. I know of one who does, in fact," he said.

"You?" She narrowed her eyes skeptically.

"Well," he said, allowing a bit of levity into his voice, hiding the agony burning over his shoulder, "I have been known to make noble gestures. But I spoke of my friend Dimitri, who is the Earl of Corvindale. He has not fed on a mortal for more than a hundred years. He is, in fact, searching for a way to break the covenant with Lucifer."

"Impossible," she said.

"I know it. But he's trying. He rarely comes out of his study for any reason except to search out new manuscripts or writings."

"And so that is why…" Her voice trailed off, and she rubbed her lips together thoughtfully.

Giordan suspected he knew what she'd been about to say. Although he hadn't been there, he was aware of the night in 1690, in Vienna, when Dimitri's house had burned. That was the night that Cezar had forced his way into the place and presented Narcise as an offering to his host—who had declined, having not the least bit of interest in her.

How Dimitri could have been indifferent to the woman in front of him, Giordan couldn't imagine, but he was grateful for that fact in many ways.

"What's in the box?" he asked, once again noticing the small metal chest that sat amid the sorts of accessories the Marquis de Sade might use.

"If you truly mean me no harm…please don't open it," she said quickly. That tension had returned to her beautiful features.

"It must be your Asthenia," he said. "And your brother allows it to be kept in here with you, when you are already at a disadvantage?" Anger chilled him. Cezar Moldavi was one Dracule who deserved to burn in hell for eternity.

Instead of responding, Narcise merely looked at him, which was as close to an admission as he expected.

"Perhaps someday you'll trust me enough to tell me," he continued.

He stood, walking over to the bottle of whiskey, and poured himself another drink. As he sipped, he turned back to look at Narcise. Overwhelming desire caused his heart to stutter and his breathing to alter, but he buried it firmly.

Not now.

Not here.

Not tonight.

He gripped his glass tighter, focusing on the scent of the alcohol and not the essence of woman that filled his consciousness. Not the enticing curve of her jaw, one that he suddenly wanted to brush his lips against, nor the ivory column of her neck, so slender and elegant.

"Why did you do this?" she asked.

"A variety of reasons, all of them—well, most of them—quite noble."

Narcise's eyes lifted, focusing on him over the rim. "Such as?"

"I'd seen you fence, and I wanted to test your skill myself. I wanted the opportunity to talk to you."

Her eyes had narrowed and she flung the rest of her whiskey down her throat. "But we did not fence, Monsieur Cale," she said, her voice even smokier, now baited with whiskey. "And you knew that I wasn't at my best—"

"Which was precisely why I chose this way to do it. I wasn't completely certain I would best you, of course, and so I thought it best to ensure that it all worked out in my favor." Giordan realized that he didn't at all mind admitting that fact. However… "I realize you don't know me very well, but I confess that I find it no little insult that you assumed I wanted to win so that I could lock you in a room with me and rape you." He sipped from the drink, his fingers so tight around the glass he feared it might shatter.

Her chin had snapped up at his blunt words, a shocked expression flickering across her face. "Why should I have thought any differently?" she asked…but the tone in her voice wasn't accusing or even defensive. It was weary.

"Because," he replied, watching her, "when you fed on me three weeks ago, I didn't so much as breathe lustfully in your direction, Narcise. Although all I wanted to do was drag my arm away from your mouth and push you up against that wall and dig my own fangs into your shoulder…and then your arm…and your breast…the inside, that very tender, most sensitive part of your thigh…" His voice grew lower, unsteady and rough. "And then I would use my tongue, long and slick and warm…all along your skin."

She gasped audibly, and the color rose higher in her face. Their eyes met, and he allowed her to see the glowing flame of desire in his. The bald need.

"I wanted to fill my hands with you, taste you. I suspect you'll be rich and warm, like a custard, sweet and yet strong. I wanted to slide my warm body against yours, feel the two textures of our skin melding. The heat generated by the friction."

He knew his words were so soft they barely reached her ears, but the rise and fall of her chest and the growing blaze in her eyes told him that she heard him.

"When you sank into me," he continued, making love to her with his words, caressing her with his tones, "I realized it was *you*. It would only be you. Narcise."

She moved sharply, that high color easing from her cheeks. "Lovely words, Monsieur Cale. But what a ridiculous thing to say, from a man who will live forever."

Giordan shrugged and concentrated on the way his feet were planted on the floor. Rooted, cemented there, keeping him from moving to her, and taking her face into his hands to show her how certain he was. "I've never felt that way before, Narcise. And I've lived a long time."

He felt the weight of her own gaze on him, and saw the bare hint of a glow there. His gums tightened, swelling more, and he thrust away the memory of her mouth closing around his arm, and her lips tracing the ridges of his wrist. He couldn't dismiss the memory of her tongue sliding through the heat of his blood, and the need burning in her eyes.

"I said I'm not going to touch you," he heard himself saying. "But that doesn't mean that you cannot touch me."

5

Narcise's breath caught and a rush of heat flooded her.

That very thought, that very temptation, had been teasing her, and now it bloomed, full and hot and sudden, in her thoughts.

"You would allow that?" she said carefully.

"I would welcome it," he replied. His voice, so low and filled with desire, sent a stab of desire into her middle. "Narcise."

The thought was titillating…and freeing. To have control, here, in this very chamber that epitomized her captivity, her complete dependence. And to have such a man beneath her hands and body and fangs.

His unique scent, fresh and warm, tinged with cedar and wool, had already seemed to overtake all of the other smells of memories—dark, awful ones—in this chamber, and now sat fully in her consciousness, reminding her of how he tasted and felt.

"But then…" *No.* She shook her head.

Temptation thrilled her…and eased into despair. But no. How long would his resolve last, if indeed he truly had resolve and it wasn't merely a trick?

As if he read her mind, Cale said, "I won't touch you. Even if you bid me." He glanced at the manacles on the wall, then back at her. His eyes challenged her, dark and intense.

Narcise was aware of a light fluttering in her center, broadening and spreading like the delicious heat of a fire on a cold Romanian night. Those compelling eyes still fastened on her; he walked over to the smooth white wall, marred only by the chains that hung there.

"I understand why you hesitate to trust," he said, slipping one of the cuffs over his wrist and locking it into place, where it held his wrist just away from his head. "Perhaps this will help." Then, unable to close the other manacle with his chained hand, he stilled and met her gaze. A sharp twinge pierced her inside.

"Narcise. Believe me when I say nothing you could do would make it more difficult for me than standing here, keeping my word not to touch you."

Trust me, he'd said before. He seemed to be saying it again, wordlessly this time.

She looked at the band encircling his wrist, wide and, she knew, cold. He would give her that control?

Wholly? Willingly?

In a place where she'd fought for so long to keep her own?

The irony touched her deeply.

And then all mundane thoughts of irony and the like fled as she realized what she had. Here. Giordan Cale: handsome, strong and virile. Offering whatever she wanted, great or small, as she wished.

Narcise's mouth dried and she found it hard to swallow as she walked toward him, her bare feet padding from cool stone floor to lush rug back to stone again.

Her middle was filled with fluttering moths, her gums swelling as they pushed out her fangs.

All the while, their eyes met and held, and it seemed as if she could feel his heart, thudding inside her own chest. Their heartbeats pounded together, their breaths seemed to work in tandem, and for the first time, in this room, she felt…womanly.

Womanly, and powerful, in a way she hadn't felt since she'd loved Rivrik.

Standing there in front of him, Narcise lifted his free arm, and felt the little ripple of a shudder beneath his skin. Her upper fangs brushed her lower lip, and without thought, she took him and brought his wrist toward her mouth.

Cale went still. Even his breath ceased as she watched the blue veins seem to surge and pulse amid the tendons in his golden skin. Instead of plunging in her fangs, Narcise flicked her tongue over the delicate ridges there, tasting the salt on his warm flesh, sensing the flavor of his scent and the essence of lifeblood pounding beneath its thin covering.

When she lifted her face, she heard the soft hiss of his breath and saw the faint smile lifting his lips. There was heat in his eyes, but no tension, no conflict in his face. Merely pleasure.

For some reason that comforted her, and she allowed her eyes to narrow and crinkle at the corners. Allowing almost a smile. And then she clicked the second manacle around his wrist, and stood back to survey her captive.

As the thought flitted into her mind, at first her reaction was one of horror that she should even have thought the word. She knew what it was like to be a captive, held immobile and helpless and at the mercy of the whims of others.

But this was different, she told herself. He gave up control willingly. He offered. He *wanted* to be here, he *wanted* her to touch him…and whatever else she chose to do.

And, she found, there was no doubt that she wanted to do…many things.

That alone was a welcome revelation, a relief, to a woman who hadn't willingly responded to the touch of a man for decades. For once the fangs protruded and the bloodscent filled the air, and the penetration began, even Narcise couldn't control her own body's instinctive reaction. But those occasions hadn't been real pleasure, or true satiation. They'd been wrung from her like some unwanted and terrible purging.

But now, tonight, this was for her. *All* for her. And Cale seemed to have understood that.

"Are you going to stand there all night while the blood flows from my arms," he said in that mellow voice, "and make me only imagine what you might do? Or are you going to kiss me and make the discomfort worth my while?"

"I never kiss," she told him, nevertheless moving closer. Her fingers itched to tear that shirt away and see what was underneath. She had a sudden fantasy of muscles shifting and bulging from the effort of pulling on the chains, in his biceps and rippling over his chest, and she wanted to see if it could be real.

His shirt was made of the finest linen, warm and damp from his skin. She tugged it loose from his tight breeches, noticing the very healthy bulge rising behind them. The sight and accompanying thought sent another spear of lust into her belly, and she boldly smoothed her hand down over that tempting ridge.

Cale gave a soft sigh and when she looked up, his

smile had grown that much hotter and his eyes darker. "Is it becoming warmer in here, or am I imagining it?" he managed to say.

"I'm perfectly comfortable," she replied and smoothed her hands beneath his loose shirt. His firm belly, warm and textured with a light dusting of hair that she imagined would be as dark as that on his head, skittered and trembled beneath her fingers. And as she slid her hands farther up beneath the shirt, she covered hard slabs of pectorals and then her fingers curled up over smooth shoulders. The tips of her fingers brushed over what must be the ridges of his Mark from Lucifer: slender, raised, veinlike markings spreading from beneath his hairline down over the back of his shoulder. As she slid over that unholy branding, her own Mark twinged and she brought her hands to rest flat on the front of his chest, pressing into the wiry hair growing there.

Narcise was aware of him watching her as she stepped back and removed her hands from those warm planes, then realized there was no way to pull the shirt over his head while his wrists were chained.

"Cut it if you like," he said, reading her thoughts. "I have many more."

"As you will," she replied, but instead of reaching for one of the daggers, which had been used on her, she grasped the shirt at his throat and ripped. The heavy linen made a satisfying, powerful sound as it tore, and left his chest bare to her avid eyes. "It's no wonder Suzette talks about you the way she does," she commented, and tore one of the sleeves free, jolting his arm against the wall.

The chains clinked with her violent movement, but he made no attempt to pull or wiggle in his confinement. She eyed the bulge of muscle in his arm as his elbow bent in an L-shape, his wrist fixed at the level of his head. His skin, even beneath his shirt, wasn't the normal pasty-white of the sun-banned Dracule, but was golden, as if tanned by a sun that never touched it.

"In what way does Suzette talk about me? I do hope it's—" His breath caught as she plunged her fangs into the soft inside of his bicep, and he gave a short, sharp groan as his lifeblood burst free.

The taste and scent of his skin, so silky and soft around that firm bulge of muscle, mingled erotically with the rush of coppery blood over her tongue, and Narcise closed her eyes as a long-subdued desire rushed through her. His bare chest brushed against her cheek, and the long line of his legs paralleled her body as she pressed flush against him.

The hard rise of his cock nudged her hip, so close to that suddenly throbbing, hot and damp center between her legs. She held on to his forearm with one hand, and the other planted flat on the rough hair covering his chest. Texture, taste, scent…and his lean, muscular body sand-wiched between her and the wall.

She pulled away after two long drags on his veins, swiping her tongue over the wound in a delicate little farewell, and looked up at him.

His eyes burned bright red-gold, and yet the centers were dark and intense. He had a sort of pained half smile fixed on his full lips, a bit of fang showing. For a moment, she almost shifted to cover them with hers, to taste him in yet another, more intimate way.

But she didn't. Instead, testing herself and testing him, she stepped back, realizing that her breathing had become unsteady and shallow. Her nipples swelled behind the bindings she wore beneath the suddenly too-tight tunic.

"More," he said, his eyes compelling her. "More, Narcise. I want to feel you against me."

She saw no reason to hesitate, and peeled off the close-fitting tunic. The freedom to do what she wished, to be in control and to enjoy the pleasure of the moment, emboldened her. Flinging the shirt aside, she untucked the binding around her breasts and began to unroll it, conscious of his intense regard.

Her relief at the release of her bosom was echoed softly by his rough intake of air when she pulled the last strip away and at last jounced free. She raised her arms, feeling the pleasant sensation of her breasts lift prettily.

"More lovely than I'd imagined," he said, the timbre of his voice skimming over her like a low and deep caress. "Will you take your hair down?"

"For one who has given over control," she said wryly, "you certainly have many requests, Cale." But nevertheless, sparked even further by her power and the pleasure simmering beneath the surface, she began to pull the pins from the huge knot of her hair.

"My given name is Giordan," he said. "Use it."

Narcise paused in the process, one heavy hank of hair tumbling down her back while the rest remained anchored in a sagging bundle. It was the first time she'd heard that tone of command from him. She found it curious...and unsettling.

As if reading her thoughts, he spoke again. "Very well, then, *cher*. No real intimacy yet. No kissing, no familiar names. When you've come to trust me, then I would that you'd call me Giordan. But to me, already you are Narcise." His eyes blazed fiercely, not with lust or desire, as before, but now with annoyance.

"I think you're mad, Cale," she said. "We've hardly met, and barely spoken. How can you say such absurd things when you don't even know me?" Of course, she was thinking of Rivrik, back when life was life and not infinite rote…and much easier than this. Back when she knew she would die someday, and when she was naive and young and in love with someone who truly knew her.

Cale gave what passed for a shrug, and despite the awkward angle of his arms, it was smooth and laced with conceit. "Sometimes, a man just knows." His eyes fastened on her, the glow receding into an intense brown-blue gaze.

Unbalanced and unsettled by the certainty in his voice, she yanked a few more pins from her hair. Narcise was mollified when she saw the way his eyes narrowed in appreciation as she combed her fingers through the thick tresses.

Her hair was one of the reasons for her great vanity, for it hung to her hips. All one length, it was a pure blue-black, thick and smooth as a waterfall even after being bound up in braids or twists. Next to her pearly skin and brilliant blue-violet eyes, the color was intense and striking.

Now she stood there, bare from her ankle-length breeches up, her hair swinging around her shoulders and waist. His eyes never moved from her as Narcise came closer, feeling the gentle sway of her bare breasts, nipples tight and high and throbbing to be touched. Her fangs were still extended and she allowed their tips to show just below her upper lip.

As she drew near, she scented his arousal, smelled it rolling off him in waves, and her stomach tightened and pitched in response. Lush and heady, it filled her nose and swelled her veins, settling into her so that she swelled and dampened and throbbed. She pulled out of the pleasure for a moment to remind herself: this was so different from the other times, when the overwhelming

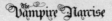

scent of lust was pungent and stinging, and as repugnant as the bitter smell of death.

Now, The Chamber was filled with the scents of desire, male and female alike, mixing and stewing together to create an even headier perfume. The last bit of his lifeblood lingered in the air and she sniffed, drawing it in, tasting it once again.

"Narcise," he whispered, his voice taut and low.

She came to him, her hands settling on his hips, then sliding up over the ridges of his belly and the rise of the planes of his chest...and brought herself closer. She arched a bit, lifting her breasts so that her hard, sensitive nipples brushed against the wiry hair there, rubbing lightly back and forth against him as their bellies and thighs pressed together. The light prickling sensation against her breasts and nipples was pleasant and tingly, offset by the hard, hot length of his cock against the rise of her pubis.

His chest moved against her, expanding as he drew in deep, ragged breaths, and when she became bold enough to look up into his eyes, the stark desire there shot a spike of lust in her own belly. His lips were parted, showing the sharp, strong gleam of his fangs. She felt a little shiver of want, imagining those sharp points sliding into her skin, and the glorious release of her surging blood over his warm lips.

The soft clink of chains, every nuance familiar to her, told Narcise precisely what he was doing—shifting, clenching his fingers and tensing his muscles. But he wasn't struggling to free himself. He didn't pull or twist as she'd done, trying to loosen them.

Now, she slid her hands back down along his torso, pausing to unlace his breeches and drawers, and then tugged them down over his lean hips. His cock surged free as soon as it was able, thick and tumescent, and Cale gave a soft sigh of relief at its release.

Narcise eyed him appreciatively, her mouth watering a bit and her quim full and tingling with interest and curiosity. Her cheek brushed deliberately against the hot, velvet skin of his erection as she worked his breeches down from knee to ankle, and she inhaled the very male, very aroused scent emanating from that center of heat.

When she got to the floor, he obliged by silently lifting his long, elegantly arched feet, and she slipped the tight breeches away. And then she settled back, her palms flat on the cool stone floor, and looked up at him.

Magnificent. She didn't think she'd ever seen a more perfect specimen of maleness—and, unfortunately, she'd seen far too many. He was as sleek and muscled as Michelangelo's statue of David, and even had the same head of thick, curling hair.

Or perhaps she was merely inflicting such a comparison on the moment, as she didn't generally stop to admire—or criticize—the bodies she normally came in contact with.

"I cannot help but wonder if your silence is due to disappointment or awe," he said, a bit of taut humor in his voice. "I hope it's the latter that has you dumfounded."

"Oh," Narcise said, her eyes traveling up along tight, muscled calves and impressively sturdy thighs, "I think it is safe to say that Suzette did not exaggerate."

She pulled to her feet, unwilling to remain in such a supine position any longer and, tossing her hair back over her shoulder, stripped off her own breeches and drawers.

His rushing exhale was audible, and when she stood in front of him, as naked as he, the heat in his eyes nearly set her on fire. The chains clinked audibly and she saw the muscles in his arms tighten even more. His cock twitched enticingly.

"What now?" he said in a dusky voice.

Narcise couldn't remember the last time her body felt so warm and lush and alive, swelling and throbbing with arousal. Power and desire gave her courage, and she stepped away for a moment, presenting him with her backside as she went over to the array of daggers and whips. The edges of her hair brushed pleasingly over the top of her buttocks.

"You've vowed not to touch me," she said, picking up one of the finger-length daggers. She remembered this one, remembered the tiny little cuts that had been made all down one side of her torso, little Xs, neatly and carefully so that a delicate patchwork of red had been left. Time to banish that memory. "And you've claimed that I can do anything I wish."

"Indeed," Cale replied. His voice, still dark and low, was a bit stronger now. Perhaps a bit wary.

Narcise walked toward him, feeling the hot glow in her eyes and the insistent press of her fangs. She held the slender dagger, sliding her fingers thoughtfully over its hilt. The Devil's Mark on her own shoulder throbbed and swelled in encouragement.

"Do you like pain, Monsieur Cale?" she asked when she came to stand very close to him. So close that his breath stirred her hair, and she could smell the blood leaping beneath the wound she'd given him. Her mouth watered at the memory of his taste and scent, and she swallowed hard.

His glowing eyes, still dark and intense at the centers, bored into hers. "You may do what you will, Narcise, I will not fight you. But I am not one who enjoys receiving—or inflicting—pain on my lovers."

The rumbling sound of those last syllables—*my lovers*—sent another shock of desire into her center. Such a beautiful voice, and the caressing of those syllables was a figurative stroking of her skin. Such an intimate word, so foreign to her, so out of reach. To be one's lover presumed a span of time. Perhaps even some tender emotion.

And…the bald truth in his words, for she could read it in his eyes, released a last bit of tension she hadn't even realized existed. *I am not one who enjoys receiving or inflicting pain.*

"Very well," she said, and raised the dagger. With a sharp, deliberate movement, she sliced a nick in the soft part of her palm.

The blood burst into a thick red line, half as long as her finger, as Cale gave a little jolt, then went still.

Narcise tossed the dagger away and lifted her hand, the bright red blood shiny and slick on the plump skin. "Taste," she said, bringing it to his mouth.

He hesitated, and she could fairly see his fangs quivering with need as she brought her hand to his lips. The chains shifted and clanked, and his torso pressed against hers, hot and damp.

"You aren't breaking a vow. You won't be touching me," she said when his only reaction was a slight flare of his nostrils, followed by a ripple in his throat. "Just taste. Sip."

He moved then, at last, his mouth covering the soft, blood-drenched skin of her hand. His lips were warm and gentle, full but firm, as they covered and caressed the wound there. The effect was the same as if he'd covered her breast with his lips, or her quim with his mouth: sensual and erotic, soft and sleek and cunning. He used his tongue to slip around, just as she had done to him, lapping and stroking the sensitive flesh, sucking and drawing in her blood. The release of pressure that had been building inside Narcise swelled and washed through her as he teased and licked with his magical mouth.

Though his teeth and fangs scraped against her, and though he gave a soft, deep groan in the back of his throat, he never drove them into her flesh, penetrating and taking more than she was offering.

Narcise, her body damp and loose, pressed herself all along the front of him, sliding and rubbing for her pleasure as much as to tease him. As he licked at her hand with full, slick lips, she curved her fingers around his cock, moving them idly up and down the length of it. He jolted and trembled against her, pulling away from her wounded hand to rest his head back against the wall as she stroked faster, then slower, then faster, faster, faster—

"*Narcise!*" he groaned, and she felt his body ready, gathering up.

"Not quite yet," she warned and slowed her last slide. Then, removing her hand, she drove her fangs into the soft part of his shoulder.

He jolted again, and cursed in pain and relief as the blood burst into her mouth like a hot, coppery orgasm. Narcise's world turned warm and damp, pounding and pulsing, as she drew on him, hard and fast, desperate and needy. Her vision darkened and became red; her consciousness was filled with the texture of sweet, bloody ambrosia and damp skin, and an erotic mélange of sensation.

Now they were vibrating against each other, the rich smells of arousal thick and full, the taste of his lifeblood filling her mouth, and her own, still on his breath. She released him and bit again, roughly, driven to devour him, to take him all in—taste, scent, touch—singe her tongue to explore those small wounds, the curve of his shoulder and neck, the taste of his skin, salty and hot.

Her bloody hand curved around his cock and guided it to her, as she lifted on her toes. She raised a leg, settling it around his hips, and he groaned in desperation when he was unable to help steady her, to settle her in the right place, and she felt the tension rippling through his body. But Narcise had an arm around his neck, her ankle curved behind him, opening her legs so that he could fit into her. She was swollen and ready and with one measured thrust, she impaled herself against him.

Cale gave a sharp cry, echoed by her own gasp at the intense, brilliant pleasure. *Oh my, oh my*...was all she could think as every bit of awareness faded into a ball of heat that expanded as she moved against him, and he thrust smoothly, forcefully against her.

She wrapped her other hand around his neck, too, fairly hanging there, and planted her feet against the wall at his hips so she could leverage herself within the pounding rhythm.

The ball of heat and pleasure grew and swelled until it filled her center, rolling into a great undulating explosion of pleasure that had her crying out, and then sobbing with relief and satiation as he shuddered his release against her.

She felt the tremors through her body, inside and against her, for a long time…and after a while, she realized she was sliding down off him, her knees weak and her limbs loose and soft.

The wall was cool and smooth under her fingers, and she heard the faint clinking of the chains, the soft rasping breaths of his pleasure and the stone floor beneath her toes.

After a long moment, she opened her eyes, stepping

away from his warmth with a shameful little stagger. Her
fingers trembled, but there was a warmth in her belly that
had spread throughout and made her want to smile. And
perhaps even to cry.

"Narcise," he said after she'd stepped back and gathered up her tunic and breeches, then turned to pick up
the dagger and to return it to the table: focusing on
those mundane tasks instead of the tender emotions that
seemed to be threatening.

There was an odd note in his voice and she looked
over to see—

"How did you do that?" she said. He was standing
there, one of the manacles hanging free. A chill raced
over her.

She didn't need him to answer, for she realized that his
free wrist was the one *he'd* clasped inside the manacle.
And that he must have connected it loosely or even not
at all…so that he could—

"You could have freed yourself at any time," she said,
needing to speak the words out loud in order for them
to penetrate. As she watched, he reached over and unlocked the wrist manacle she'd connected. It wasn't difficult: there was a small little pin that held it closed and
could be adjusted by the size of the wrist. Her world had
begun to tilt.

"You can trust me, Narcise," he said.

Something unsteady bumped in her heart and a little coil of fear started in her belly. Her Mark twinged
sharply. Now that he was free, now that she'd aroused
his lust and shared some of herself with him, he'd take
and *take*—

Narcise shook her head to force away the rising panic,
and realized she still had the dagger in her hand, behind
her back, and she gripped the hilt comfortingly. The blade

was cool against her bare skin, but she shifted so that Cale couldn't see it. She wouldn't allow him to touch her. He'd promised.

By now, to her faint surprise, he'd pulled on his breeches, and then scooped up his shirt. "But of course I want to stay, Narcise," he said, his voice very even and very low, his eyes penetrating. It was as if he could see the change in her emotion: from ease to terror. "However, I'm not going to impose my presence on you any longer, for the temptation to forget my vow is much too great. Particularly after...*that*." The low rumble caught on that syllable and dropped even lower as he made a slight gesture toward the wall of chains. "But I'll return. Until then, remember what I said." His gaze held hers for a long moment, as if to nudge her thoughts.

Trust me.

It's only you, Narcise.

Sometimes a man just knows.

She shook her head, more in confusion than negation. In an absurd display of betrayal, her body still hummed and the little knot in her quim still throbbed pleasantly even as she sifted through truths and lies, flattery and appreciation.

"Thank you," he said softly. "I pray you are safe until we meet again, *cher*."

And then he unbolted the door and slipped through, closing it tightly behind him.

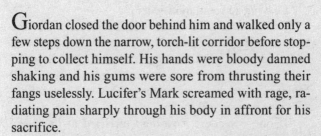

6

Giordan closed the door behind him and walked only a few steps down the narrow, torch-lit corridor before stopping to collect himself. His hands were bloody damned shaking and his gums were sore from thrusting their fangs uselessly. Lucifer's Mark screamed with rage, radiating pain sharply through his body in affront for his sacrifice.

It had taken a good deal of control and prudence to turn and walk out of that room, and if he weren't certain his every movement was being accounted for, he'd stand here longer.

That was, in fact, the only reason he hadn't dragged her out with him to freedom.

He looked around, sharpening his thoughts to take in the details of his surroundings. Of course he'd passed through this same area some hours earlier, when he was following Narcise…but understandably, his mind had been elsewhere and he'd been in no state to absorb all the details. Unlike The Chamber he'd just quit, this space was roughly hewn stone walls and an uneven floor. Very different from the dining room that doubled as a fencing arena.

But of course he was already considering how to get Narcise out of this place. It wasn't something he could rush into, much as he wanted to—*needed* to—get her free. He must plan his steps carefully, he must be patient.

For surely Cezar wouldn't even allow him free access after his "winnings"—and, ah, yes, there it was. The sound of approaching footsteps. Someone had heard the door opening from some nearby vantage point, or there was some other notification that he'd left. Perhaps a bell that rang in an above-stairs chamber.

"Leaving so soon, monsieur?"

Giordan was more than mildly surprised to see the host himself striding toward him, bringing that patchouli and cedar scent into the narrow corridor. "Yes, indeed."

"I trust that there were no problems, no concerns?" Moldavi asked, his eyes bright and his voice placating. "All was to your...liking?"

"If one considers a woman terrified at the mere thought of being touched by a man no little problem, then, no, I had no problems." It was only with great difficulty that Giordan was able to keep the great loathing from his voice and expression.

"She did not give you difficulty?" Those eyes looked closely at him, then slipped away to scan over his torso as if to look for signs of wounds or injury. An unnaturally slender brow lifted at the sight of the bite marks on his bicep.

"But of course not." Giordan was fairly certain there had been no witnesses—either visual or aural—during the events of the evening, for he surely would have scented the presence of anyone near enough to see or hear. But, yes, he had been a bit distracted, so he couldn't be completely certain. "I had all that I wanted, and now I have finished."

"Very good. Very good. It's just that I find it unusual for a man to leave my delightful sister any earlier than he must, hmm?"

Giordan gave a meaningless shrug and said nothing more as they walked along the corridor.

Moldavi continued smoothly, "Would you care to join me for a drink, then? I have just received a most delightful vintage from Barcelona. They are calling it a champagne, but of course that is impossible if it is grown in Spain, is it not?"

Giordan hesitated for a moment. He wanted more than anything to get away from this abhorrent man, out of this dark, close place and back to his own…but the more time spent in his presence, here in the highly secure, subterranean locale, the more he could learn about its layout and his host's habits…and the sooner he could find a way to relieve Cezar Moldavi of his favorite plaything.

His fingers curled into each other as he thought of having to leave Narcise here…but he forced them to smooth out. *Patience.*

Thus, although he truly wanted to be alone—with his thoughts, his memories, his fears—his concern and care for Narcise's future easily prevailed. "Perhaps…perhaps, yes, for a brief time. I would be delighted to sample your offering. It sounds most intriguing." He kept his voice mellow and even enthusiastic with effort.

Moldavi's face changed, a brief contortion, and his eyes widened a fraction…then it was gone. "Please, then, with me," said his host in his imperfect French. "And, if you like, Cale, I would be happy to provide you with new attire. I suspect you don't wish to be traveling back to your home in nothing but breeches. I have retrieved your coat from our dining area, of course, but perhaps you would accept my gift of a shirt and shoes as well."

Giordan realized that his host was correct, and that he hadn't given his bare feet, legs and chest any thought at all. *Ah, Narcise. You've already destroyed me.* "I would be very grateful."

As he walked along with Moldavi, Giordan considered the option of killing the man right here, right now. It was an efficient way to resolve things; one he'd employed far too many times, if the priests had anything to say about it. Which, of course, they didn't. It was a plain truth: Giordan had grown up with violence and poverty all around him, and was more likely to kill a man who crossed him than he was to waste time trying to find other resolutions.

That was yet another reason, he was certain, that Lucifer had found him an appropriate addition to the Draculia.

Killing Moldavi would end the man's domination over Narcise, and they would find their way out of this labyrinthine lair beneath the *rues* of Paris.

But Giordan was forced to reject the fantasy nearly as soon as it presented itself, for a variety of reasons, the simplest being, he didn't have a weapon. It wasn't as if he could choke the man to death or pummel him into the ether like one could do on the streets. Either a wooden stake or a sword that would take the man's head off were the only ways, and aside of the wooden sconces, there was nothing else that would work. And to tear down a sconce, break it into a ragged point and then attack Moldavi…even Giordan wasn't confident it could be done quickly and without mishap.

Aside of that, to do anything that would make the man suspicious would ruin any chance he might have of further access to Narcise.

Patience.

"So you have lived in Paris since you were a child?" Moldavi asked as they approached a heavy wooden door.

"Yes. Although the place I lived while a boy was much different than Le Marais," Giordan said with a sidewise, wry smile.

"I have come to prefer Paris myself," Moldavi said. "Romania is rough and wild with its own beauty, but also dark and sharp and difficult to navigate…and I find the City of Light a much welcome change." He had the key on a ring at his waist, but there was a guard stationed there to provide additional security.

"Although I travel much now for business purposes, I always return to Paris, for it's my home," Giordan replied.

It appeared even the guard didn't have access to the door, for it was his master who used the key to unlock the door. From what Giordan had observed on his journey to and from, the single purpose of this corridor was to provide access to The Chamber where he and Narcise had been. There was no other entrance or exit along here, no other rooms, and certainly no other way in or out of the room in which they'd been.

He wondered, suddenly, and with a painful shaft of horror, whether Narcise was kept in that place of torture all the time, or if she had some other sort of living space.

They walked through the door and Giordan took in the details of what he'd only vaguely noted the first time through. This underground tunnel had been in Paris much longer than Moldavi had.

"How did you come to choose the catacombs as a place to live?" Giordan asked as they passed along the corridor. What he really meant was how had Moldavi taken over control of these underground tunnels where varlets and vagrants had lived for centuries. "I would have thought you'd prefer a château or some other mansion."

The walls of this hallway were lined with neat rows of skulls, their empty eyes and toothy upper jaws an eerie and morbid decor. Above each row of skulls were lined several layers of large bones—femurs, he guessed by the size of them, with the joint ends facing out. They made for bumpy texture, and the hollows provided homes for spiders and other insects.

Giordan made no attempt to hide his surprise that a man as refined as Moldavi—at least in attire and his selection of food and drink—would choose to live in such base surroundings. But then again...this was a vampire who bled children to death and who imprisoned his sister for the pleasure of others. He tightened his jaw to control the rage. Perhaps he would kill the man now.

"It is a bit gauche, isn't it?" his companion replied, brushing a hand lovingly over one of the skulls. "But I find it such an interesting topic of conversation. At the least," he said with his faint lisp, "they are long dead and gone and we don't have the rot and smell of the decomposing bodies in the...the place where they are moving all of them now...what is it called?"

"The Ossuary," Giordan replied, having regained control of his temper. He noted that the skull-lined corridor had branched off into two different directions and that they'd taken the eastern route. "In the old stone quarries."

He recognized that the tunnels they now traversed were old quarries as well, but that these bones must be the original ones from the fifteenth and sixteenth centuries. The placement of these bones decades ago were the inspiration for the disposal of the bodies from the overcrowded church cemeteries, the newest wave which had begun thirty years earlier from parishes like Holy Innocents.

Giordan had traversed many of these underground tunnels even before he was turned Dracule, and now he was redrawing a map in his head. Combining his memory of the network and the actual route they took, he was attempting to connect the two areas. That would come in handy if—*when*—he helped Narcise make her escape.

They came to another door at a T-intersection of the corridor. When they passed through the entrance into a hallway that looked exactly like one in his own home, Giordan realized that Moldavi must simply use the skull-lined quarry as a conduit between his torture chamber and his real living space.

This suspicion was confirmed as they strode through, chatting amiably about a variety of things, and Giordan smelled Narcise, among other aromas. She obviously spent much time here, as did Moldavi and others.

That was an optimistic sign. If she were kept here, in this furnished, plastered and painted area, Giordan would have a much better chance of freeing her from it. And perhaps not quite as many nightmares about her cloistered in the torture chamber.

"Please, sit," Moldavi offered as a steward opened a tall, white door at the end of a gently ascending hallway. Inside there were many comfortable chairs and a roaring fireplace. "I hope you do not mind," his host said, gesturing to the flames. "But I tend to easily take a chill and I prefer a blaze in every chamber."

"I find it rather chill and damp beneath the ground, so I welcome the heat," Giordan told him.

Glasses clinked and Moldavi offered him a small ornate vessel shaped like an upside-down bell. They talked for some time about the spice ship, and all the while

Giordan kept his ears and nose attuned for the presence of Narcise.

But it was when Moldavi, after a long moment of silence, said, "I find that I will need to be absent from Paris for a week or more to attend to a business interest in Marseilles," that Giordan's body came to full awareness.

Something prickled over the back of his shoulders and he sipped the very fine sparkling wine that had come from Barcelona. "Do you travel by coach or horse?" he asked just to keep the conversation going, even as his mind worked madly. He kept his eyes heavily-lidded and his attention purposely jumping about the chamber. "I cannot help but admire your selection of artwork," he said. "Perhaps you've noticed I am a patron of Monsieur David."

"I did notice," Moldavi replied. "He has given my sister painting lessons, and in fact, that is one of her works." He gestured to a small square painting, surrounded by an ornate frame as wide as the image it embraced.

Giordan had already taken note of the dark, stark image of a city beneath the moonlight. The rows of buildings appeared like angry gray teeth thrusting up into a dark sky. Out of politeness, he looked again, and then, because he couldn't appear too interested, he drew his attention away almost immediately.

"I see little resemblance between her work and that of David," he commented, thinking of not only the lack of hue but also the subject matter. Monsieur David generally concentrated on portraits rather than landscapes, and even his stark portrait of the murder of his friend Marat wasn't as angry and undulating as Narcise's world.

How does she live?

Cezar gave a short laugh. "I certainly concur, but the

painting keeps Narcise occupied." He spoke as if she were some young girl who tended to be around underfoot.

Giordan had to raise the drink to keep from speaking his mind…and from lunging for the repugnant being next to him…and found that his fangs threatened to clink against the edge of the delicate glass. He drew in a slow breath and sipped, willing his teeth to resheath themselves, his eyes to keep from burning with an angry glow. *Calm.* "I suppose she cannot practice her fencing all day," he managed to say.

Aside of his surprise that the painting was Narcise's, Giordan was also taken aback that Cezar obviously allowed his sister to interact with people—men—other than when she fought for her own body. Through general conversation with Moldavi and others of those who moved in their circles, he was aware that Narcise often helped her brother entertain, and of course, very occasionally accompanied him on social engagements. He also realized why Narcise had seemed to be so familiar with, and interested in, the David painting in his own parlor.

"No, indeed not," Moldavi agreed. "But a thought has just occurred to me."

Giordan raised an eyebrow in question and tried not to look back at that dark, hopeless painting.

"I must be gone for a week perhaps, as I mentioned. I have no desire to bring Narcise and the entire household with me. Perhaps since you both are so appreciative of Monsieur David—although for different reasons, I venture—perhaps you might be willing to see to Narcise in my absence?"

Giordan went cold for a moment but recovered immediately as he saw the trap. *Clever, Moldavi. Very clever.* It wasn't difficult to force a grimace of distaste. "I hope you won't think me rude if I decline," he said with a self-deprecating laugh. "I expect to be very busy in the next fortnight, and might even need to travel outside the city myself." He watched the other man closely and was rewarded when he noticed the slightest release of tension in his fingers.

Giordan had obviously made the right move in such a blatant denial of interest.

But whatever it was that Moldavi intended, Giordan had also learned one other thing: without a doubt, the man was exceedingly cunning.

He would have to be very careful in how he proceeded. To give a man like Cezar Moldavi any sort of knowledge was also to give him the greatest of power.

And to make a move in haste or desperation could be a fatal mistake.

Trust me, Narcise.
I pray you are safe until we meet again.

Narcise woke suddenly, those words echoing in her mind. Remnants of dreams. As she stared into the soft candlelight, a bitter laugh formed in the back of her throat, startling her with its ferocity, and she pressed her lips together.

Trust me, Narcise.

Her fingers shook as she skimmed them over her naked belly, then curled them between her breasts, where her heart beat roughly, and held her hand there. Oh, yes, she had a heart, and though it had become enclosed by stone, she still felt its soft core.

What had Cale meant by saying such things? Particularly the absurd *I pray you are safe until we meet again.*

Dracule didn't pray.

And how would they ever meet again? Did she even want to meet him again?

A little twinge deep inside told her that, yes, she did. She would. He had touched her without actually *touching* her.

Climbing out of her bed, Narcise let the covers fall. It was always damp and cool here, below the ground where Cezar insisted on living. Even here in her private chamber, which was comfortably appointed with an attached parlor furnished with upholstered chairs, a mirror and dressing table, a wardrobe, and even a place for her easel and paints, the chill was never fully banished. There were no windows, of course, and the only indicator of time was a clock which she kept wound.

A stone and brick hearth held the fire that never ceased blazing, and it was only when she drew near it that Narcise was able to completely stop the little shivers of cold and dread. She stood there now, staring into the tongues of flame, feeling its warmth seep into her skin, heating the sheer lace gown she wore.

The orange and yellow fire mesmerized her, and Narcise felt her eyes begin to burn from the heat and lack of moisture from not blinking. But deep in the hot glow, she saw Giordan Cale, in her mind, strung up on iron manacles, his dark, intense eyes boring into her.

Trust me, Narcise.

He'd certainly proven his trust that night. She shivered, but not from the chill. No, thoughts of Giordan Cale invariably brought heat, not cold, to her body.

Yet, it had been more than a week since he'd left The Chamber, closing the door behind him and leaving her to her thoughts and confusion—not to mention a warm, sated body. Since then, she'd drawn and dreamed of him, even as she tried to keep herself from hoping…for something.

A log shifted in the fire, loud and sudden, sending sparks scattering on the hearth. The noise brought Narcise from her musings back to the reality that she was still Cezar Moldavi's sister, still his toy and bargaining chip, and still unwilling to trust anyone.

Unwilling was the wrong word. She was *unable* to trust.

With a sudden burst of frustration, Narcise turned from the fire and rang for Monique, her maid. Monsieur David would arrive soon for their weekly lesson, and he did not like to be kept waiting. And since the murder of his friend David Marat, he'd become even more ill-tempered and fanatical. Narcise had mused privately more than once that her brother either paid the artist exceedingly well for his continued lessons, or that he had some other hold over Monsieur David that required the man's presence on a weekly basis, despite his complete immersion in Robespierre's movement.

It was ironic: despite the fact that Narcise was Cezar's prisoner, in many ways he treated her as a beloved sister. She had lovely, fashionable clothing, comfortable accommodations, activities to keep her mind occupied and her body in good form, and servants at her beck and call. She was invited to participate in her brother's social appointments, which most often occurred safely in his own residence, and was treated as respectfully as he was.

The one thing she had no control over was her body.

But that was something she would change. She must. And nary a day went by that she wasn't considering some plan or possibility, gathering some information and tucking it into the recesses of her brain. After decades of captivity, most prisoners might have long given up hope of escaping or changing their situation, but Narcise would not. After all, she had immortality. She had forever.

She watched and listened, honed her fighting skills, made friends with some of the lesser servants and slowly, but surely, built a refuge within her prison.

Perhaps it was Monsieur David's fiery rhetoric, fueled by the Revolution happening beyond the walls of her homelike prison. Perhaps the artist's determination and belief that one should rule oneself, that no royal family or clique had the right to impose control over another, had given Narcise hope. After all, if an entire city, no, a *country*, could overthrow its reigning family and weaken the grip of an entire privileged class, why could one woman not overthrow her own personal dictator?

By the time the maid Monique had helped Narcise with a simple day dress and covered it with a painting smock, she had hardly enough time to plait her mistress's hair in a fat black braid.

The knock on the door to her adjoining parlor heralded Monsieur David's arrival and Narcise followed her maid into the next room. Monique answered the door to the artist as Narcise began to sort through her canvases, but when she turned to greet her teacher, she faltered.

Confused, but recovering, she turned to her maid. "Monique," she said in a brusque tone, "you may go. Bonjour, monsieur." Something was not right, and awareness teased her consciousness along with an odd mixture of scents lingering in her nose. She swallowed, tasting and smelling a familiar presence.

The artist, wearing a low-brimmed hat that showed his dark brown curls, strode into the chamber with his familiar satchel of paints, brushes and palette. He appeared to have had his hair trimmed since she'd last seen him, a week earlier. His long coat, perhaps one too long for the summer, swirled about his powerful, breech-covered legs as he placed the bag on a table.

"Bonjour, mademoiselle," he said. His words were thick and oddly pronounced due to a tumor that deformed his cheek and mouth, but were perhaps a bit deeper in tone today. "Shall we begin? But no, you are not yet ready for me." His disgust at the delay was clearly apparent in his voice and stance, and Monique, intelligent girl that she was, beat a hasty retreat.

David was not known for his patience nor his tact.

By now, Narcise's palms were damp and her stomach had filled with swirling, fluttering emotions. Was it possible? "Of course, Monsieur David. I am nearly ready. I was only looking for the camel hair paintbrush that you insisted my brother have made for me."

All of her brushes had handles made of bamboo or light metal, for Cezar would not allow anything resembling a wooden stake into her chambers. Her rooms were regularly searched for such contraband as well.

The door had closed behind Monique, and for the first time, the man's eyes, still shadowed by the wide brim of his hat, met Narcise's. The irises were brown, flecked with blue and ringed with black, and the last time she'd seen them, they'd been hot with desire.

Narcise's stomach did a quick flip, leaving her unsteady and weak. It was *him*. She'd scented Giordan Cale beneath the cloak, hat and satchel that also smelled of Jacques-Louis David, but until their gazes locked, she wasn't certain.

She gave a little warning shake of her head even as she turned to gather up her painting accoutrements, trying to keep her suddenly nerveless fingers from dropping the brushes and palette. "Ah, here it is," she said, producing the brush in question. She could see, now that she actually looked at him, the way his right cheek bulged—just as Monsieur David's did. It changed the shape of his face, and along with the heavy brim of the hat, there was little to see unless one looked very closely.

"So now you are at last ready for me?" he asked, still in that thick voice of disguise, still managing to make it sound annoyed. "But you will not need that brush today."

You are at last ready for me.... His words held the most subtle of underlying meanings that made her cheeks warm like that of a schoolgirl's.

"But of course, monsieur. I believe that our last lesson was in relation to perspective." As she spoke the words, Narcise wasn't certain whether Giordan Cale was at all familiar with the particulars of drawing and sketching, and she hoped she wouldn't inadvertently expose his masquerade.

For, although at least in her chamber she had privacy from prying eyes and ears—she knew this because she examined every inch of wall, floor and ceiling every month to ensure it—Narcise also knew that at any moment...

Ah. There it was. The knock on the door.

"Come in," she called, trying not to sound breathless as she dug through her paints. Cale removed his coat to lay it over one of the chairs, but he still wore his hat, and she was suddenly nervous that it would cause comment, or that he would need to remove it.

Cezar's trusted steward, Belial, entered the chamber. "Bonjour, Monsieur David," he said with a bow. "What is your desire today?" His sharp eyes scanned the room, and Narcise held her breath, praying that Cezar's sired vampire wouldn't notice that this David was several inches taller and with broader shoulders than the previous one had been, and that there was another scent mingling in the room with them.

Cale didn't pause in his action of moving a stool to the center of the room, and perhaps his half-bent, facing-away position helped to camouflage his physical appearance.

"I shall have the usual, of course," he said in that clumsy voice, and with the same peremptory tone David always used. He fussed with the stool as if needing to position it just perfectly in the light. "Mademoiselle, I shall act as your model today to continue your lesson on perspective. The very brim and angle of this hat, which I have borrowed for such a purpose, will be an excellent study in the aspects of perspective. You will need a charcoal and several soft lead pencils. Put away the paints, mademoiselle. I have already told you you won't need the brush today. How many times have I said that you must start with the drawings and sketches before you can think to paint?"

Narcise forced herself to relax slightly. He sounded just as Monsieur David would have. Cale had obviously planned this well—but what *was* he planning? "I am sorry, monsieur. It is just that I ordered new paints and hoped to be able to use them today."

"Always so impatient, the women, no?" Cale said to no one in particular, but Belial gave a soft knowing chuckle.

"I will shortly return with your refreshments, monsieur," the steward said.

He left the room as Cale ordered, "Mademoiselle, please. You are wasting my time."

The door closed behind Belial, and Narcise turned to face Cale. "What are you doing here?" she demanded in a low voice.

"Can we be heard or seen?" he replied in matching

tones, looking around the room. It was clear he had something in his mouth that caused the deformity of voice and
face, but now his tones at least sounded familiar.

"No, but Belial will return shortly. How did this come
about?" Narcise's hands were shaking, trembling furiously, and she could not understand her reaction to this.
What did it mean? Why was he here? And why did she
suddenly feel such warmth and light inside her?

"I told you you could trust me, Narcise," he said, sitting on the stool. "Get your papers ready and begin to
draw, or I fear Belial will be suspicious. Once he is gone
again, I will tell you more."

She did as he bid, feeling his eyes on her as she pulled
out the rough papers that curled from being rolled for
storage. A hunk of burned coal and her Italian pencils—
too slender and short to be used as wooden stakes—
joined the parchment on her drawing table, a few stones
anchored the paper from rolling up, and then Narcise
got to work.

She noticed that Cale had arranged his position on
the stool so that he wasn't directly facing the door, nor
the table where Belial would place the tray of coffee and
sweet breads when he returned. And once she acknowledged that added attention to detail, along with the deliberate tilt of his head to shadow his face even further,
she concentrated on her own work.

Despite his disguise, what a pleasure it was to draw
the man she'd previously had to sketch from memory.
She saw, too, that he'd affixed some sort of false, pa-
pier-mâché nose to his elegant one, widening it slightly,
and as she looked even closer, she noticed faint markings on his face, smudges to emphasize lines and non-
existent dimples.

Narcise had become so engrossed in her work, drawing the angled guiding lines for the hat that would give the sketch depth and an accurate sense of space, that she was startled when the door opened and Belial strode in.

But she felt his sharp eyes scan the room, and her drawing, and was pleased that she'd accomplished as much as she had. The steward set the tray on the table then approached her as if he were master of the place, looking over Narcise's shoulder—something that he occasionally did, but never in the presence of Cezar. She heard, and felt, him test the air about her in a soft, long intake of breath. The fine hairs at the back of her neck lifted and prickled, but she didn't move except to continue her work.

"You are very talented," he said, low and much too close to her ear and Narcise tensed. "Perhaps you will give me some private lessons?"

She resisted the urge to spin and shove the dog away for his boldness. Cezar had left three days ago, and had named Belial head of the household during his absence. Apparently this expression of trust had given the man an unwarranted sense of entitlement.

"Perhaps you will leave me to my work," she replied from between tight jaws. "Your smell is disturbing me."

She felt him stiffen behind her then relax slightly. "Is that so?" he said, obviously attempting to force amusement into his voice. "But I cannot say the same for you, Narcise." He drew in another long breath near her ear. "Your scent is as enticing as you are."

"Cezar doesn't value you that much, Belial," she warned. "You are replaceable and I am not." Rather than fear, it was anger that made her hand unsteady. As if her brother would allow a servant to touch her. Even he was not so base.

The steward made a sound filled with arrogance, but

Narcise had no concerns about anything he might attempt. And despite the annoyance, she was glad his attention was focused on her and not Cale.

She dared a glance at the model sitting on his stool, and caught a flash of fiery eyes beneath the brim of his hat. Firming her lips she sent a silent warning back at him and resumed her drawing. She didn't need Cale's anger, nor his meddling in this.

"You've completed your task, Belial," she said, replacing her pencil that drew light, thin lines with the heavier charcoal. Broad strokes emerged, dark and bold, filling in the shadows beneath the curve of the hat brim. She itched to work on those lips: so full on the bottom and with a soft line along the top one that would require delicate shading. "You may leave."

"So I am distracting you?"

"No," she said, putting the charcoal down and fixing him with fury in her eyes. "You are tempting me to introduce you to my saber. Intimately."

Belial's eyes flashed red, but he drew himself up and away. "Do not be so certain of yourself, Narcise." And with that comment, which she assumed he meant to sound ominous, but which nearly made her laugh, he turned and stalked from the chamber.

"Cock-licking snake," she muttered. Belial was a fool who'd become too important for himself. She took out her annoyance on the charcoal, crumbling a corner of it and creating an unnecessary smudge when she raked it too hard across the page.

"Does your brother allow all of his servants such freedom?" Cale asked quietly.

"He won't come back until the lesson is finished," she told him. "We are private. And, no, Cezar would not allow such effrontery if he saw it. Everything must be well under his control, and a servant—no matter how trusted—who oversteps his boundaries will find himself turned out or otherwise disposed of."

"Good." Cale moved, sliding off the stool. He raised a hand to his face, and the lump in his cheek moved, then disappeared as he caught whatever it was in the palm of his hand. "Peach pits," he told her with a sidewise grin. "Two of them, in fact." He placed them in a handkerchief on the stool. When he took off his hat, then tousled his curls from where they plastered to his skull, she found herself wanting to assist him.

But Narcise remained in her place, a distance away. "Are you going to tell me what you're doing here?" She noticed a fat black spider making its way along the edge of one of the wood planks on the floor.

"Since I doubt your brother would allow me to court you in a normal fashion, I decided I had better take matters into my own hands." A glint of humor that she'd come to realize was part of his personality shone in his eyes, and then it disappeared.

"Court me? Are you mad?" No man *courted* the sister of Cezar Moldavi. They merely took—or, at least attempted to.

"I would have come sooner, but the arrangements took some time. But in the end, Monsieur David was grateful for my large donation to his cause, and the extra time with which to spend it. Are you well?"

She realized her brows had drawn together in a frown. He spoke to her with such familiarity; as if they'd known each other forever, as if they were friends and intimates. "We've only met twice," she blurted out, hardly realizing what she was about to say. "But I feel rather as if I've come to know you even more than that."

He still wore the false nose; perhaps that wasn't so easily removed and replaced as the other elements of his disguise. Nevertheless, it was clearly Cale, with his steady eyes and the full lips that had traced the oozing blood on her palm so tenderly. "I couldn't be more pleased to hear that, for I feel as if I've known you forever…even though I hardly do, in all the ways that matter. I must know, Narcise…have there been any other fencing matches since our last? How have you fared in them?"

She knew what he was asking—whether there had been any other men since him, and whether she had been forced or not. "There are not so many now who are brave enough to face my saber," she said by way of answer. "Few men are willing to expose themselves to the possibility of the humiliation of being bested by a woman."

"Which is precisely why I took measures to make certain I would win," Cale replied. His roguish smile was infectious enough, even from a distance, that she couldn't keep her own in check.

A ridiculous thought: that he was here to court her. Yet, deep in the softest part of her stony heart, she felt a twinge of lightness. A girlish leap inside the hard heart of an old crone.

"But you did not answer my question," he pressed. He was leaning against the table where Belial had set the tray—still some distance from her. She noticed absently that the spider had made its way into the center of the room and was heading toward the opposite side with eight-legged efficiency.

"Other than ours, I haven't lost a fencing match for more than five years," she told him. "And before that, after the first five years in Romania, before I had my lessons, it was a rare night that I lost. Perhaps two or three times a year."

Cale's eyes were somber now. "I'm sorry it was that many times."

"So am I. But I've become stronger for it," she said, in a reminder to herself as well as to him. "And no one has touched me—against my will," she added with a quick glance at him, "for many years."

"Will Belial bother you? Cezar is gone, is he not?"

Narcise waved the steward away with a charcoal-smudged hand. "If he acts inappropriately, I know how to handle him."

"I have no doubt of that."

He didn't speak after that, but his eyes scanned her. The hunger therein was bold and obvious, but again, he made no move toward her. Narcise wondered about that, and felt herself tensing in readiness. And, if she must be honest, anticipation.

"Are you and David lovers?" Cale asked abruptly.

She couldn't control a shocked expression, nor a shiver of distaste. "No, of course not."

"Good." He nodded once. With a deliberate movement, he smashed the spider under his foot, as if to emphasize his response.

Narcise blinked then redirected her thoughts. "Once again, I must ask, Monsieur Cale, why you have gone through so much trouble to come here."

"I wanted to see you, of course, but I didn't want your brother to know it," he explained.

"Because he wouldn't like it?" Narcise frowned. "I am not so certain of that. He was mightily impressed that you won our sword parley, and I believe he finds it amusing that you're very well-matched in skill with me. He wants to forge a business relationship with you."

Cale was looking thoughtful. "I'm not certain whether he would or wouldn't like it, but either way, I'm not inclined to give him the benefit of the knowledge that you belong with me."

She drew herself back in affront. "I don't belong to anyone." A blast of rage shuttled through her, but when he lifted a hand she allowed him to speak.

"I said you belong *with* me, Narcise. Not *to* me. We belong together. I can feel it, and you will, someday, as well."

She looked away. "You're mad." But even she knew her words sounded weak and unconvincing. The truth was something tugged deep inside her, throughout her whole being, when he was near. This was so different from any of the other men who'd claimed to love her, to want her, to own her.

It was different because, damn the Fates, she felt it, too.

"He knows that I could take you away from him, from here," said Cale. "He knows that I'm the one."

Narcise raised her eyebrows skeptically.

"When you trust me." He smiled, but this time there was a bit of an edge to it. "And since I cannot come near you today or that low-crawling rodent will smell us, you'll see once again that I mean to take nothing from you that you aren't willing to give."

The flash of disappointment took her by surprise, and yet at the same time, Narcise felt a tide of relief sweep over her. "That's why you asked if David and I were lovers," she said wryly, a twinge of annoyance replacing her relief.

"No," he said.

She waited for him to elaborate, but he did not. A heavy silence descended, one in which the drumming of her heart seemed to grow louder, filling the chamber, and his as well, and she swore she could hear them beating in tandem. Warmth and softness flooded her, and if she didn't know that it was impossible for a Dracule to enthrall another Dracule, she would believe it was happening.

"And so," he said after a long moment, breaking the connection, "these are your private apartments—where you sleep? Where you paint, and entertain?"

"I do very little entertaining, as you can imagine," she replied, picking up the charcoal, then choosing one of the heavy pencils instead. There was a place that needed a darker shadow, but it was at the outside corner of his eye and required a delicate touch. "But I paint and draw here. There is another larger room where I practice with my sword."

"Does Cezar allow you any freedoms? Do you ride, or shop, or visit the cafés and museums?"

"I do not leave this premises without him," she replied. "I haven't been on a horse in years. He brings entertainment here, and the seamstresses and cloth merchants. He's afraid to go above ground very often."

"It must be related to his Asthenia. Despite my generous bribes, no one has even a suspicion of what it is," Cale said. "Do you?"

She shook her head. "Do you not think I would have found a way to use it by now if I did? It is an immensely well-guarded secret. I do not believe there is anyone beyond Cezar and Lucifer himself who knows."

"But what of his makes?" Cale asked. "Would it not be clear from them?"

It was a logical question, for when a Dracule sired, or made, a new vampire, his or her Asthenia was passed on to the new immortal. In addition, the immortal gained a unique Asthenia of his or her own. Thus, the further down the evolution from Lucifer's personally invited vampires, the weaker and more vulnerable the makes were, for the more Asthenias they acquired.

But Cezar was much too smart to make such a mistake. "Contrary to what my brother implies and wishes for people to believe, he has not made any *vampirs* himself. At least, of which I'm aware."

That surprised Cale, for his brows rose in shock. "How can that be true? He is known for his clan of loyal servants—most of them makes—and for his influence over even the mortal world in Paris."

"But it is true. For many years, he held three Dracule captive and forced them to sire *vampirs* for his use. Early on, he used me in the same manner." She spoke matter-of-factly as she reshaped the line at the lower part of his ear.

Cale seemed to digest this for a moment. "Very clever. And if the sires of the vampires are under Moldavi's control, then so are the makes themselves. But you are his sister, and you cannot guess what his Asthenia is, even now?"

"All I can suspect is that it is something so common that it keeps him away from the mortal world unless the environment is very much controlled."

"Then I must count myself flattered that he accepted the invitation to visit my club."

"He admires you—your business acumen, and your wealth."

Cale nodded. "Many do," he said with that sudden smile. "I am gifted in that way. But I think your brother is more interested in my Chinese contacts, and the partnerships for the opium I can help him get."

"Cezar won't allow himself to be weak enough to become an opium eater," she told him. Then she added, "Perhaps you could sit again, monsieur. I cannot seem to get this particular…" She squinted, forgetting what she was about to say as she tried to imagine the shape that the now-absent hat had made above his right ear.

Cale sat, an amused smile softening his mouth. "So he does not want the opium for himself?"

"Oh, he does, but he doesn't indulge very often. He avoids anything that lessens his control of himself or a situation."

"I have come to that conclusion."

"Now, if you could cease from speaking for a moment, monsieur," she commanded. "I must get your mouth."

"I will if you will continue talking to me."

"Very well. Cezar wants the opium for his own occasional use, but also so he can use it to influence and control not only his allies, but also the powerful people in Paris. Mortals and otherwise. They'll buy it from him, or he'll gift them with it in order to get what he wants done."

Silence descended again as she concentrated on making the shape of his mouth perfect. With an artist's detachment, she drew the lips and shaded them, the top lip always darker than the bottom because of the way it was formed and the way it slanted out and curved into the seam of one's lips…but as she finished, her femaleness began to take over. Remembering how those lips had molded to her palm, the slip of his tongue over the sensitive skin there, and the delicate brush of his mouth, hot and tender…she had to close her eyes for a moment to steady herself.

"When you trust me enough, you'll kiss me," he said, reading her thoughts with uncanny ability. Her eyes shot open and were captured by his. "And," he added, "you'll tell me what was in the little lead box in the other chamber."

Narcise licked her own lips nervously, and felt his eyes slip to her mouth. If nothing else, the man owned his control. His desire, his taste, for her was palpable, undulating through the chamber. Her own want made her fingers shake so that she couldn't finish the stroke.

"Feathers. Brown sparrow feathers," she said softly, ignoring the sharp slice of pain from Lucifer's Mark. Even though it was no great secret—many of her rivals obviously knew what was in the lead box, and Cale could easily find out himself. But he asked, and she wanted to give him the information freely. She wanted to give him something of herself. "The first thing I saw when I woke the morning after…the morning after Luce visited me…was a sparrow, singing in the tree outside my bedroom window."

He nodded in acknowledgment. "Thank you, Narcise. That's a beginning. And that's all I need from you now."

He looked as if he were about to say something more, but then his body tensed. At the same time, Narcise turned to look toward the door. She heard the footfalls, too. By the time Belial and Monique entered the chamber, Cale had stuffed the peach pits back into his mouth and replaced the hat. He was holding a cup of the coffee, and a piece of the sweet bread David enjoyed in the other hand.

Narcise positioned herself closer to Belial in order to distract him from Cale as the latter packed up his satchel and prepared to leave. She was favored with one covert glance, warm and intense, from beneath the hat brim, and then her false tutor was walking out the door.

She wondered when and how she'd see him again, and realized all at once how badly she wanted to.

Was she falling in love again?

G iordan Cale found a way to visit Narcise three more times during her brother's absence in Marseilles. Each time, he took her by surprise, each event was carefully planned and executed, and each time, he remained at a physical distance from her—despite the fact that she could feel the heat and desire between them the moment he walked into the chamber.

If he was trying to prove his trustworthiness to her, he was succeeding. If he was trying to breach the walls around her protected heart, his attempt was formidable.

Although she didn't fully understand why Cale was so intent that Cezar not know of their meetings—after all, he'd been instrumental in that first night they spent together in The Chamber—Narcise didn't argue, nor did she attempt to make their liaisons open. Instead she found herself growing more and more enamored with him, with his sense of humor and element of levity, and more and more desirous of tearing off his clothes and kissing him.

When she thought about what it would be like to cover those warm lips with hers, to taste a bit of lifeblood if she nipped one of them, mingling with their lips and tongues…to have their bodies lined up, mouth to mouth, breast to breast, hip to hip…Narcise could hardly imagine why she'd resisted so far.

But kissing, in her mind, was the last frontier of intimacy. The one thing that she could control; the thing that the men who wanted her body didn't particularly care about. Kissing, which was often the first stage of love and lust—and had been for her and Rivrik—was now the last step for her, and one she guarded jealously.

When Cezar arrived from his travels, he called her to his private parlor within hours. As he always did when they met alone, he had a tray of three brown sparrow feathers sitting on the table next to him. They were close enough to sap her strength, yet far enough away that she could talk and move, albeit a bit more slowly than usual. But most of all, they were a deterrent to her getting close enough to attack him.

He'd made that mistake once, fifty years ago. One thing about Cezar—he had absolute attention to detail, and a long memory.

"You look well, dear sister," he said, his eyes scoring her. He didn't appear pleased, but then, he never particularly did. "How have you been amusing yourself during my absence?"

"Other than fending off the hot-breathed stink of your friend Belial, nothing out of the ordinary," Narcise replied flatly, selecting a seat as far from the feathers as possible. Already, her body felt slower and heavier, and her lungs tight and constricted.

"Belial?" Cezar's face tightened, and for a moment, she felt a notch of pity for her brother. To believe that one of his most trusted allies and servants—for no one was a confidant of Cezar Moldavi—would betray him and his trust in that way was a blow to his carefully controlled world. "He attempted to touch you?"

Narcise gave a particularly unladylike snort. "He went further than that, dear brother," she said with a sarcasm-laden voice. "He wore a ring of feathers around his wrist one day when he came to deliver some wine to me, and attempted to convince me that I should allow him to feed on me." The tremor was more from anger than anything like fear; Belial was a make, and she could squash him like a bug if he didn't have the cowardly feather brace-let on his arm.

"Indeed." Cezar's voice was cold. "Did he succeed?"

She shrugged nonchalantly, despite the fact that her blood had begun to surge and race. "He did not, which was fortunate. I would have been powerless against him in the presence of those feathers—for no sooner had he backed me into a corner than one of the fabric merchants arrived. Monique interrupted and I was forced to decline Belial's proposition."

It must have been coincidence that the fabric merchant had, in fact, been Giordan Cale, in another of his dis-guises. He had sensed her upheaval, and when she told him about Belial, he became so still and quiet that she feared he would expose his identity and attack the ser-vant. It was only her assurances that she was untouched and that Cezar would manage the problem on his return that kept Cale from throwing off his cloak and wig and going after the man.

"I suggest," she now told her brother firmly, "that you keep him away from me in the future. Or I'll kill him."

Cezar nodded, and it was to her credit that he didn't ask how she would do that. "I'll see that he won't bother you again. Perhaps you'd like to take matters into your own hands?"

Narcise smiled. "It would be my pleasure."

"Very well. I don't wish you to kill him," Cezar ordered. "But do whatever else you wish. I'll arrange for him to select his sword tomorrow night." He picked up his ever-present glass and looked into the blood-red liquid that clung to the sides when he swirled it. "But tonight, we have been invited to Monsieur Cale's private club."

Narcise's heart skipped a beat. "Have you accepted the invitation?"

Cezar looked at her as he raised the glass of blood-drenched Bordeaux, one of his favorite drinks. She wondered whose blood was in there, and shuddered at the thought—the certainty—that it might be that of a child. He sipped, then drew the glass away. "I want you to seduce him."

She didn't have to feign surprise, and quickly changed her expression to include distaste. "I have no desire to seduce anyone, let alone Monsieur Cale. Might I remind you that I've already been at his hands. Against my will."

"Consider this a different test of your skills. I'm not altogether certain you'll succeed, in fact, Narcise. And that's precisely why I wish for you to do so." He tapped his fingernail against the side of the glass.

"No," she said.

Cezar turned to look at her fully, and a dart of fear shot through her. "Are you certain of that?" he asked, the hiss in his voice more pronounced. "Perhaps I'll give you to Belial after all. And Morderin as well." His eyes burned orange-yellow. "I could dress you in that special cape I've had made for you…and then let you fight your way out of their hands."

Narcise swallowed. The cape…the very words made her knees weak and her stomach swim. It was soft and light and made of dark, gossamer lace, and it was lined with sparrow feathers. The very thought of those feathers, in such abundance and such proximity against her skin made her feel faint.

He'd forced her to wear it one time, merely, he said, to see if it would fit. Thank Luce it had only been for a few moments. Belial and Morderin had had to hold her upright while her brother draped it over her shoulders, for she not only had no strength to stand, but the pain was so excruciating, she felt as if her skin was burning off. She could hardly breathe when it was on her, and even when he'd first pulled it out of the lead chest, her body had gone numb and weak with paralysis.

Perhaps if she wore it long enough, she'd die. And perhaps that was why Cezar hadn't yet employed it other than that time.

"Very well," she replied, forcing her voice to be strong.

He gave her a brief nod. "Excellent. And, now, of course, once you seduce the man, he'll want to keep you."

She was relieved that her gaze had been downcast when he spoke, otherwise, she might have given away her feelings. "Don't they always?" she muttered loudly enough for him to hear.

"They do," he replied. "But you might wish to stay with a man like Giordan Cale."

Again, she kept her eyes down, praying he wouldn't feel the way her heart leaped in hope. They would be at Cale's house tonight. Perhaps she might never have to leave.

"To ensure that you don't find yourself *convinced* to stay," he continued smoothly, his lisp whistling more loudly again, "or if you don't do precisely as I bid, I have a few reasons that might assist you in complying with my desires."

Her heart swelled with dread and now she looked up at

him, certain that naked fear and loathing showed in her eyes. "You are pure evil," she said even as he gestured to the curtained window on the opposite end of the room.

"All Dracule are evil at heart, darling Narcise," he reminded her. "After all, we wouldn't be Dracule if we weren't self-serving and greedy. Please. Open it and see."

She stood on shaking knees, her belly swishing with nausea. The curtains covered a window that led not to the outside, of course, for they were underground, but that gave visible access to the next chamber. She was fairly certain what she would find when she opened the drapes.

But she had to be certain; she had to know what he would use to bind her to him this time. The heavy drapes swished open and she only needed a quick glance to see what was there. "Lucifer's dark soul," she whispered when she saw the children.

"One of them is a prince," her brother told her proudly. "Or a comte or something of that nature. The royals are desperate to save their children from the guillotine, and will do anything to protect them—including pay for their safe passage to Romania."

There were a dozen or more, of all ages from toddler to young teen. Mercifully all were sleeping—drugged, she assumed—which explained why she hadn't heard cries or shouts from the next room. "That's where you were," she said, her voice still low, but now it was shaking. "When you claimed you went to Marseilles."

He nodded, tapping his fingernail against his glass again. "I'll take one for every hour that you disobey me, or that you are gone," he said. "They'll be awake and aware, and know everything that's happening to them. I'll even let the others watch in anticipation."

"And if I comply? Will you release them?"

His brows lifted as one M-shaped line. "But of course

not. I went through considerable trouble to obtain them. However, if you comply with my wishes and commands, I will leave them asleep until I am in need. They'll never wake from their drug-induced state, and feel nothing when I feed." His eyes danced. "I confess I rather prefer that option, for to feed whilst the young ones fight and cry is rather upsetting to the digestion and detracts from the moment. But if their blood is laced with the opium of sleep, it's all that more pleasurable for all of us. The choice is up to you, my dear sister."

Narcise felt unfamiliar tears gather at the corners of her eyes. Only Lucifer could be more black-hearted, more evil than the man sitting across from her. And yet…she remembered him when he was a boy, playful and yet awkward—only five years older than she. He'd played with her, plaited her hair, helped her care for her dolls, took her for long walks to pick the rare flowers that grew in the mountains. And then when he turned twelve or thirteen, everything changed.

"What has happened to you, Cezar?" she burst out. "How could you have changed so? You used to dote on me, and I was no different than the little girls in there. Now you would bleed them to death."

"We will leave at half past eight. Wear the black dress," he told her, his eyes cold.

"I have no black dress," she replied, turning from the window as she pulled the drapes closed. Black was for widows or mourning, and as often as she felt dark and drab, it wasn't a color she wore. Although perhaps after tonight…

"You do," he said, and gestured to a large white box. "And when you are ready to leave, attend me, dear sister. For I have a new piece of jewelry for you."

* * *

Giordan wasn't surprised when he received word that Moldavi and his sister would be accepting his invitation for that evening. He'd waited until the day after Moldavi returned from his travels and then extended the invitation under the guise of welcoming him back.

Interestingly enough, although he hadn't specifically invited Narcise, the response had indicated that she would attend as well.

He sat thoughtfully, awaiting his guests' arrival, pondering the next step in this imaginary chess game with Moldavi. Perhaps tonight, at last, he could somehow extricate Narcise from beneath her brother's thumb, stealing her away forever. After all, how could Moldavi stop him, in his own house?

Tomorrow, perhaps tomorrow morning, he would slide into bed next to the woman he loved.

Less than an hour later, Narcise entered Giordan's private parlor on her brother's arm. He sensed her presence even before Mingo announced the Moldavi siblings, and allowed his conversation with Voss and Eddersley to trail off.

When Giordan turned and saw her face, he knew immediately that something was wrong. That knowledge was closely followed by the shock of attraction and desire that assaulted him when her brother removed her cloak, revealing her gown.

Merde.

The chamber had gone silent and all eyes focused on Narcise. Giordan tore his gaze away, his mouth dry, fury pumping through his body, tightening his fingers, and he glanced at Cezar Moldavi. The man had a tight smirk on his face, and he was looking directly at him.

Take care. The warning was to himself and served as

a mantra to control his reaction. He met the man's eyes briefly, forcing himself to keep his expression blank and certain he failed, then lifted his glass.

If his hand was unsteady, it was camouflaged by the way he sloshed the drink in it. "To Mademoiselle Moldavi," he said, "the first *woman* to ever rend Eddersley speechless."

Since Eddersley's sexual preferences were well-known, Giordan's jest served to break the tension in the chamber, and everyone—except the Moldavis—laughed, including Eddersley himself. Then his friend caught Giordan's eyes for a moment, and he saw the same shock and distaste lingering in that of Eddersley's.

Narcise, once disrobed of her cloak, had hardly moved more than a step into the chamber. Giordan was compelled beyond imagination to go to her, but somehow, conscious of Moldavi's regard, he refrained, keeping his shoes rooted to the rug.

Instead he watched as Voss made a straight line toward the woman, trying not to want to put the man's head through a wall.

Giordan found himself unwilling to chance looking at Narcise, yet unable to put the image of her out of his mind. Her face, ivory with nary a hint of color to it tonight, was stark and bare. Even her lips were pale, and her eyes had that dull look he'd seen before—a look he hadn't noticed since the last time she was here. Her night-black hair was pulled back from her face, and twisted and braided into some huge, intricate knot at the back of her head. Diamonds hung from her ears, long teardrops nearly brushing her shoulders, and more of them sparkled around the bulging knot of her hair.

But it was her gown—what there was of it, and gown was not really an accurate term—that had struck every man in the room dumb. It was unlike anything in the shops of the modistes anywhere in Paris, and Giordan couldn't help but wonder where Moldavi had had it made. The dress was in the style of centuries ago, that of a medieval lady: a simple, high-necked frock that laced up between the breasts and along the sides, clinging to every curve of the body from shoulder to knee. From there it flared out in a train onto the floor. Her sleeves were tight from shoulder to elbow then flared in long points nearly to her feet. And though the cut of her attire was unusual and revealing, it was its very substance that caused comment—for the entire dress was made only of black lace.

The gown clung to Narcise and revealed more than any whore's undergarments ever had. It was clear to Giordan that she wore no corset, no chemise or undergarments of any fashion. The only nod to propriety—not that such a thing existed in the world of the Dracule—was a black silk triangle at the juncture of her legs, and the triangular panels of her skirt, where it flared below the knees, were alternating black silk and black lace. Even the bodice was lace. Her breasts were uncovered, her nipples hidden by accident or design by a heavy part of the lace…but even the undercurves of her breasts were evident.

He knew without a doubt that Moldavi had forced her to wear it, and Giordan burned to kill the man. But something else bothered him, and it was the only reason he didn't pin Narcise's brother to the wall with a stake: the look in her eyes.

His Narcise, the one he'd come to know and respect and love, might not choose on her own to wear such a gown. But, even if forced, she would never show shame or even submission while wearing it. She would walk boldly into a chamber and ignore the openmouthed gaping of every man in the room.

There was something else.

It took him some time, mingling with the other guests, directing his vintages about, but Giordan at last made it to Narcise's side. She'd hardly moved from where she entered the room, and he could see the drawn expression in her face, the emptiness in her eyes even more clearly as he approached.

"Find some other skirt to chase," he told Voss flatly. "She's mine."

Voss's quickly checked surprise told Giordan that he, at least, hadn't sensed the sizzling connection between Narcise and him. And Voss, no matter how much he enjoyed variety in the shape of women, was not at all a stupid man. He gave his host a brief salute with his glass and sauntered away, a bemused smile curving his lips. One thing about Voss: he never tired of the courting, the chase or the variety.

"What is it?" Giordan asked immediately. "By the soul of Luce, Narcise, what has he done?"

"Don't you wish to compliment me on my gown, monsieur?" she asked in a detached voice. "It was specially chosen to help me in my task of seduction." Her cool smile didn't reach her eyes. They remained blank, blue circles. Her cheeks were pale; her lips were nearly colorless.

"And who are you supposed to seduce?" he replied with ice in his veins.

"Why, you, monsieur," she said, leaning into him, placing a slender hand on the center of his chest. "I am to seduce you. Here. Tonight."

Giordan stared down at her, his heart thumping madly, her scent and her very proximity luring him into distraction…yet he knew he couldn't allow his brain to go to mush. It was the first time she'd touched him since the night he spent hanging from a pair of manacles. The sight of her in a gown that amounted to nothing more than a lacy glove, along with her pronouncement, set his thoughts to reeling. But…

"I cannot help but wonder," he said carefully, resisting the need to touch her, to close his large hand over the one that rested on his shirtwaist, "why you seem to be less than eager. Is seducing me still that revolting to you, Narcise? I thought…I'd hoped…"

He stopped, aware that he sounded pathetic and desperate. If the woman hadn't come to feel anything for him in the last weeks—which had been tortuous for him, being unable to touch her with anything but his eyes—perhaps he was wasting his time trying to convince her otherwise.

"It's Cezar," she whispered, seeming hardly to be able to form the words.

But before she could continue, Narcise clamped her lips closed, her eyes focused on something behind him, which could only be the man in question. Giordan felt and scented her brother's presence, that heavy and familiar aroma, tinged with something else he found inexplicably unappealing.

He felt the weight of the man's attention on them, and then it lifted and moved on.

"But then, mademoiselle, perhaps we ought to commence with the seduction. I am certain you know precisely how I feel about it." He managed to make his words sound light, despite the dark overhang of the situation. "Will you put on a good performance for your brother? And should I pretend to resist, or should I drag you eagerly from this chamber as I've longed to do these last weeks?"

The column of her throat, slender and elegant and so

very bitable, convulsed as she swallowed hard. *What is it, Narcise?*

"Be reluctant," she whispered as if she could hardly form the words. "I believe he is testing you—or us—somehow."

That chill came back, ice in his veins again. Then Giordan pushed it away. The man was in *his* home. He could do nothing.

Yet…he'd been in Dimitri's place, that night in Vienna, and somehow Moldavi had caused the building to burn to the ground and resulted in the death of Dimitri's mistress.

"Very well," he told her, turning slightly away. "I will play the reluctant target. For now. But take note, Narcise…once you are in my bed, my chamber, you'll never leave it. I won't let you go back with him."

He'd delivered these last words in an undertone for her ears only, but she stiffened and curled her fingers into the lapel of his coat. "No," she said. "I cannot stay. I won't stay, Giordan."

He stilled. Her refusal, coupled with her first ever use of his intimate name, told him much. Yet his emotion that overrode it all was that of anger. "Do you think I won't be able to protect you from him, in my own home?"

"It's not me. I don't fear for me any longer. It's…there are children. Hostages."

So that was it. "I'll kill him then. Now." He turned away, already considering where the closest stake or sword would be, but she caught his arm. Her fingers felt frail and he could easily have shaken her grip away.

Her words were low and desperate. "If he doesn't return tonight, the children are to be given to the servants to be fed on. They'll tear them apart. There's one in the carriage, waiting now with Belial. It's a girl-child, a young one—no more than eight. His orders are that if he doesn't return to them by midnight, Belial can do what he wishes." She seemed out of breath, exhausted by this long speech. "There is no way. Not tonight. One more night…it will make little difference."

Giordan was aware of a numbness creeping over him. "There must be a way. There is a way, Narcise. You have no idea what I'm capable of," he said, thinking back to those days on the streets when sticking a blade in someone who crossed him was as common as sleeping in the gutters.

"Please," she said, and she stumbled into him a bit. Her eyes were dark blue pools. "I can't risk it. Not tonight. It must be when he isn't expecting it, when he hasn't planned it all. Tonight is a test. Do you not think he will have considered every possible outcome and planned for it? Whatever you might attempt…he'll be one step ahead."

Then she smiled, but it was tight, and it worried him—along with the fact that she seemed to underestimate *him*.

Yet, when she pressed her body against his, the warmth from her presence, her heavy, erotic scent, the feel of her curves, all set his skin to tingling and his gums to swelling. She murmured as she looked up at him with hooded eyes, "I am certain we'll both enjoy what's to come. Can we not leave it at that? Just for tonight?"

"Very well," he said, yet unwilling to put the possibility of her freedom from his mind. But if she was willing and able to return with Cezar to save the children, how could he argue with her? Giordan wasn't certain he'd be able to make the same choice, but he must respect hers.

He slid an arm around her slender waist, pulling her close to him so that her breasts pressed against his chest. Surely she could feel his cock filling out his breeches. He was already imagining pulling the pins from her heavy hair, peeling the lace from her curves, sinking his teeth into the soft side of her belly while his fingers found her swollen quim. His breathing became rough and unsteady, his fangs long and hard.

"May I succumb to your wiles now, then, Narcise? Have I been reluctant enough?"

"Yes, I believe I've done my duty and convinced you," she said, and for the first time, he saw a spark of heat in her eyes.

"Will you allow me to touch you tonight, *cher?*" his voice dropped low. "Are you willing? Tell me the truth, Narcise."

"I am more than willing." Yet…something still lurked in her eyes. Some hesitance.

Confused and angry with whatever it was, he nevertheless offered her his arm. "Shall we? I'm certain you'd prefer all of this to happen somewhere a bit more private."

When she hardly moved, he looked down at her again. Her eyes had that dull look, her lips were slightly parted. She was either deathly afraid or in great—*hell.*

"Where the devil is it?" he demanded, taking her shoulders and turning her to face him. Fury at his stupidity, his blindness rushed over him. "Where's the feather? You're wearing one, aren't you?"

She nodded slightly, relief swimming in her eyes. "Around my neck. But not…here." Her eyes focused on him, and now he recognized the pain behind the emptiness. "He can't see…."

"Yes, here," he said in a low, furious voice. But he turned so that his body blocked the view of anyone watching.

Cezar would die. Slowly. Giordan would ensure that it took days. Perhaps weeks.

He found the slender golden chain at her throat in

seconds, and began to pull it from her gown. It was very long, and the single feather that hung from it had been slipped down the back of her gown, between the lace and her skin. Which meant it had been burning into her for at least an hour.

No damned wonder she'd hardly moved. She couldn't.

Giordan snapped the golden chain and pulled the feather away, already seeing the relief in her face and eyes. Color came back into her skin and life in her blue-violet irises.

"Now," he said, "let me have you."

Cezar Moldavi watched as Cale led Narcise from the chamber. It had been a battle between them, he noted with satisfaction. She'd had to beg and plead, to coerce.

That Cale hadn't immediately followed her like a besotted dog from the parlor gave Cezar hope. Perhaps he was wrong.

After all, every test he'd given Cale so far had turned out to be unnecessary. How many men would have declined the offer to "watch over" Narcise during her brother's absence?

And even if Cale was smart enough to see that he was being set up and to refuse the offer of having—what was it they said here? *carte blanche?*—with Narcise, surely he would at least have attempted to visit her or otherwise see her during Cezar's absence.

But, no. All of his prying eyes in the household had assured him that Giordan Cale hadn't so much as sent a message to the Moldavis, let alone attempted to call, until the day Cezar returned.

Anticipation bubbled deep within and it was all he could do not to smile broadly. He knew nearly everything he needed to about Giordan Cale. The last would become clear tonight, and then he would determine how to proceed.

A burst of laughter from the corner drew Cezar's attention to Lord Eddersley, the dark, gangly fop from London. He subdued the sneer that threatened his upper lip. Men like him, so open and obvious about their preferences, disgusted him.

Cezar turned away, sipping the fine vintage Cale had poured tonight. The man had excellent taste, along with his broad shoulders and thick, curling hair. He could hardly wait to taste the man himself.

8

Now let me have you.

Cale's words rang in Narcise's head, and now that the agonizing feather had been removed from the back of her dress, she could actually *feel*. And breathe. Her strength came rushing back, the numbness deserted her.

She wanted him to have her. Her fingers shook, her belly fluttered and leaped, she wanted him so badly.

He directed her out of the parlor, the door closing behind them and shutting off the voices and revelry—and Cezar's watchful eyes. They were walking rapidly down a corridor furnished with an occasional painting, as well as several tables with statuary, vases and other items. Cale led her past several closed doors, and she was certain he meant to take her to his bedchamber. *Once you're in my bed, my chamber, you'll never leave it.*

Her heart slammed behind her ribs, and she nearly pushed it all away: Cezar, the worries, the children… and gave in. For she knew he was right. Once she was in his bed, safe and sated, *loved*, she would never be able to make herself leave.

So she must not go there.

She stumbled purposely and when he paused to see to her distress, Narcise wrapped her arms around his neck and pulled him toward her, backing herself against one of the doors. Before he could speak, or even react, she sank her fangs into the side of his neck.

Cale went rigid, and she felt his body jolt in a great shudder as the hot blood coursed into her mouth. He swore, in some low, dark curse that she couldn't hear. For a moment, she nearly forgot her purpose...the pleasure was so intense, so long awaited. And they were in this together, as equals.

Equals.

The realization surged through her, strong and powerful, and she dragged deep, pulling him into her mouth, all the hot, coppery flavor of him.

He groaned deep and low, the cords of his neck swelling in response beneath her mouth. She pressed herself all along his body, feeling the welcome ridge behind the crotch of his breeches, the heat and strength she desired and no longer feared.

"Narcise," he managed to gasp, but his hands had covered her breasts, finding her tight nipples through the rough lace, and he seemed unable to finish. Molding her curves, sliding a thumb over her breasts, he had her flat against the door, his head tilted back, baring full, throbbing veins as she drank. His pulse pounded, sending little surges of his lifeblood into her mouth, and she sucked and licked, using her lips and tongue to taste him. He was rich and sweet, strong and yet comforting. Familiar.

She felt for the doorknob she knew was behind her, and uncaring what sort of room they would stumble into, managed to twist it. The door gave away behind her as she withdrew from the hot, soft skin at his neck and backed inside, pulling him by his lapels into the warm, dimly lit chamber.

"Out," she heard him say roughly over her shoulder. As she tore at his coat, yanking it from his shoulders, she was aware of some sort of skittering movement, quick and clumsy, and then the stirring of the air as the chamber's previous occupants quickly vacated.

Cale muttered something unintelligible, whipping the coat to the ground as she fumbled with the tie at the throat of his shirt, aware that his rich red blood had stained the white cotton. She tore it away and there was his bare chest beneath her hands again, as warm and solid as she remembered it.

He was pulling at the pins in her hair, yanking haphazardly and dropping them to the wooden floor with little scattering sounds. "So beautiful," he murmured, sliding his hands into her hair, lifting its weight from where it rested at the back of her neck, untangling the mass of coils and braids and twists, spreading it wide and full so that it shimmered down her back. She felt it through the thin lace, heavy and warm, and then he lifted the whole of it to one side, baring her neck.

"Narcise?" he asked, his voice rough in her ear, his other hand firmly on her arm.

"Yes—" She'd barely breathed the syllable when he slammed his fangs into her at that soft, sensitive juncture of neck and shoulder. She gave a little shriek of pain and pleasure, and he stilled for a moment, one hand cupping her shoulder, and the other curved around the back of her head, holding her steady when she would have sagged weakly.

The release of pressure inside her, fairly exploding into his hot mouth, combined with the sting of pain and the sensual tracing of his lips made Narcise weak and dizzy in the most pleasurable sort of way. Her lips moved in a smile, taut with need but real nevertheless.

It had been so long…so long since this pleasure hadn't been taken from her, *forced* from her. So long since it had been good, pure pleasure instead of terrible and dark.

But her knees were buckling and she grasped at the remnants of his shirt, holding on as he drank deeply. One of his hands slipped down to drag her bottom close, her torso sharply against the cock raging behind his tight breeches. She arched low, pressing against the tempting bulge, rubbing her own swollen self against him in the rhythm they both craved. Their breathing matched and mingled, hard and rough and heated, spreading over her skin where he latched on to her shoulder, his tongue caressing her behind his fangs.

There was a clink, and a jolt, and she realized they'd bumped into a table or something, and the next thing she knew, something was behind her legs. The arm of a sofa.

"Let's do it horizontally this time," he murmured, releasing his fangs and then sliding hot, slick lips over her wound, tenderly, gently, to close it up. She shivered at the sensation over her taut, sensitive skin, closing her eyes as her body seemed to turn to liquid, hot and pounding inside. Her breasts strained behind their lace confines, the rough material erotic and irritating to her thrusting nipples. But the pleasure rolling from belly to quim, undulating through her limbs, was delicious and unbearable, and Narcise found herself sighing and moaning in delirium, needing more.

Then he was easing her to the floor, pulling her down with him onto a thick rug. The glow of a fire spilled in a golden pool on the red wool. "The sofa…too narrow," he murmured, pulling at the laces that bound her into the sleevelike dress, opening it along the side of her torso, pulling it with gentle hands, her skin freed from the rough lace, open to the heat of the fire, and then—

Oh.

He bit her there, in the soft side of her belly, just above her hip, and Narcise jolted as pleasure shot to her quim in a hot, soft swell, then burst into a spiral of release. Her breathing went out of control and her world turned dark and red, pounding and rising, her center throbbing and pulsing as warmth and release surged through her.

"So you like that?" he said, his voice deep and filled with delight.

Then he—Giordan—was over her, one hand moving up under the lace to cover the top of her breast, smoothing his palm rhythmically over the needy tip of her nipple, and the other sliding up beneath her skirt, behind the black satin triangle between her legs.

His lips moved over the soft, delicate skin of her torso's edge, sipping and gently sucking at the new wounds there. Her belly shivered and trembled, and when his fingers found her swollen quim, slick and full, she closed her eyes and breathed long and deep. The pleasure and need rose again immediately at his touch, and she could picture his long, elegant fingers as they explored, stroking her back to a new peak.

"Yes," she murmured, arching into his hand, but he pulled back, teasing his fingers along the inside of her thigh, then up and away to look down at her. She was aware of his weight bearing down on her, solid and comfortable, one solid leg between hers, the other alongside the outside of her thigh.

"Kiss me," he said, his hands now covering her shoulders through the flimsy lace. "Narcise." His eyes bored into her, penetrating the haze of her pleasure, and she recognized the need, a vulnerability there—not so very different from what hers had been.

A rush of warmth, of certainty and desire, spread through her.

She cupped his warm face, sliding her hands along his jaw, felt the faint tremors deep beneath her fingers, the beginning of stubble on the very bottom of his chin. Her thumbs crept up along the sides of his face, her fingertips in the thick curls around his neck.

His gaze never wavered, dark and heavy on her, drilling deep into her soul. Deep into her damaged, warped, damned soul. Her heart shifted, shuddered and broke open.

He'd given her back so much: herself, her freedom, her body.

When she pulled, guiding him down, he lowered his face to hers. He murmured her name against her mouth, then their lips met gently, fusing together without hurry.

Giordan sank onto her, gathering her close as he shifted to go deeper, delved into her with soft lips and sleek tongue, still scented and flavored with the essence of her own lifeblood. Tears prickled at the corners of her eyes, such relief and emotion swelling strong inside her, bursting to come out from this unfamiliar intimacy.

The kiss turned from a sweet proclamation of tenderness, then to something fierce and hungry. Their tongues clashed and stroked, delved deep and furious, their lips catching on fangs and scraping tender skin. Little surges of blood mingled with the kiss, mixing with their breath, tasting sweet and thick as their bodies slid and bumped against each other. His fingers moved between them, pulling at the buttons of his breeches, the back of his hand sliding teasingly against her swollen center.

Narcise helped him, blind but efficient, and heard the

soft scatter of the buttons as they flung beyond the rug to the floor. Quick and furious now, her skirt was flipped up and aside, his breeches and drawers yanked away until the heat of him lay against her thigh.

"Giordan," she pleaded, spreading herself up and against him freely, wantonly, and she heard his great gust of relief as he found the hot, sleek place between her legs.

They both gasped when he filled her with one sharp movement, and then there was no longer time for play. He seemed to have run out of patience and teasing, for no sooner had he slid deep than he was moving again, harder and faster, bending forward to nip at her mouth, to slick up another taste of her as her hips moved to meet his rhythm.

The rug burned into her buttocks and Narcise felt her hair caught beneath her shoulders, but that discomfort was lost in the hot, driving pleasure that she suddenly reached in an explosion of pleasure, grasping it just before he did. He made a low noise, strangled and deep, and thrust deep and hard one last time, then buried his face in her hair and collapsed into her arms.

Narcise closed her eyes, her body still shuddering pleasantly, rippling from her center out to each finger and toe, remembering what it was like to feel happy, and complete after this…and not dark and damaged and used.

His lips moved against her neck, saying something she couldn't hear, but the gentle movement sent delicious little shivers along her shoulder and she smoothed her hands all along his back.

The curling, rootlike ridges of the Devil's Mark bumped beneath her fingertips on one side, and she felt the faint pulsing therein. She wondered if he'd done something to anger Lucifer, or if his Mark was always full and throbbing like that.

Hers rose and fell depending upon her mood and that of the demon who'd put it there, and right now, now that she was sated with pleasure, it was hardly a twinge over her shoulder blade.

Giordan—he was no longer merely Cale to her— shifted and pulled away, his hands sleek and smooth as they moved down over her throat and shoulders. "I hope you don't mind my saying that you're the most beautiful woman I've ever known," he said. "But you're also the strongest. Here." He rested his fingers over her heart. His eyes burned dark and steady as he looked down at her, his lips, those perfect ones that she'd learned so well from her sketching, were full and glistened a bit.

She shifted and he eased back farther, helping her to sit up.

"Narcise," he began, covering her with his eyes, determination in his jaw.

She knew what he was going to say, and she stopped him with a finger over his lips. "Don't ask me to stay. I can't—"

"I wasn't going to," he said, easing away from her fingers. A note of annoyance colored his tone. "I was going to say, I think it's important to keep this from your brother."

"Why—and how? He ordered me to seduce you—he'll smell you all over me," she began, confused and yet relieved that he wasn't going to try to convince her to stay.

Giordan was nodding. "I know. But why? To see if it would work? To see if we have an attachment?" He frowned and Narcise was surprised when a wave of affection swept her at the sight of the furrow between his brows. She wanted to touch it. She wanted to touch him again, everywhere, in fact…to lie next to him in a soft, luxurious bed, naked and sated, and to hear him talk. He must have noticed the heat in her eyes, for he paused and, eyes narrowing with desire, he bent forward to kiss her.

Another sweet brushing of lips, but then she slipped her tongue out and there was still the essence of blood on him, and the kiss became deeper and more thorough. She curved an arm around him, sliding it along the curve of his bicep as a tingle began to grow inside her again.

When he pulled away, it was with obvious reluctance. His brown-blue eyes, ringed with black, now glowed with fire again. But then he blinked and it eased into seriousness. "I don't trust anything about him, or anything he does," Giordan continued. "But it seems as if he is trying to push us together. And if he wants that, then there's a reason to benefit him. I think it would be best if you went back alone, and I'll be along shortly. He'll know you did what he bid, but he doesn't need to know that we…well, that it was like this."

His voice dipped low and sent another pang deep in her belly.

Narcise leaned forward to capture his lips again, sliding seductively against his mouth, her hand flat on his chest. "Very well," she said, and left.

Giordan took his time returning to the parlor, partly to allow Narcise to make her appearance first, and partly because, aside of getting new clothing, he had things to attend to.

Narcise might think she was returning with her brother tonight, but that wasn't going to happen. He'd take care of Moldavi himself, and then attend to Belial and his hostage in the carriage. Voss and Eddersley would help, and after that, they'd all go back to Moldavi's residence.

Then all of the child hostages would be free, as would Narcise.

Giordan slid a stake into the inside pocket of his coat. A different weapon than what he used on the streets—then it had been a slender but wicked blade that slid between ribs like butter—but they were both used in the same way.

He was waylaid by a question from one of his footmen, and then Suzette, who'd been entertained by one of Giordan's male vintages, caught him in the corridor to ask when he might plan another party. "I was hoping for a rooftop ball," she suggested with a smile. "During the full moon would be perfect."

Giordan smiled. "Very soon, *ma cherie.* Perhaps within a week." He could introduce Narcise to his friends, and he imagined that she'd enjoy the fresh air.

He excused himself as quickly as he could and returned to the private parlor at last.

The first thing he noted was that Narcise wasn't there. He frowned; she'd had ample time to return. Then, when he scanned the chamber and realized that Moldavi was absent as well, his stomach plummeted and a rush of anger stopped him cold.

"Where are they?" he asked Eddersley, who'd paused to look at him as if he were mad.

"The Moldavis? They left. Perhaps a quarter of an hour past."

Giordan rushed out of the parlor, knowing it was futile, that they'd already gone…but somehow hoping that he was wrong.

But he wasn't. Outside, beneath the swath of stars and sliver of moon, he found one of his grooms and demanded to know where the Moldavi carriage was.

When the groom explained that it had left some time earlier, and that, *oui*, the mademoiselle was with her brother, and, no, she was not in distress, she was walking of her own volition, Giordan stepped back and whirled away. His heart pounded violently and he knew his eyes were burning red and gold, fairly flaming with rage.

He had a terrible, sinking feeling that he'd never see Narcise again.

9

It was more than three weeks after Narcise seduced him that Giordan received word from Cezar Moldavi.

At first, he had no concerns about the silence. Playing the game he and Narcise had agreed upon, he waited for two days before contacting Moldavi again, under the guise this time of formalizing the details of the spice ship. When there was no response to that dangling carrot of business investment and money, Giordan was concerned, but not terribly so.

Perhaps Moldavi had been called out of town again.

He attempted to visit as Monsieur David again for Narcise's painting lesson, at least in order to see her, and ensure himself that she was well. When he was turned away from the door with the explanation that mademoiselle was no longer interested in lessons, Giordan had that awful sinking feeling again.

What did that mean?

Another attempt to deliver fabric as an elderly merchant as he'd done once before was also foiled when he was advised that no one was in residence to see him.

Thus Giordan spent the next two weeks in varying

stages of fear, fury and loathing. The helplessness was the worst. Was she alive? Was she dead? Was she here in Paris? Had she been fencing? Winning or losing?

He made personal calls three times after that, and each time he was turned away with vague explanations that the master was gone.

He began to plot with Eddersley how he might gain entrance to Moldavi's lair through the catacombs, sneaking in through the rear.

He paid Mingo handsomely to debase himself and attempt to seduce any or all of Moldavi's servants regardless of how homely they were when they visited the market, providing his own steward with enough funds to pay for an entire ship in order to incent tongues to wagging. The only information he was able to glean was that the mademoiselle was cloistered in her private apartments and had hardly been seen for more than a week. However, she had had no visitors at all.

"But she *is* well?" he demanded, his fangs flashing, his hand pressing his valet and steward's chest against the wall.

Mingo's eyes widened and he nodded. "So far as I can ascertain, she is well, sir."

Giordan remembered himself and released his servant, turning away with trembling hands and a stomach that gnawed with emptiness. *I should have forced her to stay with me. I shouldn't have let her leave.*

At last, he received a response to the five messages he'd sent, and the three he'd left in person. It was absurdly mundane: *I would be honored by your presence this evening. Moldavi.*

He had four stakes secreted on him when he entered Moldavi's stronghold, and was determined to use at least one of them before he left. As he'd anticipated, three of them were discovered by the butler when he was offered entrance at the street level. But the fourth one remained tucked in the underside of his loose shirtsleeve.

Whatever he'd expected, Giordan had not anticipated the beaming, cordial host who greeted him as he entered the spacious, well-appointed parlor they'd used previously.

"I'm so terribly sorry for the confusion," Moldavi said, gesturing to a pair of chairs pulled up cozily next to a piecrust table.

As always, he was dressed formally in well-tailored clothing: a snowy-white shirt, brocade waistcoat, knee breeches and stockings. Instead of the wigs currently in fashion, Moldavi wore his hair combed neatly over his face and ears, and his wide-jawed face was clean-shaven. Several rings winked on his fingers as he gestured with his speech. "I understand you've been attempting to reach me. It was terribly rude of me not to provide an explanation for my sudden departure, and that of my sister, from your engagement a few weeks ago. I was called away on an emergency, and quite frankly, I was too distracted to even think to send you an explanation or apology."

Giordan accepted the speech in silence, eyeing the man thoughtfully, but he did not take one of the offered seats. *He's lying as easily as the Seine in its bed.* And there was a different air about him tonight, one of anticipation, perhaps, or nervous energy.

"And Narcise—I'm afraid the servants didn't quite understand. I would certainly have allowed you to call on her in my absence…but apparently, that was not made clear to them." Moldavi, also still standing, opened a small cupboard, peered at the cluster of bottles within and selected one. He examined the label, then returned it with a *tsk*, clinking around until he chose a second one.

"Ah. Perfect," he said in satisfaction. "I do hope you like it," he added, glancing at Giordan.

"I wasn't offended that you left my gathering as much as I was concerned," Giordan offered as his host poured two glasses at the sideboard. The titillating scent of fresh blood mingled with liquor filled the room. He wondered uncomfortably from where the blood had come. "After all, that night I had been the recipient of an unexpected gift," he said. "I hadn't had the opportunity to thank you."

"Indeed. I do hope you enjoyed it," Moldavi said, handing his guest one of the glasses, brushing his fingers as he did so. "In all honesty, I wasn't certain if it would be to your liking. In fact, I'd rather hoped it wouldn't." The other man's eyes fastened meaningfully on his and for the first time, Giordan saw something there besides cunning and intelligence.

Admiration.

Fascination.

Desire.

He recognized it and nearly stepped back, his stomach twisting unpleasantly, shock and comprehension rendering him silent. All at once, the dark memories rushed to the forefront of his mind—the grasping hands in the alleys, the smell of men, the humiliation and pain.

Giordan shook the images away and speared Moldavi with his own flat gaze. "As a matter of fact, that evening was *very* much to my liking," he replied so that his position couldn't be misunderstood. "Where is she?"

All pretense had dropped; they were man to man, staring at each other, no longer hiding anything.

"She's gone," Moldavi said.

"I want to see her."

Moldavi shrugged. "She has no desire to see you."

"You're lying," Giordan replied with confidence.

"She's in love with me." He knew it for a fact; he never doubted it, for though she hadn't said the words, she had proven it when she kissed him.

She'd kissed him more than once, more than in the heat of passion, more than when he'd asked it of her. She'd kissed him with love and tenderness, and freely. He had no doubt of her feelings for him, and every bit of confidence in her brother's attempt to manipulate.

"And, to my dismay, you're in love with her," Moldavi said. He pulled something from his pocket. "You hid it very well. I wasn't certain at all, for you seemed immune. I had hoped—" He shook his head, pressing his lips together in dismay as he cut off his own words. "This is what confirmed it for me."

He held a long, slender gold chain with a single feather dangling from it. The one Giordan had removed from Narcise and tossed to the floor of his parlor the night she'd seduced him.

Moldavi's smile was a bit crooked. "If you didn't love her, you wouldn't have noticed or cared. Nor," he added, "would you have visited her disguised as Monsieur David."

Giordan couldn't keep his eyes from flickering in surprise. "You knew of that?"

His host's lips twisted in reluctant admiration. "Not at first. You fooled everyone. Not until after I found this—" he gestured with the feather "—and began to suspect. But when I went into her chamber and scented you in there…" His voice trailed off, his eyes settling heavily on him. "I've become quite familiar with your scent."

Giordan kept his face blank despite the increasingly uncomfortable churning in his belly. He was emotionless, feeling not even the animosity or affront he should. He tried to picture how Dimitri would respond in this situation: cold and lethal. But Dimitri had not lived through what Giordan had.

"I suppose I could consider myself flattered, but I do not," he replied coldly. "You understand, I have interest in only one member of the Moldavi family."

"I was afraid of that, Giordan—ah, forgive my informality. I've long thought of you that way. These last few weeks have been rather difficult for me, not knowing for certain. Particularly the time we spent in here after you fought with my sister that night." His dark gaze settled meaningfully on him.

Giordan realized with a start that that night, he'd been sitting in this very chamber dressed only in breeches, and likely smelling of arousal and maleness after the session with Narcise. His mouth dried and he realized now what he'd scented beneath Moldavi's cologne of cedar and patchouli. It was the essence of desperate desire that he'd found unpleasant.

Moldavi continued. "I had held out hope that you might be of the same mind as Eddersley—albeit much more subtle and reserved about it. After all, no man could resist Narcise and you appeared to do so."

"A man who doesn't force himself onto a woman isn't necessarily a molly," Giordan said with disdain. "He's a gentleman."

"Despite your protestations to the contrary," Moldavi said as he moved away from the sideboard and closer to Giordan, "I happen to know you're no stranger to buggery, particularly from your teen years." His eyes burned red and hot.

Giordan went cold, and for a moment he couldn't breathe. "The correct term would be rape," he said from between numb lips. He tried to summon the dark rage that he knew simmered deep inside, but somehow Moldavi's words and knowledge had catapulted him back to those dark days and evil memories. They'd grabbed hold of him and smothered his instinctive response, setting him off balance and out of sorts. He felt as if he were swimming deep in a very murky pond: half-blind, sluggish, breathless.

Moldavi seemed to realize this, and he was now standing very close to him. His scent rolled off in heavy waves, thick with lust. "Why are you here, Giordan?" he asked, the sibilant hiss very pronounced in his voice. A fang flashed, the gold chip in it winking coyly as he looked up at him.

"You know why I'm here. I want Narcise."

"Hmm. Yes. I wonder what you're willing to do to have her." Moldavi reached up as if to touch him, and Giordan knocked the man's hand away with a sharp, controlled movement.

"You overstep," he said with a calm he didn't realize he currently possessed. The anger simmered faster and harder now, nearer to the boiling point. He stepped back and took a large sip of his drink. When he raised his arm, the weight of the stake shifted in his sleeve, reminding him that he did have a chance to end this now.

"You want Narcise, but so do so many other men, Giordan. It's really quite a quandary for me. She's very valuable in a variety of ways—you understand why I cannot give her up. Because, of course, if you fancy yourself in love with her, you'll want her with you—at least for a time. Decades perhaps. And then what would I do?"

"You can have the ship," Giordan said. "All of it. Two ships if you want."

"Shall we make it three?" Moldavi asked with an intimate chuckle. "No, no, I don't want that. Although from what I understand, you can afford it." He clicked his tongue, his eyes dancing with pleasure. "Forget about the stake you have hidden on you, Giordan. You can't murder me. Do you think I'm that much of a fool? What do you think will happen to Narcise the minute you attempt it?"

"Why should I believe you?"

Moldavi sighed. "For an intelligent man, you're being tiresome. Have you not learned that I don't make mistakes, nor do I make empty threats?"

Giordan could hardly disagree. All along, he thought he'd been clever, but it appeared that Moldavi was a step ahead of him. "What do you want? My house in Paris? Four ships? Access to my bank accounts? You can have it all."

The other man continued as if he hadn't spoken. "She's perfectly content here, Giordan, truly. We've come to an arrangement after so many years and I rarely have to discipline her anymore. She's kept in comfort, like a princess, dressed in the most fashionable of clothing. She has everything she could want. And she hasn't lost a fencing match for years—except to you." His voice dropped and his eyes heated again. "I did particularly enjoy watching that."

"She's a prisoner."

"I prefer to think of it as house arrest," he replied with a smile that showed a tip of fang. "I have something else I'd like to show you. Something special I've had made for Narcise."

He walked over to a table. On top of it was a box, and Moldavi turned to lift the lid.

With a sharp jerk of his arm, Giordan had the stake through the loose cuff and into his hand. He launched himself across the room, and in a half breath he had Moldavi against the wall, slamming the slighter man there with his hand, the stake poised.

"By the Devil, you *are* magnificent," said Moldavi in a rough, breathless voice. His eyes burned with an orange glow.

"I want Narcise," Giordan said from between tight jaws.

"She isn't here," replied Moldavi, his gaze growing hotter. "I took the precaution of removing her from the premises." He looked up into Giordan's eyes, his lips parted slightly in a provocative show of fangs. "There's only one way for you to have her."

Revulsion and fury took hold, and Giordan slammed the stake down into Moldavi's chest, propelling himself closer with the effort. The man jolted, grunted against him but something stopped the pike from penetrating fully. Armor.

His adversary looked up at him, his pale, beringed hand suddenly fisted in Giordan's shirt, holding him still, leaning into him with his own vampiric strength. His fangs were fully visible, his breathing rough.

Luce's black soul.

Giordan pulled free and spun away. His heart was pounding, his stomach roiling, the stake useless in his hand. "What do you want?"

"Don't be a fool. You know what I want." Moldavi's voice was hard, and yet sensual at the same time. The words hung there for a moment.

He stepped away from the wall where he'd remained after the attack, and adjusted his waistcoat. "Perhaps you'd like a bit of incentive, Giordan? I wanted to show you what I've had made for Narcise. What she'll wear when I give her to Belial if you and I don't come to an agreement."

He turned back to the table and finished removing the top to the box. As Giordan watched, his host removed a lacy, filigree object that looked like the same black lace of Narcise's gown. It was a cloak or cape, and it shivered and flowed as Moldavi shook it out, holding it by the collars.

Then he turned it around so that Giordan could see the other side.

It was lined with brown feathers. Rows and rows of them.

"No," he whispered, turning to Moldavi in shock. *"No,* by hell."

"Now, then," he said. "Are you ready to negotiate?"

"Negotiate?" Giordan said. The numbness had eased away to cold fear and impotent anger. "You seem to hold all the cards."

Moldavi liked that, and he laughed with delight. "I do hold most of them, that's true. I spend much of my time arranging things."

"I want Narcise," Giordan said, his lungs aching, his knees watery. "Name your price. Whatever it takes to get her out of here."

Moldavi showed his fangs, a light dancing in his malevolent eyes. "I want you."

Even though he'd expected it, Giordan couldn't control the sharp, dark twist in his middle. "Be more specific," he managed to say.

"Three days and three nights. Naked. Willing." Moldavi's smile couldn't even be described as maniacal; it was too calm and controlled. Satisfied. "Is that specific enough?"

~ II ~
Liberty

10

March 1804

Every so often, the memory came hurtling back into Narcise's mind.

Although it was more than ten years since Giordan Cale had destroyed her, every nuance of the moment, every sight, sound, color, scent…even the remembrance of the way her being simply *stopped* and then imploded… it all came back.

As if it were happening again.

Anything could trigger it: the sight of a piece of charcoal on her drawing table. The sound when her maid dropped a handful of hairpins that scattered on the floor. The glimpse of a head of brown curls. The scent of a peach.

Whatever it was would send her mind shooting back to that moment when she walked into Cezar's private chambers.

Even now, her belly shuddered, threatening to send her last meal spewing forth, but try as she might, Narcise couldn't keep herself from going back there, reliving the very minutiae of a time she'd kill to forget.

She'd been looking for her brother—something she generally avoided doing, but there was no help for it, for she hadn't had a fencing lesson or a painting session for three weeks, including a false one with Giordan Cale—and she wanted to find out if and why he'd canceled the meetings with her tutors.

Cezar had been unusually absent since the night he'd brought her back after she seduced Cale, and Narcise had welcomed the reprieve, knowing how difficult it would be to hide her feelings about Cale in front of her brother. Fortunately Cezar had been in a relatively fine humor and had actually released most of the children he'd had captive. Perhaps that should have been a warning sign to Narcise, but at the time, she was merely grateful those lives had been spared.

She'd also expected to hear from or to see Giordan himself…but three weeks had passed since she seduced him, and she'd seen and heard from no one. Including Monsieur David and her fencing instructor. But it was Giordan's absence, of course, that tortured her the most.

And that had her active mind making up scenarios and explanations—none of which were pleasant in the least. The worst of them all was the image of him with another woman, or *women*, perhaps…being the jovial, sensual host she knew him to be…and providing all form of hospitality.

Or perhaps now that she'd actually seduced him, that they'd actually been together, he'd moved on to another conquest. That was the Dracule way. Her heart grew cold at the thought.

Had she trusted him only to be betrayed and set aside?

At last, after neither David nor Cale appeared for her

lesson for the third week, she went in search of Cezar, noting vaguely that all of the servants seemed to be otherwise occupied. His private parlor, where he kept the dish of sparrow feathers, was empty, but...

She stepped just inside the door, despite the deterrent of the feathers. She smelled him. *Giordan.* Giordan had been here recently.

The flush of a thrill warmed her and her heart began to pound with hope. She had no doubt, no doubt at all that Giordan would find a way to free her from Cezar. He'd been here, recently, very recently. Earlier today.

It was at that moment that two things happened: the first—and now, much later, she understood the significance—was that the ever-present tray with feathers was not in the chamber. The second was that she noticed that, across the parlor, the door to Cezar's private bedchamber was slightly open. And there were sounds and scents coming from inside...heavy, erotic, strong scents.

Even now, in her mind, her memory of it, Narcise screamed at herself *don't go over there...*

But she did. Whether she realized what it was, whether it was the scent on the air, permeating the chamber, or whether there was some other reason she was compelled to walk on silent feet over to the chamber door...

To peer around the crack and to look in...*no, no, noooooo, don't*...but she does it again...she looks in...

At first, she doesn't realize what she sees. It's the scent of arousal...heavy and thick...of lifeblood and eroticism and man.... It catches her, giving that little tug in the center of her belly that spears down low and causes desire....

The chamber is lit well enough by the blazing fire that Cezar always keeps, and several lamps, turned up to a golden glow. There is a massive bed, its curtains pulled wide, to one side. A large divan and two chairs are ar-

ranged in front of the fire. A table covered with glasses and bottles sits next to it, and even from here, she can see that three of the four bottles are empty. The scent of whiskey and blood mingle strongly with musk and virility.

There are two people, not on the bed, but on the divan, directly in front of the raging fire, opposite the door around which she peers. Since her brother's varied proclivities aren't unknown to her, she's not surprised to see that he's with a man.

She can't see well, she's not even certain why she's compelled to watch—perhaps the scent hooked into her mind and dragged her there—but the first glimpse of a pale, slender hand curling over a strong, sleek shoulder makes her breath seize.

There is a cast of amber light over his skin, over the familiar golden curve of arms and shoulders now marred with bitemarks, shadowed by the flickering fire...the golden brush of lamplight over the strong profile with the patrician nose, so handsome, so perfect...the glow creating a nimbus from behind thick, dark curls, and an unholy halo around an even darker head adjacent to his.

She can't breathe. The floor is falling away from her feet as if she is standing on a house of cards, and her body ceases. Everything halts: breath, heart, sensation, emotion.

His rich, tawny skin is slick with perspiration, shadowed from the hands on him...his face half turned from the door, etched tight with pleasure and pain. His lips, drawn back from his mouth in some sort of groan or grimace as fangs drive into his shoulder...

For all of the details of that moment, Narcise remembered hardly anything of what happened afterward. She must have made her way from the chamber, she must not have screamed despite the shrieking and wailing inside her, stumbling from the private parlor, somehow back to her own room before her body began to feel again.

Shattered.

And then, after that, it was dull and empty.

Sometime later—days, she thought, based on the number of times a servant came for her to feed…but she had no true concept of time for a while—Cezar sent for her.

She had no choice but to answer his summons, hardly aware of what she was doing. When she walked into Cezar's private parlor, the conduit that had led to her destruction, Giordan was there.

Cezar was sitting in one of the chairs, looking complacent and relaxed. "You have a visitor, Narcise," he said with great congeniality.

"He's not *my* visitor," she managed to say. Despite her best efforts, her voice shook. Rage and pain threatened to erupt.

Cale turned from where he'd been standing in the corner, his back to the room, his broad shoulders straight with tension. His eyes were bright—too bright. And yet the skin around them was tight. He was fully, formally dressed, but his clothing was wrinkled, less than perfect.

He looked weary—and well he should, based on what she'd witnessed. Narcise's stomach threatened to revolt just then and despite the fact that she hadn't fed for who knew how long, she knew something would come up anyway.

"Narcise," Giordan said. His voice was rough and low. But anger and command hummed beneath.

Why was he angry with *her?*

She couldn't—she fled the room, the world spinning into hot red nausea. She couldn't think, couldn't comprehend, could hardly feel. Nothing but the raging whirl of her emotions.

He came after her, out of the chamber into a corridor that was uncharacteristically deserted. "*Narcise.*"

His scent came with him—and with it, a revolting mix of opium, hashish, whiskey, blood. And Cezar. She steadied herself against the wall, trying to block the images that assaulted her, that matched the stew of debauchery emanating from him. The scents of his betrayal.

Somehow, from the depths of herself, she managed to find words. His words. "'It's you, Narcise. It's only you.'" She threw them back into his face, the ones that had sustained her for weeks. "You disgust me."

"By the Devil, you can't truly believe—"

"I don't have to believe. I *saw.* You." Her voice broke and she felt herself falling back into that chasm of desolation and grief, a whirlwind of blackness. Disbelief and pain. Such pain. She had to get away from him. A roaring filled her ears, the deep, dark roar of hatred and agony. *"Get away from me."*

He stepped toward her, grabbing her arm. "Do you have any idea what I've done for you?" His voice raw, his face, terrible, was close to hers. She hardly heard the words, for they were lost in the horrible swirling scent of blood on his breath, the smells of depravity and sweat and other darkness.

She talked over him, the roaring in her mind and heart blocking his words as she spewed her pain onto him. "You've completely destroyed me. Something even my brother wasn't able to do, in decades." She jerked her arm from his fingers with a sharp movement, turning away, starting back down the corridor. "Get away from me." Her voice threatened to break, but she wouldn't allow it. "*Get away.*"

He'd said she was strong. Oh, he had no idea how strong she was. Her hand closed over a doorknob and she turned it, not caring where it led, hardly aware of what she was doing. *Have to get away from him.*

"By the Fates, Narcise, listen—"

"I can't bear—" She shoved a hand over her mouth to hold back the vomit, and stumbled through the door. As she slammed it behind her, falling against it, trying to breathe something other than him and his depravity, he slammed against it, rattling it in its hinges.

And then he was gone.

He didn't remember leaving Cezar's subterranean residence after those nights of hell.

In retrospect, a decade later, Giordan wondered that the man even allowed him to do so—but then, of course, by that time, Cezar had gotten all that he'd wanted.

At least, for the moment.

With Narcise's hate-filled, witchlike visage burning in his memory, her acid words screaming in his mind, Giordan found himself raging blind and lost through the streets. Violence pounded through him, his abused body weak and overused, his hands, his very skin a reeking reminder of the hours and days past.

He had no real memory of where he went and what he did once out of Cezar's place: it was dark, and his world became a hot, red rampage, filled with the taste and scent of blood, the heat and suppleness of living flesh, the rhythmic pulsing against his body, the slap and thud of flesh against flesh. There might have been screams, shouts, cries, moans and groans. There were certainly deaths and injuries.

Giordan's vision burned with red shadow. It was as if coals had been shoved beneath his lids and seared into his irises, coloring his sight.

He supposed he went mad.

Do you have any idea what I've done for you? His own hoarse words rolled in his brain, over and over, desperate and angry even as he sought relief. She wouldn't even listen.

She wouldn't *listen*.

He woke sometime, some hours, perhaps days, later in one of Paris's narrow alleys. Tucked back in a corner. Alone.

That moment was clear in his mind even today, a decade after: that moment of reemergence, of clawing up from the depths of a heavy, dark sea. As if he'd dragged himself awake from the worst of nightmares.

But it had been no nightmare, those three nights of hell. And what he'd thought of as the light at the end of the tunnel, as the prize for his endurance and existence through hours of torture, turned only into the slap of betrayal. And the hot memory of humiliation.

Narcise.

Giordan rubbed gritty eyes with trembling fingers that smelled of blood and semen and opium and filth. He saw that the alley was hardly wide enough for him to extend his legs, but so long that he could see only that it angled into nothingness.

The walls on either side of him loomed tall and windowless, like dark sentinels. The brick was cold against his bare back, chill and rough with dirt, sticky with unidentifiable substances. Even springy with a bit of moss. The ground below, uneven with cobbles and filtered with a random tuft of grass, seeped damply into his breeches.

All at once, Giordan became aware of the sun. It emerged from a heavy cloud as if a curtain had been drawn away. The golden light spilled into the alley next to him and would soon filter over the spot where he lay.

At first, he didn't have even the energy to pull to his feet. Nor the desire.

His mind was stark and empty, devoid of thought, even emotion. Just...empty.

Finished.

She'd finished him.

But then, as the base need for self-preservation stirred with the shift of the sun, Giordan prepared to heave himself upright.

At that moment, he saw the cat.

She sat there, pale and blonde against the shades of indigo and violet and gray that filled the alley. Her blue-gray eyes were fixed on him in that way of her race, unblinking and steady.

But there was no miffed accusation in this feline's stare. Her tail, which curled comfortably around her, had no annoyed twitching at its tip. She exuded peace.

She looked just like the cat who'd stared at him from a nearby roof some weeks ago. Just after he'd met Narcise.

Giordan realized belatedly that some of the weakness in his body stemmed from the presence of his Asthenia, positioned just-so in front of him. She sat just far enough away that he wasn't breathless and paralyzed, but close enough that he felt the essence of her presence like uncomfortable waves.

And he realized that, until she moved, he could not escape from the alley.

"Scat!" he said with as much sharpness as he could muster, but at the same time, a wave of grief for his own fat orange Chaton roughened the back of his throat. "Move!"

The cat looked at him, her eyes intelligent and steady. And she didn't move.

Even when he threw a stone toward her, she didn't

flinch. She hardly deigned to notice when the rock scuttled across the stones next to her.

Giordan looked up and saw the light blazing above in a perfect, cerulean sky. Hot and yellow and bright. The beams had begun to fill the alley in an ever-widening triangle of light, turning the stones lighter gray, glazing them with hints of yellow and rust, coloring the random tufts of grass green.

It was only a matter of time until the rays would fall onto him; now they eased slyly against his breeches and filtered over the heel of his battered boot.

He pressed himself up against the wall, crouched in the corner, glaring at the cat.

"Move!" he shouted again, and looked for something else to throw at the stubborn creature. There was nothing. He managed to work one of his boots from his foot—a very long, difficult process in his weakened state—and when it finally came free, he flung it clumsily toward the thing.

It tumbled just behind her and she barely lifted her chin as it thudded onto the cobbles.

He began to heave himself to his feet, but at that moment, the cat decided it was time to move…and she sauntered toward him.

As she came closer, the rest of Giordan's strength fell away. His lungs slowed their movements, his chest felt heavy and constricted and his muscles ceased to respond.

Giordan sank back onto the ground, leaning against the wall as the cat positioned herself directly in front of him. So close he could see the gray and black flecks in her unblinking eyes, and even the fact that she had whiskers in both white and black. Her ears were two perfect triangles sitting at the top of her head, and her fur was lush and long like corn silk. He had a moment of madness and nearly reached to touch that soft fur.

Feeling ebbed from his body and he closed his eyes against the nothingness that swept over him. Blankness… something even beyond paralysis.

After a moment, he opened his eyes and saw the sun just peeking over the roof above him. Soon, it would be directly overhead, pouring into the alley.

He'd burn.

If the damned cat didn't move…he'd burn. He had nothing to cover himself with, nowhere to hide.

"Go!" he shouted, but his voice was weak. And perhaps it even lacked conviction.

The cat, of course, didn't move, and although she continued to watch him with those wide eyes, her expression was not haughty.

It was determined.

Giordan closed his eyes when he felt the first brush of the sun's warmth.

It was an impossible juxtaposition of pleasure and pain…the warmth, as if someone's hand brushed over him, warm and tender…and yet edged with sharpness, bespeaking of the agony to come.

He huddled against the building, curled up like a cat— or a fetus—pressing as close against the bricks as he could. But the back of his shoulder was exposed, the only part of him that he couldn't keep in the shadow, and the sun's rays inched inexorably closer until at last they seared into his sensitive flesh.

A wave of agony screamed through him and he realized from deep inside the white pain that it was coming from his Mark.

The light poured onto him, battling with the dark, undulating roots that branded him Lucifer's. They writhed and screamed with their own pain as the sun burned and burned and burned.

The last thing he remembered was a light…bright and white and pure, burning inside his mind.

Clarity.

And a voice, deep inside him, that said, "*Choose.*"

In the decade that followed Giordan's betrayal, as the Reign of Terror in Paris ended and the Revolution metamorphosed into a new era under Napoleon Bonaparte's leadership, Narcise came to a realization: despite her inability to banish the memory of what Cale had done to her, there were other men who wanted her, ones who could love her. At least for a time.

There were other men who, if she found one who was infatuated deeply enough, could perhaps finish the job Giordan had begun—or at least had made her think he'd begun; she had no reason to believe Giordan had ever even truly meant to free her.

She firmly pushed away her pang of unease as she remembered his face during their final confrontation. Everything from those moments was a blur of pain and darkness, of sordid, hedonistic smells assaulting and pummeling her with the knowledge of what he'd done… everything except the dull shock in his eyes.

Narcise shook her head to banish the image.

Now, perhaps she could find a man who actually would help her escape from her brother.

She didn't have to love him, or even care for him— she wasn't certain she could ever open her heart again.

She merely had to make them want to help her.

Because it had become clear to her, with a bitter and terrifying finality, that she had no chance of escaping Cezar on her own. For too long she'd held out hope that she could find a way…but he was too smart and cunning. There were sparrow feathers, it seemed, everywhere in the house and in its adjoining tunnels, and he kept anything that could be considered a weapon far from her except when she was forced to entertain. Nor could she trust any of the servants, for they were all bound to her brother.

She was utterly alone, and felt that loneliness more acutely than she ever had before—now that she realized what it was like to love someone, and now that she had lost hope of finding escape on her own.

But if she had nothing else, she had strength and determination: the same characteristics that had helped her become a nearly undefeated swordswoman and had kept her from going mad during the years of rape and molestation.

Perhaps that was why Lucifer had chosen her. An iron core beneath a seductive, beautiful woman was a formidable weapon.

And so she looked more closely at her opponents when she faced them. Sometimes, she even allowed one to win, just to remind herself that she could still feel. Pain, pleasure, apprehension…whatever.

Just so she could feel.

London

Chas Woodmore was surrounded by *vampirs*, which would normally be a convenience rather than a concern, since he was, in fact, a *vampir* hunter. And a damn good one at that.

Some called those who shared his occupation Venators, but that was a completely different society—in fact, it was an entire family from Italy that spent their lives hunting and slaying the half-demon vampires that had descended from Judas Iscariot.

Woodmore happened to specialize in the hunting and staking of the very different *vampirs* that originated in Romania, where Vlad Tepes, Count Dracula, had made his own deal with the Devil in the late fifteenth century. Unfortunately for his progeny, the unholy covenant applied not only to Vlad himself, but also to any of his descendants selected by Lucifer to participate. They had to agree, of course, just as Dracula had done, but Luce was a master at manipulation and it was rare that any of them declined his juicy bargain—partly because it was most often made during their dreams.

Thus, some of the Dracule embraced their newly immortal lives, complete with bloodlust and damaged souls that belonged to the Devil for all eternity, and some of them existed more judiciously, realizing only after the fact that perhaps it hadn't been such a good deal after all....

And then there was Woodmore's employer, Dimitri, the Earl of Corvindale, who fought the regrettable bargain with every breath he took, every single day.

It was because of his association with Corvindale that Woodmore was not only surrounded by some of the less rapacious *vampirs* at this very moment, but also comfortably unarmed—and playing cards with the lot of them. This lot happened to be safe from Woodmore's lethal stake because they were of the mind that, for example, one didn't have to murder a mortal in order to feed.

And Woodmore happened to be losing tonight because of one Mr. Giordan Cale, who seemed to have some sort of magic about him when it came to having the winning hand every time. Or at least when the pot was very large.

"By the Fates, Giordan," Corvindale said in disgust, tossing his cards onto the table. "You dragged me out of my study for this? What precisely is the benefit to me of being relieved of three thousand pounds in the space of two hours?"

A fleeting smile curved Cale's lips as he collected the pound notes and coins from the latest winning pot. "A change of scenery," he suggested mildly. "Perhaps even some social discourse, no?"

Although he spoke excellent English, he had a trace of French in his pronunciation. Woodmore knew that Cale was originally from Paris, but had left the city ten years ago, near the end of the Reign of Terror, and hadn't returned. He'd been in and out of London for the past decade, but they had only become acquainted a few weeks ago.

"Corvindale? Social discourse?" Lord Eddersley laughed, his gangly hands bumping the table, making the coins clink. "But Luce's hell hasn't yet frozen over."

The earl slid his companion a dark look, but Woodmore wasn't certain whether it was because he took offense, which was bloody unlikely, or because he didn't want to be here in the private apartment at White's gentlemen's club in the first place. His employer—which was a loose term, for they were more like associates working toward the same goals than master and minion, and, aside of that, a gentleman never actually worked *for* anyone anyway—rarely left his study unless it was to seek out more ancient books or parchments to add to his collection.

Brickbank, a baronet from Derbyshire who was also a member of the Dracule, gestured to a hovering footman for a refill on his whiskey, complaining, "Wish those Brits would run that damned frog Boney out of Paris. Damned tired of drinking this rot from Scotland. Miss a good Armagnac."

"Those Brits? Do you not consider yourself one of them?" Cale asked, sipping his own "rot."

"I'm too old to be a damned soldier," Brickbank replied, and all of the *vampirs* laughed. Even Corvindale managed the sharp bark of a chuckle. Of course they would: each of them was well over a century old, and they looked no more than in the prime of their lives. "And I don't give a bloody damn about their Prinnys or their Parliaments or anyone's cock-licking emperors."

Woodmore wouldn't trade places with any of the Dracule, even to live and be forever young and virile… for when they died, they belonged to Lucifer. Even *vampirs,* like their mortal counterparts, had the illusion of free will and some choice to be good or evil; still, a life of taking sustenance from other living creatures, of the uncontrollable bloodlust that came with it…of being cloistered from the sun, and *knowing* that one would spend eternity in the bowels of hell—whenever eternity struck—such a life was repulsive to Woodmore.

That was, perhaps, the only reason he and Corvindale had become friends—because he knew that more than anything, the earl wanted to sever his relationship with Lucifer. As proof, for over a hundred years, the earl had refused to feed as the Devil intended, and instead resorted to butchers' bags of blood for sustenance.

Among the Dracule, this long-term abstinence was routinely blamed for the earl's irritable disposition and dark personality.

"But of course Corvindale can get anything through the lines," Cale said with a sidewise glance at the man in question. "He's hardly noticed any inconvenience from the war between our nations, despite the problems crossing the Channel, have you, Dimitri? He's kept me in supply of my favorite Bordeaux as well."

"You have a stash of Armagnac?" Brickbank said, looking at the earl in surprise. "And haven't brought it here to White's? Should move the game to Blackmont then."

Corvindale shot another dark look, this time aimed at Giordan Cale, who smiled as he lifted his own glass to drink. "Naturally I've charged you a substantial fee to keep you in such supply," the earl replied to Cale.

Woodmore hid his own amusement. The last thing his employer wanted was people at his home, bothering him while he was trying to immerse himself in old scrolls and ancient languages. Searching for a way to break the covenant with Lucifer.

Which was why Woodmore felt particularly grateful that, some years back, Corvindale had agreed to play guardian and guard for his sisters should anything happen to him. He had three younger sisters—Maia, Angelica and Sonia, the latter of whom happened to be ensconced far north of London in a Scottish convent—and a dangerous occupation of which none of them were aware.

"I'm of a mind to take the game to Rubey's," said Cale, "if we're talking of moving it. I suspect Dimitri has supplied her with some excellent vintages as well— and she won't make us leave so she can hole herself up in her study."

Corvindale glanced at him, lifting one eyebrow with skepticism. "Spying on your potential competition?"

"Not any longer. She's convinced me that it would be futile for any establishment of mine to try to compete with hers here in London. Now I'm attempting to persuade her to take on an investor—namely me—to make some improvements to the place. Aside of that…ah, well, she meets another criteria of mine and she's been rather accommodating." Cale smiled with exaggerated modesty.

Woodmore, along with every Dracule in London, was well-acquainted with Rubey's—the luxurious brothel that catered to *vampirs* and, occasionally, a select few mortals who were aware of the Draculean underground. Rubey, a mortal herself, was a formidable character who reminded Chas of his half-part-Gypsy great-grandmother in personality, if not looks. She was sharp in business acumen, quick of wit and overly generous with lectures and advice—wanted or otherwise. Nearing forty, she was also very attractive, if not a bit long in the tooth for him.

Because he needed to be so ingrained in his employer's world of the Dracule, he'd visited her establishment on more than one occasion. But the most recent incident had been when he was too far into his cups and he ended up in one of the bedchambers with a female *vampir* make. That night of heat and pain and passion had been his first—and last—intimacy with a *vampir*, and one he did not intend to repeat…despite the fact that the very memory haunted him.

He tried to feel only revulsion for the night of debauchery, but even two weeks later, the marks from bites he'd begged for in the blur of drunkenness and lust hadn't quite healed. And remnants of the night's pleasures still weaved within his dreams.

As he picked up his drink, Woodmore noticed a little spider making its way along the edge of the table between him and Cale. He lifted his hand to smash it, but the other man raised his palm and said, "Allow me." And as he watched, Cale scooped the spider onto one of the playing cards and dropped the creature in a corner, where, presumably, it scuttled away to safety.

Woodmore couldn't help but eye the man curiously—a Dracule, sparing the life of a spider? Perhaps he felt some sort of bloodsucking kinship with the critter—and noticed that Corvindale had been watching as well with a bemused look on his face.

The earl looked as if he were about to comment, but he was interrupted by Brickbank.

"Woodmore, heard you tried to hang Cale on a stake, few weeks back," said the man, peering into his glass as if hoping it would change to something French. "Something about smoke explosives?"

"It would have been unfortunate if Woodmore succeeded," Corvindale said dryly. "For Cale still owes me for the last shipment."

"But since the casks are nearly empty, that would have been to my benefit," Cale retorted, giving rise to another round of laughter.

"It wasn't my best effort, that attempt," Woodmore admitted ruefully, thinking about how the little packets had fizzled and not puffed into a thick cloud of smoke when he'd thrown them into the fireplace. That had made it difficult for him to distract his victim. He looked at Cale, acknowledging at least privately that the man could easily have killed him that night. But for some reason, like the spider, Woodmore had been spared. "But as it turns out, it was for the best. Corvindale tells me you're intimately familiar with Cezar Moldavi and his place in Paris."

The last vestiges of levity drained from Cale's face. Corvindale said something sharp under his breath and Woodmore glanced at him, but the earl was watching as his friend raised a glass to sip.

"Dimitri is correct," replied Cale, his eyes iced-over brownish gray.

Unclear as to what had provoked such a turbulent response, Woodmore nevertheless continued. "He's the sort of bastard that deserves a little less efficient way to die than a simple stake to the heart, the damned child-bleeder."

"On that, at least, we are all in complete agreement," said the earl.

Indeed, the stories Woodmore had heard about Moldavi were enough to make his blood run cold. He found it disturbing enough that these immortal men, beholden to the Devil, needed to drink blood to live, but to take from *children*…and to leave them to *die*… It was tales like these that only confirmed for him that his dangerous mission was the right thing to do.

And the only reason he hadn't attempted the assassination of the beast so far was that he knew he needed a perfect plan in order to outsmart Moldavi.

He looked at Cale. "I need to find a way to get in to his hidey-hole so I can kill him. Corvindale is financing the effort, and he'll get me across the Channel."

One of the reasons Woodmore was such an effective *vampir* hunter was his ability to sense the presence of a Dracule, and thus identify them easily. Even members of the Draculia couldn't identify each other merely by sight, or smell, but even as he sat here in the midst of them, Woodmore's belly was filled with the familiar sort of gnawing-itching sensation that indicated the presence of a *vampir*. He became used to it after a while, as one did with a smell or aroma, but it was always present. Another advantage was Woodmore's ability to move about in daylight, and his innate fighting ability and speed. And then there was his lack of an Asthenia.

Of course, being mortal, he had any number of things that could slow, weaken or even kill him.

Cale gave a brief nod. "I'm willing to assist in any way. I am more than passing familiar with the place." He drank again, draining his glass, and set it deliberately at the edge of the table nearest the footman, who responded immediately to refill it.

"There's a sister," mused Brickbank. "Dashed beautiful, according to Voss. Can't remember her name."

"Narcise," said Cale quietly, curling his fingers around the refilled glass. "I believe her name is Narcise."

"Yes. She'll be included in my plans as well," Woodmore said. He knew from experience that some of the most vicious and bloodthirsty *vampirs* were the female ones. "Two for the price of one, Corvindale. She's rather accomplished with the épée, I hear."

"The saber, if I recall correctly. And rather than be your target," Cale said, setting down an empty glass again, "you'd be better off utilizing her as an accomplice. There is no love lost between her and her brother and she'd like nothing better than to see him skewered on a stake." His mouth twitched in a humorless smile as he added, "Unless things have changed in the last decade."

"I can't imagine they have," Corvindale replied flatly, confirming for Woodmore that he was definitely missing some underlayer of conversation. He would get the story from Corvindale later. "He is the worst sort of dog."

"What of the Astheniae? Do you know what theirs are?" he said, looking at Cale.

"But of course, no, or I would have employed it myself. No one knows Moldavi's weakness. But because he keeps himself so cloistered, the assumption is that it's something very common."

"And the sister? Narcise? Do you know her Asthenia?"

"I do not."

"Poor bastard Sabbanti died fifteen years ago," Brickbank commented. "His was pine needles. Didn't last more than five years before he got staked."

Woodmore glanced at him with a wry smile. "He was one of my first slayings, in fact. I was sixteen."

"Thought it was an unfortunate accident," Brickbank replied, clearly stunned. "By Luce's bollocks!"

"That's how I make most of them look. I don't need the damned Bow Street Runners sniffing around, complicating things. They get in my way often enough as it is."

"It wasn't long after that when you attempted to stake me," Corvindale said. "Naturally you didn't have a chance at succeeding."

Eddersley, whose eyelids were always half-closed, suddenly looked interested. "You tried to slay Corvindale? And you're still alive?"

Woodmore nodded. "He took the opportunity to educate me on the precise angle with which to employ my stake—I was slightly off, and therefore not nearly as accurate as I am now. And then the lesson deteriorated into a philosophical conversation about how, just as with mortals, there are good *vampirs* and evil ones, and then on to covenants with the Devil and how to break them when they are, indeed, unbreakable."

"I merely convinced Chas that he should exploit his quite exemplary skills toward ridding the earth of those Dracule who have a different perspective of how to live as immortals, among mortals, than we do. Rather than hunting us."

"You mean, those who choose not to do business with you, Dimitri, or who otherwise compete with you," Cale said. "You're a ruthless bastard in your own way." His glass had been filled and then emptied a third time, and the congeniality that was normally in his expression had completely disappeared.

"Aren't we all?" Corvindale replied evenly, but, yet, there was no dangerous glow in his eyes. Instead his gaze was somber. "And isn't that precisely why we're sitting here—Woodmore excepted, of course? Because we're all ruthless bastards, selfish and violent and lustful? That's why Lucifer came to us with the offer in the first place. And not a one of us has changed since then."

"Change?" Brickbank echoed, sloshing his drink. "Why the bloody Fates would we change? Live forever. Women—or men," he added, glancing at Eddersley, who didn't look particularly sleepy at that moment. "All we want. Power. Money. All of it. No one can touch us." His eyes gleamed with pleasure.

"But therein lies the flaw," Corvindale said, crooking a finger to have his own glass refilled. "We do not live forever. At least, here, on earth." He gestured to Woodmore. "And some of us leave this place sooner than others, thanks to our friend here. At some point, we are beholden to Lucifer. We belong to him."

Corvindale's deep bitterness effectively flattened the congenial mood, and they lapsed into silence.

Woodmore was fascinated and horrified in turn by the depths of this conversation. They were saying the very things he'd struggled with ever since he came to know Corvindale—and realized it was possible that all *vampirs* weren't deserving of being hunted and killed in cold blood.

In fact, he suspected that Cale knew full well that his accusation wasn't quite accurate—Corvindale didn't employ Woodmore to simply assassinate his competition, or even those with whom he disagreed.

Woodmore certainly made threats to those who interfered or otherwise attempted to sabotage the earl's business ventures, but his slayings were confined to those who were more like Cezar Moldavi, those *vampirs* who fed greedily and left their victims to die, or who otherwise used their strength and constitution to violate and terrorize mortals simply for the pleasure of doing so.

Because they had given away their conscience with their soul.

Thus, his occupation as a *vampir* hunter was one that brought Woodmore both revulsion and satisfaction. He associated socially with the very race he stalked—how much better it was to know well what he hunted—while picking and choosing among the servants of Lucifer to slay some and protect others.

It made for many dark, empty nights, lying in bed or in some form of transport, wondering if he truly had the right to be judge, jury and executioner of these men and women.

But he, of all men, was particularly suited to the task. And it was a cross he must bear.

11

Two months later

Despite being at war with England, Napoleon's Paris was surprisingly easy to enter, particularly with the resources of the Earl of Corvindale to grease palms and ensure that certain eyes turned blindly away from certain things. And for a gentleman like Chas Woodmore, whose Gypsy heritage gave him an almost Gallic appearance, the blending in was even simpler.

It was the getting out of the city that would be the problem.

But for Chas, there was only one element of the plan to be concerned with at a time, and the first was to gain entrance to Cezar Moldavi's house.

It was past noon, well into the afternoon, as he walked along a *rue* in Le Marais. Although this was the area where the wealthy lived, the street was busy—filled with servants walking to and from the market, deliverymen and the residents rumbling along in their carriages on their way shopping and to other social engagements. No one would take note of yet another courier with a small paper-wrapped packet, particularly since he was dressed so as to be unremarkable in simple clothing and sturdy shoes. He'd settled a simple cap on his head, which had the result of covering much of his thick, dark hair and shading his face. It also made him appear younger.

Nevertheless, Chas knew it was highly unlikely he'd actually make it out of the city. If he succeeded with his plan to assassinate Moldavi, and possibly the sister as well, regardless of what Cale had told him about her, then he would have the greatest chance of making it back to London. In that case, he'd only have to contend with getting past the soldiers at every corner of the city.

He couldn't help a rueful smile, imagining Corvindale's reaction if he had to carry through on his promise to take in Maia, Angelica and Sonia in the event of Chas's demise. Maia, the eldest of the sisters and his junior by nearly ten years, would have plenty to say about it as well. Chas could already imagine her, with her hands on her hips and her foot tapping in annoyance. She was used to being in charge and managing the household, notwithstanding the dubious assistance of their chaperone Mrs. Fernfeather.

But there was no one better equipped, nor more trustworthy, than Corvindale to protect his sisters if something happened to him, and as such, for the first time in all of his travels, Chas had left instructions with Maia to contact the earl if he didn't return or otherwise message her within a fortnight.

That was how long Chas expected it to take to infiltrate Moldavi's homestead—if things went smoothly— and get close enough to his target, then get out of the city. He'd have one chance to drive the stake home, and God willing, he'd succeed.

The *rues* were just as dirty and crowded in Paris as

they were in London, Rome and St. Petersburg. He happened to prefer the countryside to the big, loud cities, perhaps because he was fairly forced to frequent them—and their seediest, most dark and unsavory places—in search of Dracule. As he avoided a steaming pile of dog shit in the center of the walkway, which was really just the edge of the street, he pictured for a moment the small estate he'd just purchased in Wales, with its neat, unassuming manor house tucked amid rolling green hills.

It was likely he'd never have a chance to enjoy the place. He'd acquired it secretly, in hopes that it would be a private haven for him if he needed to hide his sisters from danger. For, just as he attempted to rid the world of *vampirs*, so were there *vampirs* who were bent on ridding the world of him...and who wouldn't hesitate to use Maia, Angelica and Sonia to do so.

Thank goodness at least Sonia was tucked safely away at St. Bridie's. The last time he'd seen her, when he'd come to visit, they'd had a terrible row. A flush of guilt warmed his cheeks as it occurred to him that he might never see her or any of them again. *God willing I'll make it up to them all.*

Then he realized he hadn't been paying attention to the numbers on the houses, and had nearly missed Moldavi's.

Here it is.

He walked past the columned, whitewashed front of the narrow but imposing three-story building, his attention moving from thoughts of his sisters and sharpening as he observed the area. A maidservant rushed past, carrying three large parcels that obstructed her view, and nearly collided with two footmen who were standing in the center of the walkway. Two carriages passed each other, harnesses rattling, hooves clopping. Someone shouted across the way from an unshuttered window, and there was a bellicose response from another window in the next building. Moldavi's house, while it looked the same as the ones surrounding it, was the only one that seemed devoid of life.

From Giordan Cale, Chas knew that the house itself was only the facade of Moldavi's residence, and that most of the living space was underground in well-furnished but windowless chambers.

The servants—mostly *vampir*, but some mortal—lived in the aboveground floors, where heavy curtains were drawn over the windows during the day. It was also where merchants entered and deliveries were made, and these upper floors were the way Chas would gain access to the house. He just had to wait for an opportune time…or to create one himself.

The improved smoke packets that his friend Miro had made for him were in his coat pocket, but those were best used inside a confined space. And since this was his first visit to the area, he didn't intend to do anything more than get a sense of the area.

He'd continued on his way to the end of the block. The houses that lined the thoroughfare were all similar to each other in design, with classical columns and landings. Built close together, these structures were part of an architectural revival that had swept Paris during the Revolution. Along with the city's rebuttal of all things royal had come the desire to eliminate the opulence and richness the ruling class had imposed upon it.

Thus, the nouveau style embraced the simplicity of the Greeks and Romans along with symbolizing the rise of the bourgeoisie and their own seal on the city.

The scent of spring roses and lilies caught in the breeze as he walked past neatly trimmed gardens around to the next block. There was a small alley between two of the houses that abutted Moldavi's, and he turned into it, still carrying his package.

The alley was deserted and he walked purposely along toward the rear side of Moldavi's house. If anyone saw him, he was delivering a package to Monsieur Tournedo—and could someone not direct him to whichever of these houses belonged to the gentleman, *s'il vous plaît?* If no one did, he'd have the chance to explore the rear of the house.

During sunlight was the best time to attempt to break into a *vampir* residence, for a good portion of the household would be asleep. He just had to find the right time.

And then as luck would have it, an opportunity presented itself. Looking back, Chas knew he couldn't have planned anything better.

All at once, he heard a loud crash and clatter coming from the street in front of Moldavi's house. The horrified whinny of a horse, followed by a scream and lots of shouting. More whinnies and even a terrible, agonized shriek from one of the beasts. Whatever had occurred, it wasn't good—likely an animal would have to be put down—but it was also a guaranteed distraction to anyone in the vicinity.

Sure enough, as Chas peered around the corner toward the mess on the narrow street, he saw crowds gathering. Like executions, accidents drew the morbid as well as the curious. Which included, more often than not, everyone in the vicinity.

"It was a cat! She ran in front of me and I could not stop!" a driver was shouting.

"But you should have been looking!" raged another. "Now see what you've done!"

People were streaming from their houses, shouting encouragement and orders, crying out in shock and horror. Dogs barked and whined, and warning bells began to ring. Even a gunshot sounded, momentarily tempting even Chas to investigate further.

But, no…he had much more important and satisfying things to attend to. *Bloody damned child-bleeder.* He was looking forward to seeing the man cower in fear for his life, knowing that only the thrust of a stake was between him and eternal damnation.

His lips settled in a feral grin that no one could see, he eased back behind the house. If anyone in the Moldavi household was awake, it was certain they'd be either looking out the front windows or standing on the front porch. Chas had the perfect opportunity and had to work quickly.

As trees gave shade, and thus provided shadow from the sun streaming inside the house through a window, he avoided the windows near the large oak that grew on the north side of the building. Best to find entry through a chamber that was less likely to house a Dracule. And the higher the chamber, the less likely it would be occupied when the master lived belowground. He eyed a window on the third floor and noted the sturdy brick edging around its gabled roof.

Just then, a streak of blonde shot around the corner of the house. It was a light-colored cat, and it appeared to be the one that had caused the ruckus out front. Once safely under a yew against the house, the feline stopped and looked up at him with unblinking gray-blue eyes.

"*Merci,*" Chas murmured to the creature as he slipped his package, coat and cap behind the bush and pulled a rope from inside his pocket. "You've given me an exceptional opportunity." He swung the rope up onto one of the window gables and pulled tight when its hook caught around the lip of the peak.

The cat meowed, and to his amusement seemed to nod and then preen in acknowledgment, then ducked under the bushes and out of sight. The rope safely in place, Chas tested it and then began to climb.

He was quick and efficient, his movements smooth and sleek, and moments later, he pulled himself onto the ledge of the window to peer in carefully. Empty of everything but a rug and a single chair. He smiled, but there was also a nudge of disappointment that no one was waiting to try to stop him. It had been some time since he'd been in a good fight.

Gathering up the rope, he looped it out of sight onto the top of the little roof so that it would be accessible on his way out.

Then, grateful for the continued chaos from the street beyond, he climbed into the chamber and walked silently to the door. Before opening it, he waited for the familiar sensation to come over him…the sort of itching in his belly that told him a *vampir* was near. The closer one came to him, the deeper and more violent the odd feeling he had in his gut.

There was a time not so long ago when Chas would have sneaked through the home of a Dracule and staked any *vampir* he encountered—often while in their beds, sleeping away the daylight. Even after he met the earl, and learned that at least one of Lucifer's stewards was not quite the evil being his granny's stories had made them out to be, he hadn't become any less discriminating in his work.

But in the last few years, since he'd come to know Corvindale's friends and realized that despite the fact that they had all tied their souls to the Devil, there were various degrees of immorality and violence, Chas had become less rigid in his choices. In his mind, every *vam-*

pir could be a threat to mortals, but there was a divide between those who truly were, and those who simply tried to live and let live.

He heard nothing alarming and went out the door into the corridor on silent feet. A little twinge in his belly told him a Dracule was near, but it was so subtle that he knew it wasn't in close proximity.

As he made his way through the house, mentally reviewing the rough sketch of a map Cale had made for him, it became obvious that the top floors of the house were empty and unused. That made his job even easier, for he'd be less likely to encounter anyone as he made his way to Moldavi's private quarters below the ground.

Nevertheless, he utilized the servants' stairs down through the back of the house, noting to himself that there were no enticing smells coming from this kitchen. Draculean households didn't really need to cook much.

The twitch in his gut was getting stronger, and he slipped a stake from one of his inside pockets. But as he passed silently by the main foyer of the home, which was furnished so as to impress any casual visitors, he saw that a cluster of people still gathered in front of the house and glimpsed the gleam of shiny black paint on the side of an upended Landau.

It was safe to say that everyone awake in this house was out in the street.

As he made his way toward the staircase Cale had told him led to the underground apartments, Chas couldn't resist thinking: *Could it simply be this easy? This Providential?*

Sonia would say, yes, if he was doing God's work, the Hand of the Almighty would arrange things so that it would happen. But Chas didn't fully believe that such blatant miracles occurred like chess pieces being rearranged on their board.

His favorite Biblical maxim was "God helps those who help themselves." And that was what he was doing.

He'd just about reached the entrance to the lower level when his belly gave a sharp twist and the odd itching feeling became uncomfortable. Just then a door opened in front of him.

Chas reacted before the *vampir* had the chance to see him: he lunged for the unsuspecting man, grabbed his arm and had him pushed against the wall, forearm up against his throat, before the sot could take a breath. All in complete silence.

The *vampir* goggled up at him, his eyes wide and shocked. Then they narrowed a bit as he seemed to catch his breath.

"Where's Moldavi?" Chas asked in a soft voice, the stake's point just beneath the servant's waistcoat, pressing gently into his breastbone as his powerful arm eased up on the man's throat.

He felt the footman draw in a breath and just before the bastard was about to shout an alarm, he jammed the stake through shirt, breastbone and directly into his heart.

His victim jolted, shock rushing back over his face, and Chas felt him shudder…then all life abruptly cease. Swearing to himself—for now he had the smell of fresh blood in the house, not to mention the problem of a dead body to attend to—he wiped off his stake and stuck it back in his pocket. Then he heaved the corpse over his shoulder and slipped quickly back the way he'd come, toward the servants' entrance.

Opening the back door, he dumped the corpse into the space between the house and the thick yew and boxwood that grew close to the wall, hoping it would obscure the body for some time.

Back inside the house, he moved with silent speed back to where he'd been when he encountered the *vampir*, all the while waiting for a renewed itch in his belly that told him more Dracule were near.

Before he started down the stairs, he paused, waiting, listening…feeling. There was a sound in the distance, voices rumbling…and the niggle started in his gut again. But it was some distance away and he started down into the depths of Cezar Moldavi's lair.

There was a sort of finality about it. Perhaps it was because going below the surface was akin to being buried, perhaps because there was no way out but the way he came—or through the skull-lined catacombs on the north side—but Chas felt his nerves string tight. He was on his guard as he'd never been before, listening for the sound of approach, paying heed to his body and its innate signals. He had his stake in one hand, and his other fingers curled around the butt of his pocketed pistol.

Aside of it being cooler, and lit only with oil lamps and no natural light, the subterranean corridor appeared no different than one above the ground. It was painted and furnished, lined with doors just as any other hallway in a well-appointed home. But here he moved with more caution, listening at every door to see what he heard and felt.

The voices had become more distinct and Chas more cautious as he made his way along a stretch that seemed to make a large U-shape. When he reached a large door from which the voices seemed to be coming, he stopped to listen, scanning the hall as he pressed his ear to the wood, careful not to touch it and make it jolt in its hinges.

"And Corvindale," said a male voice beyond the door.

A little prickle scooted up his spine and Chas pressed

closer. He couldn't make out all of the conversation, but he heard snatches of it.

"In London?" came a different voice, with a bit of a hiss to it. That must be Moldavi. "But of course. Perhaps you'd like to go, then, my dear?"

"Of course. I'd be more than delighted to see Dimitri again," came a husky female voice. She must be sitting closest to the door, for her words rang fairly clear. "Since Vienna, you know." She gave an arch laugh.

That had to be the sister. Chas leaned closer, his gut filled with that gnawing feeling from the proximity of *vampirs*.

Despite what Giordan Cale had implied about the sister Narcise being more of an ally than a threat to his mission, Chas had reserved judgment. Her brother might use and abuse her, but that didn't mean that she wasn't malevolent in her own way. Anyone that close to Moldavi was most likely tarred with the same brush, and from the sound of her, he wasn't far off in his estimation. A beautiful woman with fangs was a formidable force, particularly for a man.

A fourth voice joined the conversation—another male, which cooled any thought he might have had about bursting into the chamber. With four Dracule against one mortal—even with the mortal being himself—the odds were not in his favor. Chas heard something about spice ships just as something moved in the air behind him. He spun around in time for a slender, four-sided silver blade to rest right in the center of his chest.

"You don't look like much of a fencing instructor," said the woman holding the épée. This particular blade's tip wasn't blunted, however, and Chas could feel its point digging into his skin.

"What does a fencing instructor look like, per se?" he replied, keeping his voice quiet.

"For one thing," she replied in a voice that was low and dusky and threatened to wrap around him like a velvet rope, "he would normally be armed with a blade of his own, instead of a stake." She was strikingly beautiful, with deep blue-violet eyes and ink-black hair. So much so that he felt a little tremor of awareness beneath the adrenaline shooting through his body.

Now things were going to get interesting.

"Ah, yes," he said, easing a bit away from the tip of her blade, feeling the door behind him and still taking care not to jolt it. *Damn.* He'd been wrong; this had to be the sister. "Perhaps it was an oversight."

"Perhaps." She followed him with the tip of her épée, and those lovely eyes narrowed. "There is only one way to find out then, isn't there? We shall have to fence, and you will prove to me that you are accomplished. This way." She used the tip of her weapon to prod him away from the door.

"But of course," he replied readily, his brain working quickly.

Getting away from the others would hopefully give him the opportunity to disarm her without creating a disturbance that would bring Moldavi and his companions rushing from the chamber.

"I trust you have a place in mind?" he added. *And not on the other side of this door…*

"Walk, monsieur," she said, not yet drawing blood, but coming dangerously close to doing so. He didn't want that scent in the air, so he complied.

Chas walked quickly. If this was the sister, she was certainly not the downtrodden, dead-eyed creature Corvindale had described—a fact which heightened his suspicions even further. Perhaps that was the way things had been a hundred years ago in Vienna, but things had obviously changed. His fingers tightened around the stake.

"Here," she said in that low voice when they came to a door near the end of the U-shaped corridor. "Open it and go in. Slowly."

Feeling the sharp implement in his nape, Chas did as she bid and walked into the room. He took an instant to confirm that no one else was waiting beyond the entrance, and then he reacted.

Holding on to the edge of the open door, he used its leverage to whip himself around and behind it, away from her sword. She made a sound of fury, the blade clashing against the door, but he was already ducking below and erupting back out from its shelter, rearing up and knocking her against the wall on the opposite side.

A gasp of surprise burst from her as she slammed against it, her breath knocked out for a moment, and her lips curled back as she swung the blade down clumsily. He ducked again and, on her downswing, he slammed his entire body against her sword arm, smashing it against the wall, blade impaling the floor instead of his arm.

With his foot, he slid the door closed as he pushed his forearm beneath her neck and held her there.

Her eyes stormy, her breasts heaving between them, she glared up at Chas. A little ripple of attraction shivered through him, and he pushed it firmly away. She was a *vampir*, and lived to seduce.

Her breathing eased. "There is no doubt, then. You're Chas Woodmore."

12

Narcise recognized both surprise and satisfaction in his eyes. His body still held her sword arm in place against the wall. And his arm, wedged beneath her chin, was making it difficult for her to swallow, but despite the stake in his hand, she had no fear.

If he used it, then she hoped he'd make it quick and put her out of her misery.

But if he didn't…perhaps he was the man she'd been waiting for.

"You've heard of me?" he said, easing up the slightest bit on her throat so that she wasn't looking up so sharply.

"But your reputation precedes you, Monsieur Woodmore." She switched from French to English, with which she was more comfortable even after more than a decade here in Paris.

Indeed, everyone knew of the fearless and clever *vampir* hunter Chas Woodmore. How he'd somehow scaled a sheer cliff and sneaked into the mountaintop castle of the bloodthirsty Darrod Firvin to stake the man in his sleep. And how he'd tricked the princes of Tylenia and

Tynnien into climbing aboard a small ship so that he could slay them as well.

The Dracule all murmured of the dark-haired Gypsy gentleman who slipped in and out of the shadows like a *vampir* himself, silent and deadly like a servant of Death. Ironically those who told the tales were ones who'd never actually met the man, for those who did weren't alive to tell the tales.

Which was probably why no one had included in their tales the fact that he was handsome as a dark angel, with thick black hair and intense green-brown eyes. And that he smelled like danger, tight and dark and manly. She scented a bit of blood on him, too, but it didn't smell like it would be his.

"My reputation?" White teeth flashed in his swarthy face, and he inched his arm away a bit more, but kept her sword arm pinned to the wall with his solid body. "Is that so? And here I thought my accomplishments went largely unnoticed."

"I do hope you don't find such modesty too painful," she replied. "And I would appreciate it if you'd either drive that stake into my heart or remove your arm from my throat."

"You don't have a preference?" he asked. He seemed sincere.

Narcise shrugged, and she realized that although she'd managed to catch her breath from their brief battle, she still felt a bit breathless. This man might be more than a match for her. "There are advantages to both."

"Drop your sword and I'll release you," he said.

She complied, and he kicked the épée across the floor of her parlor. When he stepped away, his arm moving from her, she adjusted the sleeves of her manshirt, pulling them back down over her wrists. "Why are you here?"

He ignored her question and asked, "You're Narcise?" She inclined her head and felt his eyes sweep over her. Before she could react, his hand whipped out and grabbed her arm, pulling it away from her body. "How did this happen?"

She didn't have to follow his gaze to know that he was speaking about the bruising around her wrists from the manacles. That was nothing compared to the marks on the rest of her body, which was the reason she was wearing men's clothing today. She couldn't fit in her gowns without a corset, and it was simply still too painful to be laced into one.

"I lost a fencing match," she told him, forcing her lips into a rueful smile, meeting his eyes blandly. "It happens occasionally."

He watched her closely, as if searching for a lie, or waiting for more information, and then released her arm. "What happens when you win?"

"Whatever I choose," she replied. "What are you doing here?"

"I'm a *vampir* slayer," he reminded her.

"Then why did you not slay me?" she asked, moving her arms back and away from her chest to give him a good target she suspected he wouldn't use. "I thought Chas Woodmore was merciless."

"You might be more beneficial to me alive than dead. Where's your brother?"

"Are you truly here to kill him? I'd lead you to him in a breath if I—" Narcise stopped, her blood running cold. "He's coming. They're coming."

She could hear the voices, and knew they'd smelled the faint blood and perhaps even the new scent of Chas Woodmore. Or that her brother had become suspicious

when she didn't return to the parlor, which was where
she'd been going when she came upon this *vampir* slayer.

Woodmore looked as if he were ready to either lunge
at her or duck behind the door, and Narcise made a quick
decision. She was going to get away from Cezar, and this
man was going to help her.

She opened her mouth and screamed as she dove for
the épée on the floor.

One moment Chas was ready to duck into the bedchamber beyond the open door to hide from Moldavi,
and the next, his sister was screaming for help.

Cursing, he spun after her as she rose to her feet, her
sword back in hand. "You," he snarled, deciding he'd take
her to hell with him. "I knew better than to believe them."

But her eyes had widened with fear—something he
hadn't seen before, even when he had her plastered, immobile, against the wall—and just as the pounding footsteps reached the door, she whispered, "I'll save you.
Help me. Please."

When the door burst open, Chas got his first glimpse
of Cezar Moldavi. But he didn't have much time to observe the man in detail, for he was followed by three
other *vampirs*, and they were all red-eyed and fanged-
teeth. They surrounded him without hesitation, blocking the door.

"What is going on here?" said the man who was presumably Moldavi himself. Slight of stature, dark hair
with an odd, wide jaw, and rings glinting on all of his
fingers.

Chas stilled, his attention bouncing around the chamber to see what might be utilized for an escape, or at least
for a weapon. The thing about stakes; they weren't good
for distance. One had to get up close.

Narcise, the madwoman, had her sword, and he looked down to notice that it was once again thrusting into his chest. "Look who's arrived for a visit, dear brother," she said. Her expression had changed into something hard and blank.

"Do I know you?" Moldavi asked, making a little hissing *tsk* sound. "Monsieur?"

Chas hardly took note of the other three *vampirs*, assuming they were the ones who'd been speaking with Moldavi earlier, and instead focused on gauging the distance and angle it would take him to thrust his stake into the man's chest. He flickered a glance at Narcise, trying to read something in her eyes that would either support or deny her previous plea of *Help me.*

What exactly was she asking him?

"We've never met," Chas replied to the man who'd walked around him as if he were a piece of furnishing he was considering for purchase. The hair at the back of his neck lifted, prickling uncomfortably at the man's frenetic movements.

Darkness rolled off Moldavi in silent waves, burning in eyes that seemed calm, but lurking deep within them was an odd light. He was too quick, too odd in his movements, yet the underlying energy bespoke of paranoia battling with control. There was no doubt in Chas's mind that this man was malevolence personified.

"Too dark and swarthy for my taste," Moldavi murmured to one of his companions—not his sister. "But who are you, then, and what are you doing here?" he said, standing in front of him.

"It's Chas Woodmore," Narcise said, sending Chas's shocked attention back to her.

How in the Devil's name is that going to save me?

Moldavi stilled and his eyes narrowed. "You're Wood-more?"

"I'm here to kill you," said Chas, never one to beat around the bush.

Moldavi turned to look at his companions, chuckling, and Chas felt the tip of Narcise's blade shift a bit. Whether by accident or design, he didn't know, but he didn't hesitate.

The next moment he was spinning away and then lunging toward Moldavi, stake raised to his shoulder. No one could react in time to stop him, and Chas felt a surge of triumph as his powerful thrust embedded the stake into the back of the man's torso. Right at the heart.

But instead of feeling the soft inside, the give of the heart after breaking through the skin next to the spine, Chas felt a shock of pain jolting his arm as he realized he'd struck armor—something metal, based on the strength of the reverberations trammeling through his limb.

He swore as they descended on him then, all of them, fangs flashing, eyes red, hands tearing and clawing. He still had hold of his stake and, using his legs, he twisted and bucked, stabbing indiscriminately as countless hands and feet grabbed and kicked him. He felt something give in his shoulder, the tearing of skin, the burst of blood from his upper arm.

Something sharp slammed into his back, then his gut, and one of them yanked him up and threw him through the air. He hadn't caught his breath when he slammed into the wall and the world, mercifully, went black.

His last thought before tumbling into darkness was *Corvindale is going to kill me.*

When he opened his eyes again, Chas found himself reclining on a chaise or some sort of divan. A fire roared nearby, heating his skin uncomfortably. His body ached, his head pounded and he was thirsty.

It took him a moment to realize that he was dressed only in his breeches and that his wrists were tied on either side of him, restrained with leather thongs to the foot of the divan. His legs were also immobilized in the same way.

Something moved in his periphery and he looked over to see Moldavi, who'd shifted into his line of vision. He was with a young woman who seemed to stumble as she walked along with him.

"I have my own special armor," Moldavi said without preamble, directing the woman to sit on a chair directly in front of Chas.

"My informants neglected to share that detail with me," Chas replied wryly. "If they even knew."

"It's saved my life more than a dozen times. Would you like to see it?" Moldavi pulled off his shirt to reveal a slender, ashen-gray chest dusted with shiny dark hair.

The man was slender, nearly skeletal, and at first Chas saw nothing that could be considered armor except for a dark circular shape over the center of his chest. It gleamed and he saw that it was metal…set into his skin.

"Look more closely," Moldavi said, leaning toward him, gesturing to his breastbone. "Do you see?"

And then Chas understood. The faint octagonal outline on—no, *beneath*—his skin, covering the entire breastbone and over his chest, was larger than that which was exposed beneath the skin. No larger than the spread of a hand, the whole was nevertheless generous enough to protect the heart from any stake.

"It's… Your skin has grown over it?" Chas asked, fascinated and horrified at the same time.

Moldavi nodded complacently. "Some years ago I realized how prudent it would be to have a permanent protection. We Dracule heal so quickly, of course, and so I made a place for the medallions of protection—I have one on my back as well, of course—by cutting a place for it in my skin. Oh, it didn't hurt, don't be concerned. And it makes me feel quite powerful. I kept the medallions there until the skin grew back over them—most of the way, as you can see, some of it is still exposed. I rather like the appearance of it. I have similar protection in my neck, of course. For, you see, now I can't be killed. Even by the fearsome Chas Woodmore."

Moldavi shifted, now standing behind the woman. He moved her hair away, leaving a shoulder and the side of her neck bare. "You come from London, do you not, Chas Woodmore? Where you live with your three very lovely sisters?"

A shock of fear speared his insides. "You seem to be more familiar with me than I am with you."

"Oh, I am very familiar with you, Monsieur Woodmore, and Maia, Angelica and…Sophia? What was her name?" He gave a brief smile, licked his lips, then bent slightly to sink his fangs into the bare shoulder of his companion. She tensed, stiffening at the pain, then relaxed.

The spike of worry for his sisters turned into a deep, heavy bolt of revulsion as Chas watched Moldavi gulp the coursing blood. His throat, visible above an elaborate neckcloth, convulsed as his jaw moved in the same rhythm—as if he couldn't get enough of it fast enough. The woman's reaction was nearly as unsettling: she closed her eyes, her face tightening with some expression that was neither wholly pain nor wholly pleasure.

As he fed, Moldavi watched Chas, his burning red-gold eyes fastened on him as if gauging his response.

Chas wanted to look away, but he could not, and he felt his own body begin to stir in response.

No. He tried to force his attention away, but found himself trapped by the hypnotic gaze. The sounds of rushing blood and the quiet *kuhn-kuhn-kuhn* of Moldavi's drinking filled his ears. Chas knew he was being enthralled, but in his weakened state, he could hardly drag his eyes away. Desire tingled inside him, teasing and coaxing a deeper response and Chas tried to focus on the pain throbbing through him instead.

Moldavi released the pinch of pale flesh between his fangs, lifting his face with a slow smile. Blood stained his gums and the edges of his teeth, and Chas fancied he could even smell it on his breath.

"Very satisfying," Moldavi said, looking at him. "Would you care to sample?" He smoothed his finger over the oozing wounds on the woman's shoulder, offering a red-tipped digit to Chas.

He turned his face away, noting the pillow behind his head. His heart pounded rampantly as his stomach squeezed with queasiness.

"No? Perhaps another time then. I hope you won't think me rude, dining in front of you, but I offered to share, and you declined." Moldavi licked the woman's shoulder, which Chas didn't see, but he could hear the sounds. Sloppy and wet, yet sensual.

He swallowed, his throat prickly and rough. His cock had begun to fill and he willed it to subside.

"Now," said Moldavi, pulling the woman's hair back over her shoulders, patting it into place and then giving her a sharp gesture to leave, "back to the matter at hand. London…and your informants. I must assume Dimitri has sent you here."

"No one sends me," Chas managed to say, relieved that

the feeding was over. The tightness in his belly released just that little bit, and he began to focus on his wrists… if there was anything that might be loose or weak. "I go where I will."

"But it is well known that you and Dimitri—what does he call himself in England? Corvindale?—are associates. I find it unlikely that he hasn't at least encouraged you to find me. There was an incident in Vienna, you see, some years back…and Dimitri hasn't quite gotten over it."

"I needed no encouragement to come after a child-bleeder," Chas told him.

"Oh, who has been telling tales? *Tsk*." Moldavi stood and turned toward the blazing fire. When he shifted back around, he was holding a slender metal spike, hardly thicker than the tine of a fork. It glowed white-hot for a moment, then settled into red, then black.

A ripple of fear coursed along his spine, and Chas steadied his breath. *This is going to be unpleasant.*

"Perhaps you might tell me a bit more information about Corvindale. What his recent investments are, per-haps?" Moldavi smiled and that slender spike moved closer to Chas.

He steeled himself, his heart ramming furiously. "I'm not privy to that information," he said.

Moldavi's fingers curled around Chas's immobile arm, the digits ashen in color next to his olive skin. "I'm cer-tain you know something."

Chas shook his head, and groaned at the sharp pain as the spike slid through the soft part of the side of his arm and emerged on the other side. He closed his eyes, shuddering as the little rod burned his flesh, inside and out. Agony reverberated from that center of pain, dull-ing his thoughts and thickening his mind.

"Perhaps you might know when he is going to leave

the country again? I've found it impossible to send any-one inside Blackmont Hall, for he has it well secured. If he travels, it will be much easier for me to…renew old acquaintances."

Through the haze of pain, Chas saw that Moldavi had turned to the fire, and then back again, holding another of the slender metal spikes. "Anything you can tell me will speed things up a bit here," Moldavi said with a smile.

Chas managed to shake his head, and wondered yet again what Narcise had been thinking to say *I'll save you. Help me.*

The woman was obviously addled, or else she was a consummate actress. Just as unpleasant and self-serving as her brother.

Moldavi pinched a piece of flesh at Chas's side, along his firm belly. "My," he said, his voice shifting lower, "there isn't much here to work with, is there, Woodmore? Nevertheless, I shall prevail."

He looked at his victim and said, "What about Gior-dan Cale?"

Chas tried to shrug, but feared it came across as more of a convulsion than anything else. He braced himself, but it wasn't enough to prepare for the sharp, searing pain as the thick needle went through the flesh of his abdomen.

"Giordan Cale," said Moldavi again, more urgently. His eyes glittered. "I understand he is in London now. What do you know of him?"

Chas opened his mouth to speak, and perhaps might have said, "Nothing." At least, that was what he at-tempted to say, but it wasn't the answer Moldavi wanted. A rough jab through his bicep had him jolting and cry-ing out in pain, and then before he could react, a second one in his other bicep. He was pinned to the divan's upholstery.

"Giordan Cale," Moldavi said again. "What is he doing? Where is he? Where does he go?"

"I don't…know…much…." Chas stammered. "Water…?"

Something splashed in his face a moment later, and he choked but licked his lips to get the essence of the water. Before he could fully recover, Moldavi had something else in his hand.

Another metal object, this one with a blunt tip that glowed white-hot. "Tell me everything you know about Giordan Cale. Everything. Everything."

"Why?" he managed to ask. Why this obsession with Cale?

Moldavi's only response was to pull his teeth back in a feral smile and jam the poker into the top of his shoulder.

The smell of burning flesh had Chas arching and twisting in his position, his body fighting the thongs as agony shot through him…from his shoulder, from the back of his knee, from the inside of the crook of his arm…all of it turned white-hot and red as he babbled.

He didn't know what he was saying, but the questions over and over were about Cale, Cale…always about Cale.

At last pain claimed him, and he eased into a world of peace.

When Chas peeled his eyes open next, he could hardly breathe for the pain. Nor could he focus, for the room tilted and spun so violently, he had to close his eyes. But someone was prodding him to move, forcing him to stand, to walk.

Through a haze and with pure determination, he gathered his strength—both mental and physical—and concentrated on moving, thinking, banishing the agony. His

eyes opened, his gaze focused, his limbs began to cooper-
ate—if sullenly—and his thoughts cleared…albeit slowly.

He wasn't restrained, and was led into a room that was
well-lit with many lamps and torches, along with another
roaring fire. One side of the chamber was lined with a
small dais, on which a dining table sat. Moldavi and another four or five companions sat at the table, which was
littered with cups and goblets, bottles and flasks. They
looked up at his entrance, and Moldavi said something
that made one of them laugh, and the others look at Chas.
At first he thought he was hallucinating from the pain
when he recognized the short-statured man who was soon
to be formally crowned the Emperor of France. But he
blinked and refocused and could only come to the conclusion that he recognized him correctly.

The remainder of the space was empty, long and narrow and open. The only other furnishing was a long table
at the other end, and from here, he was fairly certain he
saw two long blades lying on it.

As Chas stood silently in front of the table, flanked
by two burly—if unintelligent-looking—made *vampirs*,
he tried to assimilate the fact that Napoleon Bonaparte
was *here*.

There'd been rumors of Moldavi's allegiance to an
alliance with the new emperor, but for him to be so intimate and in such close quarters was unsettling. It appeared to be a social engagement…but nevertheless, to
have a powerful man so enticed by one like Cezar Moldavi…well, the Dracule were infamous for remaining
uninvolved with politics or authority.

Perhaps it wasn't such a bad thing if Bonaparte was
engaged with the likes of Moldavi—it might keep him
from the invasion of England that Westminster seemed
to think was imminent.

Despite the obvious political fascination, Chas reminded himself he had more pressing matters to attend to. As he stood there, trying not to let his knees buckle, he realized he still wore his own breeches. They were sweat and bloodstained, but they were *his*, and that meant the inside pockets still held the little smoke packets he had.

If he could get close enough to the fireplace and toss one of them in, an explosive puff of smoke would—God willing—roll into the chamber and give him the element of surprise…and the chance to escape. Hopefully after he sent at least one of those bastards to hell on his way out.

Now that he knew Moldavi had protection, it made for a more difficult process. But there were other ways to get to the heart—through the throat, or shoulder, for example—although that would be much more difficult than pinning someone through the chest.

But he was still alive, and he had options, and Chas focused on those thoughts, even going so far as to slyly move his arm along the side of his breeches to confirm that the slender smoke explosion packet was still there.

It was.

Yet, he was still wavering on his feet. His body protested with every movement, and the burns and piercings were tender and inflamed with pain. He wasn't certain how long he'd been here—hours, days, weeks?—but certainly he hadn't eaten for a very long time. The gnawing in his belly wasn't merely due to the presence of the Dracule.

The chamber door opened and in walked Narcise. She, too, was flanked by a pair of guards. She was also, again, wearing men's clothing—tight breeches and a close-fitting tuniclike shirt. Her hair shone like blue-black coal from where it was pulled back tightly into a knot. Her feet were bare.

She didn't acknowledge him at all, and instead faced her brother and his companions. "What do you want?" she demanded.

"Entertainment, of course, my dear sister," Moldavi said. "We have an esteemed guest tonight—" he nodded to Bonaparte "—and I have promised him something very thrilling. I hope you will do your best to make it so." Then he gestured to Chas.

Narcise turned as if noticing him for the first time. "Him? You want me to fight him? What sort of entertainment would that be? The man can barely stand," she scoffed.

Chas lifted his chin in annoyance. He wasn't exactly ready to collapse, and he certainly didn't feel as if his knees were going to give way. In fact, he was feeling stronger—and more furious—by the moment. More determined to get out of here alive, but taking one or two of the *vampirs* to hell first.

I'll save you. Help me, please.

If there was a woman in the world who didn't need his help, it was Narcise Moldavi.

And if she thought turning him over to her brother for torture was a way to save him, she was even more disturbed than he'd thought. As far as he was concerned, all deals were null and void.

"You're correct, my dear sister...which is why I thought we might want to even things up a bit." He lifted his hand from a small box on the table, withdrawing a long cord. Chas saw that he was holding a leather thong with two feathers dangling from it.

She blanched, and even Chas could sense the tremor shuttling through her. Something changed in the chamber, some sort of ebbing of energy or life...and he realized that Moldavi must be holding Narcise's Asthenia.

Feathers.

"You'll fight to the death. There will be no stopping until one of you is dead," commanded their host, tossing the chain to the floor in front of the table.

Narcise stiffened and Chas felt her shock.

"Yes, you've heard me correctly. He's a *vampir* hunter, is he not? A killer? And that is what he came here for. I'd hate to disappoint him, and have him return to Dimitri only to complain about my lack of hospitality. Wood-more," Moldavi said, looking at him, "if you succeed in killing this lovely sister of mine, I will generously allow you to go free…back to your own sisters."

The words dangled there enticingly and Chas glanced at Narcise. Her face had gone blank and her eyes empty, and for the first time, he realized what Corvindale had meant by describing her as having dead eyes. One of her guards lifted the feather necklace and slid it over her head.

She shuddered visibly this time, and he could see her breathing change.

"Or you can slay him," Moldavi told her. "Which is what I fully expect you to do. After all, you have had so many years of instruction. You should be able to best a wounded mortal."

He settled back in his seat, a complacent smile hovering over his lips. "Arm them," he said, nodding to one of the guards.

As they faced each other moments later, each brandishing a long, gleaming blade, Chas gathered his strength and steadied himself. The sword, which would normally be comfortable in his hands, felt heavier than usual. Awkward and wearing. He looked at Narcise.

She was moving slowly, as if she had difficulty breathing, and he knew it was because of the feather necklace.

That would make things all the more simple for him. Not that he truly believed Moldavi would set him free if he killed Narcise, but he intended to win and then, hopefully, set the smoke packet afire.

"Begin!" commanded their host with a clap of his hands.

She staggered, and he could see real pain in her face. He had a momentary pang of sympathy for her…for, despite the fact that he was hardly as powerful and agile as he normally was, he was certainly mobile. She hardly seemed able to move.

She lunged toward him suddenly, her aim off and the sword jamming into the ground next to him. Their bodies clashed and he automatically reached out to steady her. As they bumped together, almost like two lovers embracing, she whispered, "Help me. Escape."

He stumbled back and whipped his blade around, wondering if he'd heard her correctly…wondering if it were another of her tricks. Her face tightened, her teeth bared in great effort as she lifted her sword and raised it over her head in a stroke that left her body wide-open for his blade.

Chas knew it was his chance, and he realized, as their eyes met when he swung his weapon around, that she knew it. At the last minute, he lowered his blow—which would have easily cleaved hand from wrist, head from neck, and hand from wrist again—and turned the blade to its flat side.

It struck the side of her torso, sending her staggering in the direction of the fire…which was precisely his intent. He came after her, and said, "Just as you saved me?" as he slammed the blade against her rising one.

"Was the only…way…" she muttered, and he saw a wave of effort crease her face.

Chas's knee buckled and he stumbled into the wall, his sword scraping along the floor as he used it to regain his balance. Hell, it was like fighting when he was in his cups. He wondered if the spectators found the sight amusing or entertaining.

They were near the fire now, and he had a decision to make. Trust her, or slay her, which would be easily done. Either way, he had one chance to use the smoke cloud. She seemed to have regained a bit of ferocity, somehow, and was coming at him again. "Please," she said over the clash of their swords.

Her eyes met his in that instant between the silver blades, and he saw pleading there. And desperation. Chas spun away, thinking suddenly of Sonia, and the argument they'd had when he visited her.

Who made you God? she'd said. *Who gave you the right to judge who lives and dies? I should think you of all people would understand why they did it.*

The pang of conscience, combined with the fear that he'd never see her again, and never be able to set things right—for he'd had his own harsh words: *We all have our God-given abilities, and some of us actually use them, Sonia*—unlocked something deep inside him.

Narcise was more familiar with the makeup of the house. Having her with him might slow him a bit, but at least he wouldn't get lost.

He could always slay her later if he had to.

"Be ready," he said, parrying sharply at her, lunging at her. The more he fought and moved, the easier it seemed to get. His body was returning...even as hers slowed. Although their conversation was soft, lost in the noise of battle and their distance from the spectators, he took care to keep his face away from Moldavi when he spoke.

She met his eyes, hers wide and hopeful, if glazed,

and he reached into the pocket of his breeches with his free hand. "Thank you."

He had the packet, he was lining them up alongside the roaring flames. "Way out?" he asked, slamming his blade against hers to muffle their conversation.

"There," she gasped, her eyes going to the corner as she raised her blade weakly.

She was so slow and clumsy that he sliced along her arm without meaning to, and heard a shout from the dais: "First blood!"

Chas saw a small door in the corner and noted that it was far from the dais. Perfect. He might have a chance after all…as long as Jezebel wasn't leading him into a den of lions or something worse. Like a locked door.

"Locked?" he asked, circling around and creating a vicious thrust that clashed with her sword.

"Don't…think…" she gasped. "No."

He flipped the packet into the fireplace as he eased her toward the corner, waiting for the telltale explosion. Hoping to hell Miro's chemistry worked as well now as it had during their trials.

He was just about to give up when there was a soft muffled *boom!* and something shot from the fireplace.

Sparks and coals blasted into the room, and in the moment of surprise, he grabbed Narcise, half lifting her against his hip, and ran unsteadily toward the door, sword still in hand.

People were shouting and Moldavi was giving orders, but Chas ignored everything but the door. They had to get around the table and off the dais, and across the room… and he had the element of surprise. The puff of smoke rolled into the chamber, more slowly than he would have liked, but it was effective enough. His legs wobbled, his arms trembled and Narcise was little help in an ambulatory fashion. They fell into the door, the momentum of his running clumsy and imprecise.

She shifted, gave a groan of exertion…then all at once, she was moving. The door opened and they burst out of the room.

Narcise turned, suddenly strong and quick. "Help me," she said, leaning against the door as something slammed against it from the other side. Chas found the wooden bar and fit it across, barring the door, and then she said, "This way," and started down a dim corridor.

She must have lost the feathers along their way through the chamber, or maybe even yanked them off her neck, because now she was faster and more agile than he.

Chas wasn't about to complain; he still had his sword and a partner who seemed able.

They were going to make it.

She ran and he followed, his legs protesting, the aches in his torso screaming, but this was for life—the pain could go to the Devil. He was going to make it.

They came to the end of the corridor—a large, locked door—and just as they approached, a *vampir* guard turned to see them.

Chas didn't hesitate; it was second nature for him to duck under the attacking man, spin—albeit wobbly—and come back around from behind with the blade of his sword at neck level.

The man's head rolled to the floor in a gush and splash of blood, but Chas didn't hesitate. He went for the door, looking for the lock, and realized that Narcise wasn't with him.

Turning, he saw her, pale-faced, half-collapsed against the wall. The blood. It had to be the blood. He grabbed her arm and towed her toward him, but her eyes were rolling back into her head and she was having trouble breathing.

She collapsed into his arms and he realized it wasn't the blood—*vampires* craved it, but it didn't make them faint.

"Where's the key?" he demanded, hearing shouts in the near distance. Damn the vampire sense of smell… they could track them as well as a dog could.

She murmured something he couldn't understand, and saw that she was severely incapacitated. Then he realized, through the intensity of the moment… "Feathers."

Narcise nodded, barely, and he realized why she'd never escaped on her own. Moldavi had the entrances and exits lined with feathers, or somehow used them to block it for her. He glanced around but didn't see any sign of them…but for all he knew, they could be embedded in the door frame. She shuddered and tried to grasp him, but her fingers were weakening.

Now he didn't know if it would kill her to go over the threshold—assuming the feathers were there, and in great numbers, obviously—or whether once past, they would no longer affect her, even if she was so greatly weakened. But either way, he had to decide to take the chance, or leave her behind.

"Where's the key?" he demanded again, then realized the guard was there for a reason.

Gingerly, still holding Narcise up with one hand, trying not to step in the pool of blood—he didn't need that scent clinging to him as well—he fumbled around the vampire's body.

Just as the voices turned down the hallway, and he could feel the pounding of feet on the floor, he found the key hanging on a ring at the man's waist.

Chas yanked it, praying it would come free, and the

man's body jolted in protest. He used his sword to slice down blindly and cut the bloody thing from his waist, taking a chunk of clothing and skin with it.

Key in hand, a weak and useless Narcise over his sword arm, he lunged for the door. They were coming, and he nearly dropped the key from his weak and clumsy fingers…but he fit it in as their pursuers appeared in the hall behind them.

Fifteen feet away and the door opened. Chas lunged through and dumped Narcise on the floor as he spun to close it behind him, struggling with the lock again in the light of a dim sconce.

By the time he had it in place the force of the others on the opposite side had the door surging in its hinges. "We've got to get out of here," he said, turning to gather up Narcise again.

But, praise God, she was on her feet—if pale—visaged and wide-eyed…and she was bloody damn smiling. He yanked the torch from the wall, even though she wouldn't need light in the dark, and they started running together.

"We made it," she gasped. "We made it. We're in the catacombs."

Chas looked around and realized they were in a stone-hewn tunnel lined with…skulls. Giordan Cale had described it to him, and had even drawn a rough map of the tunnels that Chas had committed to memory.

She was right. They'd made it.

And despite the fact that he hadn't accomplished the task for which he'd come, he felt more than a little satisfied.

13

Narcise drew in the fresh, cool air and felt the tears gather in her eyes. *Free. I'm free.*

It was well into the night, and Paris lay beyond her, around her…waiting for her. Paris, and the world…all of it, waiting for her.

Yes, she'd been out of the apartments many times in the years of living here…but this was different.

This time, she didn't have to go back. This time she wasn't accompanied by the insidious darkness of her brother, whose presence clung so heavily even when he was absent.

This time she was *walking*, on her own two feet, instead of being transported in a dark vehicle with guards.

"Are you coming with me?" said Woodmore in an impatient voice. "Or are you going to stand here and wait for them to catch up to us?"

"With you," she managed to say, terrified at the thought, as he grabbed her arm and began to walk off briskly.

He had her clutched to his side, a bare-chested, battered man towing along a slender effeminate partner. At least, that was what she thought they might look like. And, apparently, even such an appearance wasn't remarkable enough to glean notice from anyone else.

"Where are we going?" she asked, still drinking in the air, the activity of people walking and talking and laughing. There were women smiling slyly, with red lips and very low bodices…there were lanky youths watching from the shadows…there were couples, strolling arm in arm as if they had nowhere to be…and no one to escape from.

A group of the emperor's soldiers wandered past, leaving Narcise to wonder if they knew their master was several feet below them, eating and drinking with a *vampir*.

"I don't bloody damn know, but wherever it is, we don't have time to dawdle," Woodmore replied. "Nothing went as I planned."

There were smells, too…lovely smells of spring flowers on the breeze, and fragrances from some of the well-dressed (and not so well-dressed) women strolling by. She scented sausages and cheese and wine and ale, cakes and bread and crepes all offered for the late-night patrons. A rolling lust for a cake, iced with cream, surprised her. She hadn't had a sweet—or at least, hadn't enjoyed one like that—since she was a girl in Romania. And beyond the food, there was the underlying stench of sewer and refuse, the damp and algae of the Seine, coal and wood smoke, and blood.

The bloodscent was coming most strongly from the man next to her, mingling with sweat and burned flesh, and it teased her…for it had been some while since she'd fed.

A blonde woman wearing a long, simple dress was standing near one of the columns along the Tuilieries. She seemed oblivious to the passersby who jostled through the narrow walkway beneath the covered promenade, bumping into or next to her.

She was watching them closely, but her calm gaze wasn't unsettling in its intensity. Instead, Narcise felt a wave of peace slip over her as their eyes met. The woman smiled as Woodmore fairly dragged her past and the Mark on Narcise's back twinged painfully. It surprised her, for Luce hardly ever expressed his annoyance with her. Perhaps because she never had much chance to make a choice that would annoy him.

The first step. Those words rang in her head and Narcise smiled to herself as she happened to meet the blonde woman's eyes. She nodded at her, although of course there was no possible way the woman could know why she was nodding. But, yes, this was only the beginning.

It occurred to her, then, as Woodmore snapped his hand at a hackney cab—then decided not to climb aboard when a well-dressed gentleman pushed his way ahead of them—that she didn't have anywhere to go herself. She had no money. She knew no one—an uncomfortable memory pinched her belly and she thrust away the thought of someone she did know—and didn't know whom to trust.

But then a name did appear in her mind. Dimitri, the earl, in London. Cezar hated the man ever since he ended a business association with him when Dimitri learned that Cezar was a child-bleeder. And…there'd been that night in Vienna, when Cezar had offered Narcise to Dimitri.

Although she'd been dull with pain from a feather bracelet, Narcise still remembered that night…the cold, dark man who looked at her with a modicum of sympathy, but not even a flicker of lust.

She would go to him. Any enemy of Cezar was a friend of hers.

But in her fantasies, when she'd planned to make her escape, it was much less chaotic. Narcise had imagined a scenario in which she'd slipped from the house with a bag on her shoulder when the place was quiet and everyone was sleeping or otherwise distracted. Or that she'd be standing over Cezar's headless body saying a fond farewell as his blood coursed onto the floor.

Just as Woodmore said: Not as planned.

But, nevertheless, it had worked.

"Here," he said suddenly, towing her into a shadowy alcove.

The next thing she knew, they were at the backside door of a small public house that smelled of old ale and stewing meat, and Woodmore was negotiating in rapid French with its proprietor. He flashed that white smile, made a lewd gesture and then produced a small pouch that clinked—which she swore he hadn't had moments earlier.

The pouch's contents seemed to be the deciding factor for the proprietor, and the door opened wider. She felt the man's amused grin on her as Woodmore led her inside and then directly up a set of dark, dingy stairs where the smell of coitus and ale clung to the walls. She wasn't certain whether the proprietor recognized that she was a woman and not a man, but in either case, it didn't matter.

After all, this was Paris.

And the recently liberated Narcise had no qualms about following the *vampir* hunter into a small bedchamber lit only by the glow of a lamp.

"Shut the door," Woodmore ordered, and when she turned back, she saw that he'd sat on the bed.

For the first time, she noticed how much difficulty

he seemed to have breathing. His torso and arms were a mass of cuts, bruises and large burns. "You're hurt, what—"

"You just noticed this?" His voice was harsh. He seemed to struggle for a moment, then added in marginally softer tones, "I need to get cleaned up. They're going to bring a bath."

Even his sharp words didn't offend Narcise. She was *free*. Nothing would upset or annoy her now. Yet, she felt that she owed him some explanation. "It was the only way to get him to allow us to fight."

"And how precisely would fighting have helped us if one of us was dead? Or did you simply plan to kill me— but then how would that benefit you?" His voice was rough and unsteady.

"I didn't expect him to make us fight till the death. I thought I would allow you to win, and then you would take me to…well, it doesn't matter now, does it? We are here, and I'm free. Thank you. Do you need food? And where did you get the money? Surely you didn't have it in your breeches all this time."

"I venture to guess that such a bulge would have been noticeable," he said, flashing a surprise smile. "At least, in certain places. I lifted the coins from the sot who stole our hack. He'll never miss them, and I can't draw on my resources until tomorrow."

She'd walked over to turn the light up and by then, a knock sounded on the door. She opened it to reveal a maidservant with a jug of ale and a platter of cheese and bread. The girl brought it in, put it on a table, then turned to the cold fireplace.

"I don't believe they have your particular vintage," Woodmore said, gesturing to the food.

Narcise nodded, and realized again that it had been

more than a few days since she'd fed, and with the hint of his bloodscent—just barely oozing—still lingering, her gums began to contract and her breathing roughened. Her glance went briefly toward the maidservant and she considered the possibility of enthralling the girl so she could feed, but when she felt Woodmore's eyes on her, she discarded that idea.

If he was like any other man, he'd enjoy the erotic sight of two women in such an intimate arrangement, and then she'd have another problem on her hands if he wanted to participate. The last thing she wanted or needed was another man trying to control her—or to have her bloodlust take over. Woodmore might be a mortal, but he was a legendary one in her world. He wouldn't be easily denied.

She turned her attention away from him and back to the fact that she would have to find a way to feed. She'd never actually had to arrange it for herself; Cezar had always, as part of her captivity, provided a servant—a male as often as a female—or other mortal for feeding.

But this was a problem she welcomed.

A fire now blazing in the grate, the maid stood and gave a short bow, then left the chamber.

Woodmore had taken a few swigs of ale, and was selecting a piece of cheese when he looked up at Narcise. He didn't speak, although he seemed to be searching for something to say…and then he returned his attention to the tray. She realized she was trying not to breathe, for the chamber—especially the bed—reeked of coitus and perspiration, and over it all was Chas Woodmore's scent. His blood.

Narcise suddenly felt awkward and out of place. And, all at once, exhausted. Her knees wobbled and as her head spun, she reached blindly for the chair and eased herself into it.

But she was free. A smile erupted, happiness welled inside her so much that her Mark twinged again…and suddenly, tears flooded her eyes. The tears rolled down her cheeks, catching her by surprise—she hadn't even realized she still knew how to cry—but all at once, she was sobbing uncontrollably.

A handkerchief was thrust into her face, and she took it blindly, gratefully—and at the same time, ashamedly. She'd been through so much…why, now when she was happy, did she have to show such weakness?

The cloth smelled like Woodmore, of course, but dense and thick—rough with blood and sweat and pain and the pleasant smell of his skin and hair, too. She dried her eyes and lifted her face to find him watching her with a detached expression. "Thank you."

"I have three sisters," he replied with a shrug. "Sobbing females don't unsettle me in the least. And I suspect you have more of a reason to cry than Angelica did when her favorite yellow gown was stained with ink."

Narcise gave him a wavery smile and wiped her nose again. "I cannot remember the last time I cried," she told him. *Not even ten years ago.*

Another knock came at the door, and Woodmore answered it this time. She noticed the way his feet scuffled a bit when he went to open it, as if he could hardly lift them. He held on to the door while a half-full tub was brought in, followed by five huge pails of steaming water, and she suspected that he was doing so in order to keep his own knees from collapsing. There was a drawn tightness in his face and around his eyes.

But now that she'd become fully aware of his scent, Narcise found herself noticing his bare torso, half illuminated by the glow of the lamp. He was tall and the skin of his chest and ridged belly was as dark as that of his hands and face. He had dark hair trailing down his stomach, into the sagging waistline of his breeches, and up to a full expanse of it over his chest. His arms were rounded with muscle, scarred and marked, but powerful nevertheless.

Her eyes started to heat when she thought about the texture of his skin and the essence of his lifeblood, and she had to look away. It was a reaction she couldn't completely control, but she could hide it, for it didn't mean anything.

After the water came the maidservant who'd brought the food, and this time she was carrying a pile of cloth and a small pot of unguent. These she left near the bath, and Narcise realized it was for Woodmore's injuries.

When the door was closed once more, and they were alone, Woodmore turned to her. He seemed even more unsteady, and she thought he actually swayed on his feet. "I don't expect you have delicate sensibilities, but if you do, you'll either have to leave or close your eyes."

"I don't have anywhere else to go," she said quietly.

He gave her an inscrutable look and turned away. And then all of a sudden, he made a sort of half turn, as if to grab for the chair, and he began to sink.

She heard him groan a low curse just before he hit the floor with a dull thud.

Narcise rushed over to kneel next to him on the ground. "Woodmore?" she said, and went to shake him by the shoulders…but stopped when she realized that would mean closing her fingers over two ugly burns.

She saw the red oozing from his arms and the sides of his torso, recognizing Cezar's handiwork with the metal spikes, and wondered how he'd managed to do what he'd done—fight her, carry her, run and slay and even pick a pocket—with these sorts of injuries.

At the same time, she felt a wave of remorse that she hadn't noticed how badly he was hurt during their fencing match. Of course, she had been a bit distracted… but she should have at least gauged his weakness as her rival if nothing else.

"Woodmore!" she said more urgently, still hesitant to touch him. But when he still didn't move, she had to, and was shocked to find his skin flaming hot. He moaned, rolling his head to the side as her fingers brushed over his shoulders.

He couldn't remain on the floor. Narcise picked him up awkwardly—he was long and loose-limbed, and heavy even for her—and got him to the bed. And then she began examining him in detail.

She'd had enough injuries of her own, inflicted by Cezar or any number of his friends, to recognize all of the different manifestations of burns, piercings, cuts and bruises. She'd also had some experience in caring for them, although she wasn't certain whether washing and cleaning injuries on mortals would even help, since they could die from injury and she, of course, wouldn't.

But she did the best she could, using the warm water and the dubiously clean cloths that had been brought in with the unguent to wash away blood, sweat and grime. Narcise even immodestly stripped away his breeches, leaving him fully naked, so that she could examine him for other wounds. A particularly nasty one, which had been hidden by the trousers near his right hip, had her sucking in her breath in alarm.

Even in the faulty light, she could see that whatever had gone through his skin, and out the other side, had taken the fabric of his breeches with it like a needle and thread. The injury was rough and dark, and little frayed threads and pieces of cloth decorated the opening.

And it smelled. They all smelled of course, but this one had a wrong scent to it. An ugly, thick, roiling sort of stench that was so unpleasant it didn't arouse her blood-lust, even as undernourished as she was, and succeeded in masking some of the other enticing scents as well. She cleaned it carefully, probing to get the remnants of thread and wool from inside, and knew she was doing a good job when he flinched and moaned in his fever. But the injury would bear watching, for it might not heal at all.

The rest of them, ugly as they were, evil and dark, were painful but should heal. This one on his hip…perhaps not.

By the time she finished, the sun was rising and casting yellow beams through the window. Dangerous to Narcise, but at the same time, she hadn't seen the sun for more than a decade.

So she stood at the window, carefully to the side, and watched as the golden glow painted the rooftops and buildings clustered around this dingy little public house—so crude and dirty and simple compared to her previous residence, but so welcome.

She couldn't see much aside of the walls across the street and down the alley, for the buildings were close, but just the glint of yellow made her chest expand with pleasure.

No, she couldn't walk out into it, she couldn't bathe herself in its rays nor pick flowers on the mountainside as she'd done with Rivrik…but at least now she could *see* it. And she could smell the warmth as the beams baked the edge of the cotton bedding or heated the wood of the window shutters.

And perhaps…if she were brave…she could walk out into it with a cloak over her head and shoulders, thus allowing the rays to seep through and warm her through the shield.

She watched from the window for a long while, simply observing the way the shadows changed, shortening and then disappearing, and then beginning to fall toward the east…how the light changed the scene of busy Paris, the carriages and barouches, the merchant carts and the shops' awnings from dull shades of gray to every color imaginable.

She was weak and hungry still, but she couldn't leave in search of someone on whom to feed. And she couldn't go down to the public room of the house and lure someone up here…could she?

So Narcise ignored the insistent waves of weakness and light-headed moments and watched from the window, wishing for her paints or at least a pencil.

When Woodmore groaned, drawing her attention from the scenery, she went to his side. He opened his eyes, but they were dull and feverish, and his skin was still hot despite the fact that the fire had long subsided into glowing coals.

The water from the basin was cool, and she used it to dab at his forehead, uncertain what else could be done for him. His glassy gaze didn't seem to be able to focus, and his lids fluttered as he moaned and muttered things she couldn't understand.

Narcise felt a stirring of panic when she checked the worst of the wounds again and saw that it was puffy and foul-smelling still. The blood crusting and oozing, its edges stank and she knew something had to be done, or the infamous *vampir* hunter would die—and in such an inglorious fashion.

At first, she simply didn't know what to do. She couldn't leave during the day to go in search of a physician, nor did she have any funds to pay for one. The pouch he'd lifted from the nabob who'd taken their hack was empty.

And aside of that, she was feeling weary and nauseated herself, from lack of feeding and sleep.

Very deep inside her, Narcise was also terrified that if she left this sanctuary, Cezar or his men would find her and take her back to the hell she'd been living.

She looked at Woodmore, who, despite his fever and the shuddering breaths he was taking, still appeared capable and intimidating—even with his eyes closed. He was so dark and exotic looking next to the undyed linen sheets, his overlong, thick hair tumbling over his forehead and clinging to his neck from the heat of his skin. But his face was tight and flushed and his pulse thumped erratically, its sound seeming to fill her ears.

But…she had to do something.

She was a Dracule, she had the ability to enthrall even if she couldn't go out in the daylight. How foolish of her to waste time when she did have the means to do what had to be done!

It had been so long since she'd been on her own, making her own decisions. Much more than a century. Still, to have stayed hidden and helpless like a trembling rabbit was not admirable in the least.

Unwilling to leave Woodmore alone for too long, she rang for one of the servants. A young woman came and Narcise gave her instructions in her imperfect French: she needed a physician immediately for her companion.

Then, assuring herself that Woodmore would sleep—if not restlessly—for a bit longer, she left the chamber quickly. Down the back stairwell she went, and then into the public room where it was crowded with people, noise and smells. Smoke and sweat were strong enough here to gag her, along with the layer of stale ale and old wine and a myriad of other aromas.

Nervously she looked about and settled her attention on an old, fat man who was waddling unsteadily toward the door. He was well-dressed and clumsy with drink.

Narcise, who was thankful to still be dressed as a boy, kept her face averted and hoped not to draw attention as she made her way to meet her unsuspecting mark. At the door, which fortunately led into a small alcove to keep the snow and rain from pouring into the pub itself, she met up with the fat man. He was irritable, which made her feel even more justified in drawing him into a bit of her thrall whilst she relieved him of the wallet he held under his coat.

It was done more quickly and easily than she'd even imagined, and Narcise, flush with funds and a different sort of confidence that had nothing to do with swordsmanship or even her beauty, slipped back up to the chamber she shared with Woodmore. She would feed later, after she'd seen to Chas, and when she could find a more private place.

But that incident seemed to be the most optimistic part of the day. When the physician arrived, he spoke French too rapidly for her to completely understand... yet the idea that Woodmore was in dangerous condition became very clear.

Narcise watched as the *docteur* used a sharp knife to cut into the swollen and infected wound, then scooped away the foul-smelling green pus that erupted from it. He cleaned it and wrapped it and gave her a list of instructions that was only partly clear...and then he left, taking a good portion of the fat man's money with him.

Not long after he left, a knock sounded at the door, drawing Narcise's attention abruptly from her patient.

She quickly covered Woodmore with a sheet and then bade the servant to enter.

It was a young man who'd come to collect the tub and pails. He looked at Narcise, who'd just taken her hair down and whose shirt still clung to her body curves, and she saw a flare of interest in his eyes before he turned to gather up the items.

Her heart began to thump harder and her gums constricted. *No, not here...but why not? It's more private than belowstairs.*

She swallowed hard and tried to ignore her increasing light-headedness and the gnawing in her stomach.

"Could you build up the fire again?" she asked, hearing the duskiness in her own voice. "It's chilly in here."

"Certainly, madame," he replied, and set the pails on the ground. His gaze lingered as he walked past her, and she felt a little nudge in her center.

He's willing.

He doesn't know what it is you want.

She bit her lip, trying to keep from scenting the young man, who was lanky and blond and had an alluring, masculine scent laced with innocence. He couldn't be much older than twenty.

No...

But yes. A streak of pain flamed over her shoulder and down the side of her back and Narcise gasped. The sudden filling and pulsing of her Mark was like a branding iron of Lucifer's temper.

"Madame?" the youth asked, turning from the fireplace to look at her in concern.

"What is your name?" she asked, breathless with pain...and anticipation.

"Philippe," he said, and she felt her eyes warm into a strong warm glow.

"Philippe," she replied, stepping closer to him. "There is something else you could assist me with."

His breathing changed, deepening and slowing, as her eyes burned into him. *Oh, yes.* Narcise's fangs erupted swiftly and she could scarcely breathe.

"Will you?" she asked, holding out her hand. Her heart beat savagely in her breast, and she could smell his desire, his interest wafting through the air.

He stepped toward her, his eyes heavy-lidded and his mouth full and sensual. "What is it?" he asked.

She could wait no longer; hunger and need drove her and she fairly flung herself at him. His arms went around her, his fingers pulling at her shirt, but she had hold of his shoulders and slammed her fangs into his flesh.

His gasped *mon Dieu* rang in her ears as the flood of ambrosia poured into her mouth. Narcise clung to his shoulders as she forced him back against the wall, drinking and leeching from his warm, youthful flesh. His hands moved over her, pulling at her clothes, dragging the shirt up over her back so he could touch her skin.

She felt the rise and swell of his cock against her, and the soft moans from the back of his throat as she swallowed and sucked deep drafts of lifeblood. Pleasure and arousal, along with strength, rushed through her. Her breasts tightened, becoming sensitive behind their loosened bindings. Damp and heat pounded through her as she licked and drank, the young coppery blood filling her mouth. His chest rose and fell against her breasts, and his hands moved around to cover them, sliding down over tight nipples to the swelling center between her legs, frantic and desperate for his own release.

Narcise might have gone on for too long if there hadn't been a dull noise from behind her. The thump brought her back to the moment, to where she was, what she was doing…and that she and her victim had sagged into a heap on the floor, his hands tearing at her breeches.

She pulled her fangs away, breathing as if she'd been running, and felt her partner—for he wasn't precisely a victim—shuddering against her. He muttered something low and desperate in her ear, grinding the bulge in his trousers against her hip as his mouth found hers. He was sloppy and warm, and the taste of his own blood must have excited him, for he pulled her closer, urgent and needy.

Narcise twisted her face away and returned to his shoulder to lick at the bitemarks she'd left there. It made the wounds heal quickly and cleanly, and helped the blood to stop flowing.

As she pulled back, a glance behind her indicated Chas Woodmore, completely naked and wavering on his feet, clutching the bed as if he were about to pitch over any moment. The feverish light was in his eyes, but determination tightened his face, and she saw that he held a piece of splintered wood in his hand.

Their eyes met across the room, and she recognized horror and revulsion burning there…and yet an underlying layer of lust that was echoed in the lift of his own cock.

Her insides jolting in surprise and something else she didn't understand, Narcise turned away and pulled herself and her victim to his feet. He sagged against her and she propped him against the wall with one hand, much stronger now that she'd been nourished, and yanked his sagging breeches back up into place. His cock still filled them out, but she had no interest in this young, lanky man. The image of another male body—mature, muscled and powerful—had lodged in her mind.

Yet, the blind lust had eased and she was back in-

side her own control—if not fully aware of Chas Woodmore in a completely different way. Another dull thump
had her attention swiveling back to the *vampir* hunter,
even as she restrained Philippe's enthusiastic and insistent hands. Woodmore had managed a step or two, then
collapsed once again.

Narcise turned her thrall back onto Philippe with new
intent, and coaxed him into her world. This time, she
lulled him into a dreamlike state that would eliminate
from his memory everything that had happened since
she turned her thrall on him.

When she finally released him, he was back in front
of the fireplace and she was sitting in the chair just as
she had been. Woodmore, whose gaze burned in its own
mortal fashion as he dragged himself back to his feet,
had sunk weakly back onto the bed in a feverish stupor.

"*Merci*," she told Philippe as he gathered up the pails
and tub. The marks on his neck were hidden by his shirt,
and hadn't left even a drop of blood on the pale linen.
"Would you be so kind as to bring a new bath?"

"But of course, madame," he said, his eyes still a bit
feverish…as if he couldn't quite remember what had happened, but sensed that something had.

She smiled at him and gave a little flare of glow in her
eyes, then sent him on his way.

Then she turned her attention to Woodmore. His
breathing was off rhythm, rough and ragged, and if anything his skin had become hotter. His cock had softened
back into a relaxed state, and his eyes remained half open
but unfocused.

Narcise's trill of panic returned and she looked again
at the wound on his hip. It was likely causing the fever.
The swelling around it, and the stench… The physician

had helped, but the smell told her that he'd not been able to stop the infection.

And then a thought struck her. It was so unexpected, and yet so logical she could hardly believe it hadn't occurred to her before.

If there was bad blood there, gathering and clotting around the wound…she could take it away. She could draw the infection from him, and then use her lips and tongue to cleanse and heal in their own effective way.

It could work.

And, she thought, swallowing hard as she looked down at his tight, battered body…it would give her an excuse to taste him.

Something she hadn't realized how much she wanted.

14

Chas opened his eyes to find bright sunlight blazing through a half-shuttered window.

He lay there for a moment, looking up at the wood-beamed ceiling festooned with random cobwebs, then off to the side and around an unfamiliar chamber. He couldn't remember where he was or how he'd come to be here.

Yet, shifting in the bed on which he lay, Chas felt hardly a niggle of concern. There'd been many a night that had taken him places he hadn't expected to go; many times he'd awakened after too much drink or women or both…quite often after routing a group of *vampirs*.

But as he turned, he saw her, lying on her side on the bed next to him. And with that sight came the rush of memories—some strident and clear, others murky and hot and red.

But first, before he tried to make sense of what was real and what had been dreams…he just looked. Such beauty, such exquisite beauty was breathtaking. Even in repose, she appeared unimaginably lovely.

Her cheek, perfectly ivory, without a flaw, rested on

hands folded as if in prayer—an irony in and of itself. The position caused her already full, sensual lips to plump out even more enticingly, and an endearing pudge to her face. Her eyes were closed of course, but that was one thing he remembered clearly: the intense blue-violet color in them, ringed with black, flecked with dark colors.

Long, shiny hair, the color of coal, clung to her face and throat, tumbling into a pool on the bed between them. He reached over and touched it to see if it was as silky as it appeared.

It was.

He could see the shadow of her breasts where they showed through a low neckline of the chemise she was wearing, the curve of them as they bunched up against the mattress. A ripple of attraction seized his belly, but he ignored it.

This was Narcise Moldavi.

He was in bed with a *vampir*—and one he'd meant to kill, at least at some point.

Chas sat up gingerly, noting that Narcise slept on the side of the bed farthest from where the sun would stream through the window, and felt the remnants of aches and pains throughout his body. His naked body.

With that realization of pain, more details came filtering back…Cezar Moldavi and his metal spikes and the burning poker…the fencing match between him and Narcise…the smoke packets that had worked almost as well as they had during their trials…perhaps they'd gotten a bit damp during the trip across the Channel.

Things were murky after that. He remembered everything being slow and dark and red, of pain and agony with every movement, the world tilting and spinning. There were times of running, stumbling along as if forever and ever…up some stairs…

Here. Into this chamber.

There things turned darker and hotter, and memory confused with dreams and nightmares. He closed his eyes and saw an image of Narcise, rising naked and glistening from a bath...*there*, in the corner...of her with eyes red-gold and hot, her fangs long and white and lethal... *blood*...there was blood and pain, and he had an image of her on top of someone, tearing into him...

Narcise stirred next to him and then she opened her eyes.

When she saw that he was awake, she sat up abruptly. "You're alive." Her eyes were wide with shock and happiness, making her even more beautiful with her dark hair swirling about her shoulders against a thin white shift.

Chas felt another loosening inside his belly, deep and fluttery. She was right there, she was lovely and sensual and they were alone. He wasn't so weak that he couldn't reach over, pull her to him—

He closed his mind to the temptation. She was a *vampir*. She'd coerce, coax, lull...seduce him...drag him into the Devil's dark world.

"I don't remember much," he said.

"You nearly died," she said. "From an infection. The doctor came, more than once, but he wasn't certain if you'd live."

Chas sank down onto his back, remembering even more. The screaming pain on his side, the cool, quick hands administering to his wounds, the haze of heat and confusion that followed, Narcise... He stopped his thoughts, afraid of where they were about to lead. It was impossible not to be attracted to her.

He tightened his lips. That was Lucifer's game, wasn't it? She was irresistible for a reason.

"What day is it? How long have I—we—been here?" he asked instead.

"Nearly a week," she told him.

"A week?" Shock and concern almost had him sitting up again. "It's been a week since we left your brother?"

Narcise nodded.

Good Christ, Corvindale was going to be furious. Surely by now Maia had followed instructions—reluctantly of course—and contacted him about Chas's disappearance.

He turned his gaze back to hers. "You stayed here with me?" he asked.

"Of course. I wasn't going to let you die." She frowned irritably. "I'm not my brother."

An image of Narcise, bending over him, her slender hands on his skin, flashed into his mind with sudden clarity. Bending over him, near his—

Despite his lingering weakness and the raw pounding in his head, he sat up abruptly, yanking the coverings away from his right hip, knowing what he would find....

"What have you done to me?" he demanded, staring at the four neat little marks on his flesh. Repugnance and fury rushed over him as his belly tightened and fluttered. He stared at her, not trying to hide his revulsion. "You *dared?*"

Her eyes had widened again, then returned to normal. She tightened her full lips and lifted her chin defiantly. "The infected wound wasn't healing, and the doctor could do nothing more for you. There is something in the saliva of a Dracule that promotes healing, and so I thought to help you by applying it."

Chas heard what she was saying, but it took a moment for her meaning to penetrate the fury. "There are bitemarks," he said, still angry...feeling violated and unsettled, particularly by the sordid image that went along with the knowledge. Narcise, bending to him…her sensual lips closing intimately over his skin, the pain of penetration, but the release from swollen veins…nausea mixed with that shiver of lust, deep in his belly, and Chas swallowed hard.

This is what they do. They enthrall. And lure.

"I hoped that drawing out the poison, whatever was infecting you, removing it from your body, would help, along with my saliva. Whatever it was, it worked to keep you alive."

He looked away, his heart beating too hard, his fingers curling into the blanket. "I'm finding it difficult to be grateful," he managed to say. "But I suppose I must be."

She'd withdrawn from the bed in the face of his blatant anger, and now she looked at him from where she stood on the other side. "At least you're honest," she replied, and turned her back to him.

As he watched, at once struck by the intimacy of sharing this space with a woman he mistrusted, reviled and yet desired, she began to braid the inky waterfall of her hair.

"Did you enthrall me?" he asked, lifting his head, still on edge and furious as he watched her slender shoulders and the delicate edge of her shoulder blades through the thin chemise. She had sleek and elegantly muscled arms, unlike any he'd ever seen on a woman, and he could see the roundness of her buttocks, the curve of her hips. He hated that he wanted her, that his body was changing and responding to her mere presence.

Narcise had stilled at his question, then turned slowly back to face him…so slowly, it was as if she were in agony. "Did I enthrall a helpless man? An unwilling one?" Her deep blue eyes were both fierce with rage and awash with pain. "If you knew what I've lived through, how I've been violated over decades of captivity, you would never have asked such a question."

Chas felt as if he'd been struck, and he let his head fall back onto the pillow. Mortification and shame warred with that lingering revulsion and distrust, and he stared at the ceiling, utterly aware of her, knowing he'd wounded her deeply...asking himself why he cared.

She was a *vampir*. A handmaiden of the Devil. One of a race who preyed on living creatures and took from them, who'd given their souls for immortality, power, money...vanity. The very act of their feeding was an inherent violation of life and liberty. They were conscienceless, depraved, self-centered creatures, with Corvindale being the only real exception he had encountered—the only one who didn't find it agreeable to feed on living humans.

Chas had been gifted with the ability to sense, stalk and slay these creatures—he knew there was a reason he had. That he was meant to do this as surely as a priest was meant to consecrate the hosts.

But.

Narcise had finished her braiding in silence and now she walked over to the single chair on the other side of the chamber. Chas noticed how she avoided the sunlight spilling through the window, but that she looked at it with longing.

Yes. These were creatures who'd given up the light to live in darkness. And sometimes, they regretted it.

"What do you plan to do next?" she asked.

"I need clothing and food," he replied, "and then I must send word back to London. To my sisters."

"London. Is that where Dimitri is? I'd like to find him,

and see if he would…well, I know he and my brother are sworn enemies. And I hope that he might help me."

"Corvindale? He might be willing to be of assistance. I suppose you want me to bring you to him."

Her expression, which had been taut with anger and hurt, lightened. "Is it possible? To get to London, through the blockade?"

He had a mild wave of surprise that she would even be aware of the war between England and France, but then he recalled who her brother's companion was. Surely even Narcise had been privy to some of the political discussions between Bonaparte and Cezar. "Yes, but it will take some preparation."

It could be a fortnight or more, and all the while, Corvindale would be saddled with Maia and Angelica. Chas would never hear the end of it.

Then a terrible thought struck him, turning him ice-cold. Moldavi would want revenge on him for escaping, and for taking Narcise with him. And the first place he'd look to do it would be with Maia and Angelica.

He was up and out of bed in an instant. "Where are my clothes? My breeches? My shoes?" He must send word to Corvindale, at least, that the girls would be in danger. The room tilted but he didn't care.

"They're gone. You only had your breeches, and they were so—"

"I need something, I must get word back to London." He looked around the chamber as if expecting clothing to materialize.

She'd risen from the chair and before he'd even taken a step, she was handing him a neatly folded pile. "You didn't allow me to finish. I was able to obtain clean clothing for you."

Chas took them silently. If he weren't so intent on

getting out of the inn to see to business, he might have been chastened by her tone. But he couldn't worry about that now. Moldavi had had a week. A *week*. Through his alliance with Bonaparte, he could have sent people after Maia and Angelica already, crossing through the blockade.

His knees wobbled a bit as he drew on the breeches, but Chas ignored it. There'd be time for weakness later. The shirt fit well, but the boots were a bit tight—although certainly adequate. As soon as he was dressed, he started for the door…then stopped, with his hand on the knob as he turned back to Narcise.

"I'll be back as soon as I can. I trust…I trust you'll be well alone here?"

She lifted her brows in a wry expression. "I've been alone for the last week, Woodmore. I suspect I'll do just fine in your absence."

Narcise wasn't at all oblivious to Chas Woodmore's revulsion toward her. She didn't completely understand it, but it gave her a sort of comfort, knowing that he wasn't about to force himself on her.

Or try to, anyway.

She had no worries about protecting herself from him. Aside of the fact that he was still weak enough to be wavering while on his feet, she was also, of course, stronger and faster than he was even in his prime. Nor did he seem inclined to attempt to slay her, either…although she wasn't completely certain he wouldn't try.

The last week of tending to him, however, had helped to ease Narcise into her new life: a life where she was beholden to no one, a life where she made her own decisions, procured her own nourishment, clothing and even drawing supplies.

Nevertheless, she was never wholly comfortable leaving the public house—especially at night, when she knew Cezar or his makes could be out looking for her. She'd become adept at enthralling mortals to gain whatever it was she needed: pencils and paper, a pouch of *sous* or *livres*, clothing for herself or Chas…even a full, hot vein on which to feed.

Philippe had visited her chamber more than once. She wasn't certain if it was coincidence that he was always the one to bring new water for the bath, or whether he sensed that there was a reason he was drawn to this particular chamber.

Until now, Narcise had always approached feeding as some necessary evil akin to submitting to her brother's friends. A mortal was brought to her, and she fed. Or, during the span of months when she attempted to starve herself rather than submit to Cezar, a jug of fresh blood was forced down her throat.

There was a residual layer of eroticism that always aroused her when she was in such an intimate situation, but it never required satiation—at least on her part.

Philippe seemed eager enough, and more than once during the three times she'd enthralled him had he managed to get himself—or herself—half unclothed. There were moments when she nearly allowed herself to finish what they, or more accurately, their bodies, obviously both wanted…but she never could succumb so far.

For decades, she'd protected her emotions and her heart—not to mention her mind—by separating herself from the reaction of her body and keeping all but the physical response locked deeply away. She was fully aware of that, cognizant of that steely control.

The one chink in that armor had come with Giordan,

and since then, she'd melded it back together so tightly she suspected it would never soften again.

Now that she was free of Cezar, however, Narcise realized there could be a chance for her to open herself again. And after ten years, she hadn't forgotten nor forgiven Giordan. No, in fact she burned with revulsion and loathing for him…but she remembered how it had felt to be awakened. Not with malice or control, or even by reflex.

But with love and affection.

Neither of which, of course, young Philippe possessed toward her—but at least he had no malice or control.

Or so she was thinking as his insistent hand slipped beneath the hem of her chemise. Her fangs pulled free from his flesh and he tried to find her mouth, desperate for a kiss, but she refused, nipping instead at his ear and feeling his cock slide against her belly through layers of cloth.

"*S'il…vous plaît,*" he whispered thickly, and when she pulled away, he frowned petulantly.

Narcise shook her head, looking into his glazed eyes, knowing that he didn't truly know what he was doing—or wanting—any more than she ever had during those dark nights in The Chamber.

She released him, pulled him free from her thrall and from her arms, and was just stepping back when she heard the doorknob rattle.

Philippe was still too numb and slow to react, or even to understand what was happening, but Narcise knew, and she turned away an instant before the door opened. Chas swept into the chamber in the dark swirling scents of wine and power.

Later, she never fully understood why she felt the need to try to hide what had been going on—but it didn't matter. Chas's eyes flashed to her and then around the chamber. The expression on his face spoke clearly of his disgust and aversion.

"Leave," he snapped at Philippe, the poor confused boy, who stumbled awkwardly from the room with, Narcise knew, half-formed memories of a very intimate situation.

She had a moment to wonder briefly if he'd ever come back, but then irritation and affront spurred her to face Chas. "If you're afraid your sensibilities will be offended, perhaps you should knock the next time you decide to enter."

"Perhaps it would be best if you found another place to…do…that. I don't wish to be any sort of party to your depravity." His eyes flashed with that cold loathing…yet Narcise felt a shifting in his breathing, an awkwardness in his heartbeat. He strode across the chamber, much steadier on his feet than he had been when he left. She scented food along with the heavy weight of wine, tobacco and smoke, and realized he must have eaten belowstairs. And, from the smell of it, drank quite a bit of wine.

She knew her fangs were still slightly extended, and that her eyes had just banked from their burning glow, but she turned away.

"I have no choice," she said. "If I don't feed regularly, then it becomes more difficult for me to control my…" She bit her lip, her cheeks warming.

He'd walked over to the window and snapped the shutters closed, as if shutting out the cool night air would cleanse the room of tension. In fact, it did just the opposite—trapped the scent of blood and wine and musk, and of Chas Woodmore and his energy, his nobility, all the more tightly into the chamber.

Narcise felt a stirring low in her belly, a little flutter that she hardly recognized. *No. Not him.*

She turned, fighting to pull her fangs back into place. Perhaps she should leave. The sun had nearly set. She could do what she needed to do away from his judgmental, greedy eyes.

"Word is out that we've escaped from your brother," Chas said flatly. "Not only does he have his makes pouring through the streets and along the Palais searching for us, but because of Bonaparte, he's got the soldiers on the watch during the day."

A tremor of fear shivered in her belly. "Are we trapped? Will they find us?"

"Of course we aren't trapped," he replied, disdain replacing revulsion. She found she preferred that reaction to the disgust in his face. "I can get us out of Paris and across the Channel, but it will take more planning than I'd anticipated." His face turned expressionless and his eyes skirted away. "We'll have to stay here for a few days longer."

Narcise nodded. A bolt of relief that he didn't intend to leave her alone made her smile a bit and relax. She wasn't quite ready to be completely on her own yet, particularly in the same city where her brother lived.

There was still that blind fear of being found, and dragged back to his chilly, dark chambers. "Did you send word to Dimitri?" she asked, sitting on the edge of the bed. "How will you get a message through the blockade?"

"We have several methods of communication. In this case, I used a blood pigeon, which navigates across land and sea, and will find the particular person to whom it's trained to scent by following his or her blood."

"It smells Dimitri's blood from London all the way here?"

"No, no. We have many pigeons cloistered about the city, and they each have a location to which they fly, or return home. Once in the vicinity of its home area, the bird will scent the blood and go directly to its master, wherever he is." Chas had taken a seat in the chair. He rested his elbow on the table next to him and turned up the gas lamp for the darkening room.

"You're very concerned about your sisters," she said, wondering what it would be like to have a brother like Chas Woodmore instead of Cezar Moldavi.

"Our parents died more than ten years ago, and since then it's been just the four of us. We're very close, of course, but I travel a lot, and so they are often left to their own devices under the watchful eye of their chaperone. But I miss them always, for each of them is so different."

"Tell me about them. I've heard rumors…your family is quite special, isn't it? You have what is called the Sight?"

"Thanks in part to my great-great-grandmother, who fell in love with her late husband's groom. He was a Gypsy and since she'd already been married once according to her father's wishes, now that she was a widow she decided she'd wed whoever she wanted. And so she married her groom. Her great-granddaughter, my Granny Grapes, used to tell us stories about *vampires* when we were younger."

"That's why you are so successful with hunting the Dracule. Who could be better than one whose family comes from Romania? How did you ever decide that it was important to seek us out and kill the *vampires?*"

Chas rose abruptly and walked to the bellpull, ringing it sharply. "Forgive me, but it seems odd to be talking about such things with you."

"Because you're sworn to kill me? But you haven't. In fact, you helped me. Perhaps you aren't such a merciless hunter after all."

He looked at her suddenly over his shoulder. "Perhaps I am. Perhaps I am only now planning how to slam a stake into you, pinning you to the bed." His eyes were dark and glittering. And that was when she realized how very drunk he was. "Or perhaps there are other thoughts weighing on my mind."

Narcise's breath clogged and a sharp spear of desire shot through her belly. Her first reaction wasn't revulsion, however. And that frightened her nearly as much as the thought of being taken back to Cezar.

She was saved from replying by a knock at the door, and as Chas was speaking sharply to whoever had come, she went over and opened the shutters again. Drinking in the cooling air, scenting the chill breeze wafting from the Seine, mixing with smoke and trash and stewing meat, she looked out over the street below.

What if Cezar was out there, right now, looking for her? What if he looked up and saw her peeping down at him? Or across the way—there were windows across the narrow street so close she could jump to them.

Narcise ducked back inside the chamber and realized she and Chas were alone again. "Your sisters? It's said it is they who have the Sight," she said, hoping to keep the conversation light…at least until one of them decided to go to sleep.

"The two younger ones do," Chas replied. "After a fashion." He still stood at the door, now positioned there with his arms folded over his chest. "But Maia, the oldest, who is still younger than I am by nearly ten years, does not. However, she makes up for it by commanding every aspect of everyone's lives in the entire household."

His lips relaxed and nearly eased into a smile—the first one she'd seen on him, it seemed. The effect was very nearly devastating, giving him a soft, sensual look in a highly shadowed face. A dark angel, she thought again—and not in the same way of Lucifer.

"I can hardly imagine how she and Corvindale will get on," Chas continued, the smile going even wider. "For in my extended absence, I've arranged for the earl to attend to them."

"You speak of her with such affection," Narcise said. "My brother cared for me so much that he sent Lucifer to me." She made no effort to hide her hatred and bitterness.

"And so that is how it happened? You blame your brother?" Chas's voice was whip-sharp and filled with judgment.

But Narcise had come to terms with her fallibility long ago. "I blame my brother only for begging Lucifer to turn me Dracule, for sending him to me, but it was of my own will that I agreed to it."

"He came to you in a dream?"

"He came, as I believe he must always do, at a most crucial moment, and yes, in a dream. Where one is the weakest, the most vulnerable to his suggestion. I know of no one who was given the opportunity and who declined the Devil's bargain. If I ever met such a person, I would like to know how he did it."

She closed her eyes for a moment, curling her lips into themselves. "Someone once said to me that I was the strongest person he'd ever met. But by the time I became strong, it was much too late." Her insides heaved at the memory of Giordan—and she locked it back away. "I'd already given my soul."

Someone knocked at the door again, and Chas, who she realized had been waiting for the arrival, opened it. A servant brought in a large jug of ale and two cups, placed them on the table, and left without a word or glance at either of them.

Glad for the interruption and the distraction, Narcise watched as her companion sat back down at the table and poured himself a cup of ale.

"Do you want some?" he asked, then commenced to pouring one for her without waiting for a reply, then set the cup near the opposite edge of the table. He settled back in his seat and took a drink.

She walked over hesitantly and picked up her serving, sipping the strong, bitter drink. It was heavy and warm, and she didn't particularly care for it…but she found that having something for her hands to do, and her mouth and thoughts to focus on, was a good thing.

"What was the crucial moment?" he asked, pouring another slug into his cup.

"Why do you want to know? So you can find a way to my weakness and slay me?" she shot back, affronted by his curiosity when he seemed so reticent and judgmental.

"Perhaps I only wish to understand you better," he replied. His words were gently slurred. "I haven't had the occasion to converse with a *vampir* on such a subject."

"Because you're usually trying to kill them."

"Yes. I should have killed you when I had the chance," he said. His eyes were dark and unsettling. "But it would be a sin to destroy one with such beauty."

"I'm certain it wouldn't be your first," she answered, sipping again from her cup as she leaned against the wall, keeping herself distant from him. "Sin, of course."

"No, indeed not. I'm nearly as evil as you are, Narcise," he said. "What was the crucial moment? Or will you not assuage my curiosity."

"As you can imagine, vanity was my great weakness. I am fully aware of how my appearance affects those around me. Men have only lust in their eyes and hearts when they look at me, women hate me or envy me. I had a lover when I was sixteen. Rivrik. My first, and...only... in all the ways that matter." She nearly choked on the lie, but in her mind it was true.

What she'd had with Giordan could not be classified as love. At least, not anymore.

"Poor Rivrik," murmured Chas. "I can only imagine his terrible fate." He refilled his cup again, and she could tell that the jug had become much lighter.

She wasn't alarmed by his obvious intent to drink himself into oblivion, but rather curious about it. And, she suspected, in the morning he'd remember very little of what she told him tonight. "I had an injury—a burn, from an oil lamp. It was on my face, and I was terrified that it wouldn't heal, that I'd have scars forever. And that Rivrik would no longer love me."

"Because, of course, there was nothing about you to love other than your face and body," he said.

Narcise ignored him. "When Luce came to me and promised that I'd live forever, that I'd never age and that I'd heal completely...I didn't have the strength to decline. And that's how it happened."

"And Rivrik? I'm certain he was delighted to have you intact—except for your damaged soul, of course. But why would he care when he had the rest of you?"

Since these were thoughts Narcise had already considered and raged over, torturing herself with them decades ago, his words didn't sting. Too much. "He died not long after. I'm fairly certain Cezar had something to do with it."

"I'm surprised you didn't offer to turn him Dracule so he could stay with you and your beautiful, youthful self forever."

Now she was annoyed and pushed herself away from the wall. "Almost immediately after I accepted Lucifer's covenant, I realized what a mistake I'd made. I never even considered visiting such a fate on Rivrik."

"Ah, then. A Dracule with a conscience. With regret. They are so very far and few between." He upended the jug and the last bit of ale sloshed into his cup.

Then he lounged back into the chair, his legs spread haphazardly, his head tilting back so much that she thought he'd fallen asleep. But then he moved, loosening the knot at the top of his shirt, and yanking it from the waist of his breeches. He'd already toed off his boots some time earlier, and now she noticed his dark, long feet, bare on the wooden floor.

"And so, then, Narcise," he said suddenly, sitting up. His face had turned dark and fierce, and he set the cup on the table without looking. His eyes, lit to glowing by the gas lamp, pinned her gaze. "Here we are."

She opened her mouth to reply, but he'd heaved himself from his chair, and now he made his way to the other side of the table. His fingers brushed the top of it as if to give him balance, and he walked smoothly but with the slightest bit of stagger that indicated just how far into his cups he was.

Narcise's heart began to thump very hard, and her mouth dried. Even drunk and sloppy, he was dark and exotic looking. Intimidating with his superior height and broad shoulders.

Yet, she made no move to recoil or otherwise back away, even when he came right up to her. But when he grabbed the front of her chemise and slammed her up against the wall, she was so shocked she didn't have time to react before he put his face right up close to hers.

Eyes furious and dark, his lips pulled back from his teeth in a ferocious grimace, he said, "If you ever attempt to enthrall me, I'll kill you."

15

Chas opened his eyes. The room was dim with threatening dawn, a pale scrim of light cast over the furnishings.

He sat up, still feeling the remnants of last night's wine and ale. The empty jug sat on the table where he'd left it and the scent of stale hops permeated the chamber.

Narcise slept next to him on the bed, warm and close and smelling of sleep, of her. Fully clothed. Out of reach.

A rush of desire flooded him and he closed his eyes again, trying to push it away. He couldn't allow his thoughts to go along that route. Too dangerous, too degrading.

She was a practiced seductress. Aside of the fact that eroticism and sensuality always went along with the Draculia, he'd seen evidence of it when he came in upon her little tête-à-tête with the servant Philippe.

The poor sot had been out of his mind with desire and need…and the devil of it was, he had no idea what was happening. He had no control over himself or his actions.

Chas's mouth tightened and he settled on disgust. He'd not fall prey to that sort of lure. He'd never allow himself to be used thus, to lose mastery over himself. He recalled the fury he'd summoned when he dragged her up against the wall last night and threatened to kill her. He would. If she ever turned those lulling, coaxing, burning eyes on him, he wouldn't hesitate to do it.

He slid off the mattress, one of those rare people who hardly felt the effects of overimbibing. There was a dull, gentle pounding in the back of his head, but other than that, and the need for a drink of water, he felt as he normally did in the morning. Although it really was much too early to be up and about for a gentleman; normally one didn't see the light of the sun before noon.

Yet, despite the early hour and the large amounts of wine and ale he'd consumed, Chas's head was clear. He remembered everything from the evening before—including the way he'd had to fairly thrust Narcise away after getting so close to her in that moment of fury. Too close.

Especially when, after the surprise, her eyes had narrowed in interest and admiration.

He used the chamber pot—which was the cause for his early rousing—and then the water in the basin to wash his face and rinse his mouth of the vestiges of stale drink. Then he turned back to the bed.

The shift Narcise had taken to wearing as a night rail gapped away from her throat and shoulders, exposing delicate collarbones and the shadow of other delights deeper still.

Chas pivoted away, opting for the chair to finish his slumber. He remembered full well the feel of her body pressed against his when he shoved her against the wall, his face close to hers.

That had almost been his undoing…she was just *there*, in front of him. He'd even had a handful of her clothing, his fingers curling into the flesh above her breasts just before she shoved him away. His caution was just that much dulled by the drink, and the knowledge of what she'd been doing in the chamber with that servant boy still lingered in the back of his mind. His imagination filled in the details of what had gone on before he interrupted…what would have happened if he had not.

And as much as he'd attempted to drink himself into oblivion, he was fully aware of his body's response to her, his attraction to and curiosity about her.

Why did she have to be a *vampir?*

The pounding in his head had become stronger and he abandoned the idea of slumping in the chair and trying to sleep there. He'd fallen into…onto…the bed before she had last night, and she obviously had no qualms about sleeping next to him, and so why should he be concerned?

He climbed back into his place on the mattress, noting that the blankets were still warm from where he'd lay moments earlier, but that her hand had crept away from her cheek and now lay just beneath his pillow.

All thoughts of sleep fled as he settled down next to her, his face very close to hers, but yet distant enough that he could focus on her features. A soft, warm scent filtered from her hair and skin and he found it difficult to dismiss.

He found *her* impossible to dismiss.

The sun seemed to be taking her time rising today, and the chamber continued to be filled with indistinct shapes except in a rectangular patch beneath the window. But Chas could somehow make out the fringe of Narcise's dark lashes and the little accent line at the corner of her mouth. And he noticed, for the first time, a tiny beauty mark at the corner of her left eye.

Before he could stop himself, he reached and settled his hand, open, onto the cascade of hair falling over her shoulder. Slowly he traced its smooth sheen along her head and over her shoulder and arm, lightly, lightly… hardly more than a feather touch. Her warmth seeped from beneath the silkiness into his palm, and although she gave a little tremor in her sleep, she didn't waken.

Chas touched her again, sliding his fingers around a coil of hair that had fallen in front of her shoulder and hung like a corkscrew. Curling it around his finger, he rubbed the lock between two finger pads, then let it fall back against her bosom.

His heart had begun to swell and pound all that much harder, for he knew she couldn't enthrall him while she was sleeping. Which meant that what he felt—that deep tug, that insistent pull of attraction—was real. And it was strong.

He just hoped to God it wouldn't destroy him, for he didn't think there was any way to turn back.

She felt the same simmering attraction; he'd seen it when he interrupted her feeding on that youthful servant yesterday. She'd had the boy, but wanted *him*. Chas.

It was in her eyes when she saw him walking through the door.

A little pang twisted his belly. Yes, she wanted him, but he could never allow her to take from him as she'd done with the footman. He wouldn't lose that control, he wouldn't ever slip into that maelstrom of hunger and need that he'd experienced at Rubey's…that night where he was out of his mind with pleasure, with the need to have his blood freed, sopped up, drawn…

Chas swallowed the thick lump in his throat. Even now, a month later, the shame and humiliation made him ill. How could he have become so base, so depraved as to allow a servant of the Devil to control him?

But here was another temptation…a greater one. Narcise was beyond beautiful…she was also intelligent and brave. And she'd stayed with him when he was dying.

For God's sake, she'd even violated him…but to save his life.

What a turnabout that was for a Dracule.

A deep little tremor went through him and he closed his eyes. *No. Not her.*

And yet…he could not keep from touching her. It was as if a magnet drew his hand, his fingers, his attention to her.

It wasn't until he brushed a swath of hair back from her temple and cheek that Narcise stirred. She opened her eyes, and as soon as they focused, sleepiness fled. They flashed wide with surprise and then apprehension as she started with a slight jolt…and then her expression shifted just as quickly into confusion.

His heart pounded and desire shivered in his belly.

Her eyes were colorless and dark in the shadows, and he looked into them as he did the only thing he could think to do…he eased closer, sliding his hand around beneath her ear, and covered her mouth with his.

Despite the sudden rage of pleasure bursting in him, Chas took his time with the kiss…gently meeting her lips, curving into them, moving his against hers in sensual little circles.

She made a soft sound and began to turn her head away, but he slipped his fingers tighter around the back of her neck and pulled her close, turning the kiss deeper and more coaxing. He slipped his tongue into her warm, sleek mouth, pulled away and went back to nibbling on her lips, using the tip of his tongue to tease the corners. She trembled, at last kissing him back, her hand settling on his chest…not to shove him away as she'd done last night when he had her against the wall, but digging her fingers into the cloth there.

He wanted her, but he had no urgency, and their kiss went on and on…deep and long, and then gentle and seductive as they explored the taste and texture of the other.

When she twisted her face away at last, he saw that she was crying. That a little trickle had slipped from the corner of her eye and slid into the hair at her temple.

A stab of pain and fear caught him and he pulled away sharply. "What is it? Narcise?"

Good God, he hadn't expected this—from a strong, seductive woman like her.

She wiped the tear away and turned her incredible blue eyes onto him. There was enough light now that he could see how they brimmed with pain and sorrow, but she curved her lips into a little smile. "I haven't kissed anyone in a very long time."

"I'm sorry," he said uncertainly, feeling an unexpectedly soft unfurling inside him. It had been very easy to think of her as a hard, calculating woman bent on having—and controlling—any man in her path. But the expression in her face could only be described as heartbroken.

Her lips twisted wryly. "It's not for you to be sorry." Her gaze flickered away for an instant, and Chas began to ease back.

She looked at him and reached to tug him back closer to her. "Kiss me again."

He obliged, happily, despite the niggling worry in the back of his mind. He was beginning to realize that there were things about her that weren't obvious.

Her lips, so full and soft, covered his and drove all worries from his mind. He pulled her closer to delve deeper, tasting a bit of salt from her tears, and doing what he could to help her forget whatever it was that made her grieve.

Meanwhile, his free hand slid to the front of her chemise and found the little drawstring tie there. Loosening it, he slid his hand down the front of the gapping bodice as he trailed gentle kisses from her mouth along the slender curve of her jaw.

Her breathing changed when he found one of her breasts, closing his fingers around it and cupping its weight in his palm. Her nipple jutted into his thumb and he settled there, gently massaging its very tip as she shivered and sighed, rolling her body closer to him.

His breeches were tight and his shirt clinging hot and too heavy, but he was loathe to release her and take them off. Instead he pulled the drawstring even looser and tugged her bodice open more, down over her shoulders, so that he could slip south and close his mouth around her. She was sweet and warm, tinged with salt and musk, and he drew her deep into his mouth, sliding his tongue around her sensitive nipple. Around and around, darting and sleekly teasing.

Narcise arched into his mouth and he felt her legs shifting along his, capturing one of his breeches-clad thighs between hers in a sensual slide. He sucked harder, rhythmically, and she sighed, shivering against him as he dragged her hips closer.

When he pulled away to tear off his shirt, sitting back on his haunches, he saw her eyes burning, glowing red and orange and the tips of her fangs showing beneath her upper lip. A shaft of desire stabbed him low in the gut at the thought of those sharp points sliding into his flesh, of the bursting release of simmering need. He had a flash of her gouging him, goring into his shoulder or neck or arm, greedy and sensual, just as she had to that poor servant boy, and he forced himself to look away, fighting the temptation. *No.*

God, no.

Disgust made his belly pitch and swing, desire and lust weakened him, and he nearly pushed her away when Narcise reached for his bare shoulders, closing her fingers around him. But instead, he went with her, his torso warm against her breasts.

She pulled him back down onto the bed as he fought the memory of the night he'd spent at Rubey's, bitten and dragged on in a whorl of red lust. His body craved the release, his cock full and ready, the feel of the blood flowing freely into her hot mouth, the pain and pleasure of her mouth, sensual and demanding.

When Narcise's hand found the buttons on the placket of his breeches, Chas felt his whole body stiffen in expectation and control. She slipped her hand down the loosened waistband and closed around his throbbing erection, using her thumb to tease its tip just as he had done to her swollen nipple.

Somehow, her chemise had slipped away, and next went his breeches, and they were flesh to flesh. His dark Gypsy skin, textured with hair, sleek with muscle, slid against her soft ivory curves. He felt her readiness, damp and warm, and turned his mind from the burning in her eyes as he parted her legs and pulled her on top of him.

She eased herself into place and his eyes fairly rolled back into his head as they fit together in a shaft of pure pleasure. Narcise shifted her hips, rocking a bit, and he felt himself gathering up into that coil of release…and then she leaned forward, her eyes glowing, her fangs exposed.

Chas's heart thumped madly, his neck throbbing, heat rushing through his body as she shifted over him, rocking, sliding, and then easing her hands up along his torso as she bent over him. His skin burned, his fingers dug into her arms, pulling her close even as he knew he should be pushing her away…but the lust had taken hold, and the red heat caught him, and all he could think about was her pressed against him, her breasts against his chest, her face buried in his throat… He wanted that sharp, stinging pain.

No, he thought, but he wanted it nevertheless. As they strained and shifted against each other, his muscles bunching and his blood surging, her soft panting warm against his throat, he imagined the slide of her into his skin, imagined the burst of pleasure, the heat flowing into her mouth as he would burst inside her.

"Narcise," he gasped, the lust rising higher, tighter, the bed rocking and shifting beneath them. *Bite me. Take me.*

She shifted and for a moment, he thought she was about to pull away, but then her lips were warm and moist against his neck. Desire flared inside him…*yes, yes*…her tongue, slick and hot, traced the tendon, the side of his neck.

He moved faster, gathered her closer, tipped his head to the side, baring his throat and shoulder. *Please.*

Don't. No.

Please.

And then she shifted, and he felt her lips go wide against him and then the sharp stabs of pain, brief and hot, and then the burst of his blood surging free. Release.

He gave a low, agonized cry as waves of pleasure undulated through him. He exploded twice inside her, into her mouth, into the deepest part of her center as she heaved and shuddered against him, her face still buried in his neck.

Then…even as he filtered back from the edge of nowhere, the lust still vibrating inside him, Chas felt the competing rush of ugliness bubbling up. Sharp little pulses from the marks on his shoulder served as prickling reminders of his depravity, opening himself up to the pleasure of the Devil.

He closed his eyes and turned away.

Narcise slipped away from him, easing back to her side of the bed, exhausted and sated. She closed her eyes, still tasting Chas on her lips and tongue, still quivering with the last bit of pleasure.

Her body was warm and loose in a way that it hadn't been for so long. So very long. Their joining had been passionate, yet slow and tender, the desire coaxed from where she'd locked it deep inside her until it rushed out in a surge of completion.

It had been so long since she'd felt true pleasure… and yet, despite its truth, her joining with Chas left her with a hollow space deep inside. Confusion warred with satisfaction and when she felt him stirring next to her, Narcise welcomed the distraction and opened her eyes.

He'd shifted away, lying flat on his back, the back of his arm resting over his eyes. His chest—smooth slabs of muscle and dusky damp skin—still shifted with rough breathing. And a trickle of blood eased down along into the hollow of his throat.

Narcise realized that in the throes of passion and release, she hadn't finished tending to the bite. Her mouth dried in anticipation as she thought of touching his smooth, dark skin again, tasting the last bit of salt and musk mingling with the warm blood.

She lifted herself up onto an elbow, closer to him, and leaned over the rich, shining ooze. He stiffened, sensing her nearness, and she lightly closed her fingers over the squared-off angle of his shoulder as she bent to cover the bitemarks with her mouth. She'd barely begun to lick up the remains when suddenly he moved. His arm shifted, and at first she thought he was going to grab her closer to him again, but then she saw his face. Taut and dark and damp.

And then all at once, he erupted from the bed and lunged toward the table. Snatching up the basin, he vomited into it with great violence as he bent over the table. As she watched, curious and concerned, he lifted his face, swiping his mouth with a bare arm, then—all dark and naked and muscled—stalked over to the window and flung the contents out.

She winced, hoping there was no one below, and remained silent as he rinsed out the dish with water from its pitcher and dumped that below as well.

When he finished his own ablutions in the clean basin, Chas turned back to her. The expression on his face was carefully blank, but Narcise was distracted by the shiny spot on his throat she'd been tasting a moment earlier.

"Apparently I imbibed too heavily last night," he said coolly.

"You need give me no explanation for your illness," she replied, wondering why he'd felt the need to do so. And then she offered a defense of her own. "I hope you aren't under the impression that I enthralled you."

His mouth twisted as if he were either in pain or about to laugh, and he turned away, giving her another excellent view of his long, lean back and tight, square buttocks. His tousled hair nearly covered his nape, winging up every which way around his head and ears. She also noted what was, of course, absent from his muscular shoulders: the Mark of Lucifer.

"No, I am not under that impression," he replied. His

attention slipped down and Narcise realized she was still completely naked, her chemise having gone the way of the bedcoverings during their lovemaking. She also realized, with a start, that for the first time in as long as she could remember, her body remained unmarked and smooth after coitus. No bites or cuts.

Chas was moving toward her, his eyes hot and dark. And determined. "But perhaps we should try it again," he said, "to be certain."

Narcise's heart thumped and she felt her body begin to tighten in anticipation. "Perhaps we should," she replied, wondering if this time she might banish the hollowness.

She saw that he was ready for her, his cock lifting and filling, his eyes burning in their own mortal fashion. But she wasn't prepared for him to turn her around, facing away from him. He eased her toward the bed, gently but firmly, until the fronts of her thighs bumped it.

"My God," he said as he pulled the hair away from her shoulders and neck. His fingers moved lightly over the faint rise of Luce's Mark.

It grew from beneath her hair on the right side and spread down over the back of her shoulder to just past her scapula: curling, rootlike tendrils. Hers was softer in shape and lighter in color than others he'd seen, most of which looked like cracks in shattered glass.

"Does it hurt?" he asked, still gently tracing over the Mark. His voice in her ear brought deeper, gentler shivers down along the side of her neck.

"Not now," she told him, curving her hands up and around to touch the back of his head. His hair filtered around her fingers, warm and heavy, and as she combed through, a renewed wave of his scent released into the chamber.

"I've seen Dimitri's Mark," Chas commented, sliding

his hands along the curves of her torso as he lined himself up behind her. "It's thick and black and raging, as if it were filled with evil."

Narcise might have responded if he hadn't slipped his hands around to cup her breasts, if he hadn't begun to distract her thoughts by sliding his thumbs over her nipples.

He nuzzled the side of her neck, his lips full and the tip of his tongue a gentle, moist tease that sent gentle, insistent shivers through her. Narcise realized vaguely that there would be no sharp pain, no quick slide of fangs, no release from her pounding veins, and it was odd... but pleasant.

But as he eased her onto the bed, reaching around to the front of her, fingers exploring the depths of her quim to make certain she was as ready for him as he seemed to be for her, she realized what he was keeping her—and her gaze—facing away from.

Narcise could have been offended, or annoyed, but when he slid deep into place, her body welcomed him and she gave no more thought to anything except that delicious rhythm of pleasure.

And when she arched and shuddered, slamming back against his hips, her hands braced on the bed, he gave a low groan in her ear and surged one last time. She felt him find release, and allowed her arms to give way so she tumbled face-first onto the mattress.

Chas followed her, disengaging, and sliding his hand along her spine and over her bottom as he sank down next to her.

Narcise lay there for a moment, and as the last vestiges of bliss eased, she thought about what had happened... on all fronts.

He'd kissed her. He'd started this whole incident by kissing her...so intimate, so long and thorough and absent of the need for control…and she'd let him. She'd let him do something only Giordan had done. Was it to banish her memories and grief over him?

But she didn't want to think about Giordan now. He had no place in her thoughts, in her life, in this place with Chas Woodmore.

Yet… "Are we going to London?" she asked. Hadn't Cezar mentioned that Giordan was in London? Her heart seized up and she blanked out her mind.

"As soon as I can arrange it," Chas replied.

She glanced at him and noted that his face seemed only a bit less tense than it had earlier—despite two bouts of coitus. "Is something wrong? Weren't you satisfied that I didn't enthrall you this last time?"

The chagrin—and perhaps shame—showed on his face. "I don't fuck vampires," he told her flatly. "Because I don't want to be controlled."

Narcise pulled away, fury bubbling inside her. It was a welcome emotion, replacing her other softer, confused one. "But apparently you do fuck vampires, Chas, because you just did. Twice."

"I know," he said, misery flashing in his face for a moment. Then his expression was cold and flat again. "It was…incredible. You're incredible, Narcise, and, damn me to hell, I can't stay away from you." He rose from the bed with sharp, short movements. "I can't keep my hands or thoughts off you."

As she watched, confused and angry, he yanked on his breeches with a snap of the fabric, dragged on his boots and picked up his discarded shirt. "No matter how hard I try," he said, his jaws tight together, "I can't make you into the evil, manipulative demon I want you to be."

"Why do you want to do that?" she asked, affronted and yet fascinated in spite of herself. She was beginning to realize that his anger wasn't directed at her, but at himself.

"So I can kill you, damn it." With fury and rage surrounding him, Chas stalked from the room, still holding his wadded up shirt.

He didn't return until well after the sun went down, and this time, he didn't reek of drink. She'd spent the day drawing scenes from the window, using the pencils and paper she'd managed to charm from unsuspecting shopkeepers—and through Philippe—during Chas's feverish illness.

When he came into the chamber, she looked up briefly, then returned to her sketch. Much of Notre Dame's towers were visible from her window, and despite the irony of a soul-damaged vampire drawing a holy place, Narcise had spent much effort on the sketch. Now that it was getting darker, she was working from memory.

The emperor had ordered the area around the famous church to be cleared of old buildings, piles of garbage and debris left from the years of neglect during the Revolution. He insisted that the streets around the cathedral be emptied and widened for his upcoming coronation, which was to take place inside. Soldiers and city workers had been toiling over the project for the last month, and it would take well into the autumn before they were finished…or so Narcise had heard him complain to Cezar. Because of this, the coronation had been moved to early November.

"We're leaving Paris tomorrow," said Chas, sitting heavily on the bed. "I've made the arrangements."

She nodded briefly but remained intent on her work, trying to ignore the spike of apprehension in her belly.

"Your brother has the entire city looking for us," he

continued. "But he isn't certain we're even together. That works to our advantage. We have to go during the day, so I've taken precautions for you. You'll be driving a cart with a coffin in back…which will contain me—a corpse dead from the plague. I'll stuff the box with old meat beneath me so as to attract flies, and to make a stink, and will fill your pockets with it as well. You'll dress as an elderly woman with a large hat and gloves to protect you from the sun and will be taking your dead husband to the country."

Silence reigned between them for a moment, broken only by the distant shouts from the street below, and a burst of raucous laughter from the pub beneath the floor underfoot. Her pencil scratched quietly as she shaded one of the windows in the square-shaped towers.

"Do you still wish to go to London?"

At that, she rested her pencil on the paper and turned to look at him. "Only if you can suffer my manipulative, evil presence," she said stiffly.

His face tightened. "Narcise, I'm sorry if I've offended you, but understand, I spend my life hunting and killing the Dracule. It's not often that I find one worth saving."

She tossed her head and looked back down at her work, lit by a nearby lamp. To her horror, it began to blur and she furiously blinked back the tears. She hadn't cried in decades, and now in the last week, she'd teared up three times. Was she growing soft?

"Narcise," he said, his voice softer. He rose and came to stand behind her, his fingers sliding gently over her hair. "You saved my life. You stayed with me when you could have left. I was a fool for saying those things to you today. It's just that…I'm beginning to have feelings for you, and it's not what I expected."

She turned to look up at him and read the bleakness

in his eyes. "I'm sorry it's so difficult for you," she said, her voice emotionless.

He shrugged, a rueful smile curving his lips. "I am, too. Narcise, I am sorry." He drew in a deep breath and said, "I'll keep you safe. I have a secret place, a small estate in Wales where you can hide…where no one will find you."

She looked at him, her heart leaping. Wales was far from London; she knew that. "Yes," she said, knowing that her heart was in her eyes. "Thank you, Chas."

He gave that little shrug again and said, "And maybe you'll allow me to stay with you for a while." His grin was crooked.

"Of course," she said, and smiled back.

His gaze darkened and his lips parted slightly. "You are the most beautiful woman," he breathed. "God help me."

He reached for her hand and she rose from her chair, suffused for the first time with comfort and security. She trusted him, and somehow, he'd come to trust her.

As long as they made their safe escape from Paris, she would have the chance to be free of Cezar forever.

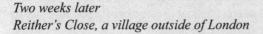

16

Two weeks later
Reither's Close, a village outside of London

Narcise paced the small chamber, trying not to imagine what was happening in the pub below. Trying not to
picture the meeting between Chas and Giordan Cale.

More than a week ago, she and Chas had arrived on
the British shore in the dead of night. *Safe.*

Between his careful planning, the *livres* and guin-
eas he'd used to grease palms and her ability to enthrall,
their exit from Paris and subsequent passage through the
English blockade of the Channel had gone expediently
and smoothly.

Without even a detour to London, they were on their
way to Chas's secret estate in Wales, but had stopped for
three nights at an inn in Reither's Closewell, a small village west of London, so that he could send word to Corvindale and wait for a response.

Everything had gone well during their stay until Chas
extricated himself from Narcise's arms—and bed—and

informed her that he was to meet a gentleman in the public room below.

When he said, "Perhaps you don't remember Giordan Cale, but he's a confidant of Dimitri," Narcise's entire world had halted.

"Not titled, but rich as Croesus and," Chas continued with a bit of a laugh, "more than a match for me. I met him when I sneaked in to stake him. Obviously we both lived."

Narcise found her voice. "Obviously."

"I can meet him below, but it wouldn't be as private if I asked him up here. Less chance of us being seen."

"No," was all she said. But inside, her body was shriveling into panic. She had to close her fingers together to hide their sudden trembling.

Was Chas watching her closely, or was it her imagination?

"Very well, Narcise."

And she wondered what, if anything, he knew about their history.

For, despite their continued intimacy, she hadn't told Chas about what had happened with Giordan and Cezar. Those events of a decade ago were no longer relevant, and there wasn't any sense in reigniting the memories, reliving that horrible time.

As she imagined their conversation, she tried not to think about the fact that Giordan would scent her the moment he approached. Her presence was everywhere on Chas, and Giordan would know not only that she was near, but he'd immediately understand the nature of their relationship.

Would he even care?

As Narcise continued to trace the boundaries of the

room, avoiding the narrow strips of fading sunlight from between awkwardly fitting shutters, she found herself wondering just what *was*, precisely, the nature of her relationship with Chas.

Not that Dracule had relationships like mortals did. After all, eternity was a very long time. Marriage was futile—at least with a mortal, who'd die long before the Dracule would, not to mention grow old and shriveled while the *vampir* remained ever young. And female Dracule, at least, didn't seem able to procreate—at least not in the way their mortal female counterparts did.

And as for love… Narcise had come to realize that love was a mortal concept. A mortal *curse*. Dracule didn't truly love, because to love meant to place someone before oneself.

And a *vampir* simply did not do that. Ever. If one even thought about doing such a thing, Lucifer burned and blazed through the pulsing coils on one's back and influenced those actions back to where they should be: to self. Of course, a Dracule was all about passion and lust and pleasure, and if one happened to give it during the time one was also receiving, then so be it.

Therefore, what had been between her and Giordan couldn't have been love. Not at all.

For more than three weeks, she and Chas had been together as partners in their escape from Cezar and lovers since that morning he'd kissed her. And since the day Chas had told her he had feelings for her, and how much he loathed the fact that he did, the bond between them had been strengthening.

Not simply a bond of passion and lust, but a layer of respect and blossoming affection. She trusted him, she wanted to be with him, she enjoyed his body. Yet, Narcise was under no impression that she loved Chas.

She sensed that she could just as easily awaken one night and realize she wouldn't truly miss him in her life. That if he left, she would be sad, but not...destroyed.

Perhaps that was because she'd come to realize one disturbing thing about Chas: he hated—perhaps even feared—her Draculean tendencies, and he loathed himself for being attracted to a *vampir*.

It was as if he were at war within himself: he wanted her to bite him, to feed on him...but he hated himself when he responded to such titillation.

Yet, he cared for her. Deeply. He brought her little gifts—flowers, lace, hair combs. Even an ivory busk, which fit into the vertical pocket of her corset, down between her breasts. No more than two fingers wide, as thin as a knife blade and about as long as her hand, it was beautifully carved with more flowers, and leafy vines, and a sun radiating bold rays.

"Because I know how much you miss the sun," he'd said when she looked at it, smoothing her fingers over the delicate design. "You can keep it near your heart."

She had. She'd slipped it into the little pocket of her corset and even now, she pressed her hand there, between her breasts, and felt the sturdy little placket there.

Then she heard the pounding of hurried, ascending footsteps and then the hasty scuff as feet reached the top, and Narcise froze, waiting. If Giordan had somehow come back with him, or—

The door to the chamber opened sharply and her heart surged into her throat as she looked at the blur of a figure rushing in. When she scented and recognized Chas, his hair dark and wild, his face tense and angry, she went even colder. What had Giordan said? What had they done?

"I'm leaving," he said, throwing clothing into his pack, hardly giving her more than a brief look. "For London. It's Voss. He's abducted Angelica."

If Chas was unsettled about being with a *vampir* himself, he was even more rigid and terrified about his sisters being abducted or otherwise seduced by a Dracule. He well knew the violence and terror that could be inflicted by one of them.

If one were to be honest, Narcise must admit that she had had more than a few pangs of envy that these three mortal women had a brother who loved them so much and was so concerned for their safety that he would risk his own life to keep them safe. And, apparently, Chas would leave the side of his lover when one of them was in danger—even if said lover was in grave danger herself.

"London?" she repeated, a variety of thoughts shooting through her brain. "But that's the first place Cezar will look for me. For us," she added.

"It certainly is, but I have to go, Narcise." Chas stopped and looked up at her. "I've made arrangements for you to stay here. You'll be safe, and Cale will take you on to Wales while Corvindale and I find Voss...."

But Narcise hadn't heard anything after the words *Cale will take you.* Her brain simply froze, her stomach plummeted and she felt dizzy. Nauseated.

I can't see him again. I can't.

The memories flooded back, the glimpses of sleek, muscled shoulders by firelight, her brother's face rising behind them, lips peeled back in pleasure and pain...the scents of depravity and the raging in his eyes. *Do you have any idea what I've done for you?*

She swallowed hard, gave her head a little shake. *No. By the Fates,* no.

"I'll come with you," she said quickly.

Chas stopped his packing and looked at her sharply. "But you don't want to go to London. It's too dangerous."

"You'll protect me," she said, smiling with a bit of seduction. Not too much. "I don't want to be away from you, Chas." She dropped her voice low, trying to keep the panic out. "You got us out of France, you've outwitted Cezar every step of the way…and London is your own city. You'll be even sharper and smarter there. As well, I'd like to meet your sisters. And Dimitri again."

His face eased just a bit. "I confess, I would rather you come with me. But I didn't think you'd want to take the chance."

"London is a big city," she replied, relief sweeping her. "There are, I'm certain, many places to hide. Aside of that, Cezar wouldn't expect us to go there, and hide in plain sight."

Chas nodded. "Then pack up. I'll send word to Cale that his services to take you to Wales won't be necessary."

"I'm certain the man didn't wish to be bothered with such a task anyway," she said, turning to stuff her own belongings—such as they were—into a different satchel.

If she'd hoped for a reply, some sort of indication regarding Giordan's feelings toward her, she didn't receive one, for Chas had already left the chamber.

Forcing herself to breathe normally, she closed her eyes for a moment and thanked the Fates—or whoever—that had helped her avoid what would have been an untenable situation.

Traveling to Wales with Giordan Cale?

Narcise would have run back to Cezar first.

London, a week later

"You're a very unusual vampire, to be sure, Giordan Cale."

He looked up from where he'd been casually feeding on Rubey's warm, creamy shoulder as a bit of foreplay and withdrew his fangs gently. Swallowing the last essence of sweetness, he smiled slightly and soothed the marks with his tongue and lips.

"In what way?" Giordan replied, settling back against the arm of the divan.

Rubey, who was half reclining on the opposite end of that furnishing, made a fetching picture. She had strawberry-blond hair that curled around her face when not restrained, and where one could occasionally find a thread of gray. Tonight she wore it in a loose tail gathered at her nape, little curls flirting with her temples and ears. Her lushly curved but slender body reminded one of a peach in color as well as in taste, and Giordan fancied she even had a permanent hint of peach brandy in her essence. It was, after all, her favorite libation, and he kept her supplied with an excellent selection of it. Her face was more striking than classically beautiful with wise green-gray eyes that tipped up at the sides and very high, sculpted cheekbones.

He'd never seen her in anything but the most expensive, fashionable clothing, and tonight was no exception. She wore silky pale green with darker green and yellow ribbons that gathered up the bodice of her dressing gown. Thanks to him, said bodice was loosened, exposing a vast expanse of breast and one marred shoulder, where thin trickles of blood gathered in the hollow of her collarbone.

"Why, and how long would it take me to count the

ways," she replied with a woeful shake of the head and the lilt of the Irish. Her eyes sparkled with wit and intelligence.

Giordan gave a brief smile and thought about loosening those ribbons at her bodice even more, but realized he wasn't all that interested in pursuing that avenue tonight.

"Perhaps I could trouble you to name just one way," he replied mildly, his thoughts slipping from the conversation to…other topics that, generally, he preferred to leave alone in the darkness. Where they belonged.

He rose from the divan, clad only in shirtsleeves and the current male fashion of pantaloons, and went to the cabinet. But of course they were in her private apartments, in a separate building from the pleasure house and the rest of her staff—most of whom were otherwise privately engaged as well.

"Very well," she replied, and he felt her eyes on him as he poured a glass of whiskey.

There were two small decanters of ruby-fresh blood from which he could add to the drink, but he wasn't certain where they'd originated, and he dared not take the chance.

Ever since what he'd come to think of as the After Hell, he'd had to be very careful about where and on whom he fed.

A lot of other things had changed as well.

"You switched the mousetraps," Rubey mused as he poured her a small glass of the peach brandy.

"And that makes me unusual? The poor creatures were being crushed in the neck by the springs of the traps," he replied, handing her the drink.

"Aye, and why should it matter to you? The mice don't

belong in my place, and I'm going to see that if they trespass, they pay the price," she replied tartly.

"A bit bloodthirsty, are we?" he asked, aware of a niggling discomfort with her choice of topic. He was different now, and even Dimitri didn't know about it all.

He just thought Giordan's feeding preferences had changed...but it was so much more than that.

"But now the new traps, they let the little bastards just get captured until they're set loose," Rubey said. "To weasel their way into someone else's house."

"Better that than yours," Giordan replied, and considered that it might be a good diversion to loosen those ribbons at her bodice after all. He settled back down on the divan much closer to her this time, his thigh lined up along where her skirts angled off the sofa.

"And then there's the way you feed," she said, eyeing him closely. "Sure as the day's long, you're not like any other vampire I've ever met. Excepting Dimitri, of course, but he don't feed on anyone anyway."

"I am discriminating in my choice of libation," Giordan agreed, sliding his fingers up to the ribbons and filtering his fingers through the loose knots. "Aren't you?" he asked with a smile.

But of course, Rubey didn't cast up her accounts if she partook of a piece of steak or a chicken leg....

He could still remember those black, bleak days when he hadn't realized what was happening, and he hadn't understood why he'd feed and then no sooner had he finished than it all came furiously, violently back up again. His mouth and throat had been scorched dry, his belly sore and weak from the constant purging. The taste of bile-laden blood, rushing back up through his throat and burning into his mouth and nose, was a disgusting, degrading sensation he'd never forget.

Thank the Fates for Drishni and Kritanu, helping him understand how he'd changed. How he must have answered the voice that said in his head: *Choose.*

How he'd found light after all the darkness. Soothing, peaceful, warm…after so many years of darkness.

If it hadn't been for them, he'd have gone mad.

More mad than he'd already been, after Narcise.

Rubey made a moue of distaste. "Sure and it's ironic, the way I run a house of pleasure for them who drink blood when the very thought of a bloody steak or the leg of a hen makes me ill. My pappa couldn't ever understand why I was happy with only potatoes and greens."

Giordan might have replied but his shift toward the ever-expanding exposure of her bodice was interrupted by a knock at the door.

"Blast it," Rubey said, disappointment clearly in her tones. "What is it?" she called.

The door eased open and one of her servants—a large brute of a mortal man named Eduardo, whom Giordan didn't wholly trust—stepped in holding a small silver tray. "A message has just arrived for Mr. Cale," he said.

Giordan took the note, which was marked with Corvindale's seal, and broke into it. *"Meeting here tonight with Woodmore. Voss still in city. Come."*

He closed it up, a myriad of emotions running through him—the foremost and strongest being pain. Darkness. But Giordan drew in a deep, steadying breath and after a moment, his red vision and the pounding, trammeling feeling eased. His fingers relaxed.

There was a time when he'd have had no qualms, no hesitation about snapping the neck of someone like

Woodmore—particularly since, several months back, he found the man in the rooms Giordan had let in London, preparing to hang his heart on a stake. Some sort of gray-black smoke was trickling from the fireplace and Woodmore was caught off guard by Giordan's wakefulness during the day and, he learned later, a malfunction of some sort of smoke explosion.

But those days of quick, efficient violence had gone, and when Giordan learned that his would-be attacker was none other than Chas Woodmore, associate and friend of Dimitri, he'd allowed it to end as a misunderstanding. He'd even helped prepare the bastard for his mission to assassinate Cezar Moldavi.

But his easy assistance was before he'd responded to Woodmore's request to meet him in Reither's Closewell… and smelled Narcise. Everywhere. Everywhere on Chas Woodmore.

Even the information Woodmore had wished to share—that Cezar Moldavi had not, in the past decade, forgotten his obsession with Giordan—didn't concern him.

After all, it had been a decade for Giordan as well. The ten years had been both interminable and all too brief, too close. Too raw.

Now, he stood and made himself walk casually over to the chair where he'd removed his shoes, sit and pull them on.

He'd known they were together, of course; that Woodmore had helped her to escape from Paris—or had abducted her. No one was clear on the details. But to smell her thus…so lush and rich and feminine. *Narcise.*

The moment was as if he'd slammed into a stone wall:

he lost his breath, he felt the shock of pain reverberating through him, he turned numb.

After, Giordan wasn't certain how he'd managed to make it through that meeting at the inn, once he'd caught her scent. It was the way it *rolled* off Woodmore, the way it seemed to permeate him and mix with his own essence…mocking and familiar and horribly insidious.

His vision turned dark and red even now. He couldn't ignore the memory of the disgust in her face, the horror in her eyes.

As if anything she could think about him was as horrible as what he'd done. *For her.*

He'd tried to explain, to make her understand…but she didn't want to listen.

She wasn't *ready* to listen.

Either she'd never loved and trusted him at all, or she hadn't loved and trusted him enough.

At it was, he didn't know whom to thank that Narcise had decided to go with Woodmore to London instead of having Giordan take her to Wales. He doubted he would have survived that trip with his sanity intact.

"Is everything all right?" Rubey asked.

Giordan wasn't certain how long he'd been silent—he'd finished dressing and was starting toward the chamber door before she spoke. "A summons from Dimitri," he said with an ironic tone. "When the earl beckons, one must answer."

She was watching him with those shrewd eyes. "When will I see you again?" she asked. Not with petulance, not even with invitation, but as a businesswoman, scheduling an engagement. Rubey was no man's woman through her own volition, and not for lack of being wooed.

"When next I need to feed," he told her smoothly, then

moved quickly back to her side. Pressing a farewell kiss to her temple, he said, "With your permission, madame."

"Of course," she replied haughtily. But he felt the weight of her curious gaze following him out the door.

The trip to Blackmont Hall, the residence of the Earl of Corvindale, was hampered by a carriage accident on Bond. Giordan didn't begrudge the delay, for it gave him more time to mull, to consider, to settle. To decide if he even meant to go.

The streets were relatively quiet, for the shops were closed this late at night, but the thoroughfares were by no means deserted. Carriages and hacks trundled by, many pedestrians skirted the shadows—some of them up to no good, some of them simply walking from one pub, club, theater, or party to another.

Giordan sat quietly in his richly appointed carriage and considered how far the bounds of friendship reached. If it were anyone other than Dimitri, he would ignore the summons. When Woodmore sent him the secret message to meet in Reither's Close, Giordan had gone, not realizing what awaited him.

But he did now. And he wasn't certain he'd be able to handle being in the same chamber as Woodmore and not think of peeling the man's flesh from his body. Despite who he'd become.

He hadn't laid a violent finger, hand, or fang on anyone since the After Hell.

Instead of dwelling on thoughts of Chas Woodmore, Giordan forced himself to review what he knew, wondering why Dimitri felt it necessary to have him present tonight.

Voss had run off with Angelica Woodmore. He claimed it was to keep her safe from Moldavi's men, who'd, predictably, followed Woodmore and Narcise from Paris.

Giordan had been in London—although with Rubey and not in attendance—the night of the abduction, when Belial and three others had entered a masquerade ball and murdered three people. That night and the next day, he and Dimitri had had to work together to enthrall witnesses and change stories. Otherwise, the news might cause a mad panic in London such as there had been in Brussels some years back after a similar occurrence. Shortly after, Giordan left to meet Woodmore in Reither's Close and break the news of Angelica's kidnapping.

But by the time Giordan had returned to London, with, presumably, Woodmore on his heels, Angelica had been safely retrieved by Dimitri.

Still, the earl was furious with Voss for taking one of the Woodmore sisters while he was responsible for them during their brother's disappearance, and by the tone of his message tonight, he intended to find Voss and square things with him. Which, in Dimitri's mind, likely meant to kill the bastard.

Ever since the incident in Vienna a century ago, when Dimitri's house had gone up in flames, there'd been bad blood between the earl and Voss. This current situation involving Angelica—which the earl would interpret as impertinent and insolent, at the very least, and a grave insult at worst—made the situation even more untenable.

And therefore, Giordan would answer the summons if for no other purpose than to reason Dimitri out of cold-blooded murder, and to help him find Voss if necessary.

Which was, it seemed, how far the bonds of friendship extended.

Blackmont Hall—which was nearly as dreary and cold

as its name and resident suggested—was surrounded by high, smooth, brick walls that were topped with sharp metal and wooden pikes and studded with gas lanterns. The two dozen lamps were lit every night and extinguished every dawn whether the earl was in residence or not. Aside of that structural barrier, Dimitri had an entire retinue of guards—both mortal and make—at his disposal, watching the sisters and the grounds.

If there was a place in London safe from Belial or unwanted guests, it was the Corvindale residence.

Giordan was well-known to the gatekeeper, and he was waved in after he removed the hat and cloak he'd donned against the ever-present drizzle. Crewston, the Blackmont butler, opened the front door and said, "His lordship is in his office with several persons. Including his young wards." His tone indicated his disdain for the inclusion of the two Woodmore sisters in a meeting clearly meant for men only. "Apparently there was some sort of *event* this evening."

Handing his hat and cloak to the butler, Giordan stepped into the foyer and stilled. *Narcise.*

Was. Here.

It was with great effort that he didn't pause in his strides, although he did slow and his movements turned jerky as he walked past Crewston down the corridor. His heart pounded, his blasted hands wanted to become damp, but by the Fates, he wouldn't allow that. He swiped his palms on his trousers and kept walking.

Pausing outside the study door, which had been left slightly ajar in—he suspected—a show of empathy and warning for him by Dimitri, Giordan listened, waiting for an opportune moment to make his entrance. The earl had given him the advantage of surprise, and he was going to make full use of it.

Someone was speaking in tones threaded with distaste. "You must be Narcise Moldavi. The vampire." He recognized the voice wafting through as that of Angelica Woodmore.

"I am." Narcise's voice was low and dusky as it always was, yet it carried a hint of annoyance. Giordan's heart thumped uncomfortably and he squeezed his eyes closed for a moment, nearly missing the Woodmore sister's response.

"Are you here so that we can welcome you to the family?" came Angelica's reply.

Clearly she wasn't any fonder of the idea of Narcise and Woodmore being together than Giordan was.

Or, no, perhaps it wasn't that the two of them were intimate that disturbed Giordan, when one came down to it. It was more the fact that she was here. He'd have to see her. He might even have to speak to her.

All the while pretending his entire insides weren't warring, desperate for her again.

"In fact, mademoiselle, I'm here, endangering my person only because of *you*." He heard the faint clink of a glass over Narcise's voice. She sounded hard and unemotional. "When your brother learned that Voss had abducted you, he insisted on coming to London, despite the danger to me."

Suddenly furious that Narcise would blame the young mortal for her own weaknesses, Giordan opened the door. He stepped inside with smooth, controlled movements, his face expressionless. "You know very well you didn't have to come to London with him. Don't blame your own cowardice on the girl, Narcise."

He couldn't have planned for a better entrance. All eyes swung to him, but he was only looking toward one pair. They flashed with bald shock and a ripple of fear… and then into cold, emotionless sapphires.

Fear, oh, *oui*, it was there. And well it should be. If she had any concept how deeply he struggled to keep himself in the light…how much, even now, after his change, he'd consider risking it, just to grab her by the shoulders, to shake some sense into her—to force her to understand, to *care* about what he'd done.…

The voice in his head, the one of the light, said: *She's not yet ready. She cannot hear you.*

But oh, yes. A woman could indeed drive a man to do what was unimaginable. To do something he could hardly conceive. For love or, just as readily, for hate.

A little shudder of nausea rippled deep in his belly and he pushed away those sordid, awful memories.

Narcise was standing near the liquor cabinet, dressed in masculine clothing. He could see that she'd been disguised as a man—and an elderly gent, if one accounted for the faint lines that had been drawn on her face to emphasize wrinkles and aging. Ironically it was Giordan who'd taught her that trick during his clandestine visits to her. Smudges added to the gauntness of her face…a face that was still as beautiful and perfect as it had always been. A mask covering perfidy and fickleness.

She held a hat that, presumably, had just been removed in an exposure of her gender and identity.

Narcise didn't respond to Giordan's entrance other than to add a flash of fangs to her sneer as she tossed the hat onto a table. Sipping from a glass of whiskey, she walked over to stand deliberately next to Woodmore.

But Giordan was no longer paying attention to her.

He'd turned his back, although he was aware, of course, of precisely where she was standing and how she'd moved. He forced his curling fingers to loosen as he looked at the other occupants in the chamber.

"Miss Woodmore, Angelica, meet my friend Mr. Giordan Cale," Dimitri spoke, rising from his seat in the corner.

"Chas, what in heaven's name is going on here?" Maia Woodmore demanded.

"I've been attempting to tell you," Woodmore replied mildly. "And I will…if we aren't going to have any further interruptions?" He glanced at Narcise, but it wasn't a look of reproach as much as it was one of affection.

Ah, the damned fool loved her.

"You're taking us home, Chas," Maia said firmly, and at that moment, Giordan felt a bit of sympathy for Dimitri. This elder of the sisters was clearly as headstrong and stubborn as her brother—and not nearly as tactful. "Tomorrow." It was more of a command than a question, or even a request.

Narcise shifted, and so did her lover. "I'm afraid that's impossible right now," Woodmore said.

"What do you mean? You're here, you're back. There's no reason for us to stay here any longer," Maia said.

"Don't disappoint the girl, Chas," the earl said. "Take her home." Then he glanced over. "Or perhaps Giordan would like to take on governess duties?"

Giordan snorted in return. "I wouldn't dream of depriving you of the honor, Dimitri." He bared his teeth in a false smile and accepted a glass of much-needed whiskey from the earl. It was all he could do to keep from slugging it down.

"But why can't we go with you, Chas?" demanded Maia.

"Corvindale is and will remain your guardian for the foreseeable future," Woodmore replied flatly, "but I wasn't going to stand aside and let Voss compromise my sister."

"I'm not compromised," Angelica said stubbornly.

"It doesn't matter," Woodmore replied, glancing around the room. "We know he was here tonight, Angelica. Whether you invited him or welcomed him or—"

"I certainly didn't invite him!" The girl was clearly outraged and offended. "I wouldn't invite a terrifying creature like him anywhere!" Apparently she shared her brother's distaste for the befanged Dracule.

"It doesn't matter," Woodmore continued sternly. "Corvindale and Cale are going to help me find him. And then I'm going to kill him."

Giordan kept his tickle of annoyance at Woodmore's assumptions to himself, and felt rather than saw Narcise move to the other side of the chamber behind him. She stayed carefully out of his eyesight. Her essence stirred the air, still as lush and feminine as it had been in Paris… but yet not quite the same.

"Since it appears that you will be under this roof for some further time, Miss Woodmore—Angelica—perhaps you might find your way back to your chambers," Dimitri said abruptly, standing from where he'd been brooding in a corner chair. "The night is waning."

Giordan, who, in some ways knew his friend better than Dimitri knew himself, suspected the man had used up his not very extensive patience. The earl's library and office had been invaded, not to mention his hermitlike lifestyle disrupted by the new additions to his household, and would be, it seemed, for sometime to come.

The earl wanted everyone gone.

In the flurry of the sisters Woodmore bidding goodnight and farewell to their brother, and the earl's insistent ushering of them out of the chamber, Giordan managed to position himself so that Narcise would be unable to quit the room without passing directly by him.

As it happened, whether by accident or Dimitri's intent, Narcise was separated from her lover and left alone in the chamber with Giordan. She would have slipped past him, the cowardly woman, if he hadn't moved a half step to stand in the way. Now she must brush against him if she meant to escape and avoid a conversation.

"Good evening, Narcise," he said.

She was close, so close, that not only her essence but the warmth of her presence surged against him. Yet, he absorbed the assault as if withstanding the force of a blow and would not allow her to escape from his gaze.

"Giordan," she replied in a voice as cool as her icy-sea eyes. An ink-black coil of hair clung to her temple as if it had been smashed there by the heavy hat.

For a moment, he wavered—the darkness, the loathing and disgust, shimmering, threatening to drop like a heavy curtain—but it was just an instant of madness. He recovered himself. "And so you have found your escape at last. My felicitations. I hope it is all that you've dreamed."

Ah, his tones were so easy, so casual and absent of irony, devoid of the shame and anger he felt. The humiliation. They were so loose, unlike his twisting insides, unlike the impossibly tight curling of his fingers.

"It is," she replied in a matching tone. It was as if they'd settled at a café and discussed the weather over coffee and tea whilst overlooking the Palais Gallery.

He made certain he showed no hint of the bloodlust that simmered beneath his skin, throbbing, dark and hot and suddenly insistent.

"My only regret," she said, still looking up at him with eyes as emotionless as a pair of black-mounted amethysts, "is that Cezar still lives."

"What is this?" Giordan responded lightly, oh, yes, still so lightly despite the heaviness threatening his mood. "Your vampire hunter could not complete the task?" Faint surprise and polite regret tinged his words. "I was under the impression that he traveled to Paris for that purpose only."

"Alas, no, for when he found there was a choice between having Cezar and protecting my well-being...well, of course you see how that turned out."

Direct and sharp, her words and meaning stabbed him deeply. And twisted, as if the blade was in his entrails, raking a cross through his insides in the manner of the Japanese *seppuku*.

Nevertheless, he kept his expression emotionless. "If only it were always so simple," was all he replied.

"Narcise." Woodmore's smooth voice interrupted from behind them.

"Chas," she said, brushing rapidly past Giordan as if he were a Corinthian column. The scent of her relief swamped him.

"I'm sorry to keep you waiting. My sisters are a bit overset," said Woodmore, looking down at Narcise and then at Giordan. Comprehension shone in his dark Gypsy eyes. "And Corvindale is fairly apoplectic that Voss has been inside Blackmont Hall."

"Not to mention the fact that his entire household has been upended," Giordan replied with a faint tinge of malice. "For the foreseeable future. I cannot say I blame him."

Woodmore continued to look at him with cool challenge and the faintest of complacence. If the vampire hunter hadn't known before, he knew now at least something of the history between him and Narcise. But if he was under the impression that Giordan would be competition for him, he was sadly mistaken.

"Indeed, and my sisters are just as disrupted. Thus, the first thing to appease everyone—including me—is to find Voss and take care of him. I don't want him anywhere near my sister. Then we can leave London." He looked at Narcise. "And go someplace where you'll be safe."

Corvindale returned at that moment. "Are you leaving now? Excellent. Good night." His expression and tone left no room for further conversation, and giving Giordan a wry look, Woodmore gestured for Narcise to start down the corridor.

"We are gone, then," he said. "Dawn is almost here. I'll see what sign I can find of Voss while the sun is up. Look for word from me in the afternoon. If luck is with me, I'll find the bastard and stake him in his sleep."

"By the Fates, you look as if you need a drink," Dimitri said to Giordan as soon as they were gone. "The Devil knows I do. Bloody damned women."

By Luce's dark soul, it wasn't a drink he needed. "No," Giordan said. "I'll take my leave before the sun is up."

And he followed Woodmore and Narcise's path down the hall, inhaling her essence in his wake.

No, indeed. It wasn't a damn drink he craved.

"You aren't truly going."

Chas paused in his packing to look up at the tone of accusation in Narcise's voice.

"Of course I'm going," he replied firmly, shoving a trio of stakes into his leather sack. "She's my *sister*, Narcise. Do you think I would leave her safety up to chance? Especially with Voss?"

Two weeks after their gathering in Dimitri's study, Angelica had been abducted by Belial. According to Voss—who'd seemed unaccountably concerned—she was being taken to Paris to be delivered to Cezar.

The other vampire had been convincing in his argument that *he,* Voss, should be the one to go after her and bring her home, despite the fact that Angelica's own brother was a *vampir* hunter. And though even Dimitri's stubborn opinion had been swayed by Voss's points, Chas wasn't about to sit on his hands while his sister's fate was in the hands of a bloody damned vampire.

Especially one who'd already attacked her once. And who'd sneaked into her chamber and done God knew what else while she was under his thrall.

He shoved a clean shirt into the pack with more violence than necessary. The only reason Voss wasn't dead right now was that he'd been wearing protective armor when Chas had seen him last, when he'd come to White's club to deliver the news that Angelica was on her way to Paris. And because the damned man was right—he *could* gain access to Cezar.

"But Voss is smart enough, and Cezar likes him because he always has information he wants." Narcise argued the same points that had been made previously. "For sale, of course. He won't be suspicious of him, so Voss will have no problem getting in. And with those smoke-cloud packets you gave him, he'll have an easy way to escape."

Chas stopped and gave her a hard look. "I don't want him anywhere near my sister. Not only do I not trust him, not only have I heard legend upon legend of him ruining women, but he is also a Dracule."

The moment those words slipped from his mouth, Chas regretted them. Not the sentiment of course, but the way he'd expressed it, for Narcise's beautiful face blanched.

"And so you can commingle with we Dracule, we damned and damaged demons…but not your sister."

Her words were bitter, and Chas felt a wave of self-disgust—for the memory of himself panting beneath her, blind with need, ensorcelled by her texture, taste and scent…and begging for her to tear into him with her fangs…burned tauntingly in his mind.

And yet…it was no mere lust that drove him. There was something much deeper in his heart. If only he could reconcile it with who she was: immortal, damaged and bound to a demon.

"Blast it, no, Narcise." He shoved his fingers through his hair and resisted the urge to throw something. "It's different for her than for me. I understand what I—I understand what it's like." He'd been hunting the creatures for years. He knew their faults, their weaknesses. Their pure center of *self.*

He fully comprehended what he was doing to himself by being with one. Unlike his naive sister.

"Well, Chas, I suggest you begin to help her understand. Because from the way she was acting that night in Dimitri's study, I wouldn't be surprised if Angelica was in love with Voss. And she doesn't know what to do about it. She probably doesn't even realize it."

Over my bloody damned dead body.

"Never," he snapped, yanking up his satchel. By God, he'd *never* wish such a thing on his sister: to be in love with one of these warped-souled beings. It was an untenable hell of its own. "And even if she fancies herself in love with him, I won't permit it. I'll kill him first."

"I'll come with you, Chas," she said, standing in a swirl of dark hair and smooth slide of her pale gown.

"Don't be a fool," he said, his voice softening. "You can't allow yourself anywhere near Cezar. Paris might be a big city, but you know as well as I do that he has spies and makes everywhere. I won't risk you, Narcise."

"It was almost impossible for us to leave Paris safely the *last* time," Narcise was arguing. "Cezar still has makes and mortal soldiers watching for us everywhere… you know it. You'll never get out of the city again, with or without Angelica. Let alone into Cezar's place."

Chas wondered whether she was more terrified that he was leaving her alone, or that he might not come back.

Or that she might have to see Giordan Cale again.

He reminded her, "But the last time *you* were with me, and he was searching for you—"

"But, Chas…"

"And aside of that, Cezar would see me. You know that for certain. He'd be delighted to welcome me back into his lair."

He didn't understand why she was being so unreasonable…so uncharacteristically weak. Narcise was the strongest woman he'd ever known—how else could she have survived her years of captivity with her brother?

Surely it wasn't just that she was frightened of being left in London. A little niggle of certainty wormed into the back of his mind and he thrust it away. No. Surely whatever had been between her and Cale was truly over and done with. The hatred between them had rolled off in palpable waves.

Between Dimitri and Rubey, who was intimate with Cale, he would find out what their history was.

"Chas, please," Narcise begged, and a wave of anger rushed through him.

"Don't insult me by implying your brother is more than a match for me," he said flatly. "If we knew what his Asthenia was, I'd have brought it to him long ago." Even as he said these words, he realized the argument was weak. But he didn't have a choice. Angelica was in danger, and he wasn't about to sit back and place her safety in Voss's hands.

And if he had the time to go to Scotland, to visit Sonia and beg her to help him one more time, Chas could learn what Cezar's Asthenia was. While Angelica had visions of people in their moment of death, their youngest sister had a different gift. She was able to see what a person feared the most—and for the Dracule, it was the Asthenia.

Chas had used Sonia more than once in the past to help him learn the specific weakness of a vampire he was hunting, but once she learned why he was asking for her help, she'd refused to be part of it. "Neither of us have the right to make such judgment," she'd told him piously.

"But you've been given a gift…and so have I," he'd argued back. "We're meant to use them."

"No," she'd said…and he'd recognized fear lurking in her eyes.

But he was certain she'd help him this time—to find Cezar's weakness, knowing that their sister's safety was at stake…yet, there was no time now. He'd have to trust Voss to carry out their plan and free Angelica…and as soon as he could, Chas would relieve his sister from the vampire's presence.

And then he'd kill Voss.

Chas looked at Narcise, filling his eyes with her. He never tired of her beauty, he never lost the awe he felt when he looked upon her perfection, and although it was blasphemy—terrible, shameful blasphemy—he thought what a boon it was that Lucifer had turned her immortal. That her looks would never fade, that her face and figure would never age.

It would have been a shame to lose such exquisiteness. Such artistry.

"You'll be safe here, Narcise," Chas said, gesturing to the stone walls around them. The quarters he'd prepared for her were in the cellar of an old monastery ruin.

Perhaps two years ago, he'd flushed out and chased away a group of made *vampirs* who'd used the place as a haven. The only access to the cellar was through an old wall in a cemetery that sat on one of the hills on the outskirts of London, and the entrance was well-hidden. Aside of that, there was a barrier of crosses and other religious markings that would keep vampires away—with only one secret passage through which one might manage to gain access. He'd had to help Narcise across that threshold in order to be safely contained, and it had been some time until she regained her full strength.

Thus, he knew she'd be safe here. Not only did Narcise, armed with her saber and vampire strength, know how to take care of herself—but no one would find her or cross over into the place…unless Chas wanted them to.

He drank in the sight of her again and felt something painful twist deeply inside him. He *would* return to her. And he'd find some way to manage loving an immortal with a warped soul.

"You'll be safe here, Narcise. He won't find you, and then when I get back we'll go to Wales."

"Very well," she acceded. Her gaze settled on him and he recognized a tinge of fear…and something softening her eyes.

His heart tripped and a wave of desire and uncertainty rushed over him. He would come back. But would she still be here?

Chas dropped his satchel and went to her, striding across the room and pushing her back against the rough wall. He took her mouth, covering her lips with his in a deep, needy kiss.

Sweet and warm and lush, she melted against him, her fingers cupping the back of his head, pulling him down into her. Chas closed his eyes, memorizing her, feeling every curve and rise of her body printed against his. *I love you.*

"Be safe," she breathed as he pulled away to catch a breath, staggered by the force of his emotions. "Come back to me." She reached up to touch his face, her fingers gentle along his jaw, brushing his hair back.

A ripple of fear shimmered in his middle. "I'm in love with you, Narcise. Make no mistake…I'll return. But…" he said, all at once knowing what he had to do. Knowing he had to take the chance. He had to *know.* "While I'm gone, you have other things to attend to."

Narcise blinked, her eyes wary and confused.

"Do what you must do," he said steadily, trying not to think of what could happen, "to let go of the past. Otherwise…" His lips tightened. "I love you, but I won't wait for you to come to love me."

No. She had to free her heart from whatever kept it locked up, away from him. And then…somehow, he'd figure out a way for them to be together.

A vampire hunter and an immortal woman with a warped soul.

As he caught up his satchel and swept from the chamber, her last words followed him. "I can't lose you, Chas."

She wouldn't.

But how would he go on if he lost her?

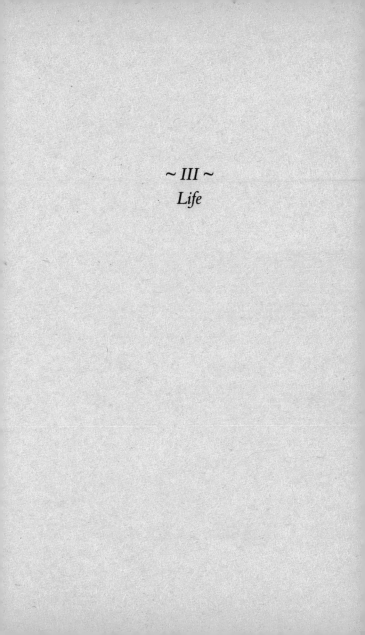

~ *III* ~
Life

17

September 1804

Narcise stared out the carriage window. The rough, craggy hills of Scotland had long given way to the more rolling familiar green ones of England, and now that she and Chas were nearing London, the land had flattened even more.

The roads were crowded now, straight, and lined with rows of houses…and the *smells!* Even if she'd not been peering from the window, Narcise would have known they were approaching the city, for the air was filled with all of the aromas and odors—pleasant and otherwise—that came with it.

Angled back from the dangerous sunlight that still managed to filter through a blanket of clouds, Narcise settled in the corner of the carriage and watched the slices of life from her restricted vantage point.

So many things had happened since her arrival in London, and that unsettling night at Dimitri's home, that she could hardly conceive of it all.

The fact that she'd seen Giordan was only the least

of it...or that was what she tried to tell herself when she woke, damp and warm, from unwanted dreams.

And dark nightmares. Narcise's insides tightened.

She glanced at Chas, grateful for a distraction. He looked almost angelic—an odd thought, to be sure, about a man who lived a life of such violence, always hunting, always killing—with the waves of his dark hair swirling around a face slack with repose. His lips were full and sensual, and his nose, straight and prominent beneath eyes fringed with heavy dark lashes.

He'd been to Paris and back since that night he'd left her in the old monastery ruins. Angelica was safely returned to London, and to the surprise of everyone, Voss had been instrumental in the girl's release. Yet, because Voss had already freed Angelica by the time Chas had found them, Cezar still lived safely in the bowels of Paris. Chas had brought his sister safely back to London, but meanwhile, he was even more determined to find a way to kill Cezar.

And now, something inconceivable had happened.

Voss and Angelica were to wed...and Voss had done the impossible: he'd somehow thrown off the bonds of his covenant with Lucifer. He was mortal and man once again, and it was only because of this change that Chas had agreed to give his permission for them to wed.

Now, he stirred, shifting, his heavy boots brushing the hem of her skirts where they mingled about her feet at the bottom of the carriage. Since all of this had happened, Narcise had seen the hunger in his eyes, the desperation and hope that somehow, something might change for her.

That she, too, might shed her allegiance to the Devil and become a mortal woman that he could love without reserve.

For, since his return from Paris, Chas had changed

as well. The pain was deeper in his eyes, grooved more sharply at the corners of his mouth, and she could fairly feel the battle he fought with himself as he came to her. He loved her, of that she was certain, but he still hated himself for it.

And, of course, love was not only as long as one's lifetime, but also a concept of selflessness…something that, still, a Dracule like Narcise couldn't fully embrace. Chas seemed even more fully aware of that than ever.

And as if he knew he'd lost a battle, but was determined to win the war by maintaining his hold, Lucifer had raged in her mind and in her body. Her Mark blazed and roiled with his fury and control, reminding her that there was no way out.

At least for her.

She hadn't even been able to leave the carriage when she and Chas reached St. Bridie's—the convent school deep in rugged Scotland where his youngest sister Sonia lived. The religious symbols and holy presence were too much for her, a woman who bore the Mark of the Devil, and she was forced to wait while Chas went inside.

There'd been those religious markings throughout the monastery cellar where Chas had left her while he went to Paris. They'd formed a safe barrier against any immortal finding his or her way into the old safe haven.

But what haunted Narcise, what she tried to banish from her thoughts, was the fact that somehow, Giordan had not only found her there…but he'd come into the chamber by crossing that barrier only hours after Chas had left.

She'd met him at the door, saber in hand, heart racing madly out of control.

"Woodmore sent me," Giordan had claimed coolly.

"He indicated there was something I was to retrieve. Now that I've arrived, I can only presume he meant you."

"Certainly not," Narcise had replied, trying to keep her breathing steady. She'd cut his hand with her saber—or, rather, he'd sliced his palm open when he yanked her blade away. And his bloodscent filled the air. Her fangs threatened to shoot free. Her knees felt as if they were about to give way. "I'm to stay here—perfectly safe—until his return with Angelica."

"And if he doesn't return?" Giordan had walked across the floor to wipe the blood from his wound. Slowly. So slowly, as if to allow her plenty of time to inhale his scent…to watch his body with its sleek, confident movements. He seemed to fill the room.

"I'll go to Dimitri. He'll protect me," she'd managed to respond.

"I never thought of you as one who needs protection, Narcise. You take very good care of yourself."

"Except when I'm locked away by my brother."

Giordan looked at her. His eyes were cold and flat brown today, icy and blank and so very angry. "Even then, you were formidable," he said. "In your own way."

"I don't know why Chas sent you here, but I'm not leaving. Especially with you. Just go." *Please. Go.*

"You don't know why he sent me here?" His laugh was more like a whip crack than a bell of humor. "I certainly do. Here, where I could smell him all over you. Where I could scent both of you on the bed and against the wall and everywhere else. The entire place reeks of you two, together. That, my dear, is why he sent me here."

She had to taunt him, to drive him away. "Then why prolong the agony, Giordan? There's no reason for you to stay and stew in your jealousy."

And that was when he'd moved. The next thing she

knew, he was there, right there, so close, in front of her. His fingers gripped her chin. The scent of his blood so close made her dizzy. The smell of him, the warmth, the familiarity… She summoned the image of him with Cezar, the two bare shoulders, one golden and sleek, the other swarthy and frail, the firelight playing intimately over them.

Nausea pitched in her belly and her awareness of him returned to loathing.

"Jealousy? You believe that's what I feel? You're a fool, Narcise." He shifted his fingers to cup her jaw no less gently. "If I still wanted you, a bloody damned vampire hunter wouldn't keep me away."

And then he'd kissed her.

Not savagely, not as she'd expected, with his eyes blazing red and his fangs long and sharp…but so gently and softly. As if he were taking a moment to savor. Lightly, lightly, over her lips…

And Lucifer's black soul, she'd kissed him back. She'd fallen into the moment of heat and desire, the memory and beauty rushing through her—

And then Giordan had thrust her away, his eyes hot and knowing, arrogance in the very essence of his body. And disgust, there, too.

"We're nearly there."

Chas's voice, rough with sleep, sudden in the silence, jolted Narcise from her memory. Her cheeks blazed with shameful heat, her heart thudded as if she'd been caught doing something she shouldn't even as she felt a renewed surge of hatred for Giordan and his games…and the twinge in her Mark reminded her of who she was.

"To Rubey's," Chas added, as if responding to her startled look. "She'll feed us, and we can rest. I can also use her messengers to get word to Dimitri and Voss that we've returned." His voice flattened a bit at the mention of his future brother-in-law.

"I thought Rubey's was a pleasure house," Narcise replied with an arch look, forcing herself firmly into the present.

Chas's mouth twitched becomingly. "It is, but it's much more than that. The Dracule also use it as a central location to meet up and for communication. She houses a flock of blood pigeons there…and sometimes, Rubey's is preferable to White's. It's more comfortable and, as Dimitri would say, there aren't any mortals about, making ludicrous bets in their blasted book. And as I said… she'll feed us. Or, me, at any rate," he added quickly.

"Did you send Giordan to me? When you left for Paris?" Narcise asked.

The bit of levity drained from Chas's face and he sat upright. His expression had gone carefully blank. "I don't know exactly what occurred between you and him," he said, "but it's clear to me that whatever it was has made you unwilling to trust or love."

Not quite an admission, but close enough.

A spike of anger shot through Narcise, and her Mark eased in agreement. "What happened with Giordan has nothing to do with how I feel about you," she responded sharply. "I care about you…I desire you and enjoy being with you. But, as you're fully aware, Chas, I'm a Dracule. I am a selfish, self-serving, damned soul—and I'm immortal. Loving anyone besides myself is in direct opposition to who I am…to who we of the Draculia are. Who Luce has forced us to be."

His face tightened and she saw the flare of hurt and anger in his hazel eyes. "You made the choice." He spoke hardly loudly enough to be heard over the rumble of the carriage. "To be that way."

Pain sliced through her, not from her Mark—it was strangely quiet—but from her heart, down to her deepest core. A choice? The thought was ludicrous. How could anyone make a clear decision when they were tricked and manipulated in their dreams by the most cunning demon of all?

In her case, it had been the choice between living a forever youthful, immortal life as a great beauty or one with a no longer perfect face, burned down one side of her cheek. The result would have been one of horror, with ropy, burned-away flesh where her smooth skin had once been.

In her dreams, Lucifer had helpfully shown her the image of what she would have been like after the burn healed…and offered her a way out. For a twenty-year-old girl whose vanity knew no bounds, there was hardly a choice. She had no real comprehension of the deal she'd made.

And…she realized later that Cezar must have arranged the incident that caused hot oil to splash and spill on her. It came from a lamp mounted high on the stairwell she frequently used. Her brother didn't want to live his immortal life alone…he wanted to live it with her.

In spite of his controlling, abusive ways, he worshipped her.

"Don't you ever regret it? Don't you ever want to change it?" Chas persisted, drawing her back from those horrible memories.

She held back a snort of disgust. "Do I want to be beholden to Lucifer? Do I want to be damned?" She shook her head, suddenly empty and dark everywhere. A cold knot sat heavily in her stomach. "Just because Voss claims a miracle happened doesn't mean it will happen to me. Hasn't Dimitri been trying for a century to break his ties with Lucifer?"

Her Mark was throbbing now, and she could feel its rootlike lines raging through her skin like tiny rivers of fire. She breathed deeply, trying to send the pain away.

Chas sank back into his corner, his expression weary and shadowed: another tacit admission. "Yes. There seems to be no way." His voice was bitter and soft. His eyes were closed and he became bathed in gray shadow.

"Chas," she began, then her voice filtered away. What was there to say? Her heart stirred for him in some soft, unlustful emotion, and her Mark raged so sharply that she had to smother a gasp. Lucifer had no patience for sympathy.

They trundled along in silence, the cloudy day filled with the sounds of city life: shouts, calls, barking, rumbling, clashing and rattling. The smells of baking bread, of coal smoke, of wet animal and roasting meat, of stagnant water and rotting waste.

Chas looked at her suddenly, from where he brooded in the corner. His eyes gleamed in the shadows and they fixed on her, dark and steady. "You once said you knew of no one who was visited by Lucifer and who yet declined the Devil's bargain. But that isn't true. You do know someone who has."

Somehow, Narcise was able to ignore the shuttle of renewed heat blasting over her shoulder's Mark. "Who is that?" she asked, suddenly feeling light of head. Suddenly afraid she understood.

"Me."

They arrived at Rubey's late in the afternoon of a dreary, foggy day.

Narcise was still stunned and silent from Chas's confession, and he, for his part, had offered no other details. When she pressed him, he merely shook his head, closed his eyes and replied, "I've never told another soul. There's a reason I don't want to talk about it."

But now, at least, she understood his consistent, barely concealed disgust toward those of her race—those who had made what he clearly saw as the wrong decision.

How fitting, in a terrible, ironic way, that he should be judge, jury and executioner of those very people. For he could have been one of them himself.

Inside Rubey's, Narcise was whisked away for a warm bath—something their hostess was particularly fond of herself, according to the maid—and Chas disappeared in another direction, presumably to eat and clean up after the grueling journey.

As she settled in the large vessel of steaming water, Narcise was offered a sip of dark red libation from her choice of three small decanters. The cup was no larger than a sherry glass, fluted with tuliplike edges, and hardly taller than her little finger.

Narcise smelled the three options and selected the lightest of them. It wasn't until she actually sipped that she realized the drink was laced with… "What's in it? Some sort of elixir?" she asked the maid, who'd begun to wash her hair.

"Mistress Rubey's finest," was the vague reply. "She 'as a few such for the likes of ye. Some-at for rest, some-at for waking, some-at for…ye ken-at."

Narcise blinked. Her English was still that bit better than her French, but this moon-faced young woman's accent was so thick and her slang difficult to follow that she wasn't at all certain what she'd just been told. But she settled back into the hot, scented water and sipped as her hair was scrubbed and her head massaged.

Sometime later, the water had cooled and the maid had gone. Narcise settled in an armchair in front of the hearth, swaddled in a thick quilted wrapper with her damp hair drying in the fire's heat. From the street below, the sounds of living wafted up through the half-shuttered windows.

The sun was nearly gone, and Narcise imagined there were young ladies like Angelica and Maia Woodmore preparing for visits to the theater or to dances…and the men to visit their clubs or to escort their women to parties. There would be courtship and romance; perhaps erotic interludes in dark corners, gossip and rumors, giggling and whispering…

And the tradesmen were closing up their shops, and the businessmen their offices, and the mamas were sending their children off to bed with or without a governess—depending upon in which area of town they lived—and the lords were leaving Westminster after a contentious day of arguments and debates.

Life.

Narcise breathed deeply of the fresh air, which was rapidly cooling with the loss of the sun. Although it was only late September, the air was damp and bone-chilling, reminding her of her girlhood in Romania.

Despite the cold and damp, she'd had a comfortable life there, for her father was a close confidant of the ruler of their province. With two older brothers, one of whom married the *voivode*'s daughter and was the conduit for Cezar's eventual gain of that throne, Narcise had been spoiled and petted and worshipped by family and neighbor alike.

She'd thought to marry one day, and the young, virile Rivrik had been her first real lover. She likely would have wed him if things hadn't changed…if Cezar hadn't found his savior in Lucifer and manipulated their lives into what they were now.

She closed her eyes and thought about where she'd been, what she'd dreamed of…and what was to become of her now.

There would be no wedding a man and bearing children, which was what she'd always hoped for as a girl. No family, no household to run. No friends with whom to gossip.

During the years of captivity with her brother, her only goal had been freedom—she'd never thought about what her life would be once she had her independence.

But now that she had freedom, now that she no longer had a goal to strive for and to dream about…what did she have?

Who would she be? What would she do, day after day? How would she pass this immortal, infinite life that would, on some Judgment Day, end with her entwined with Lucifer in hell forever?

This wasn't the first time these thoughts had entered her mind, but on this occasion, she was unable to dismiss the niggling and nagging that settled in her mind.

It had been well over a hundred years since she'd had a *choice*—what to wear, what to do, where to go and with whom to go. But now that she had it…what now?

The thought of centuries upon centuries stretching on and on into forever… The wrapper had become as stifling as her thoughts and Narcise tossed it away. Standing, she paced the chamber, dressed only in a thin, borrowed chemise, her damp hair seeping through the fabric over her back and shoulders.

Since leaving Paris, she'd either been hiding or traveling or waiting for someone to tell her what to do—none of which was particularly fulfilling or pleasant.

It was not something she meant to do for the rest of her life.

Beginning now.

Spurred by the jolt of decision, she rang for the maid. At least she could leave this room and find Chas below with their Irish-flavored hostess.

Rubey had been warmly welcoming, although Narcise had felt the weight of more than casual attention as she glanced over her. The proprietress sported shiny, curling hair that conveniently (and possibly unnaturally) complemented her name: it was reddish-blond and had been done up in a most fashionable style, with little curls around her cheeks and sparkling combs tucked in place. Her clothing was just as modern and extremely well-made, and Rubey's silk gown of robin's-egg blue had made Narcise feel as if her muslin day dress was little more than a servant's castoff, which was part of the reason she'd eagerly accepted the offer of a bath before taking any time for conversation.

The other woman was younger and more attractive than Narcise had expected, for the establishment had been a popular place for the Dracule for decades. She'd expected someone much older than the two-score Rubey appeared to be—and a well-preserved four decades she was.

The maid was as efficient and businesslike as her employer, and when Narcise was dressed in a much cleaner, softer and more becoming gown than her muslin print she took her leave from the chamber and slipped out into the hall without waiting for the maid's direction.

Rubey was obviously a successful proprietress, if the decor and luxurious appointment of her house was any indication. But Narcise wasted little time admiring the ornate mirrors and elegant furnishings, although she did pause at some of the paintings. There was a Vermeer! And a van Honthorst that made her smile because it was so appropriate for a house of pleasure: a woman playing a lute, which was a blatant sexual pun.

But even the mastery of the Dutch painters wasn't enough to keep her from her need to move. Suddenly all she wanted was to be alone, and away from everyone in this place.

She wanted to be out, under the night sky, *alone*…for the first time in more than a century.

She was done with huddling and hiding.

Narcise's excellent hearing and sense of smell allowed her to avoid the various servants and other occupants of the pleasure house, including Chas, whose voice was coming from behind a door on the first floor. The low, lyrical responses were obviously from the Irish proprietress, and Narcise didn't wait to learn the topic of their conversation.

She found her way to a side door and slipped outside.

Her hair was still damp, but despite the lift of the cooling breeze, Narcise wasn't cold. She was *free!*

This little alleyway was silent and dim, but beyond, Narcise could hear the sounds of the rest of the world. As she made her way out of the narrow space between the house and its neighbor, she felt the air stir. With the soft buffet came the scent of something familiar and pleasant…damp wool and cedar. It reminded her of Giordan, and she paused with one hand resting against ivy-covered brick.

Her heart pounded and she listened, lifting her nose to better smell the breeze…but the aroma was gone as quickly as it had come and she heard nothing. A phantom memory perhaps, or another man who wore wool and the scent of cedar.

When she moved at last, a brief shower of drops sprinkled onto her shoulders and head from the fog-drenched ivy and she stepped out into the street.

From the front, Rubey's establishment rose as high and forbidding as the home of a *duc* back in Paris, with many windows and an intimidating entrance. Narcise had learned that the proprietress actually lived in a smaller home nearby, and she wondered that a woman was able to keep up and furnish two such residences.

Then she walked brusquely past the pleasure house, with no destination in mind, but wholly aware of the fact that she had never, ever walked on a city street by herself. And that she had no one to return or answer to.

Exhilaration spurred her and she drew in a deep breath, becoming more aware of her surroundings, hardly noticing that she was the only pedestrian not dressed in a cloak or other evening wrap. Carriages clattered by, couples walked together or in groups, dogs slinked in alleys and cats peered from the lengthening shadows.

Narcise walked and walked, through the affluent residential area where Rubey's was located and, after many turns and crossing two small squares, onto a street lined with shops now closed for the evening. She passed a theater or some place of entertainment, noticing conveyances lined up, waiting for their riders to return, and night watchmen strolling along.

"Well, now, ain't this a foin surprise."

Narcise halted when a large hulk of a man emerged from a dark spot between two buildings to block her way. She realized belatedly that she'd turned down a passage that was deserted but for a slight figure in the distance, just turning the corner onto another street. It was a narrow way, with a sewage canal on one side, and lined on the other by houses or shops with dark windows—either vacant or filled with slumbering residents.

Something moved behind her, and from the corner of her eye, she saw two more shadows sliding into the glancing moonlight in her wake.

A little trip of unease quickly faded. Not only were these mere mortal men, but she was neither a captive nor prisoner weakened by a necklace of sparrow feathers.

"I tol' ye, Griff, it would be a lucky even'n', comin' out this a-way," said one of the others, nearer now, behind her. His companions laughed in agreement.

They moved closer, bringing their smells of desperation and lust, as the first one smiled and reached lazily for her. "An' she's a looker, ain't she?"

She smiled back. Allowed her eyes to glow just a bit of red. "Take your hand off me," she said calmly—and was delighted when the fool didn't comply.

Instead he laughed and tugged her closer to him so that she bumped against his torso. He reeked of sweat and smoke and old ale, and despite her height, he was taller than she. "A furriner, listen to 'er, will ye," he said. "Well, we'll 'ave to show the lady a good time 'ere in ole Londontown, aye, boys?"

The other two were just behind Narcise, blocking any escape she might attempt, and one of them slid his hand down her spine and over her rear, his fingers scoping intimately around the bottom cleft of her arse. Narcise's reflexive spark of fear at being touched dissolved instantly and she slid into action. With one smooth move, she flung the big man's hand away and spun to face the one who'd groped her.

Grabbing him by a woolen coat crusty with stains and smelling of smoke and vomit, Narcise lifted him up and tossed him into the air. His arms flailed as he flew back against a shuttered window on the brick wall.

"'Ey!" shouted the big man, as if offended and affronted by her reaction. "Wot the hell d'ye think yer doin, foin lady?" He lunged for Narcise again, but she easily ducked out of his way and then grabbed his arm, using his own weight and momentum against him.

"I told you to take your hands off me," she reminded him as she spun him sharply into the third man. They tumbled together like a load of boulders and she stood over them, looking down as they scrambled to their feet in fury. Her pulse had kicked up and she felt a rush of energy through her. Even her Mark was more at ease than it had been for days.

"Ye loose-lipped bitch," growled the big oaf, and his insult was echoed by the one she'd whipped into the wall a moment ago. The three of them, as cowards often do, shouted encouragement to each other as they bolted toward her in a rage.

Narcise didn't flinch, and in fact, was enjoying herself as she fought them off. Despite her restrictive clothing— a corset, slippers, and shoe-length skirts—and the loose braid that whipped around with her every movement, she was quick and efficient. It was a testament to their stupidity that it took three rounds before they realized she would neither go with them, nor suffer being touched. She didn't even have to bare her fangs in order to stave them off—it was a matter of strength and speed, both of which she had as an advantage over the three men.

When they were at last in an unmoving heap on the ground, their noses bloodied—the scent not even the least bit tempting to her—and lips cut, perhaps an arm broken or an eye blackened, she stood over them. "Don't ever accost a woman again. The next time, I'll kill you."

The largest one whimpered when she bared her fangs at last and swooped toward him, her eyes glowing bright and red as she yanked him up by his shirt. "Do you understand?" she demanded, breathing through her mouth so as not to inhale his putrid odor, now colored with the scent of terror.

"A-aye," he managed to say, closing his eyes and turning away as if expecting her to take a hunk out of his skin.

"Good," she breathed, and licked her lips enticingly. "Because I'll be watching you…and the next time you even look at a woman, I'll find you. And I'll be hungry." She showed him her fangs, long and wicked.

Then she smelled the pungent odor of fresh urine and shoved him toward the half wall along the sewer, satisfied that he'd been well and truly frightened. "Go off with you. All of you," she ordered, standing there in the dark street, feeling as strong as she'd ever felt—as powerful, as sure of herself.

And as her would-be attackers scuttled off into the night like frightened beetles, she felt a bubble of laughter come up from inside her. Joyous and warm, delight swelled inside her as she realized who she was.

And what she could do. And—

"How startling. I don't believe I've ever heard you laugh."

Narcise's stomach seemed to plummet to the ground. Choking off her laughter, she spun, her insides turning inside out and upside down, her thoughts scattering. "What are you doing here?" she managed to say as she swallowed her heart and felt her cheeks burn.

Giordan sauntered toward her with studied casualness. The moon was kind to him, filtering silvery light over the thick, dark curls on his head and the broad shoulders encased in a dark coat. It was open to reveal a silver-buttoned waistcoat and white shirt, brilliant and crisp, fairly glowing in the low light. His boots were soundless and his eyes dark and glittering, focusing on Narcise with unpleasant intensity. His comment had been laced with irony.

"I've been following you since you left Rubey's," he said. "At first I thought you had a destination in mind… but then I realized you were simply walking."

So she *had* scented him, and, Giordan being the cunning, manipulative man he was, had probably kept himself downwind from her as he followed her through the streets. Bastard.

Their eyes met and Narcise found that she couldn't pull hers away. Her heart pounded high in her throat and she tried to dig down inside to pull out her anger and revulsion toward him…this man who'd destroyed her.

This man who was looking at her as if he'd never seen her before.

"I thought—" She stopped herself. She had nothing to say to him. Nothing at all.

"If I didn't feel such sympathy for the way you flayed those poor bastards, I'd have found the entire scene more than a little amusing," he said, gesturing in the direction where the cowardly beetles had gone. "Is that why you were laughing?" His tone had softened, perhaps, a bit.

She drew herself up, still searching for that deep betrayed feeling, and replied, "No." Her fingers were shaking and her insides were doing unpleasant and pleasant things at the same time.

Handsome as sin he might be, familiar and beautifully scented…but she couldn't feel anything for him. Nothing but that old hatred and revulsion. She stoked it so that it burned stronger inside her, giving her a barrier behind which to hide.

She told herself that she had nothing to say to him, that she had no desire to even be near him, yet her mouth moved and the words came out before she could stop them. "Why are you following me? Surely you don't think I need protection."

"Are you going to Paris?" he asked, stepping closer, pinning her with his eyes.

"Are you mad? Go back there? *Never.*"

He nodded briefly. "I didn't think you'd be that foolish."

Giordan was very close now, standing so that his scent filled her every breath, overwhelming even that of the nearby sewer, battling for her consciousness. Her insides fluttered wildly and Narcise felt a rush of heat and desire. She swallowed hard, willing herself to step back and away…but her feet wouldn't move.

His eyes found hers, holding her gaze and her heart thumped madly as he came nearer. She took a step back and he smiled knowingly.

"What are you afraid of, Narcise?" he taunted, his gaze melting into something hot and warm.

All she need do was turn and walk away from him. There was nothing more she needed or wanted to say to him. She didn't want to even breathe him in the air.

But her knees trembled and she felt a rise of heat billowing, filling her. "I'm not afraid of you," she replied, even though her veins were pounding and surging, reacting to his nearness. Her eyes were drawn to his mouth, his lips slightly parted, full and beautifully shaped in the silvery moonlight. *No.*

"No?" he asked sardonically.

"Why were you following me? Because you thought I was going to *Paris?*" she asked, desperate to change the subject…and to ease away from him. His glittering gaze made her insides tickle and flutter.

"Either that or you were making an escape from your vampire hunter," Giordan replied. "Is that why you were sneaking off from Rubey's? Have you tired of Chas Woodmore now that he's served his purpose?"

She knew that to respond was just to bait him, to continue to keep him there, looking at her with his cold eyes. But, though she ignored his obvious lure into a discussion about Chas, she had to know something else. "Why would you think I'd go back to Paris?"

The moonbeams played over his face, swathing half of his square chin and mobile lips in silvery light and leaving the other side in shadow. His gaze searched hers and her heart skipped a little. She willed it to stop jumping around.

"Woodmore went to Scotland to see his sister. Weren't you with him?"

"I couldn't go into the convent," she replied. "Luce's hold is too strong for me to enter. But I'd like to know how you were able to enter the old monastery—"

"So that's why," he murmured, half to himself. "He didn't tell you what he learned about your brother." A little ironic smile twitched at the corner of his mouth. "He doesn't trust you. Imagine that."

"What are you talking about?" Narcise demanded stridently enough that a trio of passersby paused and looked over at them. She turned her back to them.

"Perhaps you'd best ask your lover what he doesn't want you to know," Giordan replied.

"How can you know about what happened in Scotland?" she said from between clenched teeth. How could *he* know when Chas hadn't even told *her?* He'd been vague when she asked, telling her that Sonia hadn't had a clear vision and he hoped to get a message from her later with more information.

Which meant that Chas had either lied to her or... something.

"I know because he told Rubey, and Rubey tells me everything," Giordan said. His accompanying smile was both condescending and meaningful. "She has nothing to hide from me."

Rubey. A little shaft of pain zipped through her as she realized the layers of meaning there. Narcise struggled for something to say that would wound him right back. "Rubey?"

He merely held his smile in place and looked at her.

Narcise's mouth tightened as a wave of memory and hatred rushed over her. She'd trusted him, opened herself up to caring about him...and he'd destroyed her. "I certainly hope she doesn't have a brother," she said stiffly. "I don't think she'd take kindly to a betrayal when she's served *her* purpose."

Even in the faulty light, she saw his expression settle into one cold and hard. "There can be no betrayal, for there's no love between us."

Frustration and pain reared inside her and her vision tinged red. "There's never any love with a Dracule. Lust and the moment of pleasure, yes, always...but love?" she scoffed. "Never."

"I loved you." He spoke so quietly his words were nearly lost by the sound of a passing carriage...yet they rang hard and cold and angry.

"You *used* me, Giordan. I believed you were trying to build my trust, that you truly cared about me. You did everything so perfectly when all along, you had other interests. It took me some time, but I finally realized why you never wanted Cezar to know we were...were friends.

Lovers. Because you didn't want to ruin your chances
with him. He was the bigger prize, wasn't he?"

She hardly comprehended what she was saying, just
that she'd waited so long to spew her hatred and agony
at him. She wanted him to understand what he'd done to
her. She wanted to inflict the same pain on him, but she
didn't know how, other than words. "Of course you would
want him. He was the one with the power, with all of the
money and control. I was merely a way to get to him."

"You believe that?" he said, his words choked and
low. His hand whipped out and his fingers closed around
the front of her gown. "You truly believe that I wanted
Cezar? Even after *this?*" He gave her a rough jerk and
she flew up against him.

His mouth covered hers, hard and warm and angry,
and Narcise closed her eyes at the familiar taste of Giordan, the demanding press of his lips, sliding against
hers…roughly forcing her mouth open to take the sweep
and slide of his tongue.

Her hands settled on the front of his shoulders, fingers
curling around the top of his wool coat, the edges of his
curls brushing their tips. She kissed him back, keeping
the kiss one of ferocity and fury instead of tender and
sensual, trying to remind herself how much she loathed
him…how well she'd despised him…even as their lips
mashed together, sliding and caressing in all the sleek,
sensual heat.

She pressed herself against him, angry, wanting him
to want her as much as she'd wanted him…then. Wanting
him to feel the rise of desire—and hope—only to have
it torn away.

Her breasts shoved into his chest, his arms closed
tightly around her as one hand caught the back of her
neck and held her immobile. He delved deep, matching

her now with temper, his tongue hot and slick and strong, his mouth firm and knowing. A rolling, expanding heat filled her, turning her damp and soft, in spite of the undercurrent of violence, and she closed her eyes, trying to keep hold of her hatred.

Narcise bit deliberately at his lip, her teeth sharp and fierce as she nipped, then pulled sharply, drawing blood. Her fangs had come forth and when she eased back, his red eyes glowed down at her, the tips of his fangs showing beneath well-kissed lips, now bloodied and gleaming with a red mark.

He was breathing heavily, his irises blazing around steady dark centers, and she lunged forward to taste his lips again. The bit of warm, coppery blood settled over her lips and tongue, shooting desire down, deep into her core. *Giordan.* Narcise sucked on his lip, drawing the blood, and realized that little sample was not enough.

She tore at the collar of his coat, baring the side of his neck, and pulled away from his lips. Just below his ear, she viciously sank her fangs in—hating him and wanting him at the same time. Giordan jolted against her with a low cry, and the surge of blood flooded her mouth, exploding as if released from a dam. She sighed in relief, sucking in the clean, warm lifeblood.

Desire and memories filled her, his scent and taste became her world: his strong shoulders and powerful body, the soft silk of his curling hair, the hot erection swelling against her beneath layers of clothing…it was Giordan, after so long, after such pain and deep betrayal…

And yet it was not him. Not the same.

Never the same.

He was shuddering against her, his arms tight but trembling, his body sagging somehow back against the half wall along the sewage canal. She found warm skin beneath his shirt as she tore it from his breeches, her fingers brushing the dust of hair on his belly, the smooth muscles that shuddered at her touch. When Narcise pulled away to look up at him, he bent to capture her mouth again—roughly and with some deep, driving anger, his fingers curled deep into her braid, gripping her head. She tasted heat and blood, felt his fingers tightening against her, his fangs scraping against her lips. He seemed to want to punish her.

It was a battle—their mouths, their bodies, there on the street, now in a shadowy corner: lips, hands, teeth, tongue. Hot, sleek, pounding.

He covered her breast with one rough hand, sliding his palm over her curves as she leaned against him, still angry, still hating him, but unable to stop. Unwilling to.

Narcise twisted her face away and caught against one of his fangs. Her lips split and now her own blood mingled with his, in the air and on her tongue.

Giordan stilled, his chest moving with rough heaves against her, and she saw desperate hunger in his eyes. She licked her lips, watching him, tasting the blood—their blood, together—warm and rich and potent.

"Do it," she taunted softly, holding his gaze, her breathing unsteady. "Taste me. Take me, Giordan."

He shoved her away, suddenly, his mouth flat and hard, streaked with blood. His eyes furious and filled with revulsion, burning her, as he dragged the back of a hand over his mouth.

Narcise took a breath to steady herself, her insides twisting at the ugliness in his eyes…yet her heart was pounding from desire as much as from anger. At herself and at him. She trembled with pain and lust as they glared at each other.

"See," she managed to say, licking the last bit of blood

from her lips. "Lust and pleasure, even in the face of such hatred. I could have lifted my skirts right here, but I'd still loathe you afterward."

"Narcise—" he began, his bruised lips hardly moving.

But with the pleasure and the familiarity, she'd fallen back into those horrible memories, the black, dark days of his betrayal…the pain was fresh and raw once again.

"By the Devil's dark soul, yes, I hate you. I *saw* you. With Cezar. It's hard to miss the expression of erotic pleasure on a man's face—the Fates know I've seen enough of that." She swallowed, her throat dry and scratchy. "I believed you. I believed *in* you. *You destroyed me.*" Her voice broke a little at the end and she swallowed again hard, angry at her show of weakness. "And I'll hate you forever for it."

There was a long silence as they stared at each other. Loathing and dark emotion vibrated between them as they faced each other on the dark and busy street.

"Forever is a very long time," he said at last, his voice a mere rumble.

"And we'll both be alive for it, won't we? Goodbye, Giordan," she said, and walked off, her knees trembling, her insides twisting. She squeezed her eyes closed against threatening tears.

She suspected that he would follow her again, and when she got to the end of the street, she looked back covertly.

But he was walking away, his hair and the tops of his shoulders dusted with moonlight as he strode off.

18

Giordan hardly made it around the corner before his belly rebelled.

By God, he hadn't even fed on her, but it didn't seem to matter. His body was reacting to the unfamiliar and fierce show of violence and hatred he'd just lived. As he sagged against a brick wall, emptying his stomach, he prayed that Narcise wouldn't see or hear him.

When he finally finished, still trembling with the force of it all, he swiped the back of a hand over his mouth as he walked off into the night.

Wrung out from more than simply the evacuation of the contents of his stomach, aware that Narcise hadn't finished off the bite on the side of his neck so that it still oozed a bit of blood, Giordan found himself back at Rubey's, where he'd been going when he first saw Narcise leaving. He'd been briefly at Rubey's private residence earlier, where he'd been keeping his own rooms for the last few months. She'd told him the news from Woodmore about Scotland, and Giordan was on his way to meet her at the pleasure house when he spied Narcise. He had no choice but to follow her.

"Giordan, bless the Virgin, what has happened?" Rubey said when she came rushing into the private chamber he'd taken over, ordering one of the girls out. As the current favorite of the mistress, and soon to be investor, he had that power. "Are you ill?" she asked.

Even here, in this place, he could scent Narcise…and the very aroma made his insides unsteady. "Not anymore."

Rubey came over and brushed the hair from his temples, which clung to the warm, damp skin. She *tsked* when she yanked at his shirt collar to reveal the bitemarks. "And you're about lying to me, Giordan Cale." She smelled of rose and gardenia—sweet and floral, without being too cloying.

He closed his eyes at her touch, trying to subdue the sharp, sudden yearning for something else. Something more.

Something he'd once had.

He'd betrayed his own heart and soul by fairly attacking Narcise. He'd wanted to hurt her—with words and deed—even as he desired her. Craved her.

How shameful and ironic that he'd resorted to such a frenzy. He would have sunk his fangs into her, taken and seized what she'd offered…but somehow sanity had at last reigned.

The destructiveness had come not only from mere thoughts, but from his body. He'd been in control of such fury for so long…what had happened tonight?

"What's gone on, Giordan? Will you not tell me?" Rubey, who should have been very busy attending to her girls and clients, sat next to him, giving him her full attention.

"There is nothing to tell," he said, suddenly wondering why he'd come here. He should have gone back to his rooms and sent for Kritanu.

It was the elderly Indian man who'd helped him understand what was happening to him after that pivotal, sunny day in the alley when his Mark had burned. Drishni, one of the vintages at Château Riche, had done her best to help him when he came back and kept vomiting every time he fed…but it wasn't until Giordan spoke with Kritanu that he'd begun to understand how he'd changed.

His body weakened and abused, he'd spiraled so far down into darkness and despair, violence and devastation…hopelessness…Kritanu had told him, that his mind had opened to *moksha*. Enlightenment.

That some strong bit of that powerful serenity and peace had found its way past the darkness of the Devil.

"And you're after lying to me, Giordan Cale, but I can see you won't change your mind." Rubey offered him her wrist as she eased herself back onto the bed next to him, propping up on the other elbow. "I can also see that you're in need of me in another way."

Giordan swallowed and hesitated…but she was right. His body felt so battered and tormented that he knew he needed sustenance. And although it wasn't what he craved, it was what he needed. And so he took her arm and slid his fangs in to drink.

Back when he was still recovering from the event in the alley, it was only by accident that Giordan had discovered he could still feed…if he were careful. This after three weeks of violently expelling the contents of his stomach after any attempt to gain sustenance. He could keep nothing down—and the lifeblood he ingested spewed forth with debilitating force, leaving his belly sore and his throat and mouth raw and parched.

His body was rejecting anything related to violence.

But at last, the tiny, dark Drishni came to him and offered herself. And when he felt the rush of her lifeblood in his mouth, pure and clean and sweet, Giordan nearly wept at the relief…because he *knew*. He knew she was the answer. It wasn't until later that he learned why: because she ate only vegetation, nuts and grains.

She ate nothing that had been acquired through death or violence—and it was that addiction to death and violence that his body was fighting, now that the white light of peace had found him.

During the anguish of the aftermath, Giordan could close his eyes and find the light. The same light that had flashed into his mind when he succumbed to the burning sun in the alley. *"Choose."*

Now, as Rubey's warm, clean blood flushed into his mouth, Giordan thought again how thankful he was that she could help him. And that she was willing to do so, and was intelligent and pragmatic about it all.

It would have been a great deal easier if he could have loved her.

He drank without greed, easily dismissing the little tingle of awareness and arousal that began reflexively during the process. Although her breathing shifted, and he felt her body begin to respond to him, Rubey made no attempt to touch him as she might normally do. It was as if she realized he couldn't.

"Corvindale is here," she said after a short time, perhaps after judging that the color had seeped back into his cheeks. "He has news."

Giordan withdrew immediately and looked at her in surprise. "Why did you not tell me at once?" he said, swallowing the last bit.

"I could see you were in no good mood for it. You must be attended to first."

"I'm no fragile flower," he snapped, sitting up.

Rubey offered her arm for him to finish off and patted his cheek with the opposite hand. "If you could have seen yourself, Giordan, my darling, you wouldn't say such foolish things." She ended the little pat with a tender caress over his jaw.

He frowned, but attended to her wound with his lips and tongue. She tremored a bit beneath his mouth now, and her eyes sank half-closed. He could scent the heightened musk wafting from her body and his own gave a little shiver in response.

"By the Virgin, if you weren't ruined for any other, I'd be tossing my glove into the ring for you, Giordan, rich and handsome and kind as you are," she said, her voice dusky and filled with the Irish. "But you are ruined," she said, sitting up and sliding her legs off the bed. "And so I'll tell you the bad part. That Corvindale's news is about Narcise."

"Where have you been?" Chas demanded as he burst into the chamber where Narcise was sitting.

He'd been frantic, looking for her first throughout the pleasure house, and then trying to find her by searching the streets nearby, interviewing servants and pedestrians to see if they'd noticed her. No one had, and he'd begun to be certain that somehow, Cezar had managed to take her from beneath his very nose.

Narcise leveled a calm stare at him. "I went for a walk."

There was something in her eyes, something different.

"You went for a walk without telling anyone where you were going? Did you not think I might be worried that something had happened to you?"

"What can happen to me in London? I'm a Dracule,

and use a sword better than any man I've ever met," she replied, still calm and unemotional. "No one can harm me. Nor do I answer to anyone any longer."

"What if Cezar were here? What if he'd sent his makes after you?" Chas continued, uncaring that he sounded almost as shrill and controlling as his bossy sister Maia.

Narcise—God in heaven, how could anyone be so utterly breathtaking?—fixed him with those blue-violet, black-ringed irises. Her hair hung in a long, single braid over her shoulder. He knew that it would still be smooth and straight as a bolt of silk, shimmering like a blue-black waterfall, when the plait was undone. His heart thumped and swelled, thinking about the moment they might share later, when he did just that.

Her cheeks were flushed a bit more pink than usual, and the hem of her gown was dirty and damp. The filthy, worn toe of a slipper peeped from beneath and her face had a smudge of dirt—and...blood?—on it. On her lips, too. As if she'd been cut.

"What did Sonia tell you?" she asked.

Rubey. Damn and blast. Chas sat in a chair next to the sofa on which Narcise was sitting. He'd known he had to tell her...he just hadn't been ready to so soon. He'd needed time to think about it all.

And as he sat here now, looking at her, he knew things were about to change.

"When you gave her the button from Cezar's coat, what did Sonia say?" Narcise asked again. "You told me she didn't have a clear vision."

Again he sensed that there was something different about her...something perhaps more confident, even peaceful...and yet something dark and unsettled lurked in her eyes. As if she were in some great pain.

Had he done that to her?

He bowed his head, then looked straight at her. "She did see something...I didn't want to tell you, Narcise. I didn't know what it meant, and I didn't know how you'd feel. Or react."

"What did she see?" Her voice was tight and angry.

"She always sees what it is that the person fears the most. And what she saw when she held Cezar's button was you, Narcise."

"Me?" Narcise's eyes had turned from flat and furious to shocked and wide. "She saw *me?*"

Chas nodded. Sonia had described the vision as Narcise, whom she'd met previously in the carriage, peering out from behind a fan. The ivory spindles were half-spread, covering the bottom of her chin and part of one cheek. Was the fact that her face was partially hidden somehow meaningful?

"How can that be? What does that mean?" Narcise said, but even as she spoke, he watched her face change into one of contemplation and consideration...which was just what he'd feared.

It would be just like his beautiful, brave Narcise to rush off to Paris and use herself to get back in to see Cezar. He'd intended to get her settled safely somewhere and then go back to France himself and put an end to Cezar Moldavi.

And then he'd come back to Narcise and they'd find a way to be together.

For, now that Chas had gotten the news about Dimitri's great change, even more hope stirred inside him. Just three days ago, while he and Narcise were still traveling back from Scotland, Dimitri had gone through some great ordeal to save Maia's life...and now he, too, had miraculously broken Lucifer's hold on him. Whether it was because he'd finally learned how to do it through his studies, or for some other reason, Chas wasn't certain. But the truth was, Dimitri had become mortal once again—his Mark from Lucifer had disappeared.

And the angry, austere earl had actually been seen to be smiling.

Just then, the door flew open to emit Rubey, who had no qualms about bursting into any chamber of her establishment without knocking. "Aye, I thought I heard you return. Dimitri is here," she said to Chas. "He insists upon speaking with you immediately, Chas. Voss is here as well."

He rose, at once concerned and relieved by the interruption.

"With your permission, Narcise." He glanced at her and was rewarded with a cool look that told him she wasn't finished with her pique. Ah, well, women were always annoyed about something. At least his sisters always were. He gave a proper bow and followed Rubey from the chamber.

One thing was certain. Chas wasn't going to tell Narcise—or anyone, especially Rubey—what else Sonia had seen…when he gave her a handkerchief belonging to Giordan Cale.

According to Sonia, Cale's greatest fear was Narcise. Dead.

Narcise stared after them as the door closed, suddenly furious and bereft at the same time.

The moment Rubey rushed in, she'd smelled him: smart, masculine, familiar. Giordan. *On her.*

Her throat seized up, tight and scratchy, and she'd hardly heard the ensuing conversation, for her entire body was swimming in disbelief and anger. Narcise's vision darkened with shadowy, red edges. By Fate, Giordan must have fairly run to have made his way back here to Rubey first, and without Narcise seeing him.

And then he'd gone directly from Narcise to Rubey.

From kissing Narcise, devouring her, filling his hands with her…to Rubey. The whoremistress.

Rage flushed through her, and for the first time in weeks, her Mark eased into painlessness. Narcise closed her eyes and fed it, submerged herself in the darkness of anger.

And then, just as quickly as it had come, the fury eased into something more devastating. Pain.

I loved you.

Had he really? She scoffed to herself, tried to push away the memory of his face…tonight and on that horrible day when he'd come to her afterward. Smelling of Cezar.

The starkness in his eyes had been the same then as it had tonight: deep and complete. Raw.

Narcise rose abruptly and began to pace the chamber, propelled by fear and hurt. If he'd loved her, why, *why*, had he done what he'd done? How could he?

How could he have imagined she'd accept him after he'd betrayed her? *Any* betrayal would have killed her, after what she'd experienced…but for it to be with a *man*…and her *brother*…how? How could he have thought she'd forget that?

Was it just his Draculean nature? To seek pleasure wherever it was offered? To focus on self, and only self?

Of course it was.

She was precisely the same way. The way Lucifer had turned them.

She couldn't stay here any longer. She had to have air—clean air, not breaths tainted by his scent. She wanted to be back out beneath the open sky, the stars and clouded moon. She wanted to feel that power again, that confidence and worth of self from earlier tonight, before Giordan had ruined it.

Dismissing her disheveled and dirty clothing, she strode quickly and silently to the chamber door and peered out into the corridor. It was empty, and she slipped out for the second time that night, closing the door behind her and walking down the hall toward what she recalled was the front entrance. Giordan's essence lingered, along with that of Chas and Dimitri and even Voss, she thought, but she ignored it and kept walking.

Chas would worry, but he'd have to learn that she could take care of herself. And she was furious with him as well, for lying to her. Keeping information from her.

Trying to *protect* her.

She was Cezar's greatest fear? How had she never known that?

What could that mean?

Sonia Woodmore had to be mistaken. Her Sight had to be wrong.

How could Cezar fear her when he'd had her under his control all of the time?

Narcise was just passing the door to some parlor or chamber when she heard Chas's voice. "Of course we're not going to tell Narcise. She might agree to it."

She froze.

"Do you think that's wise?" replied a mellow voice that she was certain belonged to Voss. "Perhaps she—"

"You aren't going to tell me what?" she demanded, flinging the door open. "Did you not learn anything?" she added, her voice cold as she stared at Chas.

Of the five people in the room, four faces had turned to her, and she realized with a horrid start that the fifth person was not staring at her at all because it was Giordan. He was looking down, even as the rest of the occupants of the room stared in chagrin.

And she dared not look at him, not when she knew where he'd been and what he'd been doing…not when his bloodscent lingered in the air. Not when her mouth watered at the aroma of it, and when she remembered the feel of his body against hers…only hours ago.

Instead she focused on Chas, whose countenance had gone tight with dismay. He rose from his seat. "Come in, Narcise. Apparently you *are* going to be told the news."

Aside of Chas and Giordan, Dimitri was in the chamber, of course, as well as Voss. And, to Narcise's mild surprise, Maia Woodmore was there as well, sitting next to Dimitri on a sofa. Much closer than was proper for a ward to be sitting next to her guardian.

Unlike her younger sister Angelica's had been when they met in Dimitri's study some months ago, Maia's expression when she looked at Narcise was not one of accusation nor of distaste. It was only mildly curious and laced with concern.

"And so all of you are discussing me, and I'm not invited to the conversation?" Narcise said, looking for a safe place to sit. Chas gestured to the chair he'd just vacated, but she ignored him.

Giordan was in a different seat off to the right, and Voss was in a chair next to Dimitri. There was a space on the sofa next to Maia, and that was where Narcise went. She sat, her back rigid as she tried to keep her thoughts from colliding with each other and her mind clear.

"We've received a message from your brother," said Dimitri. "I thought it best if we informed Chas immediately."

"*I* said you should be told," Maia said to Narcise. "I would want to know if my brother was doing something like this." She slanted a sidewise glance at Chas and gave a little sniff.

"Maia," Dimitri said, giving her a mildly exasperated look—mild for him, anyway—and said to Narcise, "The message arrived at Blackmont Hall earlier today via blood pigeon."

Taking care not to glance at Giordan, who sat just beyond Dimitri, Narcise turned her full attention to the formidable earl. But out of the corner of her eye, she saw the blood staining Giordan's white shirt, and the elegant shape of his wrist, settled casually on the arm of his chair. "Are you going to tell me what the message contained?"

"Napoleon Bonaparte is going to invade England in three days," he replied with characteristic bluntness. "And your brother promises to send his own army of made vampires with the emperor's mortal soldiers, to wreak havoc on this country."

"He said they'd find the children," Maia Woodmore added, her delicate face grave. "And take them."

"Maia," Dimitri snapped. "Blast it, I should have left you home."

"Then I would have just found the way on my own, Gavril," she replied. "At least we only needed one carriage this way."

"You promised you wouldn't interfere," Dimitri said from between clenched teeth.

"I did nothing of the sort. You *demanded* I promise that, but I certainly didn't. If I weren't here, none of you would tell Narcise the whole of it," the woman returned. "How can she make a decision without knowing all of it?"

"A decision?" said Narcise. "What sort of decision?" Her heart was pounding now and she felt an unpleasant twisting in her middle.

"About whether you'll go back to him," said Giordan, breaking his silence.

Quiet descended over the chamber.

"Narcise," Chas said after a moment. "You can understand why we thought not to tell you."

"No," she replied through stiff lips. Giordan had shifted in his chair, and now he was looking at Chas. "No, I do not. What did you intend to do about it, since you didn't plan to tell me?"

"That's what we were discussing when you made that most dramatic entrance," replied Voss with a lazy smile. "I know Cezar well enough, but since you know him best of all, perhaps you might have a suggestion. He promises to call off the emperor's invasion if you return to him."

Narcise shook her head, her thoughts whirling. Go back? Go back to Cezar? *Never.* But her heart was pounding and her stomach twisted nauseatingly. France's invasion didn't really matter to her—or to any Dracule— insofar as power was concerned.

But there were *vampirs* involved, and Cezar would ensure that there would be children as victims…as well as others. *Children.* If she agreed to go back, they'd be saved. She did believe Cezar would keep his word about that. He'd done so in the past, for he knew therein lay his power over her.

But to go back… She shuddered. *No.*

"I'll go to Paris," Chas said flatly. "I can get in to see him—"

"*No*, Chas," Maia interrupted. "It's too dangerous."

"Be still, Maia," her brother snapped, and received a warning glare from Dimitri.

"And you attempting to kill Moldavi wouldn't necessarily stop Napoleon," Voss added. "Although—"

"Attempting to kill him?" Chas echoed. His voice was sharp. "A poor choice of word—"

"Cezar could stop him if he wanted," Narcise said slowly. "He's got the new emperor under his thrall."

"It does seem more than a bit convenient that Bonaparte has been sitting for months with his army ready to cross the Channel at any moment…and now Moldavi claims he will invade at last," Dimitri mused. "I'm inclined to believe that your brother," he said, looking at Narcise, "is indeed behind all of this."

"And if he's influencing Bonaparte to invade, then he can stop him as well," Narcise said. And her Mark panged sharply…because she was thinking about what it would be like to return to Cezar. To put herself back under his control.

A little shiver caught her by surprise—a ripple of fear and trepidation—but then she remembered Sonia's vision. *I'm his greatest fear. How can that be? And how could I use that?*

It made her stronger. She could go to Cezar knowing that. And if he feared her, then it gave her the chance to destroy him.

If it were on her terms…

Narcise's heart began to pound harder. Could she actually go back there? She remembered the comforting feel of the saber…the way Cezar's eyes lit on her, with both delight and hate.

Another shiver started in her belly. It could be true. She *could* be his greatest fear.

"You aren't considering going," Chas said, breaking the silence. "*Narcise.*" His voice was strung tightly and she saw the fear in his eyes.

But it was the weight of Giordan's stare that she felt the most. Heavy, silent, dark…resting on her like a boulder.

"He fears me," she said, thinking aloud. "He fears me more than anything in the world."

The twinge that had begun to inflame her shoulder eased a bit more. She had power.

"But how will that help you?" Chas said, his voice low, as if he were fighting to keep it so. "Once you're back there with him, you're under his control. In that place. He's got damned *feathers* everywhere, Narcise."

"There's something else," Maia Woodmore said quietly.

"Maia, *no*," Dimitri said, his voice like a whip. "I forbid you."

She looked up at him, a steely but determined expression on her face, and lifted her chin. "*You* would want to know."

He glared at her with his mortal eyes, the burning no longer an actual glow, but no less furious. "Maia. You don't understand."

"Allow me," Giordan spoke again. He shifted in his chair, dragging Narcise's gaze toward him. His movements were so studied and casual that their easiness seemed forced. "I suspect Narcise isn't the only one Moldavi wants returned."

Dimitri made a soft, sharp curse under his breath and turned to look at his friend. "Naturally," he admitted.

"Just to clarify," Maia broke in with her imperious voice, "Moldavi promises to stop the invasion if Narcise *or* Mr. Cale returns to him. He doesn't specifically require *both*—"

"I'll go."

Narcise's breath caught at the blank expression that had settled over Giordan's face as he spoke. Like a mask. Empty, emotionless. She recognized him…and yet it wasn't truly him. His eyes…they appeared dead. And they were looking at her.

Her heart was thudding in her chest, but she wasn't certain why. The image of Cezar and Giordan rose once again in her mind and even the memory of the stew of smells around him came with it. Her belly lurched and she bit her lip, thrusting the thoughts away.

Dimitri started to say something, but Giordan's voice slashed out. "Don't be a fool. You haven't the means to stop me."

"Cale, certainly, there are other ways," Voss interjected. "Moldavi surely doesn't know about the change that's occurred with Dimitri and myself. We could accompany Woodmore and attend to Moldavi permanently."

"No," Narcise said softly. "No, I will have to go." Her Mark pulsed with anger and sharp pain, but she ignored it. "But you'll come after me. When it's safe. When I'm certain he's called off the invasion. You can—"

"Narcise," Chas began.

"Stop," she ordered, holding up her hand. "Have you forgotten? I'm a Dracule. I think only of myself. And in the end, this will serve me well. Knowing what I know about my brother now, I have more power than he realizes."

"But once you're inside there," Chas started again. "Narcise, you don't have any idea what will happen."

She fixed her gaze on him. "He won't kill me. And I can live through anything else." *But at least the children will be saved.* And the war would be stopped.

And maybe it wasn't only about her anymore.

19

"You aren't truly going," Chas said, stopping her in the corridor at Rubey's several hours after the discussion in the parlor. "Narcise." He wore a tight, strained expression.

"Of course I'm going," she replied, echoing his own response to her same question from months ago. Unlike him, she hadn't even needed to pack a bag. "He's my brother." Again, she repeated his response.

"Narcise, I— Forgive me for not wanting to tell you about…this. I was afraid that exactly this would happen. That you would go back to him…put yourself at risk." He reached for her hand, drawing her closer. "But I shouldn't have lied to you. I was wrong to—"

"You were wrong *twice*," she reminded him, but didn't pull her hand away. She needed the comfort of touch right now. "You don't trust me, and you don't believe I can take care of myself. You want to control me, just as Cezar did."

"No, damn it, Narcise…I have three sisters…it's hard for me to comprehend that a woman can be so…strong. I'm trying, Narcise."

"I don't know if I can trust you anymore," she told him. "I have a sense that you'd do it again—"

"Devil take it, yes, I would. I don't want anything to happen to you, for God's sake. I'm in love with you, Lord help me…I'm in love with a *vampir*."

He tugged her into his arms and found her mouth, bringing her body up along his tall one as he pulled her close. She sensed the desperation behind his kiss, the uncertainty in his touch…and despite the beginning flutters of pleasure, this time she couldn't forget what loomed between them. Her anger toward him for his controlling protectiveness…and Chas's own internal battle that, try as he might to overcome, was still a wide chasm.

Narcise was familiar with the anguish that played out in his face when they were together. The guilt and revulsion still warred with his desire as he begged her to bite him.

You could have been one of us. She wondered what would have happened if he had accepted Lucifer's offer. Would she and Chas have found each other, been happy together? Impossible for a Dracule.

At last he eased away, his arms still loosely around her waist, and one hand lifted to brush a strand of hair from her face. "So beautiful," he murmured, shaking his head. He looked at her, his eyes hot and heavy-lidded, his mouth swollen from the kiss.

"I'm coming with you," he told her, and she was aware of a flash of relief…then the twitch of panic. What if something happened to Chas this time? She was still angry with him, furious…but she still cared about him.

"Dimitri and Voss…they need to stay with my sisters," he added.

And they aren't Dracule any longer. Now mortals, though stronger and as powerful as men could be, the others no longer had Astheniae, nor the vulnerability to sunlight…but instead, they had many other weaknesses. They would be better served remaining with the women they loved than risking their mortal lives.

"Chas," Narcise said, pulling out of his embrace. She had to be honest. "I'm not going to change like them. I know you believe a miracle can happen…but I don't see how it can. Dimitri tried for a century—"

His eyes shone with a determined light. "But how do you know? Even Cale—"

"Woodmore." The deep, mellow voice cut in, startling Narcise as it swept over her from behind. How had she not scented him? The back of her shoulders prickled with awareness and her recently kissed lips throbbed as if filled with guilt.

"I'll be going as well," he informed them.

Her heart racing, she turned to face Giordan. "That's not necessary," she replied. Traveling with him? By the Fates, no.

She felt dizzy; he stood right before her, so close she felt his presence seeping into her. His expression had eased slightly since the conversation in the parlor, but there were still deep lines around his lips and eyes. The place she'd nipped him on his lip had dried into a slender dark line, helping to make him look uncharacteristically rugged and rough. His wound still leaked a bit and her attention was captured by the sight of the bit of blood pooling in the elegant, golden curve of skin between shoulder and neck.

Lust and pleasure zipped through her, down deep inside.

Where had her anger gone?

Giordan's expression didn't change. "I'm going. I'll be ready to leave in a quarter of an hour. Wait for me."

And he walked off down the hall, his broad shoulders seeming to fill the space, his strides easy and smooth.

When she turned back to Chas, he was watching her with an unfathomable expression.

"What is it?" she asked, aware that her fingers were trembling.

"It's him." His mouth had flattened into a white line and misery touched his hazel eyes. He slid a hand into his hair and raked it viciously through the dark waves. "It'll always be Cale, won't it?"

It's only you, Narcise. She pushed away the echo of Giordan's words from years ago. "I don't know what you mean."

"You still love him, and until that changes, you can't see anyone else. You can't love anyone else. Including me."

"I don't—I might have thought I loved him once, but not any longer. I could never... You have no idea how his betrayal destroyed me." She made her voice hard and filled with loathing, reminding herself of his sins.

And now they were going back to Cezar again. She felt light-headed and faint. Both of them. Maybe she couldn't do this after all.

Chas was looking at her, shaking his head. Intensity and anger vibrated off him. "He loves you. How can you not see it? At first I thought it was simply your disinterest. And you...you want him so badly you—"

Her mouth was trembling, but she had to stop him from talking. "Don't be a fool. He loves only himself, his own pleasure. There's no space for anyone else. And we Dracule...we live for pleasure. I do."

"Jesus, Narcise." He drew in a deep breath, covering his eyes with his hand, then sliding it down his face.

When he was finished, he looked at her. "God help me, I cannot believe I'm about to say this."

She waited.

"If nothing else, at least you'll know I've learned from my mistakes…." He shook his head, his dark hand falling away. He wasn't looking at her now; he was looking down the hall, away from her. "I gave Sonia one of Cale's handkerchiefs."

Narcise's heart stopped. She already knew Giordan's Asthenia was cats, so it would be no surprise…but why would Chas be hesitant to tell her—

"She saw *you* in the vision. Dead. His greatest fear is you dying. Why do you think he's insisting on going back to Cezar with us?"

"You must be mistaken," she whispered, frowning, fighting the shivers that attempted to take her over. "He has other reasons for seeing my brother again," she said, forcing bitterness into a voice that shook. But it was difficult. All at once, she felt off balance and confused. Weak. Even nauseated.

Chas didn't respond right away. He was looking down the corridor in the direction Giordan had gone, his face still and harsh, his lips curled into each other. White edged his mouth and around his nose.

"Are you that blind, Narcise? His only reason for going back again is for you. Don't you understand what happened?" But still, he didn't look at her. "Your brother blackmailed him into it. All of it. He was only with him in order to protect you…in exchange for getting you away from Cezar. But you wouldn't go."

Narcise put her hand out against the wall. "You're mistaken," she breathed again, trying to draw air into her suddenly frozen lungs.

But Chas was still looking away, his body rigid. "I wish to hell I was."

* * *

Giordan had no compunction about leaving Rubey's while Narcise and Woodmore were finishing their tender little tête-à-tête in the corridor.

He hoped they took their time and fucked while they were there, so he could get that much more of a head start. Never mind the way the thought made his insides roll sickeningly and darkness hover at the edges of his vision.

The sun that had burned his Mark no longer bothered him, so he was able to travel during the day. This gave him an advantage: horseback to Dover instead of the closed carriage Narcise would have to take, then across the Channel. If he could get to Cezar first...

A shudder took him by surprise and he quickly submerged it. Yes, he'd go back there. Yes, he'd do what he had to do—to save the lives of countless children and English citizens. To keep Narcise from having to.

He'd even kill Cezar if he had to...although it would probably kill Giordan as well, to do it. The remnants from his interlude with Narcise in the alley still made his insides pitch and his knees wobble.

Now, clear-minded, he understood why he'd reacted so strongly: his body and soul had been protecting him from the pain and anguish that would come from trusting his heart to Narcise again. The violent illness had been his reaction to hate and violence he'd eschewed for a decade, the reaction to a long-submerged addiction that had suddenly come rushing back: the need to hurt, to wound, to *have*.

"Ah, sister. I've been expecting you. I see that you could no more stay away from me than I could stay away from you." Cezar looked up as Narcise walked in. "And Woodmore as well. You didn't mention in your message that he would be joining us. To what do I owe this great pleasure?"

They had entered Cezar's private chambers, escorted by Belial, who stood too close to Narcise for her comfort. Her brother sat across the room at a desk. As they entered, his face changed from one of bald delight, to contemptuous welcome…to a startled, blank expression, as if he were trying to hide his true feelings.

Narcise found that both disconcerting and optimistic.

"Belial," Cezar said sharply. "Escort my sister to the dining area. I'd like her to entertain my guests this evening."

"I'm not here to entertain your guests," Narcise told him, evading Belial's reach. "I'm here to stop Bonaparte from invading England."

Lifting her nose, she breathed, trying to scent Giordan's presence. Was he here or not? When he hadn't come back at the promised time to find them at Rubey's, she'd figured out that he meant to beat them here.

They'd sent word by pigeon to Cezar to stop the invasion, for they would not have reached Paris within the three-day timeline, promising that she was on her way back to him. So far, no news of invasion had come and she believed he'd kept his word.

Of course, he knew if the invasion went forward, she wouldn't come back to him.

Narcise didn't spare a look at Chas, though she felt him tensing next to her. On the back of her shoulder, the Mark was inflamed with fury—so much that she could hardly move her arm. Even breathing was difficult. But it had been that way for two days, and she had learned to accept it.

"Ah, my darling sister," Cezar said, his voice carrying more of a lisp than usual, "the emperor will be here later this night. And if you provide enough entertainment, I am certain you can convince him to change his mind. Belial, take her." Now he seemed breathless with excitement.

But Narcise wasn't about to go quietly. For some reason, Cezar feared her, more than anything in the world, according to Sonia. The thought gave her confidence she'd never had before. She started toward her brother as Belial made a move to stop her. She flung his hand off her arm, her eyes glowing red and hot. "Don't touch me or I'll kill you."

Chas had moved at the same time, producing the short but lethal stake he'd hidden in the sole of his boot.

"Cezar, you promised me if she returned…" Belial whined, stepping back. "She owes me."

"I did indeed," Cezar mused slowly. "Perhaps I could accommodate your request tonight."

Narcise felt Chas tense behind her, but he remained still and silent as planned. She'd prepared him for her brother's malevolence. Stepping away from Belial, her heart thumping hard, she started across the chamber. The made vampire didn't worry her. It was the children in England she was concerned about. And where was Giordan? "I've returned to you, brother. You agreed to call off the invasion if I returned. Did you not miss me?"

Cezar's eyes were pinned on her, and she saw both fear and admiration therein. His throat convulsed as he swallowed, his attention avid and palpable. She halted halfway across the chamber, unwilling to get close enough for him to grab her.

"I thought you wouldn't return," he said, his voice thready. "I thought I'd lost you forever. *Narcise*."

"I've returned willingly," she told him, watching him closely. "I trust that you'll do as you promised." She didn't look at Chas.

He nodded slowly. "Yes. Belial, take them to the dining room. Go with him," he told Narcise, his eyes now intent. The craftiness there unsettled her…but she knew the risks.

She knew she wouldn't leave here soon, but she would someday. She was armed with knowledge and intent, and she had friends outside of this subterranean hole who would come for her.

Thus, for now, despite the constant throbbing and burning of her Mark, reminding her that she was doing something selfless, she would be Cezar's pet for just a little longer.

20

On her way to the dining room—the room where she had fought countless battles in front of the dais—she scented Giordan. So he *was* here. Or had been.

A little shiver ran over Narcise's shoulders. What had Cezar done with him?

She hadn't been able to dismiss Chas's dire words. If he was correct, Giordan's actions had been a sacrifice beyond comprehension. She knew what he'd suffered as a boy, in the dark alleys, at the hands of men…but all along, when the worst had happened and she'd witnessed the hedonistic scene in Cezar's chambers, she'd suspected Giordan of hiding his true self, his real desires.

Not so very different from Chas, who was revolted by her vampirism…but yet craved it, wanted *her*. He was reduced to begging her for the very thing that disgusted him.

It had all made sense to her—or so it had seemed at the time, and confirmed over the years. Giordan had really wanted Cezar all along, but could never admit it.

But Chas seemed so certain…and if Giordan truly

wanted Cezar, why hadn't he come with them when they left Paris?

Narcise's insides had been a muddle of nausea and self-recrimination during the entire trip from London, but now she must put that out of her mind. She had to be cunning and strong to survive whatever punishment her brother would mete out to her for running away.

Chas had insisted on coming with her, to her great dismay and impotent fury…yet part of her was relieved to have someone with her. She meant to use her influence with her brother to keep Chas from being imprisoned.

Knowing that she *had* influence was a nebulous thing…but it was probably the only reason she wasn't engulfed in the flames of fury by Lucifer. The continued throbbing of the Mark was painful, but not unbearable.

Inside the dining room, Narcise found that nothing had changed since her escape…only four months ago.

Four months. It had seemed a lifetime, even for one who was immortal.

But a moment after she walked into the dining chamber accompanied by Belial, everything did change. Suddenly there was a flurry of activity.

The next thing she knew, Cezar was there, standing on the dais behind the long table above her. Next to him was Giordan, a stony expression on his face. He was bare from the waist up and his sleek, tanned skin was marred with bitemarks that made Narcise's stomach turn. Two of the marks still oozed, and she could scent his lifeblood.

She heard Chas hiss behind her, and suddenly they were separated by a clan of her brother's men—Chas shoved and pulled away, held immobile by two *vampirs*, and three of the others surrounding her.

"My darling sister, I have a confession to make," he said. "I do hope you aren't too upset about it, but the truth is, Bonaparte is much too busy with his coronation to actually consider invading England. As I'd hoped, you took the bait."

Narcise tried to pull away from the two men holding her, but they were just as strong as she was. "I should have known better than to trust you," she spat.

"I could still send my army, if it would make you feel better about it all," he added. Then, when she gave him no further response, he commanded, "Strip her." His eyes glittered with delight.

The next thing she knew, they were tearing at her dress. The flimsy muslin of her traveling gown ripped easily, and they flung the remnants away as they grabbed at her corset, yanking at the laces, jerking her body every which way as they tugged it loose. She stumbled and fell, twisting as she tried to fight them off, and keep her balance. One of the three finally caught her arms and pulled them up and away from her torso so that the others could loosen the laces and pull the corset, then Narcise's light linen chemise, from her.

They allowed not even her drawers to remain, those loose, light pantaloons that covered her from waist to knee. That last bit of shield from avid eyes was yanked away by one of the makes as the other two held her arms out on either side. When they were finished, all three stepped back, leaving her to stand there in the chamber completely nude. Her skin was marked and scratched from the harsh scrape of the grommets and hard edging of her stays, along with sharp, rough fingernails, and her hair sagged from its anchor at the back of her neck—unable to be used for any sort of covering.

Cezar made a sharp gesture for one of his men to take her clothing away, and now he looked down at her with what could only be described as a vivacious smile on his face. "There, now, my dear. That is much better. Not only was that the ugliest frock I've ever seen—even you couldn't do it justice—but now we can all see what it is Belial will be fighting for."

Narcise leveled a cool look at him, hardly aware of her nudity. She'd been thus exposed many times in the past. "I suspect it will be nothing more than a distraction. Belial hasn't a chance, and you know it. Are you certain you wish to lose your most faithful servant?"

Her brother looked at her for a moment, and her heart sank when she saw the crafty look that eased into his eyes. "Perhaps you are correct, Narcise. My confidence in your ability is profound, and, to my dismay, Belial hasn't the skill to match you."

Her heart was pounding hard now and she, foolishly, glanced at Giordan. Their eyes met and the terror she saw in his nearly knocked her breathless. His face had gone white and stony, and for a moment, she thought he was going to faint.

But then her attention was drawn back to Cezar, who'd had a long, metal box brought onto the table in front of him. With a sly glance at Giordan, and then a benevolent smile at Narcise, he said, "But you must be chilled by now, my lovely sister. And I haven't properly welcomed you home. I have something for you." He started to lift the top.

"*No.*" Giordan's voice was sharp and desperate. He slammed his hand onto the top of the box, clanging the metal top back into place. His voice was low and unsteady, and she could barely hear him say, "Anything else, Cezar. Name it."

By now, Narcise's heart had plunged to her knees, which trembled and threatened to buckle. What was in the box? She glanced at Chas, who was held against the wall by one of the makes, and their eyes met. But his gaze, instead of being wild with concern or fear, was wide and intense. As if he were trying to tell her something.

Instead of being angry with Giordan for his outburst, Cezar seemed amused. "My, you are free with your promises now, Monsieur Cale. If only you'd been so accommodating a decade ago. When it really mattered." And yet, despite his cool words, he was gazing up at Giordan with such a baldly lustful expression that her own stomach lurched with revulsion.

Giordan's face was shiny and hard and she swore she could hear…or feel…the pounding of his own heart as he looked down at her brother. Cezar murmured something that she couldn't hear, but that turned Giordan's face gray. The marks on his skin stood out in sharp red-black relief against a suddenly ashen backdrop and his throat convulsed as he nodded. Once. Quickly and short.

That was when Narcise knew for certain that Chas had been right. That whatever had happened with Giordan and Cezar, it had been under duress. Her vision wavered and she was assaulted by a rush of grief and shame. *How could I?*

"Stop," she cried. Her voice rang out and drew her brother's attention. "I need no one to fight my battles for me. Release my friends, Cezar, and you'll have whatever you want."

His eyes danced and he smiled. "Take the *vampir* hunter away, then. My sister is correct: I have everything I want, right here."

He lifted the lid of the box as Giordan made a sound of protest, but it was too late. Narcise realized immediately what was inside.

Feathers. Many of them.

As Cezar reached into the box, Giordan launched himself at him, and they tumbled to the floor. Narcise started to move, whirling around to notice that Chas was gone—they'd taken him away—and then toward the dais before someone caught her by the arm. Someone else slammed into her, and she flew to the floor, her bare skin scraping across the cold, gritty stone.

By the time she was dragged to her feet, she saw that Giordan had been subdued and was being forced down from the dais and onto the same level on which she stood. By his slow and jerky movements, she could tell that he was weak or somehow inhibited—loss of blood, or for some other reason.

He didn't look at her as they pulled him past, but as they went by, Narcise smelled him, felt him, so close as he came by…and then she saw Giordan's back.

She gasped and stared, hardly noticing as Belial came up to where she stood, held in place by two strong men, and slid his palm under one of her breasts.

Giordan's Mark was…*white*.

The corded, rootlike brand was no longer black, no longer full and pulsing and throbbing…or even merely dark lines…but it was white. Nothing more than a scar… as if it had been burned away.

What did that mean? What had happened?

But she had no time to think on it, for, as Giordan was strung up by his arms on the wall, she felt her own body turn slow and sluggish.

The feathers.

Narcise turned to look, and the men holding her dropped her arms as finally she saw what Cezar was pulling from the box. Even Belial had stepped away, as if unable to stay near her for this.

She couldn't breathe, for she recognized it.

It was the cape…made only of feathers. Rows and rows of soft, light, brown…burning…feathers.

Now her breathing came fast and hard, shallow with panic as Cezar flung the cape out with a flourish, as if to shake off any dust or wrinkles. If that touched her… If he wrapped her in it… The room tilted, turning dark and off-center, and her knees nearly gave away.

"*No*," she whispered as her brother stepped down from the dais, sauntering toward her as if about to present her with a most precious gift.

"Stop!" The desperation in Giordan's cry penetrated even Narcise's terror and pain. "*No*. Don't…do…it."

"By Lucifer," Cezar said, pausing, his face hard and foxlike as he looked over. "If I had known how deep your attachment was, Giordan, I would have asked for a month instead of three nights."

"*Please*," he breathed, his voice a low, rough rumble. His eyes shone with misery and desolation. "Whatever you want."

Narcise could hardly think. Her limbs were heavy as boulders, her lungs as tight as if they were being crushed by the very same thing. Pain from the proximity of the feathers added to the paralysis, and she could feel them as their presence wafted through the chamber…but somehow, through it all, Giordan's words, his intent, penetrated.

It humbled her, weakening her even more than the feathers.

She gathered every bit of strength she could muster and said his name. "*Giordan*."

And when she did, she put every bit of apology and shame and humility in those syllables as she could.

He looked at her then, and she felt the strength of

his love and devotion for her travel across the chamber, through the pain and sluggishness.

And then she could no longer breathe. Cezar was there in front of her, his face a cold, tight mask, and with a flick of his wrist, the feathers were wafting down over her shoulders in a smothering blanket.

Narcise tried to smother the scream of agony, but even Luce's most furious blaze through her Mark was nothing compared to this. Shaking uncontrollably, she started to collapse as the soft brush of the burning feathers encapsulated her, and someone caught her on each side, holding her erect.

The pain was so great that she couldn't gasp or breathe or feel... She tumbled into a vortex of mad sensation: the softness of each feather, branding into her skin, the insubstantial weight pulling her down.

Vaguely she was aware of being held upright, and hands on her flesh...molding over her breasts and hips... the smell of lust and perspiration, heavy and cloying... some shadowy, indistinct dampness, heat, pressure...

Then, in her dreamlike paralysis, she was aware of being moved: the brush of her feet against the stone floor, the change of position as she went from vertical to horizontal...something hard beneath her, pressing the cape of feathers even more deeply against her skin.

She was aware of crying out, perhaps screaming... but she hardly had the breath to do so. A mouth was on her, hands, a body shoving against her, questing and invading...the shift as the feathers were pulled away from one of her shoulders and that pain was replaced by the sharp penetration of fangs.

And then, suddenly, nothing.

21

When Chas was dragged out of the chamber, away from Narcise and Giordan, he realized he was being given a miracle—just like that day when the cat had run into the street and caused the accident which allowed him to sneak into Moldavi's home the first time.

He still had his stake, now hidden in his sleeve during the walk to the dining chamber with Belial…and he was certain he'd be able to take at least one of his two captors by surprise.

As he faked a stumble, a quick flick of the wrist slid the weapon into his hand and loosened the guard's grip on one side of him. When he righted himself and came back up, it was with the point of the stake ready. It found its mark with the same ease and power it always did, and he breathed a silent thanks.

By the time the other guard realized what happened, Chas had him slammed face-first against the wall, the stake at his back. "Get me out of here," he said. "I want the way outside."

He had to get out of the place so that he could come back in and free Narcise. And he knew exactly how to do that, what he needed to find…for it had all suddenly become clear to him.

He'd figured out Cezar's Asthenia.

As he was observing everything that happened, from the time he and Narcise entered her brother's chambers, and his reaction to her presence, Chas suspected there was something wrong. Moldavi had seemed so pleased to see them…until they walked into the chamber.

Then, he'd ordered them out almost instantly. "Take my sister to the dining chamber," he'd told Belial.

And every time Narcise moved closer, Moldavi had slowed and changed. His breathing, his voice, even his body had tensed. He'd tried to hide it, but Chas was used to watching for the signs of weakness from the prey he hunted.

But Chas still didn't completely figure it out until they got to the larger chamber…that, he realized later, gave Moldavi a larger space in which to be confined with his Asthenia. And he'd had Narcise stripped immediately… *and her clothing taken from the chamber.*

Why would he do that unless there was something he needed to get out of the place? Without, of course, anyone realizing it.

And that was when it all crystallized for Chas. The vision Sonia had seen had Narcise in it, and it was clear that Cezar had some mixture of fear and admiration for his sister…but she was also holding an ivory fan.

And in her clothing, she had been wearing a corset… with the *ivory busk* that Chas had given her.

It was *ivory*. Moldavi's Asthenia was ivory.

The next thing Narcise was aware of was Chas's face, dark and frightened and furious, looking down at her.

"My God, Narcise," he said, touching her cheeks as he

gathered her into his arms, his eyes glistening. "I came as fast as I could. Can you… Are you… Holy Mother of God…Narcise."

The feathers had disappeared…the pain was gone…the paralysis and heaviness had eased. Her body throbbed in places, and was numb in others…but she could breathe. And think.

And remember.

She struggled to sit up, extricating herself from him. "Giordan," she breathed, looking around frantically. Had she lost her chance? Had she lost him again?

Chas's face changed and he stepped back so that she could see the tanned body, sagging against the wall, arms straight above his head. Giordan's face was half-lifted, his glittering eyes scoring her, and as their gazes met, she saw wild relief in his.

She slid off the table upon which she lay, her knees wobbly and the room spinning. Something wet oozed from her shoulder, and there was blood and dampness in other places. Her arms hurt, her back felt as if it had been seared. She saw Belial's body sprawled on the stone floor. His head lay in a pool of dark red blood, its putrid scent nauseating, nearby.

Chas caught her arm as she began to sink to the ground, and said, "Stay here. I'll see to him." His words were as taut and short as his movements, and Narcise felt a wave of remorse as she realized his pain.

She watched as he released Giordan, saw the way he sagged and pitched forward when Chas cut him free from the bonds that had held him upright, and she had to move from the table to meet him. Already, the weakness was ebbing, her legs were stronger, her mind clearer.

She looked around the chamber, and for the first time,

she saw more bodies—dead, *vampir* bodies…and then she saw her brother.

He was sitting in a chair on the dais, tied to his seat, surrounded by slender white items.

He wasn't dead…but he wasn't moving.

All at once, she had Giordan in her arms, his heavy, solid body, warm and welcome, sliding against her—and it was all she could do not to collapse into shameful tears.

How much time had she missed? How much had she lost? She'd been so wrapped up in herself, in her center…

"I'll take care of things in here," Chas said, turning from them. "See to him. I think he's—he needs…" His voice trailed away and he walked off with jerky steps.

"I'm well," Giordan muttered into her hair, but his arm was tight around her, and he leaned against her too heavily to be "well."

She smelled scents on him that she didn't care to identify, and, blinking back angry, horrified tears, she helped him out of the ugly chamber without a glance at her brother.

She knew where to go, and took him back to her own private apartments. A niggle of guilt bothered her as she left Chas behind, and she promised herself she'd go back to him as soon as she got Giordan settled.

But he was weak, with an ashen cast to his rich, golden skin, and she knew he'd need to feed before he recovered his strength. How much blood had Cezar taken from him? Had there been others who'd fed as well?

What else had happened?

The smells and marks on his body told her more than she wanted to know, and Narcise blocked her mind from thinking about it or imagining it, remembering the shiny gray color to his face. He was safe now. Cezar wouldn't bother him…or either of them…again.

When she eased him onto the bed in her old chamber, Giordan didn't release her, and she tumbled down with him, their legs bumping and sliding awkwardly together. Bare skin to bare skin, her breasts pressed up against his torso, his warm arms loose around her waist.

"Narcise," he murmured, his lips moving against her hair again, "is it really you? Have you come back to me?"

"Giordan," she replied, pulling away to look down at him. "I'm sorry. I don't even know what to… I know that I can't say anything to change what happened, to make amends for it…but…I'm so sorry. I didn't understand. I didn't—" Her voice broke at the end and despair took over. How could he ever forgive her? "So…sorry."

The Mark on her back shot a renewed blast of pain— or maybe it had never stopped doing so—but whatever the case, she felt it.

And along with the shock of hurt came an unlikely sense of satisfaction. If Lucifer disapproved, then there was something good about it.

And it had all ceased being just about her some time ago.

"Shh," he said. "Don't…say anything."

"Are you hurt? What can I…"

He covered her mouth with his, his lips warm and firm, fitting over hers with a softness that made her want to weep. His hands glided up her unclothed body, gentle and yet possessive.

"Belial," he said, pulling away suddenly, his face hardening. "He—"

"He's dead," she replied. "Chas…" She shook her head and pressed her swollen lips together.

"I would have killed him myself. Watching him—" His voice trailed off and he looked at her, his brown-blue eyes deep and filled with grief. "I knew what Cezar was going to do. I tried to stop him, Narcise."

"By Fate, I *know* you did," she replied wildly, consumed by her own guilt and shame. "Giordan, there was *nothing* you could have done—"

"I would have done anything—"

"But you already *did*," she wept. "You already *did*. And I didn't *see* it. I was too... I didn't, I *couldn't*, understand...what you'd done."

He gathered her close, but she could feel the trembling and weakness in his powerful arms. She pressed a kiss over one of the wounds on his shoulder, tasting the remnant of luscious, warm, clean lifeblood. Desire and affection rushed over her, and he shivered beneath her lips.

"You need to feed," she told him, pulling away, putting aside her own needs and desires. "You can hardly lift your arms."

"No," he murmured. "I only need you, Narcise. I never thought—"

"Please, Giordan. Allow me." She raised her arm and offered it to him, at the same time as she admired the smooth planes of his chest, dusted lightly with dark hair. "Just as you did for me."

He shook his head. "I can't. Narcise. I can't." He turned his face away, his mouth tight, his nostrils flaring as if he drew in her scent, but tried to force it away at the same time.

Something sharp and hard stabbed her in the heart. He'd fed on Rubey. She knew he had...she'd scented and smelled the proof.

If he loved her, why would he not take what she offered? Her heart thumping, an uneasy churning in her insides, she looked for something to cut her skin...just as he had, when she'd demurred his same offering, ten years ago.

A lifetime for some. But just a flash in the life of a Dracule.

"Please," she said, wanting to help him, and at the same time, wanting to erase the remnants of Belial that had been imprinted on her.

She raked her arm over the corner of her bedside table, and it did enough: leaving a slender red line that burst into shiny pearls of lifeblood.

"Narcise." He sucked in his breath and she put her arm there...but even then, he turned away. "I can't. You don't understand...I've changed. I can't."

But then he shuddered, deep in his middle as he pulled in a breath. His belly and torso flinched against hers, and all at once his mouth was on her...closing around her arm.

His tongue slid along the slender wound, leaving a moist, hot trail in its wake, and Narcise's desire blossomed fully inside her, shooting low and deep.

She rolled and pressed against him, jolting delicately when he slid his fangs into the soft side of her arm. The rush of her blood into his warm mouth, his slick tongue tasting the lifeblood was as pleasurable for her as sinking her fangs into his vein.

She tasted his salty skin, felt the racing and pounding of his pulse as it beat with her own. His eyes were closed, his face taut with relief as he drank—

Giordan abruptly pulled up, thrusting her arm away and lurching off the bed. He fumbled at the table, grabbing a small bowl from it just in time to vomit inside.

Narcise went still and cold. Did he hate her so much that he couldn't...

Slowly she eased away from the warm place on the bed, the last remnants of her pleasure evaporating, leaving her shaky and confused. His back was to her, that broad expanse with shifting muscles…and a Mark that had turned white. It covered his shoulder and down his back, smooth and light—as if he'd been tanned around it.

He looked up then, wiping his mouth with the back of a hand, and saw her. "Narcise," he said, reaching for her. "I'm sorry. It's not you—"

"It must be me," she whispered, her throat suddenly raw and dry. "You have no difficulty feeding on Rubey."

His fingers were surprisingly strong, and he kept her in place on the bed as he came back onto it. "No. I shouldn't have tried. I knew what would happen…but I can't resist you." His smile was forced and wavery, making her even more discomfited.

She blinked back tears, not even caring that she might appear weak. She *was* weak. Weak and foolish. And what she'd done was unforgivable.

You are the strongest person I've ever met, he'd said to her once.

That was before he'd really come to know her.

Giordan wouldn't release her hand. "After what happened…before…when I left, I was so dark and angry and—well, I went a little mad. I don't remember what I did, precisely, but it was violent and evil and black. I do remember waking in an alley, with no memory of anything but the realization that I didn't have you any longer—" He squeezed her fingers. "No, don't talk. You need to understand."

Narcise couldn't look at him, so she stared down at their joined hands: his dark, powerful one closed around her pale slender fingers.

"There was a cat," he said. "In the alley, and she blocked me in. I couldn't leave. And I stayed there as the sun rose, lost in that dark time—I can't describe how it was, but it was horrific. I tried to hide from the sunlight, but one part of me was exposed." He gestured to his shoulder, drawing her attention from their hands. "I saw a bright light, and this happened. I felt as if my insides… my soul…were battling. They were. The light won."

Narcise reached to touch the markings, certain that he was making the entire event seem much simpler than it had been. "Did you…" She shook her head. The white lines were no longer raised, nor was the texture any different than the rest of his skin. The change of color made the mark look almost beautiful, instead of ugly and malevolent.

"I was weak and beaten, and when I finally made my way home, I tried to feed. And every time I did…" He gestured to the bowl, an odd expression on his face. "That happened. At last, Drishni came to me and I was able to feed from her. Because she eats nothing brought to her through death or violence. Somehow, with my change, my body would no longer accept anything violent or evil. After that, I realized I was changing. In many ways."

"And so you can feed on Rubey?" she asked, knowing that her tone was stiff with hurt.

"She eats no meat. And she offers freely." His eyes searched hers. "But I don't love her."

Narcise turned away to hide the tears. What a fool she was. "And Luce?"

"He no longer owns me. Kritanu—an old Indian man who Dimitri sent after he learned about this—says that I've attained a level of *moksha* that most mortals can never reach. Because I'm immortal, still, Narcise. I still have forever."

So he wasn't like Dimitri and Voss. She frowned, her heart lightening just that bit. "You are no longer Dracule…but you aren't a mortal?"

He shook his head, his eyes steady. "I don't know what I am…but I know that I'm my own man once again. And that I have an eternity to learn what this change means. I hope…Narcise, will you stay with me?"

"But I'm Dracule," she replied. *I can't love you.*

"It doesn't matter, Narcise. I love you…and that will never change. I told you: it's only you. It's only ever been you."

"He has to die," Chas told Narcise sometime later. Much later, after she and Giordan had fully recovered in the privacy of the bedchamber. "That's why I came: to slay Cezar. Then you'll never have to worry about him again."

She nodded, imagining a life without her brother's dark shadow hovering over her. "But how can it be done? He's protected himself so well. You can't even put him on a guillotine."

"There is a way," Chas replied. His expression had been, and remained, emotionless—something that she'd come to notice since he'd rescued her from the feather cape.

When he thought she wasn't looking at him, however, she felt his eyes on her: heavy, filled with heartache.

The next day, Narcise walked into the dining chamber to watch the execution. The servants and made *vampirs* who'd lived with Cezar had either been slain by Chas or run off now that their master was a prisoner. There was no one left but the three of them and her brother.

Cezar was manacled to the high-backed chair, his arms and legs chained in place. He was also fettered at the hips so his torso wouldn't move, and a chain positioned his head and held it immobile against the back of the chair.

Narcise found the sight of her brother thus contained visually shocking—horrifying, really—and more than a bit unsettling to see a man who'd made her life so tormented now in such a crudely helpless condition.

As executioner, Chas had managed the preparations, and now he stood off to one side, sharpening a long wooden pike. It looked lethal and wicked, and Narcise shuddered in spite of herself. Giordan, who'd come in with her, had an understandably tense look on his face.

Soon, she would be rid of her brother and the threat he posed to her and the rest of the world. And then she could go on to live the rest of her life without fear.

"Narcise," her brother said from his restricted posture.

This was the first she'd spoken to him since the events of yesterday.

She walked over to stand in front of him and found his blue-gray eyes steady and clear. They fastened on her, and she felt a wave of hatred and disgust for the man who'd taken so many years of her life away. Yes, he'd given her immortality—an unwelcome gift, after all—and he'd taken so much else from her: a normal life. A family. The natural cycle of living and loving and dying.

The man she'd loved…or tried to love…for more than ten years.

"Did you come to bid me farewell?" Cezar asked. "Or to taunt me? I must congratulate you, Narcise. You've beaten me at last."

"I thought it only proper to bid you *adieu*," she replied, aware that Chas was listening. "And to make certain the deed was done. I'm sorry that our reunion wasn't as long as you'd hoped. But I'm not sorry that there will be no more children bled by you." *And that you won't live to torture me any longer.*

His face changed as he looked at her, and she saw a

flicker of something in his eyes. Not fear, not anger…
perhaps something like regret. "I have always only admired you, sister."

"Admired and tried to control," she reminded him.
"Bartered off to the highest bidder or the strongest sword.
Such admiration."

"How else was I to keep you with me?" he asked. "You
would have left the moment you had the chance. I wanted
you with me. All the time. *Forever*."

"You nearly achieved just that," she said, her throat
raw again. "What happened to you, my brother? How did
you become like this? You used to be…sweet."

For a moment, his facade crumbled, and she saw the
real Cezar: a frightened, self-loathing, insecure man.
"I couldn't find who I was supposed to be," he said. "I
couldn't accept who I was."

But then the tortured expression was gone just as instantly as it had come, and he took on a haughty face and
speared her with cold eyes. "I should have been you. I
wanted to *be* you, Narcise. Always loved, always petted
and worshipped…perfect in form and image. A woman
of unbelievable exquisiteness."

Her heart was pounding and Narcise realized that
Giordan had come to stand with her, resting his hand at
the base of her back. Comforting and supporting.

"You always had the men," her brother continued.
"They always loved you and wanted you…and I could
understand why. I admired you…even loved you…but I
wanted to be in your place." Cezar's attention flickered
to Giordan, standing behind her. A flash of regret and
admiration went through his gaze and his lips flattened
in a humorless smile. "And then he came and I knew
I'd lose you to him. And rightly so. You were," he said

to Giordan, allowing his eyes to glow a bit, "all that I'd hoped and imagined."

Narcise felt Giordan's faint shudder against her, and she eased back a bit so that she was closer to him and his hand pressed more firmly into her back.

What he'd gone through. For her.

The very thought, especially now, faced by Cezar and seeing the lust in his eyes even as he prepared to die, made her sick with regret and revulsion.

How could Giordan ever forgive her for misunderstanding? For doubting him?

"And so I'll go to my death, envying you still, Narcise," Cezar said in his lisping voice. "What an irony." He closed his eyes.

Narcise turned away, her belly lurching. It was time.

Chas was there, watching silently. "I'm ready," he said, flashing a look toward Cezar. "Let's finish this." He turned to walk away, then paused and came back. "You don't have to watch, Narcise."

"No," she replied. "I'll stay. I'll see this done."

Giordan, who couldn't witness such a deed, squeezed her hand and, after one last searching look, left the chamber.

Chas brought a chair and positioned it behind Cezar's seat. He climbed up on it, the long, lethal pike in his hand, and stood there for a moment.

"This," he said as he raised the long stake vertically above Cezar's head, "is for the children you slaughtered, and for the Jews you blamed for it. This is for Narcise, and the years of abuse in your household and for keeping her captive. And for tricking her into the covenant with Lucifer."

The point hovered directly above Cezar's dark head, and Narcise couldn't take her eyes away from him. He sat, immobile, stony, unable to move, trussed and captured, helpless—just as she had been. He stared straight ahead, his lips curved in a faint smile. But fear glinted in his eyes.

Chas would have to slam the stake all the way down, through his skull, into the brain and mouth, down his throat, and into the chest cavity...then into his heart. Narcise closed her eyes. Her brother would be killed in an instant, put out of the misery of the life he hated.

He'd be gone, sent to Lucifer forever.

No more fear, no more violence....

"Goodbye, Cezar Moldavi." Chas raised his arms, muscles tense and swollen, and just as he moved, Narcise screamed.

"No!"

She flew across the room, launching herself at Chas, slamming into him and the chair just as he brought the stake down. They crashed to the stone floor in a rough heap, the pike clattering across the ground as a white-hot blaze engulfed her.

"What the hell are you doing?" Chas said, grasping Narcise's shoulder as he pulled up into a sitting position. "What's wrong?"

She was shaking her head, her body trembling, her belly heaving. Pain screamed through her, radiating from her Mark, raging through her like a ball of fire. "I couldn't let you," she gasped, tried to speak, looking up at him through the blazing red pain that grew stronger and hotter. "Couldn't...kill him."

He's still my brother.

22

Giordan heard Narcise's scream and the terrible crash. Terror arced through him as he spun around and flung the door open, dashing back into the chamber without hesitation.

Woodmore was crouched next to Narcise, who was in a heap of twisted skirts and hair on the stone floor. Even from the entrance, Giordan could see her writhing and twisting in agony. Her silky dark hair dusted the floor, clung to her face and neck.

"What is it?" he demanded, rushing over to them, taking note that Cezar still sat, alive, in his helpless position. He saw the pike on the floor where it had rolled, and noticed the upended chair.

And the stiff, terrified expression on Woodmore's face. "She stopped me," he told Giordan. "She saved his life. And now she's…"

But he needed to say nothing more, for Narcise's low, tormented moans and the dead-white look on her face told Giordan everything.

He shoved Woodmore out of the way, pulling Narcise into his arms. She couldn't die. Not from this.

"Narcise," he said calmly and loudly, giving her a gentle shake in an attempt to pull her from the sort of seizure, the frenzy of pain. Trying to keep himself collected. "Look at me."

She shuddered and blinked, her breathing coming in short, anguished gasps. Her eyes were blank with pain, empty and lost, and he didn't know if there was anything he could do to help her...but he brushed the hair from her face and murmured, "Narcise. Look at me."

He closed his arms around her, drawing from deep within, from his soul, his core...focusing on the white light he'd found in his mind while in the alley that day. *Peace.* Light.

He held it in his heart, in his mind, as Kritanu had taught him, and looked into Narcise's fathomless violet eyes. "Look at me. I love you, Narcise. I need you...stay with me. Fight it, Narcise. Fight him."

He didn't know if she could hear him through the pain, but he kept talking to her, ignoring the solid brown boots standing next to him on the ground as Chas stared down at them.

"Narcise. Look at me. *Look* at me," he begged. If she could look at him, focus on him...

She bucked, shuddered and gasped, and beneath his hand, he felt the pulsing rage of her Mark through the fabric of her clothing. A ripple of shock flashed through him and without realizing what he was doing, he tore away at the bodice of her gown as she agonized against him. But she was softening...slowing... Was he losing her?

"My God," breathed Chas, kneeling next to them again when he saw her shoulder. "It's *alive.*"

Like black veins, tiny black snakes, Lucifer's Mark twisted and surged on her creamy skin: stark and wicked, evil emanating from the Devil himself. It *was* alive, and it was fighting—for Narcise.

Giordan didn't know exactly what to do, but he knew he had to try. He bent his head to the Mark.

His lips touched the raging black weals and he felt the sharp, excruciating sting, the bolt of peace and light meeting dark malevolence. He kissed her, his lips soft and gentle, absorbing the shock, taking on the pain... He moved his hands over those curling, twisting worms, closed his eyes and prayed.

Help me.

"She's ready," came the voice inside his head. *"Help her."*

He pulled back, needing to look in her eyes. Still covering the Mark with his hands, both of them, holding her up, he lifted her so he could look into her eyes. "Look at me, Narcise. *Look in my eyes.*"

She blinked through pain-filled eyes, focused for a bare moment and, still holding the light, warm and clean in his heart, he gave it to her. Their eyes met and he felt another bolt, a shaft of effort and then release surge through him...and into her.

Narcise gasped and looked at him again, this time with clarity and the light of serenity. Beneath his hand he felt a searing heat where Luce's Mark thrived. She screamed, then closed her eyes and sagged into unconsciousness... and then the writhing black veins collapsed.

When Giordan looked at them again, he saw they had disappeared. In their place were pure white lines marking the battle won.

"*An avatar*," Kritanu said in his precise, smooth accent. "You must have acted briefly as some sort of *avatar*, Giordan, in conducting that power and strength to Narcise. That is the only explanation I have."

He was an old man, perhaps seventy or eighty, with hair as black as Narcise's. He wore it in a long, sleek tail at the base of his neck. His mahogany skin was smooth, hardly wrinkled, and his eyes were sharp and black, like jet beads. Giordan had met him years ago when he first came to England, for Kritanu was a friend of Dimitri's Aunt Iliana.

Giordan and Narcise were all sitting with Kritanu in Dimitri's study, having at last returned from Paris only two days earlier. They'd spent nearly a fortnight making arrangements for Cezar and settling his household.

"What's an *avatar?*" Narcise asked, moving closer into the warm, familiar curl of Giordan's arm. He smelled like comfort and warm sunshine and sensuality, and she couldn't wait to drag him off to the chamber they'd been sharing and sink her teeth…literally…into him.

"I've studied every bloody religion and writings from

every age and I find it impossible to comprehend. An *avatar* is an entity from a heavenly level who manifests himself on earth," Dimitri said. The note of disbelief in his voice was nearly comical. "A god come to earth in human form. You cannot be serious. Giordan? An *avatar*?"

Kritanu smiled, his eyes glinting with shared humor. "I'm not at all suggesting that Giordan is a humanized god of any sort. In fact, that would be impossible. But, just that, for a miraculous moment, he acted as a conduit for Narcise, and the *moksha* he'd attained allowed that same window to be opened to her. She had to be ready and willing to go through it of her own volition."

"Naturally," Dimitri replied, dry skepticism still lacing his voice. "So if Giordan had attained Enlightenment ten years ago, why in the devil couldn't he transfer it to me when I was looking for it so hard?"

Maia, who'd just walked in at that moment, carrying a tray, said, "Because you didn't have a soul-deep connection with Giordan like Narcise does. Nor did you just want to be loose of Lucifer—you wanted to be mortal again, Gavril. You needed to be. So you could be with me." She set the tray down and gave him an arch look.

"A wise woman named Wayren is fond of saying that, when we are truly ready for it, we receive whatever grace it is we need," Kritanu said, accepting a handleless cup of tea from Maia. He cupped his hands around it and breathed in the scent—something exotic, like jasmine, Narcise thought. "Each has his or her own path to travel. I don't pretend to understand it all, either."

"And so Cezar still lives?" Maia said as she settled next to Dimitri, confirming Narcise's suspicion that there was to be a second wedding in the Woodmore family after Voss and Angelica. "You'll keep him alive?"

Narcise had a soft, sad pang at the thought of Chas, still in Paris, attending to the final details of arrangements for Cezar. He'd insisted on staying…perhaps because he didn't wish to witness her happiness with Giordan. He might miss even his sisters' weddings. Narcise's insides squeezed at the memory of the stark misery on his face…the emotionless eyes when she'd awakened from her ordeal to find both of the men who loved her in attendance.

And only one of them had she really wanted.

Chas would never have been truly happy with her. He couldn't accept who she was…or who she'd been; there would always be that layer of judgment for what he saw as her mistake. And he was so enamored of her beauty that he wasn't able to see the rest of her—her strength, her needs…who she was behind the perfect face and form.

"Yes. Cezar's been confined in a well-guarded prison. Narcise may wish to visit him occasionally," Giordan said, looking down at her. "Since you saved his life." His eyes were warm with affection and admiration. She was reminded again of how he'd taken his time, his patience and risked his life, to woo her and unravel her layers of distrust all those years ago.

Thank God he'd forgiven her for her blindness.

"Chas is taking care of the details. Moldavi will be kept in relative comfort, but his chamber and the hallways around it will be lined with ivory, so there will be no escape," Giordan continued.

Narcise shrugged, looking at her hands. "I realized I couldn't let him be killed. Even after everything he did, I couldn't make that choice. Because death…it eliminates all hope for change. And with what's happened with Voss and Dimitri, and even Giordan and me…" She looked up. "I suppose there's always hope that something might change."

"It's interesting to think of how the concept of karma works when one is immortal," Kritanu mused. "After all, as we believe, one normally has many lifetimes to work out cause and effect, realization and change. But as an immortal being, you will have an eternity to observe this extraordinary situation and see what happens to your brother. Now that he has been given the chance to change."

Dimitri said to Narcise, "And who knows…perhaps Cezar will be helpful to you in some other way, sometime in the future."

Later, in the privacy of their chamber, Narcise huddled in the warmth of Giordan's sleek, golden body. He smoothed his hand along her hair, from the top of her head all along its length, to where it pooled next to them on the bed. His touch was comforting and familiar and she closed her eyes at the pleasure, wondering if she ought to tell him about the other change that had happened to her. Her body seemed to have become fully alive again, functioning as any young woman's might.

"Do you want to go out tonight?" he asked. "We could try to find some excitement."

Narcise gave a little laugh. She'd told him about how she felt when she'd chased off her attackers after leaving Rubey's. It had occurred to her that she could use some of her great strength and fighting skills to do that sort of thing on a regular basis. As a sort of protective agent on the streets at night, watching for opportunities to help the vulnerable and weak.

It would give her something to *do* with her life. And although she couldn't be violent simply for her own purposes, or for the sake of hurting another, she could use her strength to help the weaker—by saving women, who, like she'd been, were controlled or assaulted by others. "I think that would be very exciting. Perhaps we could go to Seven Dials… I understand there is a public house there that attracts varlets and the bad sort—and more of Luce's half demons, too. I don't recall the name of it."

"The Silver Chalice. Whatever you wish," Giordan said, sliding his muscular leg between hers. "I don't mind a good fight myself, once in a while." He smiled, showing his fangs.

Neither of them would turn away from a fight—as long as it wasn't violence for the sake of violence. Or death. Narcise had learned that she, too, could only feed from those who consumed only sustenance without violence. *Moksha* was a powerful thing.

And Giordan had given it to her.

"I'll take you to visit Cezar whenever you like," he said, sliding those sharp fangs along the sensitive column of her neck. She shivered, then pulled away as her veins pulsed and throbbed in anticipation.

"It won't bother you…after all that's happened?" she asked, now watching him closely. "To see him?"

He shook his head, mashing those thick dark curls against the white pillow. "Not now that I have you. It was all for you, Narcise. I could live through anything, knowing I had you on the other side of it."

She squeezed her eyes closed again, the welling of guilt and misery strong and hard, knotted in her belly. "I wish I had been different."

But he shook his head again, and touched her face. "Do you not see? It was only because of what happened that I was able to change…to find that peace. And then, when you were ready, I gave it to you. If you'd left with me that day…after I was with Cezar, we wouldn't be here now, marked by light instead of dark."

Narcise sat up suddenly, the heavy weight of guilt and shame sliding away like a dark cloud. "Do you truly believe that?"

"But of course I do," he said, looking up at her. "It's often only after great despair and sacrifice that one finds what one really needs. And in an immortal life, ten years is hardly a breath."

She smiled and felt as if the warm blast of the sun had just entered the chamber. "What an amazing man you are, Giordan. I love you…forever."

"I've loved you from the moment I first saw you. There's no one I want to spend immortality with besides you, Narcise."

"How about a child?"

He stilled, looking at her with shocked, wide eyes. "But you cannot…"

Her smile grew wider. "I happen to know that something else about me has changed…and I think it's possible now."

"Then I suggest we begin attending to that right away," he said, sliding over on top of her. "Then I'll have two females I love to spend eternity with."

"What if it's a boy?"

"It won't be. I know these things…remember? I was almost an *avatar*."

* * * * *

ACKNOWLEDGMENTS

As always, I have many people to thank for helping to get *Narcise* out of the cobwebs in my head and onto the shelves, not the least including Emily Ohanjanians, my hardworking and attentive editor, and the entire team at MIRA. I couldn't ask for a better group of people to launch this series, and I'm especially grateful to Diane Mosher and Katherine Orr for their team's support.

I'd like to thank Erin and Devon Wolfe and Gary and Darlene March for the late-night boat ride that helped me to crystallize exactly how things could work out for an immortal vampiress. I'm not sure if it was the wine or the combined brainpower, but you all got me thinking on the right path, and herein is the result. Extra hugs and kisses to Darlene and Erin for doing early readings of the book to check my work as well!

Thanks to Holli and Tammy for helping me muddle through yet another book, and for your thoughtful and supportive feedback. I am so very grateful to the two of you that I celebrate Thanksgiving every single day!

I owe my brother Sean big thanks for his expertise with arson and fire—not only for this book, but for every other book that I've ever written that has a fire in it. And there are many.

Also, great big hugs to Robyn Carr for too many reasons to list, although I'm pretty sure you know them all. But I'm just going to say one word: sushi.

I also really appreciate the time given by Maggie Shayne, Heather Graham, Lara Adrian and Jeaniene Frost to read from this new series. I can only guess at how busy you are, and I can't tell you how much I appreciate the support from such talented, generous women. Thank you.

I would also like to thank Marcy Posner for being a wonderful business partner and support over the last seven years. I will always appreciate everything you've done for me.

And last, but never least, I must express my deep love and gratitude to my husband and our children for really understanding how my deadlines work, and why there are times that I just can't sit in on family movie nights. Also special thanks to MusicMan for all those lunches and breakfasts where you're throwing plot ideas out to me willy-nilly and always manage to come up with something that sticks. I love you.

SINK YOUR TEETH INTO THREE SEXY
VAMPIRE TALES FROM

COLLEEN GLEASON!

REGENCY LONDON—A DIZZYING WHIRL OF BALLS
AND YOUNG LADIES PURSUED BY CHARMING MEN.
BUT THE WOODMORE SISTERS ARE HUNTED BY
A MORE SINISTER BREED: LUCIFER'S OWN.

**Available for the first time in mass-market
paperback, wherever books are sold!**

New York Times bestselling author

RACHEL VINCENT

Kori Daniels is a shadow-walker, able to travel instantly
from one shadow to another. After weeks of confinement for
betraying her boss, she's ready to break free for good. But
Jake Tower has one final job for Kori, one chance to secure
freedom for herself and her sister, Kenley.

The job? Recruit Ian Holt—or kill him.

Ian's ability to manipulate the dark has drawn an invitation
from Jake Tower. But Ian is on a mission of his own. He's come
to kill Tower's top Binder: Kori's little sister.

Amid the tangle of lies, an unexpected thread of truth
connecting Ian and Kori comes to light. But with opposing
goals, they'll have to choose between love and liberty....

Shadow Bound

Available wherever books are sold.

MIRA   HARLEQUIN®
www.Harlequin.com

MRV1343R

REQUEST YOUR FREE BOOKS!

2 FREE NOVELS FROM THE PARANORMAL ROMANCE COLLECTION PLUS 2 FREE GIFTS!

YES! Please send me 2 FREE novels from the Paranormal Romance Collection and my 2 FREE gifts (gifts are worth about $10). After receiving them, if I don't wish to receive any more books, I can return the shipping statement marked "cancel." If I don't cancel, I will receive 4 brand-new novels every month and be billed just $21.42 in the U.S. or $23.46 in Canada. That's a saving of at least 21% off the cover price of all 4 books. It's quite a bargain! Shipping and handling is just 50¢ per book in the U.S. and 75¢ per book in Canada.* I understand that accepting the 2 free books and gifts places me under no obligation to buy anything. I can always return a shipment and cancel at any time. Even if I never buy another book, the two free books and gifts are mine to keep forever.

237/337 HDN FEL2

Name	(PLEASE PRINT)

Address	Apt. #

City	State/Prov.	Zip/Postal Code

Signature (if under 18, a parent or guardian must sign)

Mail to the **Reader Service:**
IN U.S.A.: P.O. Box 1867, Buffalo, NY 14240-1867
IN CANADA: P.O. Box 609, Fort Erie, Ontario L2A 5X3

Not valid for current subscribers to the Paranormal Romance Collection or Harlequin® Nocturne™ books.

Want to try two free books from another line?
Call 1-800-873-8635 or visit www.ReaderService.com.

* Terms and prices subject to change without notice. Prices do not include applicable taxes. Sales tax applicable in N.Y. Canadian residents will be charged applicable taxes. Offer not valid in Quebec. This offer is limited to one order per household. All orders subject to credit approval. Credit or debit balances in a customer's account(s) may be offset by any other outstanding balance owed by or to the customer. Please allow 4 to 6 weeks for delivery. Offer available while quantities last.

Your Privacy—The Reader Service is committed to protecting your privacy. Our Privacy Policy is available online at www.ReaderService.com or upon request from the Reader Service.

We make a portion of our mailing list available to reputable third parties that offer products we believe may interest you. If you prefer that we not exchange your name with third parties, or if you wish to clarify or modify your communication preferences, please visit us at www.ReaderService.com/consumerchoice or write to us at Reader Service Preference Service, P.O. Box 9062, Buffalo, NY 14269. Include your complete name and address.